DATE WITH A SURGEON PRINCE

BY
MEREDITH WEBBER

MILLS & BOON

First published in Great Britain 2013
by Mills & Boon, an imprint of Harlequin (UK) Limited.
Harlequin (UK) Limited, Eton House,
18-24 Paradise Road, Richmond, Surrey TW9 1SR

© Meredith Webber 2013

ISBN: 978 0 263 89928 3

Harlequin (UK) policy is to use papers that are natural, renewable and recyclable products and made from wood grown in sustainable forests. The logging and manufacturing process conform to the legal environmental regulations of the country of origin.

Printed and bound in Spain
by Blackprint CPI, Barcelona

Meredith Webber says of herself, 'Once I read an article which suggested that Mills & Boon® were looking for new Medical Romance™ authors. I had one of those "I can do that" moments, and gave it a try. What began as a challenge has become an obsession—though I do temper the "butt on seat" career of writing with dirty but healthy outdoor pursuits, fossicking through the Australian Outback in search of gold or opals. Having had some success in all of these endeavours, I now consider I've found the perfect lifestyle.'

Recent titles by Meredith Webber:

ONE BABY STEP AT A TIME
CHRISTMAS WHERE SHE BELONGS
THE SHEIKH AND THE SURROGATE MUM
NEW DOC IN TOWN*
ORPHAN UNDER THE CHRISTMAS TREE*
MELTING THE ARGENTINE DOCTOR'S HEART
TAMING DR TEMPEST

Christmas at Crystal Cove

These books are also available in eBook format from www.millsandboon.co.uk

PROLOGUE

'ARE YOU COMPLETELY mad? Bonkers? Round the twist?'

It wasn't often Marni yelled at her grandfather. In fact, if she'd been in any fit state to think about it, she'd have realised it was probably the first time. But this was just too much.

'It says here the man's a prince. Just because he hasn't married doesn't mean he'll be interested in some cockamamie story about being betrothed to me when he was three!'

She was still yelling, and brandishing the newspaper Pop had been reading at the same time, while the voice that lived in *her* head told her it would be a bad idea to bash an ailing eighty-four-year-old man to death, especially as she loved him to bits and couldn't bear the thought of life without him.

Except that she had to start—start imagining it, that was. Eighty-four, with a blocked valve in his heart and blocked stents in the vital arteries that fed the heart muscle.

The specialist wanted to do open-heart surgery to replace the valve and, at the same time, the surgery necessary to bypass the stents. Pop was vacillating, another cause for anger because as a nurse she thought he should have the operation. Of course he should, he was a man who enjoyed life, and, selfishly perhaps, she really, really didn't want him dying of heart failure.

'You finished?' Pop retrieved the flapping paper from her now limp grasp, and opened it up to fold it at a different page. 'For your information, he was six, *you* were three. Now, look at this page near the back.'

Ignoring a momentary pang that she could no longer see the photo of the strong-featured face, framed by a white headdress, that had started the conversation, she peered over Pop's shoulder to read what he was showing her.

Not that her mind would take in much—she was still struggling with the little gem the old man had delivered earlier, finger pointing at the picture, voice full of wonder as he'd said, 'That's Ghazi. His father and I pledged the two of you would marry. Says here he's still single. You should get in touch.'

Forget this prince business and get with it, the inner voice in her head said firmly. Pop's made it clear he doesn't want you hanging around here while he's getting over the op, no matter how much you might want to be with him. Perhaps a short contract job somewhere else?

'See,' Pop was saying, and for a moment Marni wondered if he could hear her thoughts because he was pointing at a job advertisement. 'Theatre nurses wanted for new children's hospital in Ablezia. That might be why Ghazi's out here. He's looking for nurses.'

Yeah, right, she thought. Of course the crown prince of any country would have to check out hospital staff!

But Marni ignored the voice in her head this time, intent on reading exactly what was on offer in this place she'd never heard of, which, presumably, was far enough away from the Gold Coast, Queensland, Australia for her not to be tempted to ignore Pop's plea to keep away while he went through his operation.

If he went through with the operation!

Six months' contract' extendable, the advertisement read, air fares and accommodation provided. Six months would bring her up to Christmas and if Pop had the operation as soon as possible, then he'd be well on the way to recovery by the time she got home.

Six months! It was the answer to the other problem plaguing her too—her virginity! Given six months, thousands of miles from home—*surely* in six months she'd meet *someone*…

She sighed as she looked blankly at the paper, sighing because the virginity thing, as she thought of it, shouldn't really be a problem. It wasn't as if she'd held onto it deliberately, she'd just put things off for various reasons—Pop, Nelson, her mother's behaviour—then the cruel words of the last man she'd become involved with had made her realise it was a burden as well as an embarrassment.

Read the ad!

The pay scale seemed staggeringly generous, but it was the thumbnail description of the country that made her heart flutter. Set by the warm waters of the Ablezian Sea, the country was well known for its underwater wonders—coral reefs, abundant marine life, nesting turtles on the beaches…

This idea could actually solve some problems. She could make Pop happy by taking the job and getting out of the way while he recovered, make him even happier by at least meeting this prince guy—she owed Pop that much—and maybe, as a bonus, find someone with whom to have a holiday romance, or a work romance, or even just a little fling…

'I'll get the picture,' Pop said.

Marnie lost herself in thoughts of diving into warm gulf waters and playing with the fish and turtles. She barely heard Pop as he left the paper in front of her at the breakfast table and disappeared into his study.

Nelson, who'd been with her grandfather as long as Marni could remember, as valet, butler, cook and probably secretary, appeared in his usual silent way.

'I don't know, Nelson,' she said quietly. 'It seems wrong to even think of going away. Pop's taken care of me and been there for me all these years, surely now I can be there for him?'

Nelson shook his head.

'You know he probably won't have the op if you're around, because he doesn't want you to see him weak and sick. He wants you to remember him as the strong, active man he's always been, and can be again. He's far more likely to agree to the procedure if he knows you're not fretting over him.'

Nelson paused then, with only the slightest quaver in his voice, continued, 'You know I'll take good care of him.'

Blinking back the tears that had filled her eyes, Marni got to her feet and hugged the man she'd known since the age of two, when she'd been dumped on her grandfather because her mother's third husband hadn't wanted a kid around the place.

'I know you will, Nelson, and I know you're right about him recovering more quickly if I'm out of the way. If he's so set on me leaving, I'll do it. I'll take this job and check out this prince bloke, say hi to him from Pop, and report back. Can't you just imagine it—me rocking up to a palace in the desert to tell the local ruler he's betrothed to me! I'd be arrested and thrown into the deepest, darkest dungeon, or fitted with a straitjacket, or at the very least deported on the first plane out.'

Nelson's serious brown eyes studied her for a moment.

'It would make your grandfather very happy if you did meet the guy,' he said, so seriously that Marni groaned.

'Not you too!' she protested.

'Well, he was a really nice little kid and he was very good to you, although in those days you were a right little tantrum-throwing madam.'

'I met him? I knew him? When was all this?'

Marni frowned, trying to remember, to place a time she might have played with a prince.

Not something everyone would forget!

'It was shortly after you first arrived to live with us,' Nelson explained. 'Your grandfather had only recently moved into this apartment and Ghazi's father booked out the entire hotel section for himself, his family and his staff.'

'The whole hotel?'

'He had a lot of wives and daughters,' Nelson said, as if that explained everything.

The Palazzo Versace was the first six-star hotel built on the Gold Coast, her grandfather's apartment one of a few privately owned condominiums included in the ritzy complex. As residents, they were free to make use of all the hotel facilities, the beautiful pools, the restaurants and the day spa, so she'd often played with the children of hotel guests as she had been growing up.

But one called Ghazi?

She had no memory of it at all, even when Pop returned with a box of photos showing her as a very small child with a boy who stood much taller. The photos told her they'd had fun together, two children at play while slender, black-robed figures sat in the shade by the pool.

'This is the one,' Pop, who'd been sifting through the photos, declared.

He handed it to her.

It was a more formal shot showing a tidily dressed little girl, blonde hair in pigtails, pale blue eyes looking up at the boy sitting on the arm of one of the big lounge chairs in the hotel's foyer—a white-robed boy, who was holding her hand and smiling down at her.

Even then you could tell he was going to be good looking, although the miniature white headdress he was wearing in the photo concealed all but his profile. Strong nose and jaw, a high forehead, shapely lips widened in a slight smile—

'Hey, I was looking at that,' Marni protested as Pop turned the photo over.

He ignored her, pointing at the writing on the back. The top line was in his handwriting and, sure enough, there was this nonsense about the two of them being betrothed, Pop's signature at the end of the statement.

Beneath that was a line of beautiful, flowing, Arabic script, and presumably another signature.

'Honestly, Pop, you can't read Arabic so for all you know the man's written something like, "This nonsense should make the man happy!"'

Marni regretted her words the moment they'd popped out of her mouth and she caught the hurt in her grandfather's eyes, hurt that prompted a quick hug and a totally impulsive promise to go right now and apply for the job in a country called Ablezia.

'*And* I'll do my best to see this guy but only if you agree to have the operation,' Marni added. 'Deal?'

'Deal!' Pop agreed, and they shook on it, the slight tremble in her grandfather's hand reminding her just how frail he had become.

CHAPTER ONE

WAS IT THE subtle scent that perfumed the warm air—
salt, spices, a fruit she couldn't identify—or the air itself
that wrapped around her like the finest, softest, mohair
blanket? Or was it the mind-boggling beauty of a landscape of red desert dunes alongside brilliant cobalt seas,
the dense green of a palm grove in an oasis at the edge
of the desert, or the tall skyscrapers that rose from the
sand like sculpted, alien life forms?

Or perhaps the people themselves, the shy but welcoming smile of a headscarfed woman, the cheeky grin
of tousle-haired boy, pointing at her fair skin and hair?

Marni had no idea. She couldn't give an answer to the
question of why she'd fallen in love with this strange, exotic land within hours of stepping off the plane, but in
love she was—flushed with excitement as she explored
the narrow market lanes that sneaked off the city high-
ways, trembling with delight the first time she dived into
the crystal-clear waters, and shyly happy when a group
of local women, fellow nurses, asked her to join them for
lunch in the hospital canteen.

This was her first day at the hospital, her schedule having allowed her four free days to explore her new home
before starting work, and today was more an orientation
day, finding her way around the corridors, feeling at home

with the unfamiliar layout and the more familiar hospital buzz. Now her new friends were telling her about the theatres where they all worked, which surgeons were quick to anger, which ones talked a lot, which ones liked music as they worked, and which ones flirted.

Hmm! So there *were* some flirts!

Would they flirt with her?

Seriously?

The young women giggled and tittered behind their hands as they discussed this last category and Marni wanted to ask if they flirted back, but felt she was too new to the country and understood too little of the local ways. So she listened to the chat, enjoying it, feeling more and more at home as she realised the women's words could be talk among theatre nurses anywhere in the world, except that it was never personal—no mention of family or relationships—usually the main topics of conversation among nurses back home.

But for all the ease she felt with her fellow nurses, nerves tightened her sinews, and butterflies danced polkas in her stomach when she reported for duty the next day.

'Welcome,' Jawa, one of the nurses she'd met the previous day, said as Marni pushed through the door into the theatre dressing room. 'This morning you will enjoy for Gaz is operating. He's not only a good surgeon, but he takes time to tell us what he is doing so we can learn.'

Aware that many of the staff at the hospital were imports like herself, she wondered if Gaz might be an Australian, the name a shortened Aussie version of Gary or Gareth. Not that she had time to dwell on the thought, for Jawa was handing her pale lavender—lavender?—theatre pyjamas, a cap and mask, talking all the time in her liltingly accented English.

'So we must hurry for he is not one of those surgeons who keep patients or staff waiting. He is always on time.'

Jawa led the way through to the theatre where they scrubbed and gloved up, ready for what lay ahead. The bundle of instruments on the tray at Marni's station—she would be replenishing Jawa's tray as Jawa passed instruments to the surgeon—looked exactly the same as the bundles at home, and relieved by the familiarity of that and her surroundings she relaxed.

Until the gowned, capped, gloved and half-masked figure of the surgeon strode into the room, when every nerve in her body tightened and the hairs on her arms and back of her neck stood to attention.

He's just a man! she told herself, but that didn't stop a tremble in the pit of her stomach as he looked around the room, dark eyes taking in the newcomer, his head nodding in acknowledgement, the eyes holding hers—a second or two, no more—yet causing heat to sear downwards through her body.

'So, we have a stranger in our midst,' the man who was causing the problems said, his voice reverberating through her like the echoes of carillon bells. 'And you are?'

'Marni Graham, sir,' she said, hoping she sounded more in control than she felt.

'In here I'm Gaz, just Gaz, Marni Graham,' he said. 'Welcome to the team.'

She really should say something—respond in some way—but her voice was lost somewhere in the general muddle of the new and unbelievably vital sensations she was experiencing right now.

Lust at first sight?

It can't be, Marni argued with herself, but silently and very weakly.

The man in question had pulled his mask up to cover

his nose and mouth, and seemed about to turn away, but before he did so he smiled at her.

Of course, she couldn't see the smile, not on his lips, but she was certain it was there, shining in his eyes and making her feel warm and very, very unsettled.

What she had to do was to appear totally unaffected by the man, which, of course she was, she told herself. The reaction had been nerves, first day on the job and all that. Yet she was aware of this man in a way she'd never been aware of anyone before, her skin reacting as if tiny invisible wires ran between them so every time he moved they tugged at her.

Was this what had been missing in her other relationships—the ones that had fizzled out, mainly, she had to admit, because she'd backed away from committing physically?

She shook the thought out of her head and concentrated on the task at hand, on the operation, the patient, a child of eight having a second surgery to repair a cleft palate.

'This little boy, Safi, had had his first repair when he'd been six months old,' Gaz was explaining, his voice like thick treacle sliding down Marni's spine. 'That was to repair the palate to help him feed and also to aid the development of his teeth and facial bones.'

He worked as he talked, slender gloved fingers moving skilfully, probing and cutting, everything done with meticulous care, but Marni gave him more points for knowing the child's name and using it, humanising the patient, rather than calling him 'the child'.

'Now we need to use a bone graft to further repair the upper jaw where the cleft is, in the alveolar.'

Marni recited the bones forming part of the maxilla, or upper jaw bone—zygomatic, frontal, alveoal and palatine—inside her head, amazed at what the brain could retain from studies years ago.

'If we had done this earlier,' Gaz was explaining, 'it would have inhibited the growth of the maxilla, so we wait until just before the permanent cuspid teeth are ready to erupt before grafting in new bone.'

He continued speaking, so Marni could picture not only what he was doing but how his work would help the child who'd had the misfortune to have been born with this problem.

It had to be the slight hint of an accent in his words that made his voice so treacly, she decided as he spoke quietly to the anaesthetist. So he probably wasn't an Australian. Not that it mattered, although some contrary part of her had already wound a little dream of two compatriots meeting up to talk of home.

Talk?

Ha!

Her mind had already run ahead to the possibility that this man might just be the one with whom she could have that fling.

You're supposed to be concentrating on the job, not thinking about sex!

She hadn't needed the reminder, already shocked by how far her mind had travelled while she'd worked.

And *where* it had travelled!

The man was a complete stranger...

A complete stranger with mesmerising eyes and a sexy, chocolate-syrup voice!

The operation, which seemed to have gone on for ever, wound up swiftly. The surgeon and his assistant left, although Gaz did turn at the door and look around, frowning slightly as he pulled his mask down to dangle beneath his chin, revealing a sculpted line of barely-there beard outlining a jaw that needed nothing to draw attention to its strength.

He nodded in the general direction of the clump of nurses where Marni stood, before disappearing from view.

There was no rush of conversation, which seemed weird as either the surgeons or their skills usually came in for comment during the post-op clean-up. But here the women worked competently and silently, Jawa finally telling Marni that was all they had to do.

'We have time for lunch and you're back in Theatre again this afternoon—you and me both, they have paired us for a while.'

'I'm glad of that,' Marni told her. 'I still need someone to lead me around.'

She opened her mouth to ask if the surgeon called Gaz would be operating again, then closed it, not wanting to draw Jawa's attention to the fact the man had affected her in some strange way.

A *very* strange way!

The afternoon operation was very different, removal of a benign cancer from the ankle of a little girl. The surgeon was French and seemed to think his nationality demanded he flirt with all the nurses, but his work was more than proficient and Marni decided she'd enjoy working here if all the surgeons were as skilled as the first two she'd seen.

A minor operation on a child sent up from ER, repair of a facial tear, finished off her shift, but as she changed into her outdoor clothes she wondered about their first patient, the little boy who'd been born with a deformity that would have been affecting his life. No child liked to look different from his mates…

Uncertain of protocol but needing to know how he'd

come out of the operation, Marni asked Jawa if she'd be allowed to see him.

'Just a brief visit to see he's okay,' she added.

Jawa consulted her watch and decided that, yes, he should be well and truly out of Recovery and back on the children's post-op ward.

'Of course you can visit him,' she assured Marni. 'I would come with you but I have an appointment.'

The faint blush that rose in her cheeks as she said this suggested the appointment was special, but Marni forbore to tease, not knowing Jawa or the local customs well enough.

The post-op ward was easy to find. The hospital was set up rather like an octopus with all its tentacles spread flat on the ground. The operating theatres, recovery rooms, the ICU and the administration rooms were all in the tall body of the beast, while the arms supplied different wards.

In the post-op ward, bright with murals of colourful forests and wild animals, Marni found most rooms occupied not only by the patient but by a clutch of family members as well—black-robed women, white-robed men.

'Can I help you?' a passing nurse inquired.

'A little boy who had a cleft palate operation this morning. I was one of the theatre staff and wondered how he was doing.'

'Ah, you mean Safi. Do you wish to visit him?'

'I wouldn't want to intrude on his family,' Marni said.

'You won't,' the nurse told her. 'In fact, it would be good if you could visit him. He's not local but has come here for all his surgery. The hospital takes many children from neighbouring countries because we have the doctors with the skills to help them, and this wonderful facility where they can recover, but often the parents cannot afford to accompany the child. The nurses will do their best to see these children are not too lonely, but most of the time—'

'You're too busy,' Marni finished for her. 'I understand, but I'm far away from home myself so I'll be happy to visit Safi when I can.'

Following the nurse's directions, she found Safi's room, knocked quietly then went in. The little boy turned wide, troubled eyes towards her.

'Hello,' she said, aware he probably had no idea of English but not knowing what language he might speak. 'I've come to visit you.'

She sat beside him and held his hand, wishing she'd brought a toy or a book. Although this boy was eight and she'd been only two when she'd first gone to live with her grandfather, she remembered how Pop had helped her feel at home—he'd sung to her.

Dredging back through her memory, she sang the nursery rhymes of her childhood, using her hands as she had back then, making a star that twinkled in the sky and an itsy-bitsy spider climbing up a water spout.

Safi regarded her quite seriously but when she sang 'Twinkle Twinkle Little Star' for the fourth time, he joined in with his hands then smiled at her.

The smile made her want to cry for his aloneness, but apparently the music had soothed him and he fell asleep.

Not wanting to disturb him too soon, she sat by the bed, holding his hand, her mind drifting through the memories of the tumultuous few weeks since she'd made the decision to come to Ablezia, stumbling out of the drift when she thought of her goal—*her* goal, not Pop's.

Could she do it? Go cold-bloodedly into a relationship with a man simply to rid herself of her virginity?

Hot-bloodedly if it was Gaz! The thought popped into her head and Marni knew heat was colouring her cheeks.

Think sensibly!

It wasn't that she'd thought it precious, the virginity thing. It had just happened, partly, she knew, as the result of having a wayward mother who flitted like a butterfly from man to man. But the biggest hurdle had been growing up with two elderly men who thought the world of her, and not wanting to ever do anything that would make them think less of her.

So she'd pulled back through her late teens when her friends had been happily, and often unhappily, experimenting with sex, although, to be honest, there'd never been a boy with whom she'd desperately wanted to go to bed.

At university, her lack of experience had embarrassed her enough for her to be cautious, then, probably because of the virginity thing, she'd virtually stopped dating, somehow ashamed to admit, if a relationship *had* developed, her intact state. Until Jack—

Enough brooding!

But Marni still sighed as she lifted the little fingers that had been clasped in hers and kissed the back of Safi's hand.

Who would have thought it could be so hard?

She stole silently out of the room, turning her thoughts back to the child, knowing she'd return and wondering just where she could buy toys and books to cheer the little boy's recovery.

Nelson would send whatever she wanted but he was busy with Pop—she'd check out the internet when she went back to her room.

As she passed the nurses' station, nerves prickled along her spine and glancing over her shoulder she saw the back of a tall, dark-haired man bent slightly to listen to what the nurse at the desk was saying.

Of course it's not him, she told herself, though why had her nerves reacted?

Surely she wasn't going to tingle when she saw every tall, dark and handsome stranger!

CHAPTER TWO

No Gaz in Theatre the next day or the next, and Marni decided, as she made her way down the children's ward to visit Safi, that she was pleased, she just had to convince herself of the fact. But the sadness in the little boy's eyes as she entered his room banished all other thoughts. She sat beside him, took his hand, said 'Hello' then '*Salaam*', one of the few words she'd managed to remember from Jawa's language lessons.

Safi smiled and repeated the word, then rattled off what might have been questions, although Marni didn't have a clue. Instead she opened up the folder of pictures she'd printed off the internet, showing Safi a map of Australia and pointing to herself, then one of Ablezia. Using a cut-out plane, she showed how she'd flown from Australia to Ablezia.

The little boy took the plane and pointed from it to her. She nodded. 'Aeroplane,' she said. 'A big jet plane, from here...' she pointed again '...to here.'

Safi nodded but kept hold of the plane, zooming it around in the air.

Marni flipped through her folder, bringing out pictures of a koala, a wombat and a kangaroo. She put them all on the map of Australia and when Safi picked up the picture of the kangaroo, she hopped around the room, delighting the little boy, who giggled at her antics.

'Kangaroo,' she said, hoping the books and toys she'd ordered would arrive shortly—she'd paid for express mail. She'd actually found a female kangaroo with a joey in its pouch among the soft toys for sale, and had made it her number-one priority.

Safi was jumping the picture of the kangaroo on the bed now and pointing towards her, so Marni obligingly jumped again, her hands held up in front of her like the kangaroo's small front paws. Unfortunately, as she spun around to jump back past the end of the bed, she slammed into an obstacle.

A very solid obstacle!

Stumbling to recover her balance, she trod on the obstacle's feet and mashed herself against his chest, burning with mortification as she realised it was the surgeon—Safi's surgeon—the man called Gaz.

'S-s-ir!' She stammered out the word. 'Sorry! Being a kangaroo, you see!'

Marni attempted to disentangle herself from the man.

He grasped her forearms to steady her and she looked up into eyes as dark as night—dark enough to drown in—felt herself drowning...

Fortunately he had enough presence of mind to guide her back to the chair where she'd been sitting earlier and she slumped gratefully into it, boneless knees no longer able to support her weight.

He spoke to Safi, the treacly voice light with humour, making the little boy smile and bounce the picture of the kangaroo around the bed.

'I am explaining to him you come from Australia where these animals are,' Gaz said, turning to smile at her.

The smile finished her demolition. It lit fires she'd

never felt before, warming her entire body, melting bits of it in a way she didn't want to consider.

'Well, well, well,' he said, so suggestively she had to wonder if he'd read her reaction to him. Surely not, although the smile playing around his lips—gorgeous lips—and the twinkle in his eyes suggested he might have a fair idea of it.

'You're the new surgical nurse.'

A statement, not a question.

'Marni Graham,' she said, holding out her hand then regretting the automatic gesture as touching him, even in a handshake, was sure to cause more problems.

You've fallen in lust! Twenty-nine years old and you've finally been hit by an emotion as old as time.

'It's not lust,' Marni mumbled, then realised she'd spoken the words, although under her breath so hopefully they hadn't been audible to the surgeon, who was bent over Safi, examining the site of the operation and speaking quietly himself in the soft, musical notes of the local language.

The little boy appeared to know the man quite well, for he was chatting easily, now pointing to Marni and smiling.

'You have visited him before?' Gaz asked as he straightened. 'For any reason?'

'Should I not have come? Is it not allowed?' The man, the questions, her silly reactions all contributed to her blurting out her response. 'Jawa said it would be all right, and the nurses here don't have a lot of time to spend with him.'

The tall man settled himself on the bed, his knees now only inches from Marni's, although she could hardly push her chair back to escape the proximity, tantalising though it was.

They're knees, for heaven's sake!

Marni forced herself to relax.

'Of course you are welcome to visit. Safi appreciates it and looks forward to your visits, but I wondered why you come. You are a stranger here, are you not being looked after? Have you not made friends that you spend your spare time with a child?'

The man had obviously painted her as pathetic.

'Of course I've made friends, and everyone has been very welcoming, and I've done a lot of exploring, both on my own and with others, but...'

She hesitated.

How to explain that while she loved theatre nursing, the drama of it, the intensity, she missed patient contact?

He was obviously still waiting for an answer, the dark eyes studying her, his head tilted slightly to one side.

'Like most nurses,' she began, still hesitant, 'I took it up because I felt I could offer something in such a career. I enjoyed all the facets of it, but especially nursing children. Early on, I thought I'd specialise in paediatric nursing, but then I did my first stint in Theatre and I knew immediately that's where I really wanted to work. But in Theatre a patient is wheeled in and then wheeled out and somehow, even with the good surgeons who use the patient's name, they don't become real people—there's no follow-up to find out if the operation was a success, there's no person to person contact at all—'

Aware she'd been babbling on for far too long, she stopped, but when her companion didn't break the silence, she stumbled into an apology.

'Sorry, that sounded like a lecture, sorry.'

He reached out and touched her lightly on the knee, burning her skin through the long, loose trousers she was wearing.

'Do not apologise for showing humanity. It is all too rare a trait in modern medicine where everyone is under pressure to perform and seek perfection in all they do, so much so we have little time to think about those under our care as people rather than patients. In this hospital we allow the families to stay, so our patients have them to turn to, but children like Safi, who have come from a neighbouring country, often have no one.'

'Except you,' Marni pointed out. 'The nurse told me you'd been in earlier and that you stayed with him that first night.'

'I was worried he'd be afraid, alone in a strange place, and I've learned to sleep anywhere so it was no hardship.'

Not only gorgeous but nice, Marni thought, and she smiled at him and told him so—well, not the gorgeous bit.

'That was very kind of you,' she said, 'but have you done it every night? Surely that would be too much if you're operating every day?'

Gaz returned her smile, but it was absent-minded, as if it had slipped onto his lips while he was thinking of something else.

'Not every night, no, but an old friend of mine comes in now and stays with him. It was she who heard the story of a foreign woman visiting.'

'So you came to check?' Marni asked, not sure whether to be pleased or put out. Pleased to have seen him again, that was for sure...

'Of course,' he said. 'Not because I doubted your good intentions, but to see who it was willing to put herself out for a child she did not know.'

The smile this time was the full effort, its effect so electrifying in Marni's body she hoped he'd go away— disappear in a puff of smoke if necessary—so she could sort herself out before she tried standing up.

'And now that I do know,' he continued, oblivious of the effect he was having on her, 'I wondered if you'd like to have dinner with me, a kind of welcome to Ablezia and thank you for being kind to Safi combined. There is a very good restaurant on the top floor of the administration building right here in the hospital. We could eat there.'

So it would seem like colleagues eating together if your wife or girlfriend found about it? Marni wondered. Or because you have rooms here and it would be convenient for seduction? Well, the seduction part would be all right— after all, wasn't that one of the reasons she was here?

Although annoyed by her totally absurd thoughts, Marni realised her first question had been plausible enough—a man this gorgeous was sure to be taken!

Taking a deep breath, she put the whole ridiculous seduction scenario firmly out of her head.

'I'd like that,' she said, and was surprised to find her voice sounded remarkably calm. 'That must be a part of the building I haven't explored yet. My friend Jawa and I usually go to the staff canteen on the ground floor.'

Shouldn't you check whether he's married before you get too involved? Marni thought.

Having dinner with a colleague was hardly getting involved!

Or so she told herself!

Until he took her elbow to guide her out of the room.

She knew immediately there was a whole lot wrong with it. She'd made a serious mistake. It was utter madness. That, oh, so casual touch made her flesh heat, her skin tingle and her heart race.

Although wasn't that all good if—

She *had* to stop thinking about seduction!

He dropped her elbow—thankfully—as they walked back up the corridor to the big foyer in the middle of the building, which, again thankfully, gave Marni something to use as conversation.

'It's been beautifully designed, this building,' she said—well, prattled really. 'I love the way this atrium goes all the way up, seemingly right to the roof.

'You'll see the top of some of the taller palms from the restaurant,' Gaz said. 'In arid countries we long for greenery so when there's an opportunity to provide some, either indoors or out, we make the most of it.'

The pride in his voice was unmistakeable and although Marni knew from Jawa that the locals didn't encourage personal conversation, she couldn't help but say, 'So, you're a local, are you?'

The lift arrived and as he ushered her in he smiled at her.

'Very much so.'

The slightly strained smile that accompanied the words told Marni not to pursue the matter, so she talked instead of her delight in the markets, the colours, the people, the aromas.

Still prattling, she knew, but the man made her nervous in ways she'd never been before.

The lift doors slid open, and they stepped out into a glass-sheathed corridor, the inner wall displaying, as Gaz had said, the tops of the palm trees in the atrium.

Drawn to the glass, Marni peered down.

'It's beautiful,' she said, turning to him to share her delight.

He was staring at her, a small frown on his face, as if something about the sight of her bothered him.

'What?' she asked, and he shook his head, before again, with another light touch on her elbow, guiding her forward, around the atrium to the far side, where a restaurant spread across the corridor so the atrium was indeed visible from the tables.

The place was dimly lit and quiet, only a few tables occupied.

'Are we too early or too late for the usual dinner hour?' Marni asked, desperate to talk about something—anything—to distract herself from the effect this man was having on her, especially with his casual touches and watchful dark eyes.

'Early for the diners coming off late shift, late for those going on night duty,' Gaz told her as the young man on the reception desk greeted Gaz in his own language then bowed them towards a table close to the atrium.

Gaz held up a hand and said something, and the young man bowed again and led them in a new direction so they crossed the room.

'You have seen the tops of the palms in the atrium,' Gaz explained, 'but possibly not the desert in the moonlight.'

The table was beside a wall of glass, so Marni felt she was seated in space above the long waves of dunes. The moon silvered the slopes it touched, and threw black shadows in between, so the desert seemingly stretched away for ever with a patterned beauty that took her breath away.

'I hadn't known—hadn't realised...'

'That it could be so beautiful?' Gaz asked as her words stumbled to a halt.

She smiled at him, but the smile was an effort because something in the way he said the word 'beautiful' made it seem personal—although that could hardly be true. The women she'd met here were so stunningly attractive she felt like a pale shadow among them, a small daisy among vibrant dark roses.

Answer the man, her head suggested, and she struggled

to get back into the conversation—to at least *act* normal in spite of the chaos going on in her body.

'Yes, that,' she said, 'definitely that, but I hadn't realised the hospital was so close to the desert. I've always come to it from the direction of the city, from the sea side, but the desert's right there—so close you could touch it—and so immense.'

'And dangerous, remember that,' Gaz said.

'Dangerous?' Marni repeated, because once again there seemed to be an underlying message in his words.

It's the accent, you idiot, she told herself. Why should there be some sensual sub-text when the man barely knows you?

'You have deserts in Australia—inhospitable places where a man without water or transport could perish in a few days.'

'Of course. I hadn't thought about it but it would be the same in any desert, I imagine.'

She'd caught up with the conversation, but it hadn't mattered for Gaz was now conferring with a waiter, apparently discussing the menu. He turned to her to ask if she'd like to try some local dishes, and if so, would she prefer meat, fish or vegetarian.

'Meat, please, and yes to local dishes. I've tried some samples of the local cooking in the souks. There's a delicious dish that seems to be meat, with dates and apricots.'

'And to drink? You would like a glass of wine?'

And have it go straight to my head and confuse me even further?

'No, thank you, just a fruit juice.'

Her voice was strained with the effort of making polite conversation. Her nerves were strung more tightly than the strings of a violin, while questions she couldn't answer tumbled in her head.

Was the attraction she felt mutual?

Could this be the man—not for a lifetime, it was far too early to be considering that—for a fling, an affair?

Worse, could she go through with it if by some remote chance he was interested?

The waiter disappeared and Marni took a deep breath, knowing she somehow had to keep pretending a composure she was far from feeling. But how to start a conversation in a place where personal conversations just didn't seem to happen?

Gaz saved her.

'You mentioned the souks. You have had time to see something of my country?'

She rushed into speech, describing her delight in all she'd seen and done, the beauty she'd discovered all around her, the smiling, helpful people she'd encountered.

Gaz watched her face light up as she spoke, and her hands move through the air as she described a decorated earthen urn she'd seen, or the tiny, multicoloured fish swimming through the coral forests. He saw the sparkle in her pale, grey-blue eyes and the gleam where the lights caught her silvery-blonde hair, and knew this woman could ensnare him.

Actually, he'd known it from the moment he'd seen her—well, seen her pale eyes framed by the white mask and lavender cap on her first day in Theatre.

There'd been something in those eyes—something that had caught at, not his attention but his inner self—a subliminal connection he couldn't put into words.

At the time he'd dismissed the idea as fanciful—the product of a mind overburdened by the changes in his life, but now?

Impossible, of course! He had so much on his plate

at the moment he sometimes doubted he'd ever get his head above water.

He groaned inwardly at the mess of clichés and mixed metaphors, but that's how his life seemed right now. He'd stolen tonight from the schedule from hell, and by the time he had his new life sorted, this woman would be gone.

There'll be other women, he reminded himself, then groaned again.

'Are you all right?'

The pale eyes showed genuine concern, and a tiny line of worry creased the creamy skin between her dark eyebrows.

'I will be,' he answered. 'There are some massive changes happening in my life right now, which, as far as I'm concerned, is really bad timing.'

He reached across the table and touched her hand, which was wrapped around the glass of pomegranate and apple juice the waiter had set in front of her.

'Bad timing?' she repeated.

'*Very* bad timing,' he confirmed, and said no more, because he knew that although an attraction as strong as the one he was feeling couldn't possibly be one-sided, there was nothing to be gained from bringing it out into the open. He simply had no time! No time for them to get to know each other properly.

No time to woo her.

Instead, he asked how much diving she'd done, and listened as her quiet, slightly husky voice talked about the Great Barrier Reef, a holiday she'd had in the Seychelles, and compared other dives she'd done with the Ablezian Sea.

Was he listening? Marni had no idea, but she was happy to have something to talk about and as she spoke she relived some of her underwater adventures, and remembering the joy and fun she'd experienced eased the tension in her body so talking now was easy, her companion prompting her to keep going if she lagged.

The meal arrived—a covered earthenware dish set in the middle of the table, another dish of rice set beside it. The waiter added small plates of cut-up salad vegetables and a platter of the flat bread that she was beginning to realise was part of every meal in this country.

'Traditionally, I would serve you, but perhaps you would prefer to help yourself,' Gaz said, lifting the lid of the earthenware pot and releasing the mouth-watering aroma of the dish. 'I would not like to give you too much or too little.'

Ordinary words—common-sense words—so why was she all atingle again?

It was his voice, she decided as she helped herself to rice then added a scoop of the meat dish, before putting a little tomato salad on her plate and taking a piece of bread. His voice sneaked inside her skin and played havoc with her nerves, but when she'd finished her selection and looked across at him, his eyes, intent on her again, caused even more havoc.

Totally distracted now, she picked up her glass of juice and took too big a gulp.

At least half choking to death brought her back to her senses. Marni finished coughing and, flushed with embarrassment, bent her head to tackle her meal.

Fortunately, Gaz seemed to sense her total disarray and took over the conversation, talking about the hospital, built within the last two years, and with the charge of looking after not only local children but those from nearby countries that did not have the facilities this hospital had.

'We have a big oncology department, keeping children

here during their treatment so they don't have to travel to and fro. With those children, we try to make sure they have someone from their family travel with them—sometimes, it seems, the entire family.'

His rueful smile at this confession undid all the good concentrating on her food had done for Marni, mainly because it softened his face and somehow turned him from the sexiest man she'd ever laid eyes on to a real, caring human being.

All you're wanting is an affair, not to fall in love, she reminded herself.

But at least hospital talk got them through the meal and when they'd finished, Marni sat back in her chair.

'Thank you, that was utterly delicious. Wonderful. Perhaps I could pay the bill as thanks to you for introducing me to this place? Is that allowed in Ablezia?'

She offered what she knew must be a pathetic smile, but now they'd finished eating she had no idea how to get away—which she needed to do—or what was the polite thing to do next.

Say goodbye and leave?

Wait for him to see her back down to the ground floor?

And if he offered to walk her back to the quarters—through the gardens and lemon orchard, the scented air, the moonlight…

It was too soon even to think about what might happen and the man had already said he had no time.

'You definitely will not pay when I invited you to dinner,' Gaz was saying as she ran these increasingly panicked thoughts through her head. 'It is taken care of but, come, you must see the desert from outside, where you can really appreciate its beauty.'

He rose and came to stand beside her, drawing out her

chair, which meant his entire body was far too close to hers when she stood up.

Turning to face him, this time with thanks for the courtesy of the chair thing, brought her even closer—to lips that twitched just slightly with a smile, and eyes that not only reflected the smile but held a glint of laughter.

The wretch knows the effect he's having on me, Marni realised, and found a little anger stirring in the mess of emotions flooding through her body.

Good!

Anger was good—not argumentative anger but something to hold onto. The man was a born flirt and though he obviously couldn't help being the sexiest man alive, he didn't need to use it to snare unwary females.

Wasn't wanting to be snared one of the reasons she'd come here?

Marni ignored the query and allowed Gaz to lead her out of the restaurant and along another corridor that led to a balcony overlooking the desert—the magic sea of black and silver.

She sniffed the air, then breathed it in more deeply.

'It's strange,' she said, turning to her companion, her reaction to him almost forgotten as she considered the puzzle the desert air presented. 'I know the sea is just over there, but there's no smell of salt in the air, no smell of the spices escaping from the restaurant or the lemon blossom that I know is out in the gardens down below us. No smell at all, really.'

He smiled again—a genuine smile this time, not a teasing one—but this one made Marni's heart flutter.

'The desert is a great cleanser. Over the centuries much blood has been spilled on the sands, and civilisations have risen and collapsed, their ruins buried by the sand. For people like me, with Bedouin blood, the desert is as necessary as water, for it is where we replenish our souls.'

He was serious, the words so graphically beautiful Marni could only shake her head.

And smile.

A small smile but a genuine one.

A smile that for some reason prompted him to inch a little closer and bend his head, dropping the lightest of kisses on her parted lips.

Had she started, so that he put his hands on her shoulders to steady her?

Marni had no idea, too lost in the feel of his lips on hers to think straight.

So when he started talking again, she missed the first bit, catching up as he said, 'You are like a wraith from the stories of my childhood, a beautiful silver-haired, blue-eyed, pale-limbed being sent to tempt men away from their duties.'

She was still catching up when he kissed her again.

Properly this time so she melted against him, parted her lips to his demanding tongue, and kissed him back, setting free all the frustration of the lust infection in that one kiss.

It burned through her body in such unfamiliar ways she knew she'd never been properly kissed before—or maybe had never responded properly—which might explain—

It sent heat spearing downwards, more heat shimmering along her nerves, tightening her stomach but melting her bones.

Her head spun and her senses came alive to the smoothness of his lips, the taste of spice on his tongue, the faint perfume that might be aftershave—even the texture of his shirt, a nubby cotton, pressed against the light cotton tunic top she wore, was sending flaring awareness through her nipples.

A kiss could do all this…

Gaz eased away, shaken that he'd been so lost to propriety as to be kissing this woman, even more shaken by the way she'd reacted to the kiss and the effect it had had on him. Heat, desire, a hardening, thickening, burning need….

For one crazy moment he considered taking things further, dallying with the nurse called Marni, seeing where it went.

Certainly beyond dallying, he knew that much.

Al'ana! Where is your brain? his head demanded. Yes, I thought so! it added as if he'd answered.

He looked at the flushed face in front of him, glimpsed the nipples peaked beneath the fine cotton tunic, the glow of desire in her eyes.

Yes, it would definitely have gone further than dalliance…

'I had no right to do that. I have no time. None! No time at all!' He spoke abruptly—too abruptly—the words harshly urgent because he was denying his desires and angry with himself for—

For kissing her?

No, he couldn't regret that.

Angry at the impossible situation.

This time when he turned to lead her back inside, he didn't touch her elbow and guide her steps but stayed resolutely apart from the seductive siren who'd appeared, not from the sky but in full theatre garb, then jumped like a kangaroo right inside his skin…

Obviously married, Marni told herself. Serves you right, kissing on what wasn't even a first date.

But she was too shaken by the kiss to care what the

sensible part of her brain was telling her. Too shaken to think, let alone speak.

Standing silently beside Gaz in the lift, the foot of space between them was more like a million miles.

Back in the foyer, he spoke to one of the young porters who seemed to abound in the place.

'Aziz will see you back to the residence,' Gaz told her, then he nodded once and was gone, seeming to disappear like the wraith he'd called her.

Aziz was beckoning her towards the door so she followed, deciding she must be right about his marital status if the man she'd kissed didn't want to be seen walking her through the gardens.

So she was well rid of him.

Wasn't she?

Of *course* she was!

The gardens were as beautiful as ever, the scent of lemon blossom heavy in the air, but the magic was dimmed by her memory of the kiss, and now that embarrassment over her reaction was creeping in, she was beginning to worry about the future.

She was a professional. Of course she could work in Theatre with Gaz without revealing how he affected her. Not that he didn't know, given her response, but at least she didn't have to be revealing just how hard and fast she'd fallen for the man.

Lust, her head reminded her, and sadly she agreed.

For all the good it was going to do her when he'd made it obvious he wasn't available!

She sighed into the night air. It was all too complicated!

CHAPTER THREE

HIDING HER REACTIONS to Gaz in Theatre proved unnecessary, because although she worked for five straight days, he was never rostered on in the same theatre as her.

She didn't kid herself that he'd had his schedule changed to avoid her, doubting she was important enough to cause such a change, and caution told her not to mention him to Jawa, not to ask where he was operating or seek answers to any personal questions about the man, in case she unwittingly revealed how she felt.

Besides, they just didn't do personal conversations, these Ablezians.

But her reaction to Gaz had certainly put a damper on her virginity quest, other male colleagues seeming pale and uninteresting by comparison, although she did accept an invitation to the movies from a young doctor on Safi's ward.

She'd even accepted a goodnight kiss but she had felt nothing, not a tingle, not a sign of a spark—and the poor man had known it and had avoided her ever since.

So she worked, visited Safi, and worked again until finally she had time off—three days.

Nelson had emailed to say Pop was talking to the surgeon but was still undecided about the operation, although now he could walk barely a hundred metres without tiring.

She had to forget about Gaz and find a way to see this prince! Once she'd kept her part of the bargain, Pop would *have* to have the operation. He wasn't one to renege on a deal.

And at least sorting out how you're going to approach *him* should get your mind off Gaz, she told herself.

And it did, the whole matter seeming impossible until she read in the English-language newspaper that the new prince had reintroduced his father's custom of meeting with the people once a week. Each Thursday he held court in a courtyard—was that where courtyards got their name?—at the palace, hearing grievances or problems, any subject allowed to approach and speak to him privately for a few minutes.

Reading further, Marni discovered the custom had stopped while his uncle had been the ruler but had been reinstated some weeks previously and was a great success.

She wasn't actually a subject, but that couldn't be helped. If she tied a black headscarf tightly over her hair and borrowed an all-concealing black abaya from Jawa *and* kept her head down—maybe with part of the scarf tied across the lower part of her face—she could slip in with the locals, have a minute to introduce herself and show the photo, perhaps even have a laugh with the man who'd been kind to her as a child.

The planets must have been aligned in her favour—though they'd definitely been against her last week—for the next meeting was the following day.

She emailed Nelson to tell him she was keeping her part of the bargain and to warn Pop she expected him to keep his, then went to collect the clothing she'd need.

Which was all very well in theory!

In practice, once dressed and sitting in the back of a cab on her way to the palace, a building she'd glimpsed from afar in her explorations, she realised just how stupid this was, how ridiculous the whole thing—making a deal with Pop so he'd have a lifesaving operation—fronting up to the prince of a foreign land to show him a photo of himself as a child.

The enormity of it made her shake her head in disbelief.

Yet here she was!

Huge arched gates in a high, sand-coloured wall opened into a courtyard big enough to hold a thousand people. It was an oasis of green—she remembered Gaz telling her how important green was—with beds of flowering roses, tinkling fountains, fruit trees and date palms. The garden had been designed and planted to provide shade but also to form little spaces like outdoor rooms where one could sit and read, or think, or just do nothing.

In the centre, facing the immense, low-set building, was an open grassed area and here the suppliants were gathering, seating themselves cross-legged on the ground in neat rows. Thankfully, there were not as many as Marni had expected, although, contrarily, part of her had hoped there *would* be too many and she could put off her ridiculous venture for another day.

She seated herself beside the last man in the back row, pleased it was a man as she knew he wouldn't attempt to make conversation with a woman he did not know.

An exchange of *salaam*s was enough, Marni with her head bent, not wanting to reveal pale eyes surrounded by even paler skin.

Intent on remaining unseen, she barely heard the words from the wide veranda that ran along the front of the palace. Not that hearing them more clearly would have helped.

Really smart idea, this, she thought despairingly. Just pop along to a meet and greet without a word of the language to tell you when it's your turn to front up to His Maj!

A long line was already forming and as it snaked towards the veranda the man beside her said something then stood and joined the line. Checking that it already held some women, Marni slid into place behind him, her heart beating such a crazy rhythm she was surprised she could stay upright.

The line inched forward until she could see, on a low couch on the veranda, a white-robed figure, bowing his head as a supplicant approached him, apparently listening to the request or complaint before assigning the person to one of the men who stood behind the couch.

Some people were led to the edge of the veranda and returned to the courtyard, while others were taken in through a door behind the couch, perhaps to sort out business matters or to leave more details. Whatever reason people had to be here, the line moved without a hitch, the meet and greet, as Marni thought of it, a smoothly organised process.

The man in front of her reached the steps, and although instinct told her to flee, the memory of the greyness in Pop's face held her steadfast in the grassy courtyard.

He *had* to have the operation!

The man moved on and one of the flunkeys supporting the main act waved Marni forward. Following the actions of those she'd seen, she approached swiftly, knelt on the pillow set before the robed figure and bowed her head, then lifted it to look at the face she'd seen in the newspaper back home and on billboards around the city.

The face she'd seen in Theatre, only in his snowy headdress he looked so different…

'But—you're—you're *you*,' she managed to get out before words evaporated from her head.

Gaz was staring at her, as bemused as she was apparently, although once again she suspected there was a smile hovering somewhere in his eyes.

'I am,' he finally said. 'Definitely me. How may I help you?'

The voice had its usual effect, and Marni dissolved completely into a morass of words and half-sentences that she knew were making no sense at all.

'Stupid, I knew that—but Pop needs the op—and then the photo—photos really—you were in the paper—and the job there—here—and I know it's silly but he really wanted—so I came—'

'You came?' Gaz repeated.

Marni took a deep breath, looked into the face of the man she lusted after and smiled at the absurdity of it all.

'Actually,' she said, almost totally together now, 'I came to—well, to say hello and show you a photo. Apparently we were betrothed, you see, a long time ago, and I know it's stupid but I promised Pop I'd try to meet you and—'

She was rattling on again so she stopped the babble and reached into the pocket of her borrowed abaya, but before she could pull out the photo the man she'd written off as a flunkey had grabbed her wrist in a grip of steel.

'I think she wants to marry me, not shoot me,' Gaz said, adding something in his own language so the man withdrew his hand and stepped away, leaving Marni burning with embarrassment.

Gaz took the photo, frowning at it, thinking back perhaps, looking from it to Marni, shaking his head, serious now, although a gleam of amusement shone deep in his eyes.

'Oh, but this is wonderful!' he finally declared, a delighted smile flashing across his face. 'We cannot talk now, but you have no idea how fortuitous this is. Mazur will take you to a side room, get you tea or a cold drink. I will join you shortly.'

Marni was still trying to work out the wonderful and fortuitous bits when Gaz reached out to help her back to her feet, indicating she should follow the man who'd stepped forward on his other side.

Totally bewildered by the whole charade—Gaz was Prince Ghazi? How could that be?—she followed Mazur, stumbling slightly as she was about to enter the room and realising she hadn't removed her sandals.

They entered a huge, open room, with high, arched doorways curtained in what looked like gold-coloured silk, the drapes pulled back and held with golden, heavily tasselled cords. The floor was of white marble, inlaid with coloured stones that made twining patterns of leaves and flowers, so brilliantly beautiful she had to pause to take them in.

Scattered here and there were immense carpets, woven in patterns of red, blue and green. Low settees were placed at intervals along the walls, cushions piled on them. Here and there, groups of people sat or stood, obviously waiting for further conversation with Gaz—Prince Ghazi!

'This is the *majlis*, the public meeting room,' Mazur explained. 'but you will be more comfortable in a side room.' He led her towards an arched opening to one side of the big area and into a smaller version of it—patterned marble floor, a bright rug and a pale yellow sofa with bright cushions scattered over it.

Mazur waited until she was seated on the softly sprung sofa before asking, 'You would like tea perhaps? We have

English tea or mint tea, cardamom, of course, and other flavours if you wish.'

His English was so impeccable, his courtesy so effortless he could have worked for English royalty.

Though apparently Gaz *was* royalty...

And she'd *kissed* him? Considered—well, more than considered—him a potential lover!

'Mint tea would be lovely,' Marni managed to reply, and waited until he'd departed before burying her head in her hands, desperate to make sense of what had happened.

She was finishing her tea and nibbling on one of the little cakes Mazur had produced when Gaz appeared, looking so utterly regal in his pristine white robe and starched headdress, a coronet of black silk cord holding it in place, that her heart fluttered again but this time with a degree of not fear but definitely trepidation.

'So, we are betrothed?' he teased, not bothering to hide his smile.

'Well, that's what Pop wrote, but who knows what your father put underneath—probably something about pleasing a daft old man—but it was all just a kind of a joke, me coming here. I didn't come here to hold you to a ridiculous betrothal, but with Pop so sick I made a deal with him. It's hard to explain...'

Marni was doing her best to sort things out, but she was becoming increasingly annoyed because the wretched man was so obviously amused by the whole thing while she was squirming with embarrassment.

Gaz came closer and the white gown did nothing to stop all the physical manifestations of lust that had struck Marni when she'd first set eyes on him.

Lust, she had discovered very quickly, was stronger than embarrassment, for all the good it was going to do her. This man was way out of her league in every way, so a casual affair was out of the question.

She watched him, nervous, apprehensive, wondering just what he might be thinking.

'Actually,' he said, coming to sit beside her on the couch, 'the betrothal is a splendid idea. You may not know it but I have seven sisters, six of whom are bent on finding me a wife.'

'Only six?'

Marni was interested in spite of herself, although she had to admit to a little twinge of dread as to where this betrothal idea might be leading.

'The seventh's heavily pregnant at the moment and fortunately has other things on her mind. But having six sisters producing eligible women for you almost daily is very difficult, especially when I'm trying to come to terms with this job. So your arrival has come at just the right time, and with the photo as proof that my father arranged it, my sisters can do nothing but accept it. It's perfect!'

Marni stared at him in disbelief.

'Perfect?'

'Absolutely perfect!' The dark eyes were definitely smiling.

'Are you saying you'll tell your sisters we're betrothed?'

'Of course.'

She shook her head then pulled herself together enough to demand, 'But that's all? Just betrothed? A temporary arrangement to stop them dangling women in front of you? That's all you want?'

'For the moment,' the white-robed figure replied, while Marni quelled an urge to run a fingertip along the fine dark line of his beard. 'I wouldn't rush you into marriage.'

'Marriage!'

The word came out as a startled squeak, and it was the squeak that brought her to her senses.

Mature, professional women did not squeak!

'Let's just back up here,' she said firmly, trying hard not to notice how exotically handsome he looked in his prince outfit. 'I know it was a ridiculous thing for me to do, coming here and rattling on about a betrothal, but you were meant—no, you weren't meant to be you to start off with—you were meant to be this kindly prince and I'd burble out my stuff, you'd laugh, I'd let Pop know I'd done it, he'd have the op to keep his part of the bargain, and everything would be fine.'

She hesitated then added, 'To be honest, it did cross my mind you might not be so kindly and I just might end up in a dungeon or deported at the very least, but Pop needed—'

Gaz held up his hand, the white robe falling back from his lower arm so Marni could see his wrist, fine dark hairs on his forearm, smooth olive skin...

'This Pop you talk of—he's the one who wrote on the photo?'

Marni swallowed hard, unable to believe a little bit of a man's arm could have excited her so much.

She managed a nod.

'What operation?'

Whether it was the tension of the day or her concern over Pop or simply relief to be talking about something other than her reason for being here, suddenly words flowed freely.

How Pop had always been an active man, involved in so many things, running different charities, on the boards of hospitals and refuges, years ago two stents had been put in and he'd continued on without missing a beat then suddenly this tiredness, exhaustion and a diagnosis of a faulty heart valve and blocked stents, two bypasses and open-heart surgery the only answer.

'We're sure he'll get through it, Nelson and I, but Pop feels at his age maybe it isn't worth it—'

Again Gaz lifted his hand and this time Marni refused to look at that erotic bit of forearm.

'Nelson?' Gaz asked, frowning now.

'The man who looks after Pop—he's been there for ever, looked after me as well. A kind of general factotum.'

But Gaz wasn't listening. He'd pulled out the photo and was staring at it.

'Where was this taken?' he demanded, and Marni explained.

'Apparently your father took over the whole hotel,' she added, and Gaz smiled.

'He was never one to do things by halves and I suppose if I was as young as I look then some of my sisters would already have been married, then there were the wives and the aunts and all the women the women needed to look after them whenever they travelled. But if he took over the whole hotel, where did you come into it?'

So Marni explained about the apartments.

'Pop bought one when the hotel was built and still lives there with Nelson, so when I was dumped on him by my mother, I lived there too. We were allowed to use all the hotel facilities so I probably met you in the pool or garden.'

'Nelson!' Gaz said. 'That's what brought it back to me. I kept calling him Mr Nelson and he'd tell me, no, his name was Nelson.'

He looked from the picture to Marni then back to the picture, tracing his finger across the images of the two children.

'I asked you to marry me,' he said quietly.

Being flabbergasted took a moment, then Marni laughed. And laughed!

'Oh,' she said, finally controlling her mirth, 'that's what it must be about. A child's proposal—the sort of thing that would happen at kindergarten—then your father and Pop humouring you by having the photo taken and writing on the back.'

It took her a moment to realise her amusement wasn't shared. In fact, Gaz was looking particularly serious.

'But don't you see?' she said. 'It was a joke between the two men. It's not as if it meant anything.'

Gaz continued to study her.

'Would you mind very much?' he asked after the silence had stretched for ever.

'Mind what?'

'Being betrothed to me?'

Mind? Marni's heart yelled, apparently very excited by the prospect.

Marni ignored it and tried to think, not easy when Gaz was sitting so close to her and her body was alive with its lustful reactions.

'To help you out?' she asked, hoping words might make things clearer. 'With your sisters?'

Gaz smiled, which didn't help the lustful business and all but destroyed the bit of composure she'd managed to dredge up.

'That, of course, but it's more than the sisters. I have to explain, but perhaps not here, and definitely not now. There are people I need to see, supplicants from this morning. Are you free for the rest of the day? Would you mind very much waiting until I finish my business? Mazur will see you are looked after, get you anything you want. You could explore the garden or even wander around the palace. It's exceptionally empty now without the harem, so you needn't worry about disturbing anyone.'

He touched her hand and stood up, apparently taking her compliance for granted, although, in fact, her mind had stopped following the conversation back when he'd said the word 'harem', immediately conjuring up visions of dancing girls in see-through trousers and sequinned tops, lounging by a pool or practising their belly dancing. Was it because he'd said the word with a long 'e' in the last syllable, making 'hareem' sound incredibly erotic, that the images danced in her head?

She watched the white-clad back disappear through a side door.

He *had* made it sound as if the lack of a harem was a temporary thing, a slight glitch, she reminded herself. Which meant what?

And wasn't having no harem a positive thing?

What was she thinking?

A harem or lack of one would only affect her if she was *really* betrothed to him, and as far as she could re-member—it had been a very confusing conversation—she hadn't actually agreed to even a pretend betrothal.

Had she?

And surely harems no longer existed?

Not dancing-girl harems anyway...

She pushed herself off the sofa and, too afraid to wan-der through the palace, even one without a 'hareem', she retreated to the gardens, thinking of pronunciations. Gaz with its short 'a' sound, suggested a friendly kind of bloke, sexy as all hell but still the kind of man with whom one might have had an affair, while Ghazi—which she'd heard pronounced everywhere with a long 'a', like the one in 'bath', sounded *very* regal.

Frighteningly regal!

And it totally knocked any thought of using the man to overcome her other problem right on the head! Ordinary women like Marni Graham of Australia didn't go around having affairs with kings or princes.

Even a pretend betrothal was mind-boggling!

A wide path led to a central fountain and, after playing with the water for a while, she turned onto another path, this one running parallel to the main building, leading to what appeared to be another very large building. In front of it, on a wide lawn, four boys were kicking a soccer ball. A wayward kick sent the ball hurtling in her direction and, mindful of Nelson's coaching tips, she kicked it back, high and hard, aiming it at the tallest of the boys, who raced to meet it and headed it expertly towards the makeshift goal—two small topiary trees spaced conveniently apart.

The lad high-fived all round then turned towards her, speaking quickly.

Marni held up her hand and shook her head.

'I'm sorry, I don't understand your language.'

The older boy came closer, looking her up and down, waving his hands towards her clothing as if to ask why she was dressed like she was.

She lifted up the black abaya to show her jeans and the boys laughed, the tall one inviting her to join the game.

'That's if you can run in a skirt?' His easy command of English made her wonder if he went to school overseas, or perhaps to an English language school here.

'I'm sure I can,' she assured him, and joined the boys, kicking the ball from one end of the grassed area to the other. She'd just sent it flying over the top of the topiary goal posts when a tall figure appeared, not in scrubs, or in the intimidating white gown, but in jeans as faded as hers, and a dark blue polo shirt that had also seen better days.

'Ghazi!' the boys chorused in delight. 'Come and play. This is Marni, she's nearly as good as you.'

Although he'd been looking for her, he'd hardly expected to find her playing soccer with his young nephews. The hood of her cloak had slipped off her head and her headscarf was dangling down the back of her neck, hiding the thick plait of fair hair. Her face was flushed, but whether from exertion or embarrassment he had no idea, and she was the most beautiful thing he'd ever seen.

Best not to get further entangled, his common sense warned, for all the betrothal idea was so appealing. But against all common sense he joined the game for a few minutes then told the boys he had to take their playmate away.

He was pleased to see they all went up to her and held out their hands to say goodbye, only Karim, the eldest, bold enough to invite her to play with them again.

How old was Karim? Surely not yet a teenager, although these days who knew when hormonal changes would rear their heads.

Marni had fixed her scarf and pulled the hood back over her head as she approached him.

'I do hope I wasn't doing the wrong thing,' she said, the flush still visible in her cheeks. 'The ball came towards me, I kicked it, and next thing I knew I was part of the game. They're good, the boys. I played for years myself, never good enough to make a rep team but enough to know skill when I see it.'

'They're soccer mad, just as their father is. His dream is to get Ablezia into the World Cup. For a country that doesn't yet have its own international team, it's a huge task. I'm pretty sure that's why I landed this job.'

'This job?'

The pale grey-blue eyes looked into his, the question mirrored in them.

'Ruler—supreme commander—there are about a dozen titles that my major-domo reads out on formal occasions. My uncle succeeded my father, who was an old man when I was born—the first son after seven daughters. Here, our successors are chosen from within the family but not necessarily in any particular order, but I had assumed Nimr, my cousin, would succeed *his* father and I could continue my surgical work, but Nimr the Tiger didn't want the job—his focus is on sport—and so here I am.'

Had he sounded gloomy that he felt soft fingers touch his arm?

'Is it such a trial?' the abaya-clad blonde asked.

'Right at this very moment?' he asked, covering her hand with his. 'Not really!'

The boys started whistling as boys anywhere in the world would do at the tiniest hint of romance, and he stepped back, gave them what he hoped was a very princely glare and put his hand on Marni's back to guide her away from them.

He'd have liked to tell them to keep quiet about her, but that would only pique their curiosity further, and he knew that before they'd even eaten lunch the boys would have relayed the story of the soccer-playing visitor to Alima, his eldest sister, wife of Nimr and mother of the precious boys they'd waited so long for.

'And the prime mover in the "find a wife" campaign,' he added, the words spoken aloud before he realised it.

'Who's the prime mover?' Marni asked, stopping by a pomegranate tree and fiddling with her scarf.

Gaz explained the relationship.

'Is that why they live so close? Not in the main build-ing but within the walls?'

He looked at her, wondering if the question was noth-ing more than idle curiosity, although he was coming to believe that was unlikely. He was coming to see her as a woman who was interested in the world around her, eager to learn about it and discover new things.

Could this crazy idea work beyond a pretend betrothal?

'My uncle was living in the palace when they married, so naturally he built them the house nearby. This palace is new, or newish. My father built it when he tired of travel-ling from our home in the old city to here. Ablezia came late into the modern world, and we are a people who are slow to change. Obviously when the world changed so dramatically in these parts, we *had* to change—to learn new ways, to understand the intricacies of new business structures and international relations. My father was the right man for the job, because he understood it had to happen.'

'And you?' his perhaps betrothed asked softly. 'Are you the right man for the job?'

CHAPTER FOUR

GAZ—SHE COULDN'T think of him as anything else—didn't reply, simply putting one hand in the small of her back to guide her along a path between the huge houses towards what looked like stables beyond more garden.

Not stables but garages.

'There *are* horses,' he said, 'at the old palace, but I think my father realised we'd have no use for them here, so where, traditionally, the stables would be, he built "stalls" for cars.'

'So many cars?' Marni queried, seeing the long line of garages.

Gaz shrugged.

'Oh, you never know when someone might need to go somewhere,' he said, nodding to an elderly man who came forward to meet them. The man wore the loose trousers and long tunic top common among the locals, with a snug-fitting, embroidered cap on his head.

Listening to the fluid sounds of the words as Gaz spoke, Marni felt a longing to learn the language—to learn all she could about this fascinating country, although, she realised rather glumly, once the pretend betrothal ended she'd certainly have to leave.

If there *was* a pretend betrothal...

'I was explaining we won't need a big car and driver,

but Fayyad is horrified. He feels I'm not respecting my position enough.'

Again a touch on the small of her back, and her body's inevitable response.

Gaz steered her to where a battered four-wheel drive was relegated to a car port rather than a garage, and held the passenger door open for her.

Still totally bemused by the outcome of this visit to the palace, Marni climbed in. The day had taken on a dream-like quality, and she was moving through the dream without conscious thought. Gaz slid in behind the wheel and drove out through a rear gate, waving to the two men who squatted on the ground beside the big open doors.

'To answer your question,' Gaz said, taking what seemed like a little-used track that appeared to lead directly into the desert, 'I am reluctantly coming to the conclusion that I *am* the right man for the job, although I would far rather have continued my surgical career. All I can hope is that once I've got the job sorted—I've only been in it a couple of months—I can continue operating, at least on a part-time basis.'

Intrigued by his answer, Marni turned to look at him— not a good idea, for he flashed her a smile and the reactions the light touch on her back had stirred came fully to life.

'So, what's the job, as we seem to be calling it, entail?'

Another flashing smile, though this one was slightly rueful.

'I'm still coming to grips with it, but it's mostly formal stuff—meeting representatives from foreign countries, listening to delegations from various committees, making rulings on things that are more to do with our cultural heritage than politics—we have an elected congress that takes care of politics. And then there's the entertaining—endless entertaining.'

The road had petered out and he drove swiftly and skilfully across the sand, taking a slanting line across a dune and pulling up on the top of it. Beneath them the sand fell away to rise again, and again, and again, rolling waves of red-gold, brilliant in the sunshine. Breathtaking in its beauty. Marni remembered what he'd said about the desert being as necessary as water to his people. Did he need its power now? Need to refresh himself in the same way as she looked to the ocean for the replenishment of her spirit?

She was staring at the dunes, her mind asking questions she couldn't answer, so didn't realise he'd climbed out of the car and walked around to open her door. Beyond him, she could see a low-slung shelter, dark cloth of some kind, held up in front by sturdy poles, high enough to sit under to escape the sun. In front of it a low fire burned, beside the fire were two ornate silver coffee-pots, like others she'd seen in the souk.

'Come,' he said. 'We have to eat so why not here?'

He took her hand to help her down, his words perhaps answering her question about his need for the power of the desert.

Leading her to the shelter, he motioned to a faded rug, spread on the sand and heaped with cushions. A large woven basket was set in the shade beside the rug, its lid open to reveal an array of goodies.

Marni sank onto the rug, tucking her legs sideways so the abaya fell around her. The desert was framed now by the dark material of the tent and she could only shake her head in the wonder of its beauty.

Shake her head about the fact that she was actually

here, not to mention seeing it with the man who ruled the country.

Impossible!

Gaz settled beside her, closer to the fire.

'We must have coffee first,' he said, lifting one of the ornate pots and taking two tiny handle-less cups from the top of the basket. He poured the strong, thick brew easily into the tiny cups, passing her one before setting the pot back by the fire.

'Traditionally you should drink three cups, but it's definitely an acquired taste so you may stop at one.'

His smile teased at her senses and in an attempt to settle herself she gulped the drink, tasting the gritty lees but not finding them distasteful.

'And now we eat,' he said, and she wanted to protest—to ask what they were doing there, apart from picnicking, of course. To question the betrothal stuff and try to sort out what was happening. But he was producing bread, and cold meats, salad vegetables and fruit, serving her this time, piling goodies on a silver platter, handing it to her and urging her to eat.

Looking at the food, varied and enticing, she realised how hungry she was, and, not having much option now he'd handed her the plate, she ate.

Gaz watched her while he ate, wondering about this woman fate had thrust into his life. She was using her bread as cutlery, in the local way, and managing to do it without too much spillage. And as she ate she smiled, or muttered little sounds of appreciation, looking up from time to time to ask what a particular morsel might be.

She fascinated him, and not just in a physical way, although the physical attraction was extremely strong. Could this extraordinary idea work?

It was certainly worth a try.

He thought back to the night he'd first kissed her on the balcony outside the restaurant and remembered the surge of desire he'd felt—a surge that had almost led to his suggesting they take it further...

A betrothal would put that off limits. He could hardly be seen sneaking in and out of her room, or sneaking her in and out of the palace, although...

There was no although, but what if the betrothal led to marriage?

It needn't be a long betrothal, and if the marriage didn't work he would make sure she was amply compensated—these things were understood in his country...

Marriage was the logical answer. His body tightened at the thought, but she hadn't actually said yes to the betrothal, had she? He'd have to start there, he realised as she set aside her plate, all but empty, and wiped the damp, scented towel he handed her, across her lips.

'That was amazing,' Marni told him as she put her plate down on another mat. 'Just amazing!'

He turned to her, and reached out to touch her chin, tilting her head so he could look into her face.

'I'm glad,' he said, 'and now we're both fed, perhaps we can get back to the conversation.'

'The job?'

'The job!' he confirmed. 'Actually, endless entertaining is more time-consuming than difficult. I'm concerned that it might bore you to death.'

He had moved towards her as he spoke and now he leant forward and kissed her on the lips.

Thankfully, the shock of what he'd said lingered long enough to prevent Marni from responding to the kiss.

'Won't bore *me* to death?' she shrieked. 'Why on earth would it bore *me* to death?'

Now he frowned, and his eyes seemed darker than ever, though could black be any blacker?

'You think you'd enjoy it?' he asked. and it was her turn to frown.

'Why should I enjoy it, or be bored by it?' she demanded.

His answer was a smile, and if she'd managed to squelch her reaction to the kiss, she failed with the smile.

'Because, as my betrothed, you'll be by my side a lot of the time. I know that's an imposition, but I have women who'll help you all the way. The harem will be back in the palace next week, and I've sisters and nieces and cousins, even aunts, who'll be only too happy to shop with you for suitable clothes, to set you up with anything you need, and make sure you know the protocols.'

It would have been confusing if once again Marni's mind hadn't balked at the 'harem' word. Although if it was only a pretend betrothal, did the harem really matter?

Yes!

'This harem?' she asked, then stopped as she really didn't think she could mention belly-dancing females in see-through trousers.

'The harem?' Gaz repeated, making it exotic again with his pronunciation.

He looked puzzled then suddenly began to chuckle.

'You weren't imagining a seraglio, where you?'

'I've no idea what a seraglio is,' Marni said crossly, 'but if it's scantily clad women, lounging around limpid pools eating grapes and belly dancing then, yes—that's how everyone *I* know imagines a harem.'

The chuckle became a laugh and looking at him, with the tension she'd seen earlier washed from his face, she was once again tugged into the extraordinary sensual power of this man.

'The harem is simply a group name for the women of the family—women and children, in fact. My mother is part of it, my father's other wives, aunts and cousins and even more distant relations, also friends of all the women. Some come and go but the core of them moves together.

'Right now they are all at the old palace where one of my nieces is preparing her wedding chest. Years ago it would have meant a trip to London and Paris and taking over hotels, having stores like Harrods opening at night especially for them, but now they've discovered the internet, shopping has taken on a whole new dimension.'

There was more than a touch of cynicism in his voice so it took a moment for Marni to absorb what he'd said—taking over an entire store?—and then she wondered about the wedding chest. Should she ask? No, another diversion would take her further from where she needed to be.

'Okay,' she began then found she didn't know how to continue. She gazed out at the desert sands but there was no help to be had there. *What* had he been saying before she was thrown off track?

Shopping, suitable clothes, protocol—

'Okay?' Gaz prompted gently, and she turned to face him once again, his gentle smile causing so much confusion she stuttered into speech.

'B-b-but if it's just pretend—just for your sisters—do I have to do all that formal stuff? The "by your side" stuff? I've got my job, you know—well, of course you do—so surely...'

The words fell off her lips as something in his eyes—intensity, or was it intent?—caused such severe palpitations in her chest she couldn't breathe.

It had been intent she'd read. She realised that the moment his lips, once again, closed on hers.

Her mind shut down completely.

Was it a minute or an hour later that he released her? She had no idea, only knew she felt so weak and shaken she had to lean against him, her breath coming in little gasps, her brain slowly returning to work, though not offering much by way of explanation as to why this man, of all the men she'd met in her life, should have such a disastrous effect on her.

Nothing to do with the fact he's the most gorgeous guy in the known universe, the voice in her head suggested.

There was that, of course, but why her?

He eased away, smiling at her, a teasing smile, as if he knew exactly how much damage his kisses did to her.

'I don't think we have to pretend about the attraction between us,' he murmured, and the shiver that ran down Marni's spine told her just how dangerous this situation was.

'But that's different. It's the betrothal thing—*that's* the pretence.'

She was babbling again!

'So you're not denying the attraction?'

The words may have been innocent but she heard the challenge behind them and glared at him.

Pulling herself together with a mammoth effort, she tried again.

'I'm not talking about the attraction, Gaz,' she began, then hoped she wasn't breaking some unknown protocol by continuing to call him that. 'I know I started this nonsense about the betrothal by showing you the picture and, yes, when you said it would help you out, I kind of went along with it. But appearing in public, wearing clothes, meeting people, deceiving them really, well, I don't think that's quite me.'

'You'd rather meet people naked?'

It was the glint in his eyes as much as the words that made her want to belt him one. Except she probably *would* be thrown into a dungeon if she hit the ruling prince.

Would that be such a bad idea? A nice cool jail cell with no diversions?

'You know what I mean,' she retorted. 'It's not so much the fuss and public stuff, though that's mind-boggling enough, but the—the deception. I mean, your family, your mother, people who care about you, what are they going to think when the pretence ends and I go back home?'

He smiled and took her hand, rubbing his thumb across the backs of her fingers, sending tingling messages along her nerves and searing heat through her body.

'Don't worry about that for an instant—they'll all blame me. I've been a lost cause to the family ever since I insisted on studying medicine instead of business or commerce. It's one of the reasons I thought I was safe from the ruler's job, but as it turned out, there are so many people in our parliament and public service with all the right degrees, the fact that I don't have a huge amount of knowledge about international business isn't a disadvantage.'

Somehow his mood had changed and Marni sensed hidden depths in this man, for all he joked about the 'job'.

'But you *do* know people, surely that's more important than a business degree,' she said softly, and his hand tightened on her fingers.

'Ah!' he said softly. 'So someone understands.'

Uncertain what he meant, Marnie was about to ask, but he'd turned to look out at the desert again, and she sensed a remoteness in him, as if he was disconnected by his thoughts.

Disconnected from her as well.

Did someone not want him to be the ruler?

Someone in his family?

Or did he feel detached from his family?

Had it been a real problem for him, going against their wishes to follow his own path? He had certainly seized on her silly betrothal photo, grabbing it like a drowning man would grab a tiny stick, so his sisters' representations must have been bothering him.

And now you're back at the betrothal!

Had he guessed that her thoughts had returned to it that he turned back to her and lifted his hand to tuck a stray lock of hair behind her ear?

'Maybe our betrothal could turn out to be more than a pretence, Marni,' he suggested, his voice deep and husky.

With desire?

She was still wondering when he continued, 'We may not know each other very well, but there's time enough to remedy that, and you can't deny the attraction between us.'

His eyes held hers.

No, she couldn't deny the attraction, but…

She shook her head.

'I'm sorry, but I simply cannot imagine what would lie ahead, so how could I possibly agree to anything?'

'I would be there with you all the way. I would give you every support, give you anything you needed or wanted,' he said, his voice so serious she found herself shivering, although the air was warm.

The tension in the shade of the tent was palpable now, so thick Marni imagined she could feel it pressing against her skin and taste it on her lips.

But how to break it?

'Let's just go with the betrothal for now,' she said. 'And maybe keep it quiet—just letting your sisters—your family—know. You can use the excuse of Pop's operation—blame me for not wanting a fuss at this stage. Then if you need me to accompany you to official functions, I can start slowly, so it isn't some big deal but something people gradually get used to. Would that be possible?'

He rested his palm against her cheek.

'Anything is possible,' he said, as he slid the hand behind her head to draw her close.

The kiss was so gentle she responded in spite of herself.

Responded and was lost.

Admittedly, with Pop and Nelson's opinion of her always in her mind, she'd come late to the kissing scene, although she'd eventually made up for lost time, exchanging kisses with any number of young and not so young men over the years.

But had she ever experienced a kiss that made her toes tingle?

A kiss that sent shivers spiralling along her nerves, sensitising the skin at the back of her neck, along her arms, across her breasts, not to mention other places previously immune to spiralling shivers?

Not that she could recall.

And surely if she had, she wouldn't have the other problem.

Dear heaven, she was melting, disintegrating, a helpless mass of quivering flesh.

His hand was moving on her arm, leaving lines of heat where it had touched yet still his lips held her in thrall, held her and seduced her, his searching tongue making promises she barely understood.

Eventually he lifted his head, looking down into what was undoubtedly a face flushed scarlet by her reactions.

'I'll need to find you somewhere to live,' he said as calmly as if he hadn't just destroyed any common sense and will-power she might once have had. 'The harem would swamp you, drive you mad with all their so-called help. My sister, Tasnim, the pregnant one, would be best. Her husband is away so she'll enjoy the company. She's banished all the women in her family to the main harem because they were fussing over her too much, but she'll love to have you visit.'

Still trying to collect herself post-kiss, Marni could only stare at him. Then, as the words took on a slightly suggestive air, she pulled herself together.

'I have a perfectly good little flat at the hospital,' she reminded him.

He smiled in such a way the shivers started all over again, but rather than pointing out that he couldn't be seen visiting her at the nurses' quarters, he merely said, 'Security!' and helped her up off the mat, leading her back to the car, seeing she was buckled in.

Was he really intending to go through with this absurd betrothal? Gaz asked himself as he eased the vehicle back down the dune.

He thought of the kiss and the fires it had lit within him, then shook his head at the absurdity of the situation.

Was it lust or simply one-upmanship against his sisters that was making him push it?

And if it was lust, wasn't becoming betrothed to her the one certain way of ensuring he couldn't act on the lust—well, not beyond a few very heated kisses?

Very, *very* heated kisses, he amended, thinking of the taste of her, the softness of her lower lip as he'd sucked it gently into his mouth…

He glanced at the woman who sat so quietly beside him, the colour subsiding from her cheeks. If he could only get past his visions of how good they'd be in bed, maybe he could think clearly about the future—the immediate future anyway.

Men in his family didn't marry for sex. Such appetites could be satisfied in other ways with willing partners who were well looked after financially when the arrangement ended.

Not that he'd had any such arrangements, though there'd been affairs, some almost serious, during his student and university days.

But marriage?

Essentially, one married to produce children, but also, more often than not, for political reasons—uniting warring tribes, gaining power against a neighbour, improving the bloodlines of their breeding horses or camels.

He found himself chuckling at the thought and when the blonde who'd exploded into his life turned towards him, he shared his thoughts—not the children part, but the rest.

She grinned at him.

'Well, if your camels need some improvement in their genetic make-up then even being betrothed to me might ruin your chances with someone whose father has vastly superior camels.'

He reached out to touch the silvery fair hair.

'My camels will just have to take their chances, although you have no idea what a sacrifice I'll be making. My family have bred beautiful camels for generations. And we expect to win most of the prizes at the annual camel show.'

'A camel show? The camels all on show? How are they judged?'

Her interest was so apparent he felt warmth stirring inside him—something quite different from the heat he'd experienced earlier. This was pleasure, pure and simple—pleasure at how this woman took such an interest in everything about his country, a genuine interest that went beyond politeness. He wanted to stop and talk to her again, this time about the camels—*his* camels—but the palace was in sight and he'd already stolen too much time out of his schedule.

He slowed the car then stopped so he could explain.

'I must go back to my office before someone sends out a search party, but Fayyad will drive you to the hospital and wait while you pack, then take you to Tasnim's house. Fayyad will let me know when you are on your way and I will meet you there. In the meantime, I will phone her and explain and organise a permanent driver for you if you want to continue to work while we make the necessary arrangements for our betrothal.'

He saw the objections rising in her mind but before she could launch them he claimed her lips once again, thankful for the darkly tinted windows in the vehicle for they were right outside the palace gates.

He felt her resistance, but only momentarily…

CHAPTER FIVE

MARNI SANK DEEP into the softly cushioned seats in the black limousine and battled to make sense of the day. Not even a full day, for it was still early afternoon. Yet here she was being driven to her flat under orders to pack and go off to stay with a total stranger—a pregnant stranger—who would help her deal with being betrothed to the country's ruler.

How had this happened to her?

She certainly hadn't set out to become betrothed to the man—all she'd wanted was for Pop to have his operation.

Pop!

What on earth could she tell Pop?

She heard the groan that escaped her lips then realised she needn't tell him anything—not yet. All she had to do was email to say she'd kept her part of the bargain and met Ghazi, and she expected Pop to let her know the date of his operation.

Ghazi!

The Gaz-Ghazi thing was a whole different problem. Yes, she'd been attracted to Gaz right from the beginning, but the man she'd been kissing wasn't Gaz, he was Prince Ghazi and given that the betrothal was a pretence, she really should stop responding to his—Gaz's? Ghazi's?—kisses.

Shouldn't she?

Nothing was going to come of it—of the kissing business. Given her private reason for coming to Ablezia, she might well have had an affair with Gaz if things had turned out differently, like if he'd been Gary from Australia, but she had a nasty suspicion that rulers of places like this didn't have affairs with women to whom they were publicly betrothed. With other women probably, but not their betrotheds.

And as for the other nonsense he'd been talking—about how maybe the betrothal would not be a pretence—well, that was just ridiculous. He was the ruler of his country. He might have joked about a suitable marriage for the good of his camels, but surely, in all seriousness, there would be certain expectations of him in regard to marriage—either political or familial—and she doubted she'd be considered suitable by any of his advisors or power-brokers.

She buried her face in her hands. 'Oh, Pop, what have you got me into?' she whispered, but Pop was a million miles away and hopefully in hospital so he was no help. She'd just have to sort this out on her own.

Why in the name of fortune was he doing this? The question lurked in the back of Ghazi's brain as he talked with supplicants who had been given lunch while waiting for his final decisions on their claims. His officials looked into all the claims then gave him their opinions so he could make a judgment. He discussed land rights, and the sale of camels, and fixed a bride price for the father of a young woman keen to marry out of her family—marry a foreigner, in fact.

Ironic, that! Should he be offering a bride price to Marni's grandfather?

Marni!

Her name sang its way into his conscious mind and he needed Mazur's discreet cough to bring him back to the subject at hand—an altercation over the placement of two stalls in the souk.

'Your families have worked stalls side by side for generations,' he told the two men sitting cross-legged in front of him. 'Why the trouble now?'

'It's his daughter,' one said.

In chorus with, 'It's his son,' from the second man.

'They like each other?' Ghazi guessed.

'Too much,' the father of the daughter spat. 'But she is already betrothed to a distant cousin—from when she was four—but young people these days!'

The situation was far too close to this morning's astonishing revelations, and he was feeling more and more uncomfortable as the two men explained all the reasons why their children should not marry, and therefore why their stalls should be moved so the young people were not in constant contact.

'A betrothal at such a young age need not stand,' Ghazi said cautiously, ignoring the fact that he was pushing for just such a betrothal to stand in his own situation. 'Times have changed, my friends, and if these two love each other, instead of fighting, can you not put your heads together and work out a way for them to marry and be happy? After all, you could then combine your stalls and have twice the space and twice the customers, surely. I could possibly arrange extra space for the expanded stall, by way of a marriage gift for the couple.'

Behind him, he heard Mazur's sharp intake of breath, and knew he'd overstepped some invisible barrier, but if the two young people were genuinely in love…

He heard the phrase—genuinely in love—echo in his head and wondered if he'd lost his mind.

'I want to see both of them,' he said, 'to hear from them how they feel. Make sure they are at the next citizens' meeting.'

Thus dismissed, the two men departed, united now, he had no doubt, in horror over what he had suggested.

'Genuinely in love!' Mazur mocked. 'What on earth has got into you, Ghazi? Since when was love a factor in the settlement of disputes? Or in marriage, for that matter?'

Ghazi turned to the man who was not only his first advisor but also his best friend, aware he had to be careful.

'We must move with the times, Mazur,' he said. 'You know full well that the system of arranged marriages is not infallible—many such marriages fail and many of our people seek and are granted divorces. Maybe marrying for love will be more successful—and don't start quoting me figures from the West where people do it all the time. I know about their divorce rates. But young people have always longed for love, so surely if they find it, can we deny it to them? Can we break up two families by standing in the way of these young people?'

He was obviously losing his mind, Ghazi decided as Mazur gave a disbelieving snort and walked away.

Surely it couldn't have been the couple of kisses he'd shared with Marni that had him turning an age-old tradition on its head.

Marrying for love?

No wonder Mazur was snorting.

Marni packed her things then sat on the bed in the small bedroom and tried to work out exactly what she was doing.

And why.

If you're finding it hard to make a decision, write a list, Pop had always said. That was how she'd decided which university to attend, which course to take, even, one slightly embarrassing time, which of two young men would take her to the hospital ball.

So, mentally, she made her list.

For going along with Gaz—Ghazi—on this betrothal thing was that she would be doing him a favour, and it was never a bad thing to have a favour owed.

Besides, Nelson had said he'd been a nice little boy who'd been very kind to her at a time when she'd been desperately alone and confused, so maybe *she* owed *him* one.

Then there was Pop, who'd be delighted, and by the time the betrothal ended, however they were to manage that, he'd be over the operation so could handle the news without too much of a problem.

And...

She couldn't think of an and!

Well, she could, but she'd already decided he probably wouldn't seduce her while they were betrothed.

Against—well, that was easy. The disruption in her life for a start, the hassle of whatever the betrothal would entail in the way of public appearances, the interruption to her work, having to get new clothes—

She smiled to herself and wondered if that should go on the 'for' list...

Then there was Gaz.

Was he a for or against?

A bit of both really, because as Gaz she liked him and more than liked his kisses, but as Ghazi, wasn't there something wrong with kissing him if their betrothal was only pretend?

Fayyad would be wondering what had become of her, but still she sat, looking down at her watch as she tried to work out what time it would be at home.

If she phoned Nelson, she could ask him what he thought, ask him what she should do, as she'd always asked him what to do, relying on his common sense and good judgement.

But Nelson had enough on his plate right now, looking after Pop, so she was on her own.

She stood up, grabbed her suitcase and made her way down to the foyer and out to the door, where Fayyad waited patiently in the car, climbing out when he saw her to open the back door for her.

'I need to stop at the hospital to see a patient,' she told him, feeling guilty because with all the 'will I, won't I' that had gone on in her head about attending the citizens' meeting she hadn't seen Safi for two days. 'I'll be half an hour, maybe a little more. Do you have to wait in the car, or can you go into the canteen and have a cool drink or a coffee?'

Fayyad smiled at her then lifted a Thermos and a book to show her.

'I am never bored while waiting,' he said, 'but thank you for your consideration.'

His English was so good she wanted to ask where he'd learned it but remembered that personal conversations seemed not actually forbidden but perhaps impolite. She must ask Gaz.

Ask Gaz?

Just because he'd kissed her it didn't mean…

Didn't mean what?

And surely the kisses hadn't made her feel more at ease with him than she did with Jawa, for instance?

Totally muddled, she watched as Fayyad pulled up in front of the hospital.

'I will be watching for you,' he said, as he opened the door for her, making her feel a total fool. She thanked him and hurried inside, hoping none of the nurses she knew had seen her stately arrival. But the staff entrance was around the back so she should be safe.

These niggling worries hung around her like a cloud of summer midges as she walked towards Safi's room, but vanished as soon as she entered. She'd vaguely been aware of intense activity in one of the rooms she'd passed, and a lot of scurrying further down the passageway, but surely whatever was going on, someone would have checked on Safi recently.

His face was pale but red spots of fever burned in his cheeks and his thin fingers plucked at the dressing on his lip while his body turned and twisted on the bed.

'Safi!' she said, coming to take the hand that worried at his dressing, feeling the heat of it.

She found the bell and pressed it, then grabbed a towel and ran water over it in the little attached bathroom, wringing it out then bringing it back to sponge his face and chest, his arms and legs, desperate to cool him down before the spike in his temperature could cause a seizure.

No one had answered the bell.

She pressed it again, talking soothingly to the little boy, careful not to touch the dressing as his wound was obviously causing him discomfort, or more likely, pain.

He was staring up at her, wide-eyed, panic and pain in equal measure in his face.

'It will be all right,' she said, and although she knew he wouldn't understand her words she hoped her voice would soothe him. Her voice and the cool, wet towel...

Wrapping the towel around his head like a turban so it

pressed on his temples and the back of his neck and could cool surface blood vessels in both places, she grabbed his chart. Thankfully all charts were written in English because of the imported staff, and although she couldn't read exactly what he'd been given at the last check, she could tell that it had been at ten in the morning.

Had no one seen the child since then, apart from ward cleaners and the maid who'd carried in the meal that was uneaten on his table?

Giving up on the bell, she carried the chart out into the corridor, heading for the nurses' station, needing urgent attention for Safi and ready to demand answers.

The place was deserted, although she could tell there was still a major commotion in one of the rooms she'd passed earlier and a fair level of noise coming from a room further up the corridor.

There had to be a nurse in one of those rooms.

Three nurses and two doctors, in fact, and a crash cart pushed to one side.

'She just went flat,' the nurse Marni hauled into the corridor explained, 'about two hours ago. The doctors thought we'd lost her but she's coming round now.'

Marni accepted it had been an emergency but that only accounted for three of the nursing staff.

Not that she had time to complain! She hurried the nurse towards Safi's room.

'I came to visit, and there he was, burning with fever.'

'Oh, not Safi!' the nurse wailed. 'I'll have to page Gaz—he insists on knowing any change in Safi's condition—and get a ward doctor in as well. Can you go back and sit with Safi for a few minutes?'

She looked about her and frowned as if she'd just become aware of the emptiness of the corridor and nurses' station.

'I've no idea where the others are,' she added, peering vaguely around.

'I don't care where they are,' Marni snapped. 'I just need someone to see Safi and see him now.'

She might have raised her voice just slightly, but she was pretty sure she'd kept it below a shout, which was what she'd really wanted to do.

Hurrying back to Safi's room, she wet the now warm towel and bathed him again, pressing the cold cloth on his wrists and in his elbow joints, below his knees and against his neck and head, talking all the time, wishing she knew his language, wishing she would somehow conjure up his mother for him, for his little body was now slack, his eyes closed—the fight gone out of him.

The nurse came in and Marni stepped back while the woman checked his pulse, temperature and blood pressure, then a young doctor appeared, looked at the figures and fiddled with the drip, checking the catheter in the back of Sufi's thin hand, making sure the tape was in place.

'I've been off duty for a few days but I know that since the wound in his hip where they took the bone from has healed quite well, he's been walking around the hospital, even going outside at times. He must have picked up an infection,' the nurse suggested as the doctor drew blood for testing.

An infection that could cause such a rapid response?

Marni wondered about it but said nothing—in this room she was a visitor.

And she was still angry that the rise in his temperature hadn't been picked up earlier, before he'd become so distressed.

Gaz's arrival provided answers. He must have been on the phone during his journey from the palace to the hospital, telling her, as he examined Safi, that apart from the child who'd needed resuscitation, an accident to a school bus had brought a rush of, thankfully, minor injuries to the hospital, diverting staff to the ER, then to top it off the mother of another patient in the post-op ward had gone into labour and actually given birth in her daughter's hospital room.

'Still no excuse,' Marni thought she heard him mutter, but the barely heard words were followed by a rush of orders, arranging for Safi to go straight to Theatre.

'But with his fever—with the infection still so active?' Marni protested.

Gaz shrugged.

'Unfortunately yes. His temperature rose the day before yesterday and we've had him on vancomycin, which is usually the most effective drug for multi-resistant bacteria, but it obviously isn't working. I need to remove the grafted bone before the infection spreads into good bone.'

He paused for a moment, then said, 'There are still staff problems. Will you scrub?'

'Of course!'

An orderly appeared to wheel Safi to Theatre and Marni backed out of his room so he could be moved, waiting until he was wheeled out then falling in behind the little procession.

Gaz was walking beside the gurney and turned to glance back at the woman who'd erupted into his life, spinning it in a direction he'd never expected it to take— well, not right now.

She'd come from what must have been a fairly momentous day, given the job he was thrusting her into, to see a child she barely knew, and now was quite happy to spend however many hours it would take in Theatre for

Gaz to remove the bone graft because there was no way the infection could be anywhere else.

She'd stripped off the abaya and was wearing jeans and a loose shirt, and just the sight of her stirred thoughts he shouldn't be having right now.

'I suppose the infection can't be anywhere but in the graft?'

Marni had caught up and was walking beside him, but apparently her mind was still firmly fixed on Safi. Gaz swung his mind back that way, determined to concentrate no matter how distracting he found his colleague.

'The site's red and swollen and obviously painful. The nurse who changed his dressing this morning should have noticed and alerted someone.'

'I wondered,' Marni said, 'but I didn't like to touch it.'

'You did enough, cooling him down and alerting the staff. Without you—'

He stopped, so angry, so upset for the little boy he needed his own language—and bad words from it—to release his rage.

But not at Marni!

'Thank you for being there—for caring enough to call in to see him,' he said, and lifted his hand to touch her on the shoulder. 'From me and from Safi!'

She didn't move away from his touch but turned towards him, the slight frown he'd seen before creasing the smooth creamy skin of her brow—and even a frown caused inappropriate reactions.

'But he's been on antibiotics since the operation—I saw that on his chart—and you've started stronger antibiotics—would they not work in time?'

Gaz shrugged.

'I daren't take the risk. Yes, there's risk involved operating when he's harbouring something bad, but...'

He sighed, before adding, 'I thought because our hospital is so new we'd avoid things like this for a few more years. The problem is that so many of the bad ones target bone, and the grafted bone is likely to be badly compromised.'

The crease in his companion's forehead deepened.

'So you'll take the graft out, then how long before you could do another one? You'd have to clear the infection first, and where could you harvest the bone? His other hip?'

Her mind was obviously more focussed than his had been—no inappropriate reactions for Marni!

'I'll take it out, that's enough for Safi today. Later, when we know he's clear of infection, yes, I'll have to harvest some new bone and, yes, probably from his other hip. Poor lad. He's been through so much and bears it all so bravely. I'd have done anything to have saved him from this.'

They'd stopped in the corridor outside the theatre changing rooms; the orderly and nurse pushing Sufi's gurney moved on and through the theatre's swing doors.

'Will he be able to go home to his family before the next op?'

Gaz studied her for a moment, so aware of her as a woman it was hard to concentrate on the question she was asking.

'And why do you wish to know?'

A faint colour rose in her cheeks.

'Well, if you must know, although I genuinely care about Safi and want what's best for him, I'm so darned confused about all that's happened today, and then walking along beside you as if *nothing* had happened, well, it seemed best just to keep talking about practical things rather than have a fit of hysterics in the hospital corridor.'

Her cheeks grew pinker and her eyes dropped to study the floor between their feet, and he felt an overwhelming urge to give her a hug—a big hug, a warm hug, a non-sexy hug, although how long the non-sexy part would last was a moot point.

'Me too,' he said, ignoring the urge. He touched her lightly on the elbow and waved her through the door into the changing rooms.

He'd obviously made good use of his time during his trip from the palace to the hospital, for an anaesthetist Marni had worked with before was already attending to Sufi, talking quietly to him as he set his drip on a stand and prepared to give him a pre-op sedative.

Jawa was also there and greeted Marni warmly, although she did raise her eyebrows.

'But you're off duty,' she murmured.

'And doing me a favour.'

It was Gaz who answered for her, coming into the theatre behind her.

'It is Marni who found Safi so ill,' Gaz added, causing Jawa to look from him to Marni, so many questions in her beautiful dark eyes Marni knew she'd have some explaining to do later.

Personal explaining, for all it might go against the local custom!

Three hours later, Safi was wheeled away to Recovery, the open wound where the graft having been cleaned out and left with a drain in it to leach out any more of the poison. Marni felt tears prick at her eyelids and knew it was tiredness—well, tiredness and the stress of the totally bizarre day, *and* her heartache for little Safi, who had already suffered so much, and underlying it all her worry over Pop...

Gaz caught her arm as she was about to follow Jawa

out of Theatre. He'd pulled his mask down so it hung loosely below his chin, and the fine line of beard was a little ragged. His eyes, however, still held her gaze, drawing her into the darkness...

'You are exhausted,' he said gently. 'I would suggest you go back to your flat here at the hospital but Fayyad tells me all your things are in the car. Let me drive you to Tasnim's. She is expecting you and will have waited up for you.'

Marni dragged her attention back from his eyes and nodded, too tired to argue, and anyway he was right, all her belongings were in the car. She slipped into the changing room, and again saw the questions in Jawa's eyes.

'Tomorrow,' she said to her friend. 'I'll return your abaya and explain tomorrow. I'll meet you at the canteen at ten.'

But could she explain?

Explain it all?

And how would a local woman feel about her ruler's betrothal to a foreigner?

Not to mention if she said it was a pretence.

So many questions to which she had no answers...

The ruler in question was waiting for her in the corridor.

'Is it going to cause you problems with your people, this betrothal?' she asked as soon as she was close to him. 'I know it seemed like a good idea at the time to get your sisters off your back, but what about the local population? Might they not be offended in some way? Feel I've cheated you, or you them?'

Gaz—he was definitely Gaz at the hospital—stared at her for a moment then shook his head.

'Do you worry over everybody?' he asked, the smile

in his eyes, and somehow in his voice as well, making her stomach curl.

'Of course not, but Jawa must be wondering what's going on and I wouldn't like—well, she's been so kind to me, I really have to try to explain to her before you do this breaking me to the public gradually business, and then I thought—'

He brushed his knuckles across her cheek and her mind went blank.

'That I might be lynched, or deposed, for getting betrothed to a foreigner?'

Marni managed to nod, but with Gaz so close and the sensation of that touch lingering on her cheek, she found it impossible to speak.

Or think.

And only just possible to breathe.

'Stop fretting,' he told her, 'and that's an order!'

He then put his hand gently on the small of her back—again—and propelled her down the corridor, into the car and out again only minutes later, in front of the low open patio of a house the size of a hotel.

Tasnim was a short, glowing, heavily pregnant woman wearing designer jeans—who knew designers made pregnancy jeans?—and a tight purple top stretched across her swollen abdomen.

She greeted Marni with a warm hug and made no secret of her delight.

'This will be such fun!' she said. 'I was bored out of my brain. I did keep working but got so fat I couldn't sit behind the desk any more and Yusef—Ghazi's told you he's my husband, hasn't he?—said to stop, then the wretched man took off to Europe for some round of international monetary fund talks and just left me stranded here.'

Marni could only stare at the beautiful, bubbly, excited woman.

'She *can* talk,' Gaz said, giving his sister a kiss on the cheek and asking where Fayyad should put Marni's luggage.

'Oh, Ahmed will take it.'

Tasnim waved her hand towards a white-clad figure and the luggage disappeared.

'But are you sure this is okay?' Marni finally managed to ask. 'Me being here, I mean?'

'Of course,' Tasnim told her, giving her another awkward hug. 'Not only will I have the fun of getting clothes for you—and spending lots and lots of Ghazi's money—but every one of my sisters will be green with jealousy that you're here and not with them.'

She clapped her hands.

'Oh, it will be delicious!'

'But I wouldn't want your sisters—' Marni began.

'Don't worry,' Gaz told her, resting his hand on her shoulder. 'They play these games of one-upmanship all the time, my sisters, but they still all love each other. Just wait, they'll be vying with each other to give you the best gifts, take you to the best silk shops, the best seamstresses.'

Marni closed her eyes as she realised this whole betrothal thing had spun right out of control and taken on a life of its own. She turned to Gaz so his hand fell off her shoulder, which did make it slightly easier to think.

'I can't take gifts,' she said, which was as close as she could get to protesting in front of Tasnim. 'It wouldn't be right!'

'Of course it's right,' Tasnim argued. 'You're his betrothed.'

But it's pretend! Marni wanted to yell, and as she couldn't, she made do with a glare at the man who'd got her into this situation.

Well, it had been partly her fault...

Perhaps mostly her fault...

'She's exhausted,' she heard Gaz say. 'What she needs is food, a bath and bed, and no teasing her for explanations or gossip or any chat at all!'

'Yes, Master,' Tasnim teased, 'but don't think I'm going to turn round while you kiss her goodbye. We've all been waiting far too long for you to fall for someone.'

He hasn't fallen for me, it's all pretence, Marni wanted to say, but didn't because even thinking about it made her feel a little sad and, anyway, Gaz was obviously giving his sister a piece of his mind, so stern did his words sound. Then, with one last touch on Marni's shoulder, he stalked away.

'Come,' Tasnim said. 'I won't tease you.'

She took Marni's hand and led her through a bewildering maze of corridors, across carpets with glowing jewel colours, through arches with decorative plaster picked out in gold and set with precious stones. The rooms she'd seen in the palace had been plain, though there, too, the carpets had been beautiful, but this was like some fantasy out of an old-fashioned book and, tired as she was, it took on a dream-like quality.

'Here!' Tasnim finally said, going ahead of Marni into a room the size of her entire hospital flat. A huge four-poster bed, hung with dark blue silk curtains, dominated one end of the room while the inner walls were lined with a paler blue silk, padded somehow and indented with buttons of the same colour.

'The bathroom is through that door and a dressing room through the one next to it. You'll find plenty of clothes in the dressing room because we like our guests to feel comfortable and sometimes they may not have brought clothing that will fit special occasions.'

She flung open a door into what looked like a very expensive boutique. A long rack down one side held clothes ranging from ballgowns to tailored shirts and skirts, while further down were jeans and slacks and even, she rather thought, some long shorts.

The other side of the room had shelves of shoeboxes and drawers containing exotic-looking underwear, still in its original packaging, and beyond the drawers long, filmy nightdresses.

For the harem—no, seraglio—belly dancers? was Marni's immediate thought. Wasn't this proof they still existed?

'Not that you need any fancy clothes here,' Tasnim was saying. 'Wear whatever you like. Now I'm pregnant, I do cover up with an abaya if I go into the city, but I always worked in Western clothes.'

Marni wanted to ask what work she did, to find out more about this lively, fascinating young woman, but tiredness had fallen on her like a great weight.

'Have a bath and go to bed, Tasnim ordered. 'I'll have a light meal sent up to you—just eat what you want. Tomorrow we'll talk.

'Thank you,' Marni said. 'I *am* tired.'

CHAPTER SIX

SHE'D ENTERED A world of fantasy, Marni realised when she woke in the luxuriously soft four-poster bed to find a young woman sitting cross-legged by the door, obviously waiting for the visitor to open her eyes.

'Good morning, I hope you slept well,' the young woman said, rising to her feet with elegant smoothness. 'I am Shara and I am to look after you. I shall bring you whatever you wish—some tea or coffee to begin with perhaps, then you must tell me what you wish for breakfast. Ms Tasnim sleeps late and has her breakfast in bed.'

'A cup of tea would be wonderful,' Marni told her. 'English tea if you have it. I can drink mint tea later in the day but need the tea I'm used to to wake me up.'

The girl smiled and disappeared, her bare feet making no sound on the marble floor, although Marni fancied she could hear the swish of the soft material of the girl's long trousers and the long tunic she wore over them.

Marni had a quick shower and, aware of her appointment with Jawa at the hospital, dressed in one of the pairs of loose trousers she'd brought from home, adding a tunic in her favourite deep blue-green colour.

'You dress like us?' Shara commented when she returned with the tea.

'I decided before I left home that if I was going out

in public it would be polite to follow the local customs,' Marni told her. 'In my flat, and possibly while I'm staying here, inside the house, I might pull on my jeans.'

'I am the opposite, I wear jeans outside,' Shara said. 'This is just a uniform for work.'

Marni sipped at her tea, wanting to know more—about Shara, about Ablezia, about—

'You speak such good English,' she said. 'Did you learn it at school?'

'At school and at college too, and I listen to recordings at home as well. I am training to work in hotels, you see. We are building many hotels now in our country and they will all need staff. One day, I would like to manage one, but first I must learn the basics of housekeeping, then I must learn how to run a kitchen, not to cook but to under-stand what goes on, then—oh, there is so much to learn.'

She flashed a bright smile at Marni, who smiled back as she said, 'You'll go far, I'm sure.'

'Not if I don't get a breakfast order from you,' Shara said, still smiling. 'The chef will have my head. What would you like?'

What would she like?

'What do you have for breakfast?' she asked.

'You would like to try a local breakfast?' Shara asked, obviously delighted.

'As long as it doesn't take too long to prepare. I have to be at the hospital at ten.'

Shara disappeared, returning with a round brass tray on which nestled six small bowls. In the middle of the tray round flatbread was folded into cones, the whole thing like some wonderful display made for a picture in a food magazine.

'Here,' Shara said, as she set it on the small table by an arched window. She pulled a plate out from under the bread and a napkin from beneath that again, and waited for Marni to sit. She then pointed to each dish in turn.

'This is labneh, our cheese, a bit tangy but soft, and dahl, you know dahl from lentils, and these are eggs mixed up and cooked with spices, some olives, some hummus, and here is honey, and jam, apricot, I think, and halwa—you know the sweet halwa?'

'It looks fantastic but I can't possibly eat it all,' Marni protested, and Shara laughed.

'You just eat a little of whatever you want. You use the bread to scoop it up or there is cutlery on the plate if you prefer to use that. Now, we would drink tea but tea you have had, so perhaps coffee?'

Marni agreed that she'd like coffee and as Shara disappeared once more, Marni began to eat, scooping bits of one dish, then another, trying them alone, then together, settling on the spicy eggs and labneh as her main choices and eating far more than she normally would for breakfast.

Coffee and dates finished the meal, and as she was thanking Shara, Tasnim burst into the room.

'I've come to make plans,' she announced, but before she could continue Marni explained she was meeting Jawa—and soon.

'Oh!' Tasnim was deflated but not for long. 'That is good. I send you with a driver in the car to the hospital and when you are finished with your friend he will bring you to the Plaza Hotel. The shops there are discreet and we can enjoy shopping without a crowd.'

'The Plaza?' Marni echoed faintly, thinking of the enormous, palace-like hotel she'd seen but had never visited.

'Definitely the Plaza, it is the only place,' Tasnim insisted, before whirling out of the room to make arrangements for a driver.

'You will like the Plaza,' Shara said, her voice so full of awe Marni felt even more uncertain.

'Have you been there?' she asked the girl.

'Oh, no, but I hear it is very beautiful and the boutiques there—well, they are for the very rich.'

Which you obviously are not. Marni felt she could hear Shara's thoughts. She'd know that from unpacking her suitcase.

Marni ignored the questions she'd heard in Shara's voice. She grabbed a scarf to wrap around her hair, found her handbag, then asked Shara to take her to wherever the driver would be waiting with the car.

'I daren't walk out of the room for fear of getting lost,' she told the girl, who smiled but was still treating her with more reserve than she had originally.

Treating her like someone who shopped at the Plaza!

Hell's teeth, Marni thought. Does money really change things so much?

She was early when she arrived at the hospital, so her feet took her automatically to Safi's room. The little boy was sleeping, but she'd barely registered that when her body told her who else was visiting him, although the second person had been in the bathroom, washing his hands, as she'd come in.

He was in full prince gear, so—pathetically—her breath caught in her lungs and her heart stopped beating.

'You look beautiful,' Gaz—no, he was definitely Ghazi—said, crossing the room towards her and taking her hands. 'You slept well? Tasnim is looking after you?'

He raised her hands to his lips and kissed each knuckle in turn, making it impossible for her to answer him.

Soft footsteps in the corridor made him release her

hands and step back, but the look in his eyes was enough
to bring all the embers of desire back to ferocious life.

Why *wasn't* he just Gaz?

'How is Safi?' Marni asked, in an attempt to dampen
the heat.

'He is well, his temperature is down and his sleep is
peaceful,' he replied, then he lifted one of her hands,
dropped a kiss on the palm and left the room, muttering to himself.

It had to be the stupidest idea he'd ever had, he decided as
he marched away from Safi's room. Here was a woman
he desired more than he'd ever desired a woman before
and he'd put her off limits by becoming betrothed to her.

And all to avoid the women his sisters were throwing at him!

But could he have accepted any of them, feeling as he
did about Marni?

And how *did* he feel about Marni?

He desired her but was that it? Would an affair have
satisfied that desire? Could they have shared some mutual pleasure and enjoyment then parted?

He wasn't too sure about that.

There was something about the woman. She was different, and not only in race but in…

Personality?

Guts?

It had taken guts to approach him yesterday, not knowing who he was or what might occur, but she'd done it for
her grandfather…

He needed to know her better. He'd go back to Safi's
room now.

'Sir!'

One of the junior doctors had caught up with him and

tapped him lightly on the shoulder. Had he called to him more than once?

'Your driver, sir, he has a message for you.'

Back to reality! Gaz strode towards the front entrance, aware his driver would only have sent for him if he was already late for the next thing on his interminable schedule.

Marni held the kiss in her hand as she made her way to the canteen. She felt slightly foolish. The kiss meant nothing so why hold onto it?

Did she want it to mean something?

Want it to mean love?

She shook her head at her thoughts and smiled sadly. Six times so far her mother had married for 'love' so, not unnaturally, Marni had a slightly skewed view of it.

The advent of lust into her life had really confused things, she decided as she dawdled down the corridor. Caught up in its snare, couldn't one mistake it for love?

Want it to be love?

Was that what had happened with her mother?

Again and again and...

She sighed, and put the problem out of her mind. Right now she had to get her head straight and work out exactly what she was going to say to Jawa.

Jawa!

Jawa meant passion or love—Marni had looked it up when she'd learned that most names had meanings. Ghazi—of course she'd looked it up as well—meant conqueror.

Hmmm!

Jawa was waiting in the canteen, two cups of coffee and a plate of sweet pastries on the table in front of her. Marni slipped into a chair opposite so she could look into her friend's face as she spoke.

The politeness of morning greetings and thanks for the coffee held off the revelations for a few minutes but finally she had to tackle the subject she'd come to discuss.

'You know I've mentioned Pop, my grandfather,' she began, then stalled.

'Your grandfather?' Jawa prompted.

'It's complicated, but I didn't know when I met him in Theatre that Gaz was Ghazi, your prince. The thing is, Pop had known him and his father when he was a boy—when Ghazi was a boy—and Pop wanted me to say hello to him while I was here, which was why I borrowed your abaya and went to the palace yesterday, and now we're kind of engaged to help him out with his sisters who keep finding women for him to marry.'

Jawa's eyes had grown rounder and rounder as Marni's disjointed explanation had stumbled from her lips.

'You're engaged to Prince Ghazi?' Jawa whispered, her voice ripe with disbelief.

'Only pretend—for his sisters,' Marni said desperately, but she rather thought that message wasn't getting through. 'And we're keeping it quiet but I've moved in to live with his pregnant sister, for security he says.'

It wasn't making much sense to Marni so she had no idea what Jawa might be making of it.

'The thing is, I don't know what his people—people like you—will think about it, because he should probably be marrying with better breeding stock for his camels.'

Drained now of words, Marni stared hopefully at Jawa, who seemed to have gone into some kind of fugue, although she did manage a faint echo.

'Camels?'

'So what do you think?' Marni eventually demanded, the silence adding to the tension already built up inside her.

'About the camels?' Jawa said faintly.

'No, not the camels, although apparently his camels are very important to him, but about me being engaged to him—betrothed?'

Jawa shook her head.

'I don't know what to think but if it's been arranged—your grandfather and his father—then that's how things should be. I know more of our people are marrying for love these days but arranged marriages have worked for centuries.'

'I'm not *marrying* him,' Marni told her. 'It's a pretend betrothal—because of his sisters—just while he sorts out his job—and then...'

'And then?' Jawa probed.

Marni shrugged.

'I have no idea,' she said. 'It's really all just too stupid for words, but I felt I should tell you because you've been so good to me. I'd like to keep working but we don't seem to have talked too much about that. Tasnim—that's his sister—seems to think clothes are more important.'

'Oh, clothes will be very important,' Jawa said, then she smiled and took Marni's hand.

'I only know him when he's Gaz, of course, as a colleague. He is much respected and admired. From the time he started work here, he has never made anything of his links with the ruling family and no one ever treated him any differently because of who he is. I don't think he expected to take over from his uncle, but he will do his duty well.'

Of course he will, Marni thought, feeling slightly let down, although she wasn't sure what she'd expected of this conversation.

Congratulations?

Certainly not!

Reassurance?

Of course!

'It's the pretence that bothers me,' she said. 'Will people—the local people—be upset when it ends?'

Jawa thought for a moment then turned Marni's hand in hers.

'I do not think so. They will accept his decision, whatever it is. Those who thought it was a bad idea to marry a foreigner will say at last he's come to his senses, and those who liked the idea will think, ah, that's the trouble with love because they will have been sure it was a love match.'

A love match?

For some reason, far from reassuring her, the words sent a wave of melancholy washing over Marni and she took back her hand—it wasn't the one with the kiss in it—and sighed.

Love, of course, was the other reason she had the virginity problem—her mother's version of love...

The Plaza Hotel was surely bigger than the palace!

That was Marni's first thought on seeing it as they drove up a long drive to an immense building spread across the top of a slight rise.

And far more opulent, she realised as she entered the enormous lobby so gilded and arched and carpeted it looked more like a posh showroom of some kind than a hotel.

Tasnim was waiting, perched on a chair beside a lounge setting.

'Would you believe they don't have ordinary chairs like this in the lobby?' she demanded, when she'd greeted Marni with a kiss on the cheek. 'I had to ask someone to find one for me. There's no way I could have stood up from one of those low, soft sofas without making a total fool of myself.'

Marni smiled, doubting the formidable Tasnim could ever make a fool of herself anywhere.

'Come,' Tasnim continued. 'We'll be given refreshments in the boutique. I phoned ahead and asked for my favourite one to be closed for us. The women from the other boutiques will come there with whatever else we need.'

A shop closed so she could shop? Once again Marni found herself in fantasy land.

'I've made a list,' Tasnim told her. 'I thought half a dozen everyday things for a start. Just things like you're wearing today so your way of dressing doesn't offend anyone. Then half a dozen formal outfits—two kinds—Western for entertaining diplomats and other foreigners, and Eastern for entertaining locals. And some casual clothes for at home and for when Ghazi visits.'

'I have my own clothes for at home,' Marni protested as they entered the boutique, a woman bowing them through the door.

'Nonsense! You can't be wearing the same thing every time you see Ghazi, now, can you?'

Couldn't she?

Marni felt a little lump of sadness lodged beneath her breast.

Because she knew Ghazi didn't really care *what* she was wearing?

Probably!

Although he *had* said she looked beautiful this morning...

The lump remained.

Tasnim was talking to the saleswoman, the words rattling around the beautifully set-up salon.

Marni was checked out, looked up and down, ordered

to turn around, then told to sit on a low love seat and offered tea.

She shook her head and looked about her. There was only one gown on display—a Western evening gown made of some silvery material, and sewn with beads and crystals so it shimmered under a discreetly placed light.

It appeared perfectly simple in style and cut and yet was breathtakingly beautiful.

'Local things first,' Tasnim declared, returning with the saleswoman and a young woman who was pushing a trolley hung with clothes, spectacular clothes in rich greens and blues, long loose trousers, patterned and beaded tunics that would go over them and at the end of the rack a selection of black abayas.

An hour later, Marni was the rather hesitant possessor of four new pairs of trousers and five new tunics. She'd put her foot down over Tasnim's suggestion she'd need half a dozen, listened in disbelief as Tasnim and the saleswoman claimed to have hundreds of such outfits, and had been talked into the fifth tunic because it was so beautiful.

It was the simplest of them all, not bright but a pale blue-grey with a pearl-coloured thread woven through it and the patterning around the bottom in the pointy-topped shape of the local arches, picked out in darker blue.

As for the abayas! Far from the plain cotton garment she'd borrowed from Jawa, these were woven from the finest silk, with delicate ebony bead embroidery around the hem, sleeves and neckline. Beautiful garments to cover other beautiful garments.

The fantasy deepened!

'If you choose a couple with hoods, it will save you tying a tight scarf over your hair when you go out,' Tasnim advised. 'Abayas used not to have hoods as we wore a hijab—a specially tied scarf—over our heads. But with the hoods, any of your scarves would go under the hood.'

The saleswoman hung the abaya Marni had tried for size back on the rack—on the buying side, not the reject side—and studied Marni yet again.

'Surely that's enough for one day,' she begged Tasnim, but her new friend wouldn't be distracted.

'We haven't done the scarves,' she scolded. 'If you're insisting on only having four outfits, at least you can vary them with scarves.'

Long scarves, as fine as gossamer, were produced, most in tantalising colours, all embroidered in different ways.

She was wearing the tunic she'd been unable to resist, and the woman found a scarf in the darker blue of the embroidery and draped it around Marni's head and shoulders.

'Perfect. It makes your skin gleam like alabaster and turns your eyes as blue as cornflowers,' Tasnim said, clapping her hands in delight. 'But you will need more. Darker ones are good for evening, and if you have a darker one over your hair, you can still tie it hijab style and need not pull the hood of the abaya over your head.'

Marni assumed Tasnim was talking sense but she was lost. She found herself drifting, doing whatever Tasnim or the saleslady told her, lost in the mad dream that had become her life.

The evening gowns were unbelievable—like things she'd seen actresses wearing on the red carpet when the Oscars were televised. And the names of the designers—names she'd heard with awe and had never in her wildest dreams imagined wearing clothes they'd designed.

But she was also tiring fast and after trying on and removing the sixth evening gown she found the energy to protest.

'Tasnim, we've settled on three, that's enough,' she said, although her eyes strayed to the silver creation on the shop model.

Tasnim saw her look that way then she said, 'Just one more,' and spoke to the saleswoman, who immediately began disrobing the mannequin.

'It's made for you with your fair skin and hair,' Tasnim insisted, and when Marni put it on she knew she had to have it. She'd never considered herself beautiful, but in this dress?

She remembered Gaz saying after dinner at the hospital that she was like a silver wraith—well, in this dress she almost was.

So why was that lump back in her chest and her heart hurting, just a little bit?

'Sandals next,' Tasnim decreed, and another saleswoman appeared pushing a trolley laden with shoeboxes. Marni gave up. She pushed her feet in and out of sandals, stood in them, walked around, and finally settled on a few pairs, although it seemed Tasnim was making her own decisions as at least ten boxes were piled together while the rest were wheeled away.

But when make-up and perfume were suggested, Marni stood her ground.

'I can handle that myself,' she said firmly. 'I have my own make-up and have always used the same perfume, a particular scent my grandfather first bought me when I was eighteen. I'm not changing that!'

Tasnim argued she needed more than one so she could choose according to the time of day and the occasion and the outfit, but Marni was adamant—she'd wear her own, any time, any day, anywhere!

Exhausted by the decision-making, all she wanted to do was go home—well, back to Tasnim's place, and lie on the bed, and try to make sense of all that had happened to her.

Although wasn't that bed part of the fantasy?

But Tasnim was ruthless.

'Of course we can't go home,' she said. 'We need to go over to the palace and get you some jewellery. Ghazi won't want people thinking he's too mean to give you jewellery and until he's got time to buy you some, there's a ton of stuff over there. Some of it's a bit old-fashioned, which is why we sisters all insisted our husbands bought us more—but we all got plenty of the family stuff in our bridal chests.'

Marni stopped outside the boutique to study the woman who'd taken over her life.

'Aren't pregnant women supposed to get tired and to need a lot of rest?' she demanded.

'Oh, phooey,' Tasnim replied. 'You sound like my mother. I'll rest later!'

So, to the palace they went, Marni regretting she hadn't stayed in one of her new outfits in case they ran into Ghazi, but that was stupid, wasn't it?

Once at the palace, Tasnim summoned Mazur and must have explained what they wanted for he led them through more tortuous passages, finally unlocking what looked like, but couldn't possibly have been, a solid gold door. Pulling a huge, old-fashioned key from beneath his kandora, he unlocked the door, pressed numbers on a very modern-looking security system pad, then turned on a light to reveal an Aladdin's cave of riches.

'Oh!'

Marni breathed the word, unable to believe that a picture from a childhood book could be springing to life in front of her. Yes, there were neat chests with little drawers in them, and glass cabinets with displays of stunning jewellery, but there were also open chests and large jars from which spilled what looked like all the treasures of the world.

'The children like to play with the chests and jars,' Mazur explained in a very disapproving voice. He was retrieving a long string of pearls from the floor as he spoke, and examining them for damage.

'But I couldn't possibly wear any of this kind of jewellery,' Marni protested. 'I'd look ridiculous!'

'So start simple,' the indomitable Tasnim told her. 'Take those pearls, for instance. They will go beautifully with that tunic you really like. Mazur, a bracelet or bangle to go with them and a ring, of course.'

Mazur poked through drawers, finally emerging with a bracelet that had six rows of pearls on gold wire and fastened with a gold catch.

'Perfect!' Tasnim declared. 'And now a ring.'

The ring he produced had a pearl the size of Tasmania, and Marni refused to even consider it, although a smaller ring, set with rows of seed pearls that went well with the bracelet, won her heart.

'Now that's enough,' she told Tasnim, but the woman was unstoppable. Ignoring Marni completely, she pulled out necklaces, bracelets and rings with stones that looked like emeralds and rubies. Studied them, then declared, 'No, we'll stick to sapphires because of your eyes, but now I am tired. Mazur, could you put together some sapphire sets and send them to my house?'

Mazur nodded, and followed the two of them out of the treasure trove, locking the door behind him before walking them out to the car. The driver held the door for Tasnim, while Mazur did the same for Marni, murmuring, as she slid past him, 'I am very happy for you and Prince

Ghazi.' Marni sensed the kindly man actually meant it and immediately felt depressed.

She hadn't realised just how much she would hate deceiving people—maybe not people generally, but nice people like Mazur.

Fortunately Tasnim seemed to have finally run out of steam so the drive back to her home was quiet.

'I *will* rest now,' she said, 'but the driver will take you wherever you wish to go, or you can ask Shara for anything you need if you decide to stay in your room. The boutique will package up all we've bought and send it here, probably by later today, so you can choose what you want to wear to dinner tonight.'

'Dinner tonight?' Marni queried.

Tasnim smiled.

'Did I not tell you? Ghazi phoned to say he would pick you up at seven to take you out to dinner. It will be to somewhere special so—no, I won't let you decide. I'll come to your room later and we'll decide together what you will wear. Remember, this will be your first public appearance and although as yet your betrothal is not known, people will notice you and begin to talk.'

Marni's stomach knotted at the thought, but she *had* agreed and she'd gone along with the purchase of all the new clothes so she couldn't deny being aware that they would be needed.

'Okay,' she said, letting the word escape in a sigh.

But underneath her trepidation a bud of excitement began to unfurl.

She would be seeing Ghazi—how easy it was to think of him that way after being with Tasnim most of the day—tonight!

Which was really pathetic if she thought about it. This was all pretence!

CHAPTER SEVEN

THE EXCITEMENT HAD waned by the time she was dressed, waiting with Tasnim in the big room at the front of the house. Her own reflection, as well as Tasnim's cries of delight, had told her she looked good, but uneasiness boiled inside her.

This dressing up in clothes paid for by someone else seemed to underline the fact that it was all pretence, and the subterfuge made Marnie feel queasy. It was one thing to pretend for the sake of his sisters but for other people that she would surely meet, people who looked up to him as their ruler—was it right to be deceiving them?

'Ghazi will not be able to take his eyes off you,' Tasnim was saying, 'and how he'll keep his hands off you—whoo-hoo, it will be near impossible. Such fun!'

Considering her more personal reason for being in Ablezia, Marni would have liked to ask if Ghazi would *have* to keep his hands off her, as Tasnim seemed to be intimating. But that question was far too personal—too fraught with hidden mines and traps to even consider asking.

Beside which, she was reasonably certain formal betrothals didn't include the couple going to bed together, while actually making love with the ruler of a country—

any country—was so far beyond Marni's imagining it had to be impossible!

'The car is here!'

Tasnim's—was he a butler?—appeared, and made the announcement, then vanished in his usual silent way.

'Oh, bother Ghazi,' Tasnim muttered. 'He's sent a car, not come himself, and I did want to see his face when he saw you looking so beautiful.'

'It's just the clothes,' Marni told her, using words to hide the little stirring of disappointment at Gaz's non-arrival, and her embarrassment over Tasnim's praise.

'No, it is you,' Tasnim argued. 'Of course the clothes help, but you have a serenity about you that enhances whatever you are wearing, and that's part of true beauty.'

As if! her head mocked, but Tasnim's words helped ease Marni's disappointment, and she walked out to the car, slipped into the back seat and settled her beautiful new clothes around her.

Cinderella going to the ball, was her first thought, but if that had been the case she'd have been wearing one of the ballgowns.

And glass slippers!

She sighed and wondered just what lay ahead of her on this, the second momentous day in this new, and totally fantasy, life.

Lost in her thoughts and concerns over pretence, she barely noticed where the driver was taking her until she saw the palace looming up ahead.

'We're going to the palace?'

Duh!

'No, miss, we're going to Sheikh Nimr's home. His wife, Sheikha Alima, is preparing a special banquet in your honour.'

A special *banquet*! Great!

Fortunately Gaz was at the top of the steps as the vehicle pulled up and it was he who came down to open the car door for her, taking her hand to help her out, the light in his eyes as he took in her appearance enough, for a moment, to still her nerves.

'You are beautiful,' he murmured, for the second time that day.

'It's the clothes—the dressing up in this gorgeous gear—anyone would look beautiful,' she said, trying for lightness, although her fingers clung to his for support.

His smile told her he didn't agree, and it was the smile, plus the sensations firing through her that made her remove her hand and regain some common sense.

'A banquet?' she queried.

'Only a small one,' he assured her, smiling as she spoke. 'Having put all the sisters' noses out of joint by asking Tasnim if you could stay with her for a while, I have to start the conciliation process. Believe me, growing up with seven sisters is better training in diplomacy than any university degree.'

They had reached the top of the steps, and he paused, turning towards Marni to explain.

'I have to start with Alima because she is the eldest. She has invited two other sisters, Meena and Ismah, and their husbands, as well as Nimr's brothers and their wives, the married ones. A small party and you do not have to remember everyone's names and if I don't get you inside very soon I shall have to kiss you right here and scandalise everyone.'

Marni had been trying to get her head around the names and wondering why only two sisters had been invited—with Tasnim she would now have met four of the seven—when Gaz—in a business suit so definitely Gaz—had added the last bit.

About the kiss…

So it wasn't *all* pretence…

Of course not, there's still the lust, she reminded herself, dousing her re-smouldering embers.

They paused at the front door, Marni preparing to slip off her sandals and noticing the ease with which Gaz removed his highly polished loafers.

'You learn our ways,' he said quietly.

'This one's easy,' Marni retorted, unsettled by the lust reminder as well as by his nearness.

The lust wasn't pretence.

Neither was it love!

But love's not been any part of this, the sensible part of Marni's brain responded.

And the funny lump of pain sneaked back into the middle of her chest.

'Have you an extremely tidy mind that you need to reposition your sandals three or four times, or are you having second thoughts about meeting the family?'

Gaz was waiting for her to move away from the neat array of sandals.

Marni pulled herself together and looked directly at him, hoping all her doubts and inner discussions weren't visible on her face.

'Only two of the other sisters?'

He smiled and her heart turned over.

Love not part of this?

'I'm breaking you in gently. I think you'll find Tasnim has already asked the others to lunch one day next week. Alima set the limits—ordered them all not to crowd you—and what Alima says goes with the women.'

He took her hand and placed it on his forearm, tucking her close to his side as they walked through the wide entranceway. Marni glimpsed the huge majlis off to the left, and was relieved when a white-clad servant bowed them into a smaller, though no less opulent room.

Where shades of yellow from palest lemon to deep, rich gold had been the dominant colours in the rooms Marni had seen in the palace, it was red that struck her here. Swathed red silk curtains framed arched openings into what appeared to be a courtyard garden, while deep vermilion couches were pushed back against the walls. The floor, again, was marble, but a creamy colour, streaked with red, so Marni wasn't surprised to find the woman walking towards her, hands outstretched in welcome, was also clad in what must be her favourite colour.

'My sister, Alima,' Gaz said smoothly. 'Alima, this is Marni.'

Alima clasped Marni's hands and drew her closer, kissing her on both cheeks—air kisses really, although the warmth of the woman's smile seemed genuine.

'What I wonder,' she declared as she looked Marni up and down, then down and up again, 'is how our father knew his son would be so difficult to please as far as women went, so he solved the problem early on, betrothing him to you.'

'I think it was probably a joke,' Marni said, the words popping out before she realised it was probably the wrong thing to say. But Alima was unfazed.

'My father *never* joked and, believe me, having cast upwards of a dozen beautiful and intelligent women in my brother's path over the years, I am more than ever convinced of my father's prescience.'

'You do rattle on,' Gaz said to his sister, but Marni heard fondness in his voice. 'Now, do your duty and introduce Marni around. I've told her she needn't remember all the names—in fact, any of them except for Meena and Ismah, and I assume you've seated her near them for dinner.'

Gaz—why when he was with Marni did he think of himself this way—watched Alima lead Marni into the throng, seeing the way the fluid material of her tunic swayed about her body, noticing the strands of fine silvery hair escaping from the dark blue shawl she'd draped over her head.

His silver wraith!

His body had tightened the moment she'd stepped out of the car, and he was sorry he'd chosen to wear a suit tonight. His kandora hid far more than trousers.

A string of oaths echoed through his head. He'd brought this on himself, betrothing himself to her, so if he wanted her, and he did, he'd better organise a wedding, and soon!

'Well chosen, brother!' He turned to find Nimr standing beside him. 'But you'd better secure her before my boys are old enough to challenge you. Karim is already in love with her—he talks of nothing but the soccer-playing blonde he found in the gardens.'

'Surely he's too young to be thinking of women,' Gaz protested, and Nimr laughed.

'Don't believe it for a minute. They mature early, our boys, and didn't we, as youngsters, believe an older woman could teach us much?'

Gaz laughed but he was looking around the room at the same time, and realised that not only were all four of his nephews included in the party—very smartly dressed in miniature suits—but Karim was right now chatting up Marni, making her laugh at something he'd said.

He's twelve, he reminded himself as he moved away from Nimr, easing his way through the crowd, hopefully unobtrusively but heading for his fiancée nonetheless.

'We'll have to lead the way into dinner,' he said when he arrived, taking Marni's arm in a possessive grasp. 'It's the way things are done.'

'Oh, but dinner won't be for ages,' Karim told him, 'and there must be people you have to see.'

'People Marni has to meet as well,' Gaz said firmly, at the same time telling himself he couldn't possibly be jealous of a twelve year old boy.

He was leading Marni towards Ismah's husband when two youngish men swerved into their path—Nimr's youngest brothers, unmarried as yet and more than a little wild. He introduced Marni and was pleased at their manners, although, as they moved away, Marni smiled and said, 'The wild ones of the family?'

The effect of the smile left him floundering to catch up with the question, and he had to find an echo of it in his head before it made sense.

'What makes you ask?'

Even that was a stalling tactic—he was still trying to come to grips with why a smile would stir his blood and have his body thinking about ravishment.

Marriage or distance—they were the only two options—and hadn't he promised he wouldn't rush her into marriage?

Well, not actually promised...

Although marriage hadn't been an issue when he'd asked her to pretend to the betrothal!

'They look like young men who are constantly seeking amusement—the kind that usually leads to trouble. I've met young men like them staying as guests at the hotel, young men with too much money and too much time on their hands, always looking for what they call fun but which often translates into something illegal.'

He heard the words but his mind was still following his

body down the sex trail so he took little notice, although the word 'hotel' registered enough to give him the glimmer of an idea.

'Will you give me your grandfather's phone number? I should have asked before. I must phone him to—'

Marni giggled.

'To ask for my hand in marriage? Oh, really, Gaz! That is so old-fashioned. Besides, he is in hospital. Nelson emailed this afternoon to say the operation will be within the next few days.'

The giggle—such an inconsequential thing—had further activated the inappropriate desire he was feeling, but the idea was even better now. Out there, in Australia, anything might happen...

'Then we should fly out right away. You will want to be there when he has the operation and I can stay in the hotel so I don't put your Mr Nelson out at all.'

Pale eyes looked up at him, no mirth in them now, only fear and sorrow.

'He definitely doesn't want me there, Gaz,' she said softly. 'That's the main reason I'm over here. He's a proud man and doesn't want me to see him all weak and tied to tubes in the ICU, or have me around while he's recovering. I promised him I'd stay away.'

'But you'll be riven with worry and concern and feel helpless because you're so far away.'

She tried a smile but it wavered with apprehension and he wondered if the response that burned through his body might not be more than lust.

'I'll just have to deal with it, won't I?' she said, the smile getting better. 'I promised! Besides, I'd be just as helpless there! I know he's in the best possible hands.'

'Ghazi, you must not monopolise your betrothed in this manner!'

Alima had appeared and before he could object, she whisked Marni away.

He'd drive her back to Tasnim's later! At least that way they could kiss.

But wouldn't kisses make the longing worse, the desire stronger?

Maybe putting some distance between them would be better...

Marni allowed herself to be led through the crowd, introduced to this one and that, realising Gaz had been right, she'd *never* remember all the names. Meena would be easy. She was very like Tasnim in looks.

'We are full sisters,' the pretty woman explained, 'the daughters of our father's third wife, the one before Ghazi's mother.'

'I was just thinking I'll never remember everyone's names and now you're making me realise I'll have to remember relationships as well.'

Meena touched her softly on the arm.

'Do not worry. It will come to you in time. For the moment, it is more than enough for us all that Ghazi is happy—that he has found the right woman to love.'

The 'love' word had its almost predictable effect in Marni's chest, but she was getting used to it so ignored it, reminding Meena instead that it wasn't love but an arrangement made by her father.

'Ah, but the old ones know,' Meena said. 'My marriage was arranged but when I met my husband I knew my father had been right for there was no one else in the world I could love as much.'

Intrigued by a culture so different from her own, Marni couldn't help asking, 'Were all your marriages arranged?'

The question was probably too personal but Meena didn't seem to mind.

'Not really, although when Alima was about eight she decided she was going to marry Nimr, so then our father and our uncle betrothed them. Ismah met her husband at university in America. He is from a neighbouring country and will one day rule it so our father couldn't object to him. Tasnim, of course, just told our father she was going to marry Yusef and no one could ever argue with Tasnim.'

'I can understand that,' Marni put in, but if Meena heard her she didn't show it, continuing on down or up the family tree.

'Our other sisters, well, you'll meet them eventually, but Zahrah is married to a Westerner, the son of one of our father's old friends and advisors, Maryam is married to her work, she is a doctor like Ghazi, and Rukan is married to another of our cousins. They were both betrothed to others but ran away to get married and our father forgave them both because they were obviously meant for each other.'

Just as Marni decided it would be impossible to remember even the sisters' names, Alima rescued her, taking her off to meet other guests, including Ismah, a slight, plump woman with such beautiful eyes Marni could barely stop staring at her.

'She is beautiful, yes?' the man beside Ismah said, and Marni could only nod and smile.

'As are you,' Ismah said quietly, and Marni shook her head. Among these exotically beautiful women she faded into oblivion.

Gaz returned to lead her into dinner, explaining on the way that although all those present were family, the women would still sit together at one end of the table and the men at the other.

Marni smiled at him.

'Sounds like an Aussie barbeque,' she said. 'The men in one group the women in another.'

'Here it makes sense as most of the women live with their husbands, so at gatherings like this they enjoy gossiping with the other women, and the men enjoy catching up on politics or, more likely, the latest football scores and transfers.'

'*Most* of the women live with their husbands?'

His turn to smile.

'As against the old days when they would all have lived in the harem, visiting their husband in his tent, or later his palace, when invited.'

The teasing glint in his eyes made Marni's insides flutter. What had she got herself into, and where was this going?

Had he read the questions in her eyes that he gave her hand, where it rested on his arm, a slight squeeze before abandoning her to his sisters at the women's end of the table?

To Marni's great relief the meal was not a banquet in the true sense of the word, with endless plates of food laid out in the middle of the table. Instead, light-footed serving women offered plates of this and that, placing small or large spoonfuls of each dish directly onto the guests' plates.

And contrary to her impression that personal conversation was off limits in this country, she was peppered with questions about herself, her home and her family.

'We all remember that visit to the beautiful hotel,' Ismah told her. 'Alima and Rukan were betrothed already, but Maryam and Meena flirted shamelessly with the young man who worked on the concierge desk, flashing their eyes at him and teasing him so he blushed whenever one of us came near, because he couldn't really tell us apart.'

'You flirted too,' Meena reminded her. 'And remember the day Zahrah went out without her abaya, in Western jeans and a T-shirt and her hair in a ponytail for everyone to see.'

The sisters laughed.

'Oh, I remember that,' Alima said. 'She went to Sea World to ride on the big roller-coaster and she was so sick she had to ring the hotel and ask them to send a car to take her back there.'

'And Father said she'd shamed the family and would never get a husband.'

'That's probably why he sent her to America,' Meena said, and the women laughed, as if that had been a good thing, not a punishment.

The talk turned to other holidays, other places all the women had stayed at one time or another, London and Berlin apparently favourites with them all. Sitting listening to them, Marni realised how at ease with each other they all were, even the women married to Nimr's brothers.

Was this normal in all families?

Not having one—not an extended one—she couldn't judge, but their obvious closeness once again reminded her that her position was a false one, and the niggle of disquiet that rarely left her these days began to make itself felt more persistently.

'I will drive you home.'

Gaz appeared at her side as the women left the dining room. He took her hand once again and placed it on his arm in the formal manner he had used before.

She said goodbye to the women she had met, sought out Alima to thank her for the evening, then let Gaz guide her to the door, exhaustion nipping at her heels as the tension she hadn't realised she'd been feeling drained from her.

Pausing at the front door, she managed to get one sandal on but was having trouble with the second when Gaz knelt and slipped it on her foot.

'Oh, no!' she protested, not sure whether to laugh or cry, 'that is just far *too* Cinderella! Is your car a pumpkin?'

He looked at her, bemused, but at least it gave her something to talk to him about, explaining the story of Cinderella and her prince.

'They were real, these people?' he asked, driving through night-quiet streets, the engine in the big saloon purring quietly in the background.

'No, it's a children's fairy-tale,' Marni told him. 'It's just that I can't help thinking of it.' She paused, then added quietly, 'Probably because it's easier to be thinking of my life right now as a fairy-tale than be worrying over deceiving nice people like your sisters and their friends.'

He had pulled the car over as she was talking and she looked around, seeing a long wall with an arched opening in it, an ornate gate protecting whatever lay behind the walls.

'You have the photo,' he said, turning and taking both her hands in his. 'How is there deceit?'

'It's pretence—you asked me to pretend, remember, to get your sisters off your back.'

'And it is working,' he said, lifting her hands and kissing the backs of her fingers, one by one, so she had to struggle to keep her brain working while her body melted from something as unsexy as finger kisses. 'So much so they are asking about the wedding—about when it will be.'

If finger kisses had melted her bones, talk of a wedding sent such heat washing through her she could barely breathe.

Had to breathe!

Had to protest.

'But we're doing this to give you time to get to know your job,' she reminded him, hoping he wouldn't hear just how shaky her voice was. 'A wedding, even if we wanted to marry—well, the kind of fuss that would surely entail would interrupt your schedule far more than just being betrothed. It would be a terrible distraction.'

He didn't reply, simply using his grasp on her hands to draw her closer then dropping his head to kiss her on the lips.

'This particular distraction,' he said a long time later, tilting her head so he could look into her eyes, 'is interrupting my schedule more than you could ever know. If we were married there'd be *one* distraction less.'

She frowned at him.

'Are you talking about sex? Is that the distraction that's so hard to handle?'

He kissed her again, but lightly.

'Do you not find it so?' he teased, and just as she was about to admit she felt it, too, she remembered the virginity thing and was flooded with embarrassment.

Should she tell him now?

But how?

What would he think?

That she was frigid, or had something wrong with her?

Or decide she was pathetic, locked in adolescence, as the last man she'd dated had. Christmas cake, he'd called her, apparently a foreign insult for an older virgin, dried out the way a cake did after the twenty-fifth of December.

He'd laughed at the notion that there was anything special about virginity—not that she'd considered it that way. As far as he'd been concerned, it was nothing more than an embarrassing nuisance. Men, he'd told her, expected a woman to have had experience and be able to please a man in bed.

And that had been a man she'd thought she loved!

The thought of telling Gaz—of his reaction—made her tremble. It was one thing to think she could tell some man with whom she was having a virginity-relieving fling about it, but telling Gaz?

'I think we'd better just stay betrothed,' she muttered, her voice sounding like a very creaky gate in desperate need of oil.

CHAPTER EIGHT

'ARE YOU TIRED, or would you walk with me a little way?

Marni, who'd been expecting an argument, or at least further discussion, over the marriage business, was startled.

'Walk?

'In the oasis,' Gaz said, waving a hand towards the gate. 'Have you been there?'

'I remember going past the wall on my way somewhere, but haven't been inside it. Won't it be dark?'

'Wait and see,' Gaz said. He was already opening his door, coming around to open hers and offering his hand to help her out.

He led her to the gate and unlatched it, ushering her inside onto a path between what seemed like a jungle of palm trees. The path was lit by lampposts placed at intervals, and the palms were lit from below by soft floodlights.

'It's like an enchanted forest,' she whispered as they walked through shadows.

'It has been here for thousands of years,' Gaz explained. 'There is a spring, and our ancestors built a series of narrow canals out from it so the palms would thrive. It is here for all our people to enjoy, and the dates are free to anyone who wishes to pick one or many.'

The soft air smelled sweet, and a slight breeze ruffled the fringed palm leaves, so it seemed as if they walked through a world apart.

'Will you pick one?' Marni asked, enjoying the sight of the palms growing so closely, and the little paths that led this way and that but still wondering what they were doing here, given the late hour and the marriage conversation, which seemed to have been forgotten.

'Of course, that is why we are here.'

He held her hand and was leading her to the right then to the left, taking paths seemingly at random. Yet when he answered, she'd heard something in his voice—something that was Ghazi, not Gaz. This place must be special to him—like the desert—part of who he was...

Why?

'Dates and camels, these have kept my people alive down through the ages,' he said quietly, apparently answering her unspoken question. 'The date is especially miraculous as it can be eaten fresh, or dried and kept for months while the tribes travelled across the desert. The pulp makes sweets and bread, the seeds can be ground for flour, the fibrous mass that holds the dates is used for brooms, the palm leaves for thatch. But it is the legend that brings us here tonight.'

'A legend?'

'A story like your Cinderella. You reminded me of it when you told me your fairy-tale. The date grove is the one place a betrothed couple may walk together without a chaperone.'

Marni looked around and smiled.

'I can understand that—they can hardly get up to much with the narrow pathways and the little canals and the prickly fronds of the date palms pressing in on all sides.'

'Ah, but they walk together for a reason,' Ghazi said,

stopping by a heavy cluster of ripening dates drooping from a palm. 'Our legend says if they find the perfect date, ripe and ready to eat, and they feed it to each other, not only will their marriage be fertile but they will live long together.'

'Just live?' Marni queried. She knew she should be protesting the marriage thing again, yet here she was querying a single word.

Had she been hoping the legend would say live and love?

Of course she had! It was the silly lump that kept forming in her chest causing this sudden longing for—

Love? Get over it, Marni! Love was never the issue here! It's the marriage thing you should be worrying about!

She knew he was talking marriage now so they could go to bed together—a marriage dictated by lust. Although she hadn't seen much of her mother since she'd abandoned her daughter to Pop and Nelson, she had memories of her mother's desperate search for love, and understood now how lust could be mistaken for it.

Did she want that?

No!

'Of course live,' Ghazi said, his attention still on the cluster of dates. 'Aha! I have it.'

He plucked a date and turned towards her, holding it to her lips so she could take a bite.

'Just a bite,' he warned. 'You must then feed me.'

Ghazi was watching her, his eyes intent, his fingers moving closer to her lips.

It's only a legend, she told herself, but her heart was pounding and suddenly being fed a date—well, half a date—by this man was the most erotic thing that had ever happened to her.

Her body afire, she opened her lips and bit into the sweet, juicy flesh. Ghazi's thumb brushed her lower lip and she felt her nipples peak beneath her tunic and a near orgasmic heat between her thighs.

'Now you,' he said, his voice so husky it rasped against her sensitised skin.

He handed her the date and she lifted it towards his lips, her fingers trembling as he opened his mouth and his even white teeth bit into it, taking it and her finger and thumb into the moist cavern of his mouth, suckling at them while her body pulsed with need.

He released her fingers, disposed of the seed then drew her close so they embraced within the heady scent of the dates, and her body pressed against his, feeling his reaction to the tasting, wanting him so badly she was beyond all rational thought.

Never had he held such a responsive woman in his arms—never felt a need that matched his own in its ferocity, and he'd gone and betrothed himself to her and so put her off limits for the moment. He could not tarnish her name with his family or his people by sneaking in or out of lodgings or hotels, and both the palace and Tasnim's place were off limits for the same reason.

He could kiss her, but kisses made things worse—but he couldn't not kiss her…

Ghazi groaned and held her more tightly, pressing the softness of her body against his, fitting the two halves that were man and woman together to make a whole, aware she must know just how much he wanted her.

'It's like a madness, my desire for you,' he whispered, before his lips closed on hers, seeking to devour her, to draw her body into his, to make her his for ever.

For ever?

The words echoed in his head.

Surely he didn't mean it.

Yes, he desired her, and would marry her if only to assuage that desire, but such desire—lust even—did not last for ever. He knew that from experience. Marriage, then a suitable arrangement to end it and no one any the worse off. Marni, in fact, would be better off, although he was aware her grandfather must be a wealthy man. But her settlement would certainly include a house and enough money to live on without having to work—she'd take whatever jewels he gave her during the marriage, it would all be worked out by his advisors and—

She was pulling away from him, peering up at his face as if to read it in the shadows.

'You're not with me in this kiss, are you?' she asked. 'I think it best you take me back to Tasnim's.'

He didn't argue, couldn't, yet as he walked with her, back the way they'd come, he felt a sense of loss—not for the kiss, there'd be other kisses, but because of the conclusions he had reached.

Although they had to be the correct ones, the best for both of them, surely…

Tasnim had been in bed when Marni had returned the previous evening, but Shara had been waiting up for her and Marni had asked the young woman to wake her for breakfast in time for her to get to the hospital to do her shift.

She didn't know what Gaz might have arranged at the hospital, but she was due on duty and she'd decided that was where she most wanted to be. At least there she could concentrate on work and forget all the mind-boggling stuff going on in the rest of her life here in Ablezia, as well as her worries over Pop's imminent operation.

So, early next morning, reminding Shara to explain to Tasnim, Marni went out to the car Shara had arranged for her, feeling like her real self in her uniform and hospital shoes.

Cinderella back in the kitchen after the ball!

Jawa was surprised to see her, yet pleased.

'As far as we know, there's been no change in our work schedules so if you hadn't turned up we'd have been a nurse short. We're in Theatre Three with the Frenchman for the morning, then with a paediatric orthopaedic surgeon this afternoon.

'Good. We should be busy,' Marni said, knowing she needed something—anything—to distract herself from thoughts of Pop.

And Gaz!

And *marriage,* whatever that might have meant…

Not to mention memories of the last time she'd told a man she was a virgin…

Work went well, and Marni enjoyed the sense of teamwork that was typical of operating theatres—the moments of drama, the excitement when a tricky bit of cutting or stitching was successful, the quiet pleasure when a job was done.

As they finished their shift, she and Jawa left the changing rooms together.

'Coffee?' Jawa asked, but Marni shook her head.

'I want to sit with Safi for a while. I've been neglecting him lately.'

It was mostly true, but when she'd checked her phone for messages earlier she'd found a text from Nelson telling her Pop's operation was going ahead that day.

Working out the time difference, she knew he'd be in Theatre right now, and although she knew worrying about it was pointless she couldn't help feeling anxious, tense and sick-to-her-stomach nervous. Neither did she want to return to her current abode and have to explain her concerns or distraction to the ever-bubbly Tasnim.

'So I'm really hiding here,' she said to Safi when she entered his room and settled by his bed, taking his hand in hers. She knew he didn't understand her but the slight pressure of his thin fingers told her he was glad she was there.

She sang the songs she knew he liked and watched him drift off to sleep, before picking up his chart and checking what had been going on with him.

As far as she could see, he was doing well.

Pop would be, too! If she couldn't be there, the least she could do was send positive thoughts in his direction.

You *will* get through it! You *will* be well!

'I thought I'd find you here. Tasnim phoned to say you'd sent the driver home and would take a taxi later. Drivers will always wait, you know.'

Marni smiled up at the man who'd entered the room so silently he'd been standing beside her before she realised it.

And before her body reacted?

She *must* be distracted!

'No, I didn't know that,' she said, trying for lightness, although she felt strangely intimidated by the white-robed Ghazi.

'Is it your grandfather?' he asked, pulling over a chair and sitting beside her, taking her free hand in his so the three of them were linked.

Marni nodded.

'He's in Theatre now.'

Had he felt a tremor in her hand that his fingers tightened on hers?

'I could organise a hook-up to the hospital so you know exactly what's going on,' he offered, rubbing his thumb back and forth across the palm of her hand—distracting her in spite of her concern.

'Nelson has promised to contact me when it's over and he's spoken to the surgeon,' she said, turning to look at him, reading his sympathy in his dark eyes, feeling weakness all through her that this man should care enough to be here for her.

Not that she could let him see her reaction. He was being practical—sensible—and she could do both!

'I know the routine of the op, and that makes it both easier and harder,' she said. 'They'll open his chest and bypass the two stents in his coronary arteries before opening his heart to replace the valve.'

'You've seen the operation before?'

'I worked in the cardiac theatre for a while when I was training. It's a long, hard operation, but generally there aren't too many risks.'

Ghazi took both her hands now and smiled gently at her.

'Or so you keep telling yourself,' he said. 'Now come, you need to eat. We'll go to the restaurant at the top of the building again. You can turn your phone back on up there and be ready when your Mr Nelson calls.'

Marni stared at him, feeling a frown forming between her eyebrows.

'But you've no time for this,' she protested. 'You said yourself you've got a schedule from hell and I've already taken up too much of your time. I'll just sit here for a while then go on back to Tasnim's—even phone her to send a driver if that will make you happy.'

His smile was broader this time, and it started up all the reactions her preoccupation had held at bay.

'If the country's boss can't take time out to be with his betrothed when she needs him, who can? Besides, the dinner I was meant to be attending promised to be boring in the extreme—a meeting of some world soccer association organised by Nimr—and the men attending won't know one sheikh from another. To them we're all just men in long white dresses—so one less will hardly matter.'

Still holding her hands, he eased her gently to her feet, but before he left the room, he, too, looked at Safi's chart and examined the little boy who lay sleeping quietly in the big bed.

'He seems to be doing well,' Marni said, as they walked towards the lifts.

But Ghazi's, 'Yes,' was distracted.

'You're worried about him?' she asked as they waited in the foyer.

'Worried about his family situation,' Ghazi admitted. 'I really don't want to send him home while he recovers enough for another operation, but he's already been away from home for a month and that's a long time for a child. Also, he can't stay at the hospital. I can keep him at the palace, of course. The women would look after him and there are children he can play with, but his family—'

The lift doors opened in front of them and they stepped in, the three occupants inside nodding their heads towards Ghazi, while Marni considered the conversation they'd just had.

This man was the ruler of his nation, battling to come to terms with his 'job' and to meet the demands made of him, yet he had time to worry over one small boy, or made time to worry about him.

He was special—not the boy but the man! The realisation wasn't a total shock—Ghazi had shown his empathy with people before, his being here with her tonight being one example—but...

The warmth unfolding in her chest as she pondered these things was different—not lust at all!

Oh, surely not the other 'l' word,' she thought as they left the lift and a warm hand on her back, guiding her towards the restaurant, sparked her more recognisable reactions. To fall in love with this man would be madness! They were from different worlds, so different she doubted any marriage could survive, especially if the love was one-sided.

He'd spoken the truth when he'd said he wouldn't be missed at the sports dinner, Ghazi mused as he asked the waiter for a table overlooking the desert, but there'd been many other things he could have been doing.

So why was he here?

Kindness—Marni was a stranger in his land and at the moment needed some support.

Right! said the cynic within him. You couldn't have made sure Tasnim or one of your other sisters was with her?

And was support the only reason you wanted to be with her?

Honesty compelled him to admit it wasn't.

He'd *wanted* to see her.

Needed to see her!

Not only to see her but to touch her, even just minimally as touches must be in public.

This was crazy!

This was a betrothal of convenience and somehow he'd allowed himself to become attracted to the woman.

Allowed?

Did one *allow* such reactions to happen, or were they beyond human control?

Surely not! He'd always been able to control such impulses before.

'Sir?'

The waiter had obviously asked him a question as both he and Marni were looking at him, obviously puzzled.

'Sorry!'

He dragged his mind back to the present. This was hardly the time to be questioning his behaviour.

'This time you will choose what we eat,' he said to Marni. 'There is an explanation for all the dishes in English, so you decide.'

He smiled, hoping she'd forget his distraction.

Some hope! She'd no sooner finished ordering and the waiter had disappeared than she asked, 'Are you worried about something? Is it still Safi or was it more important than you made out, this dinner you're missing? Because if it is, or if there's something else you should be doing, I'll be fine on my own. I could even go to Jawa's rooms and wait for the phone call there. She'd understand.'

He gazed at the woman across the table from him, aware how worried she must be beneath her cool exterior, yet here she was worrying about *him*! When had anyone last concerned themselves about his welfare—apart from Mazur and a couple of his closest servants?

She disturbed him in ways apart from the purely physical...

'Ghazi?'

His name, softly spoken, reminded him she'd asked a question and deserved a reply. But there was more—the name itself—more internal disturbance.

'That is the first time you've used my full name,' he said, reaching out across the table to touch her hand where it rested beside her water glass.

Her smile stirred the more usual disturbances.

'That's because when you're in your prince gear I can't help but think of you as Ghazi. Gaz is just a bloke—an

Aussie term for an ordinary man—but in that get-up you have to be Ghazi.'

She paused then added, 'But don't think you've distracted me with this talk of names. You're obviously worried about something and if it's that I'm keeping you from where you should be, please believe I'll be okay on my own.'

He had to smile.

'I know you would. I am coming to realise just how strong and capable my betrothed is, but I want to be with you tonight.' It was his turn to pause, though what he added, was, 'In many ways,' which made the colour rise in her cheeks and his own body harden.

Fortunately their dinner arrived, the waiter setting down plates and different dishes in the middle of the table, offering them first to Marni, who had chosen them.

They ate, and talked of food, but he could see her anxiety growing, and noticed the quick glances she was giving her watch.

'Come,' he said, 'we can get a snack at Tasnim's later if we're hungry, but for now we'd be better waiting somewhere quiet. I've an office here, on the floor below. I'll order some coffee and sweetmeats to be sent there and we can both be comfortable.'

The relief on her face told him he'd made the right decision, and although she smiled her thanks as she pushed back her chair and stood up, he knew all she wanted to do was be somewhere private when she heard the results of the operation.

He distanced himself when the phone rang, standing by the windows while she burrowed deep into one of his armchairs, the hand that held the tiny mobile to her ear trembling slightly.

He only heard her end of the conversation but could

tell from the relaxation in her voice that all had gone well, so he was surprised when she'd said goodbye to turn and see the tears trickling down her cheeks.

'Marni? It's all right, isn't it? I heard you saying "That's good" all the time. I realise it will be a while before he's out of the CCU but your grandfather's come through it well, hasn't he?'

Marni scrubbed at her cheeks, ashamed of her tears when everything had gone well. Far better than the surgeon had expected, according to Nelson.

'Are they tears of relief?' Ghazi asked.

He'd taken off his headdress and come to sit on the arm of her chair, his hand resting gently on her shoulder.

'Mostly relief, I suppose,' she admitted. 'I'm sorry to be such a wuss, but when Nelson said goodbye he called me "darling girl". Nelson hasn't called me that for years and I guess it just broke me up.'

'Darling girl! What a lovely phrase. He's something special, the man called Nelson.'

'He is indeed,' Marni responded, resting her head against Ghazi's side and remembering just how special Nelson had always been to her. 'Pop was very good with children but once they started to grow up, girls especially, he became…not embarrassed but less approachable somehow.

'He always blamed himself for how my mother turned out, always seeking love in the wrong places. So it was Nelson who had to check I knew about the birds and the bees—he actually used those words—and he'd call me darling girl when he talked about growing up, and give me little lectures about believing in myself, and about honour and respect and loyalty—all the things he felt were most important in the way we live our lives, all the things Pop lived by but couldn't put into words.'

She looked up at the man she'd been leaning on, suddenly embarrassed by all she'd revealed.

'Not that you need to know all that! It's just the words brought it all back. I'm sorry. You've already been so good, and here I am babbling on about Nelson bringing me up.'

The dark eyes were unfathomable, but as he moved she sensed what was coming and her body tightened as he dipped his head and kissed her on the lips.

'I think I owe your Nelson a big favour,' he said quietly, breathing the words against her skin, then his lips returned to hers and the kiss deepened, taking her away from the past and the present, to where sensation swamped all thoughts.

CHAPTER NINE

COULD SHE BLAME the relief that had set in after talking to Nelson, or was it just that this man had been so good, so kind and considerate, so *there* for her, that her response was so heated when he kissed her the second time?

Somehow, as the kiss deepened, they'd moved, Ghazi in the chair, she mostly on top of him, her arms wound around his neck, her body snuggling against his.

His hands were on her breasts, brushing across them, teasing them to a heavy longing, while his lips explored her face, kisses brushing eyelids, temple, the little hollow beneath her chin.

Her hands explored his back, feeling the hard muscle beneath the white robe, and ranged across his head, his beautifully shaped head, dark hair cut close to the scalp, her fingers teasing at his ears, wanting more contact with his skin.

Now his lips found hers again, deep, drugging kisses, while his hands travelled lower, fingers seeking sensitive parts while she squirmed against his hardness and wanted more and more of him, wanted the feel of his skin on hers, wanted to know him by touch, to tease him as he was teasing her.

Could she?

Awareness that she had never felt this way before—

had never known she could—was somewhere in her consciousness, but buried deeply beneath the sensations she was experiencing.

The sensations she was enjoying!

Inflamed by his fingers, trembling on the brink, she heard him saying something but the words didn't penetrate the fog of longing enveloping both her body and her brain.

She moved and felt a shudder of release, a promise of things to come that she didn't fully understand but knew she wanted.

Her excitement must have stirred more arousal in him, for now they were joined in a macabre dance as they tried to strip each other's clothes off, while still kissing, still touching, still stoking the fires in both their bodies.

'There's a couch, for emergency overnight stays,' Ghazi said, half leading her, half carrying her towards an open door at the side of the office.

She glimpsed a small bathroom then an even smaller room, as plain as a monk's cell, one narrow bed against the wall, but Ghazi had stripped off his robe and stood before her, a snowy-white sarong tied around his waist—untied now, the full magnificence of the man revealed.

Her lungs jammed, she couldn't breathe—had to—

He drew her close, her trousers and tunic gone, her bra disposed of next, his lips suckling on her breast, her body in a torment of need as his fingers slipped beneath her knickers, touching her already sensitised nub, and she knew the little whimpering noises were coming from her, although an occasional groan suggested he was as aroused as she was.

Now on the bed, his fingers inside her, feeling the hardness of him against her soft abdomen, need outweighing any lingering doubt she might have had—need, and fear that he'd stop if she admitted—

He mustn't rush! Ghazi told himself.

How could he not?

Control was about the last thing on his mind now this woman who'd been driving him insane with desire was finally naked beneath, or nearly beneath him.

Yet he wanted to savour this first experience of the two of them together, for her sake as much as for his, and the way he felt now he'd be rushing towards a finish like an adolescent boy!

He cupped her flushed cheeks in his hands and pressed a kiss on her lips, slowing himself down, breathing deeply, allowing her time to...

To say no?

Could he stand it?

He didn't have to—not if the way she was returning his kiss was any indication. The kiss was surely her answer to his unspoken question, a kiss that burned along his nerves while her fingers teased his skin, trailing across his abdomen, his chest, brushing against his nipples.

He knelt above her, pressing kisses on her pale skin, sliding his tongue across her nipples while she squirmed beneath the attention, her breath rasping in her throat.

Trailing kisses down her chest, he teased her belly button with his tongue. Her hands were on his head, half holding him back, half urging him on.

He kissed her lower, felt a flinch of uncertainty and returned to use his lips and tongue in torment on her breasts while his fingers did the exploration.

He felt her tightness, warmth and slickness—heat—felt a tremble that told him she was ready, more than ready, her response to his attentions exciting him beyond reason—beyond control.

He took her hand and cupped it around his length, urging her to guide him in. Her fingers were shaking, and he slid his hands beneath her buttocks, easing her off the bed so he could slide inside that hot, moist sheath.

Slide inside now in one quick thrust, the idea of not rushing forgotten in his need to take her, make her his, and himself hers in the give and take of sexual pleasure.

Her fingers slipped away, he thrust again, heard her cry out but it was too late—far too late—her movement beneath him driving him on. Her cries were different now, asking for more, needing more, seeking her satisfaction as well as his.

Her body gripped him, her legs lifted to link around his back, they moved as one until he burst apart, collapsing on her, feeling the quivers in her body that told him she had found her own pleasure and release.

But as common sense returned he realised what had happened and anger surged through him—anger at himself.

He'd taken advantage of this woman at a time when she was most vulnerable, comforting her with kisses that had led to this, never for a minute dreaming she might be a virgin. Then he'd let the desire he'd held in check since he'd first met her take over, when he should have—

Well, there was a lot he should have done.

Al'ana! How was he to know? Women her age…

He heaved himself away from her, sat up on the very edge of the narrow bed, his back to her, searching for something to say.

'You should have told me,' he finally managed, then realised the words had come out as an accusation, not an excuse.

He felt her move behind him and watched as she slid off the bed, briskly gathering up her discarded clothing, her beautiful, slim body silvered by the moonlight through the window.

His body stirred again, almost ready, but she'd straightened now and faced him.

'And have you ridicule me?' she demanded angrily. 'Tell me men expect women of my age to be more experienced? Tell me you're beyond wanting to teach a virgin about sex? I wanted it as much as you did, and I'm sorry if I disappointed you. Now, I'm going to have a shower and get dressed and I'd be grateful if you'd call a driver to take me back to Tasnim's.'

He sat on the bed as the bathroom door closed behind her, trying to make sense of the situation. First the virgin thing, then the things she'd said—she'd been *mocked* because of it?

How hurtful!

How damaging to her.

And now *he'd* made things worse.

Or he thought he probably had.

Seven sisters and he didn't have any understanding whatsoever of women and the stuff that went on in their heads.

Seduced by tears in grey-blue eyes and lips as soft as rose petals, he'd done the one thing he'd been determined not to do—made love to Marni.

And having had her once…

It didn't bear thinking about, but he did know he couldn't sit in the back of a dimly lit limousine with her while his driver took her home.

He picked up the phone and asked Tasnim's major domo to send a car to meet Marni at the entrance to the hospital, but his phone call alerted someone to where he was, because now the phone was ringing, Mazur asking him if he could call in at Nimr's dinner on his way home.

He was arguing about the uselessness of that as Marni slipped out of the bathroom, nodded once in his direction then headed out through his office towards the door.

'Wait, I'll walk you to the car,' he called, while Mazur listed reasons he should do this one thing for his cousin.

Marni turned then shook her head and disappeared from view.

Lost in thoughts of what might have been, of should she have done it or shouldn't she, and all the other questions that had arisen out of their coupling, it took Marni a while to realise the car she was entering already had a passenger.

'Are you all right?' Tasnim asked. 'I know you phoned earlier to say you'd be late home, but I was a little worried, so when Hari, Nimr's youngest brother, who was visiting, offered to come and collect you, I came along as well.'

Marni took her hand and squeezed her fingers.

'You are far too kind to me,' she said. 'I visited Safi, the little boy I've told you about, then Ghazi kindly said I could wait for my phone call from home in his office.'

'Your grandfather's operation? It was today? It went well?'

'Yes, and, yes, and, yes,' Marni said, and for a moment in her pleasure and relief at being able to report that she forgot what had happened after the phone call.

But only for a moment.

What on earth must Ghazi think of her?

How could she have been so stupid as to think it would all be okay?

'What was that?'

She turned to Tasnim, aware the other woman had said something—had sounded concerned.

'We're going the wrong way,' Tasnim repeated, pointing out towards the road.

'I can't help you but surely Hari knows the way. Ask him.'

She hoped she didn't sound as distracted as she felt. As far as she was concerned, Hari could take her out into the desert and drop her there.

Tasnim rapped on the glass that separated the passengers from the driver but when Hari didn't turn, she picked up the handpiece for the intercom, talking into it, then yelling into it.

He didn't answer.

'The wretched boy! I don't know why I agreed to let him drive us tonight. It's just that his brother's away somewhere—Fawzi, the other young one he hangs around with—and I thought he must be lonely to have come for a visit. Then when he wanted to play chauffeur I went along with it. This will be some bet they've had, or some daft joke they've dreamed up. The two of them are always up to something.'

Tasnim was sounding angry and concerned enough to distract Marni from her morbid thoughts.

'Can you phone your home? Tell someone what's happening?' Marni asked.

Tasnim shook her head.

'I was only coming for the ride to collect you. I didn't think to bring my mobile. But you'd have yours.'

Marni felt around her on the seat then remembered Hari—only she hadn't realised it was Hari—taking her handbag as she'd got into the car. He'd put it on the front seat—behind that nice, impenetrable barrier.

A smidgen of concern sneaked into her already tortured thoughts but considering Tasnim's condition, surely it was best to pretend that it was all some kind of joke.

'Well, as there's nothing we can do, we'll have to relax and go along with it,' Marni said, almost pleased to have something other than Ghazi to consider. 'Think of the baby and don't let yourself get upset.'

'Don't let myself get upset? It's ten o'clock at night and I'm usually in bed by nine these days. I was only up because Hari was there and he seemed to want company.'

Tasnim's voice was becoming more and more strident, and concern for her and her unborn child soon outweighed Marni's guilt and anxiety over what had just happened with Ghazi.

'Breathe deeply,' she told Tasnim. 'Calm yourself down. We're in the car, we're safe, and we really can't do anything other than sit back, relax and wait to see what happens.'

'I'll kill him!' Tasnim declared, leaning forward so she could hammer on the heavy screen.

'Later!' Marni said, capturing Tasnim's hands and massaging them, forcing her to lie back against the seat, talking quietly until the distressed woman calmed down.

Forget the joke, Marni now felt almost as much anger and murderous intent towards Hari but she kept it hidden, knowing the most important thing was to keep Tasnim as calm as possible. Eight months into her first pregnancy, a bout of hysterics was the last thing she needed.

'We're out on the desert road,' Tasnim told her, and Marni looked out the car windows, surprised to see the city must be far behind them for there was nothing as far as she could see—well, nothing but the dunes and sand, lit by the headlights as the car raced up the broad highway.

'It's the road to the old palace. That's Hari's joke. He's taking us to join the harem—he probably thinks that's where all the women should be.'

The idea that they were going somewhere specific seemed to calm Tasnim and she rested her head back against the seat, wriggled around to get comfortable, and promptly fell asleep.

Leaving Marni alone with nothing but her memories of what had happened before she'd left the hospital—memories she didn't want, things she most definitely didn't want to think about.

She thought of Pop instead, of how he must be feeling, picturing him in the CCU, all wired up to machines, tubes anchoring him to his bed. How he'd hate it, being so helpless, so reliant on others. Hopefully he wouldn't be conscious enough to be aware of it.

Her heart ached for him, but Nelson would be there…

The car stopped, but definitely not at any palace for, looking around, Marni could see nothing but desert and more desert, and perhaps a cloud of dust, just visible in the distance, gradually revealing another vehicle as it came into the beams of the headlights.

Hari got out of the car and opened Marni's door.

'You will die in the desert if you do anything foolish,' he said, startling Marni so much she could only stare at him.

'Die?' she finally echoed weakly. 'But you're Hari, Nimr's brother, why would you want us to die?'

'I don't want you to die, I'm just telling you what would happen if you ran off into the desert,' he said, shifting uneasily, and looking anxiously towards the approaching vehicle. 'Fawzi will explain.'

'Have we been kidnapped?' Marni asked, and Hari looked even more embarrassed.

'Not for money,' he finally blurted out. 'We wouldn't do anything like that.'

'Is that supposed to make me feel better?' Marni demanded, but Hari had moved away from her and didn't reply.

The other vehicle was pulling up now, off the road but close enough for Marni to see it was a big four-wheel drive painted in the sandy camouflage colours of desert war vehicles.

'Here's Fawzi now,' Hari said, with such evident relief that Marni knew that whatever was going on, it was Fawzi who was the organiser—Hari was the weak link, should she and Tasnim need one.

'You're talking to her,' Fawzi said as he strode towards them. 'I said no communication.'

'But she asked—' Hari began.

'Bah!' his brother said. 'Just get her in the car and no talking. Where's Tasnim?'

'She's asleep.' Marni answered for the younger brother. 'And she's eight months pregnant so whatever arrangements you've been making, I do hope you've got an obstetrician or a midwife on hand because an upset like this could bring on the birth any minute.'

Even in the dim light shed by the muted headlights she could see Hari's face pale, but Fawzi only swore— well, Marni imagined he was swearing—and waved at his brother to get her into the bigger vehicle.

'No, I'll wake Tasnim and help her,' Marni said, thinking she could slide in beside Tasnim and they could both refuse to budge. She doubted the young men would drag them out forcefully, their inbred respect for women too powerful to overcome. 'You don't want her going into shock,' she added, for good measure.

Both brothers looked concerned this time, and Marni realised, whatever was going on, and whatever they intended doing, she could use Tasnim's condition as a weapon against them.

Weapon! Was that a gun stuck in the belt of Fawzi's tunic?

If it was, then refusing to leave this car and get into the other one was no longer an option.

Marni frowned at him.

'Is that a gun?' she asked, and heard the incredulity in her voice.

He glanced down at it, telling her all she needed to know.

'Then hide it somewhere else on your person. The last thing Tasnim needs is to see people with guns!'

Especially young foolish people, she thought but didn't say.

The two young men began muttering at each other, Hari obviously getting more and more upset about the situation, but Fawzi seemed able to calm him in some way.

Marni slid back into the car and shook Tasnim awake.

'We've met up with Fawzi and have to get into his car,' she told the sleep-bewildered woman. 'I'm sure they don't intend to harm us because every time I mention your pregnancy they get worried. Let's just go along with things for now. I'm here with you and I'll look after you, whatever happens.'

Tasnim's reaction was to burst into tears, which was hardly helpful, but eventually Marni got her transferred to the other vehicle, needing the help of both their kidnappers to get the heavily pregnant woman up into the high-set four-wheel drive.

Hari left them, no doubt to drive the limo back to the city, and Fawzi drove—carefully for one so young, Marni thought—across the desert, up and over sand dune after sand dune, reinforcing—as if she'd needed it—the desolation of the endless shifting sands.

Tasnim was asleep again and Marni dozed, aware there

was no point in watching where they were going because it all looked exactly the same. Finally, he pulled up beside what looked like a small thatched cottage, half-buried in the sand.

'We are here. There is food and water, a little camping stove, beds and bedding. You will stay there. We will be watching you, though you may not see us. Just remember if you venture out into the desert, you will surely die.'

Marni didn't argue. Tired, confused and still angry with Ghazi over his 'Why didn't you tell me' question, still hurt by it, she was beginning to think a comfortable prison cell might not be such a bad idea.

With Fawzi's help she got the still sleepy Tasnim out of the vehicle and into the little shelter, lit by two small gas lanterns that threw dark shadows into the corners of the room.

She could see a couple of mattresses against one wall, a pile of bedding in a corner, a table, where one lantern and a small gas stove, some plates and cups and a kettle stood, and a set of shelves packed with what was probably tinned food—the second lantern on the top of them.

'Lie down on that mattress,' she told Tasnim. 'I'll make you some mint tea. Assuming there is mint available for tea?'

She'd turned to Fawzi, hovering in the doorway, to ask the last question and a more hesitant or unhappy kidnapper she could not imagine.

'Of course,' he said abruptly, before walking out into the darkness. She heard the engine of his vehicle starting up then the noise gradually died away.

Tasnim was lying on the mattress, shivering in the night-cold desert air. Marni found a warm duvet and tucked it around the pregnant woman, thinking, as she did so, of her far-off obstetrics training.

How much did she remember?

'I'll get some tea,' she said. 'There might be biscuits. I'll have a look. We're quite safe here,' she added, reassuring both herself and Tasnim. 'And as soon as Ghazi realises we're missing, he'll find us.'

Given what had happened, she actually wasn't sure about that statement and had said it to reassure Tasnim.

It must have worked for Tasnim nodded and snuggled into the bedding. Satisfied that she was all right for the moment, Marni stood up to explore their temporary home. Water first, to boil for tea. Four large plastic containers of it suggested their kidnappers thought they might be here for a while. Fortunately, as she doubted she could lift a full container, she found a tap at the bottom of each of them so was able to slide a cup under it and get enough water to put into the kettle.

They'd thought of everything, she realised as she picked up a box of matches to light the little gas cooker. Beside the matches was a small gas firelighter but she was too tired to work out how to use it right now.

She set the kettle on to boil and began to check the shelves—sure enough, there were biscuits. Probably because the young men liked them, she decided, but she wasn't going to quibble over the reason for their choice.

Dried mint in a plastic container—she had no idea how much to use, having only made the tea with fresh mint when she'd been living in her little flat. She guessed amounts, realised there was no teapot so she waited until the water boiled then threw the mint into the kettle, adding sugar because that would help with shock.

But by the time she was done, Tasnim was asleep again, too deeply asleep for Marni to want to wake her.

Pouring herself a cup of tea, she carried it to the doorway of the hut, holding it in both hands as she sipped the sweet liquid, looking up at the billion bright stars and wondering if some combination or permutation of their movements had dictated the events of this most momentous day.

Well, at least you've achieved what you came to this place for, a cynical voice whispered in her head. Now perhaps you can get on with your life—go on dates, have some fun!

The realisation that she didn't want to go on dates—except perhaps with Ghazi—or have some fun—except, of course, with him—made her feel so miserable she gave up on the beauty of the night sky and crept back into the hut.

CHAPTER TEN

TASNIM WOKE UP irritable and unhappy, waking Marni, who'd settled on a second mattress nearby and had finally gone to sleep way past midnight.

'We have to get out of here,' Tasnim was saying, while Marni was still shaking off the heaviness of sleep. 'We've got to get away!'

'And go where?' Marni demanded, more concerned that she was going to have to find somewhere behind the shed to relieve herself in private.

And soon!

'If we walk out into that desert we're as good as dead,' she added, heading for the door then hesitating there. 'Do you think they're really watching us from somewhere? I mean, it's not as if we can escape, is it?'

'I went behind the shed,' Tasnim told her, guessing at her concern, 'not something that's easy when you're eight months pregnant. And I don't mean to walk out into the desert, but next time they come we'll have to overpower them some way and take the vehicle.'

I rather think that's a royal *we*, and she's meaning I will have to do the dirty work, Marni thought.

But right now she was beyond caring, hurrying around behind the shed, worrying now about how they'd wash themselves *and* their underwear.

Tasnim was ahead of her, for when Marni returned Tasnim had found a basin and filled it with warm water from the kettle, smelling of mint but very welcome nonetheless.

'I've found a couple of long gowns, like the men wear in the desert. I think the boys must use this place when they come out to hunt. They look clean enough so I'm going to have a wash and put one of them on. We can use the water we're washing in to wash our underwear.'

She must have read the surprise in Marni's face for she laughed and said, 'Being the descendant of a long line of desert women,' she reminded Marni, 'I know how precious water is. Out here we don't really need our underwear so we wash it this once then put it away until we're rescued.'

'Excuse me,' Marni said, 'but are you the same woman who was telling me, rather emotionally and only minutes ago, that we have to get out of here?'

Tasnim smiled at her.

'Pregnant women get very emotional,' she reminded Marni, 'but we're also very sensible under the hysteria because we've something very special to protect.' She patted her bulging belly. 'So now we have to be practical and look after ourselves, bathe and eat, and then we plan.'

The bathing and eating part went well, but planning? Tasnim's escape ideas became more and more impossible—finding a rock and hitting whoever came over the head, grabbing the gun, hiding in the sand then racing to the car while their kidnappers searched for them—until Marni grew tired of pointing out just why they wouldn't work.

'Well, we can't just sit here waiting to be rescued,' Tasnim complained. 'I mean, Yusef's still away, and is Ghazi likely to come looking for you?'

After the way she had stormed out of his office? Hardly! But Marni didn't share that thought.

'Your staff will know you're missing and they must know you went off with Hari,' Marni said instead.

'Yes, but if Hari's not in town—if he's somewhere out here, watching us—how can they ask him where I am? And if they've really thought things through, that pair, they'll have come up with some reason why we didn't go home. They'd have told my people we were going to stay with one of the sisters or something.'

'Would your people believe them? I mean, you didn't pack anything or make any arrangements.'

Tasnim's smile was rueful.

'I do tend to be a little impulsive so although they might mutter among themselves, I doubt any of the staff would be surprised enough to be suspicious. And everyone always has spare clothes and toiletries, even make-up, for visitors. Like the stuff in your bedroom suite.'

They were sitting on Tasnim's mattress, and now she stretched out and lay down on it.

'I'm going to sleep for a while,' she said, patting Marni's leg where she still sat on the edge of the mattress. 'You keep thinking.'

Marni was relieved her companion was sleeping, but without Tasnim's chatter and flow of ideas there was nothing to stop Marni's mind drifting back to Ghazi and the events of the previous evening.

'They cannot just have vanished,' Ghazi yelled, striding about his office at the palace, glaring at his closest friends and advisors.

Unfortunately, deep down he believed they could have done just that. Marni, upset with him—hurt—over what had happened, or what he'd said, could have told Tasnim and Tasnim certainly had the guile and resources to hide them both away somewhere. In fact, the little devil would delight in the intrigue!

'I don't want to alarm you further—' Nimr's voice brought Ghazi out of his dark thoughts. '—but Alima says there's no way Tasnim would put her unborn child in jeopardy by doing something rash, and as far as Alima's concerned, leaving her home voluntarily at this stage of a pregnancy counts as rash.'

'So they *are* in danger!' Ghazi stormed, as his cousin swept away his last hope that Marni might be safe. 'Why? Who? Is it to get at me? Who have I offended?'

'At least we know they've got Hari with them,' Nimr offered, and Ghazi snorted.

'That's hardly comforting, Nimr. Those two young brothers of yours have about as much sense as the rabbits they love to hunt.' He hesitated for a moment, then added, 'Although, where's Fawzi? Maybe he knows something.'

Nimr shrugged.

'He went off a few days ago. Hunting, as you said. The pair of them are obsessed with all the old ways. They believe we should still live in tents and roam the desert sands—in the newest and biggest four-wheel drives, of course.'

Ghazi shook his head. He had no time to be thinking of Nimr's irresponsible brothers now, not when Marni was missing, perhaps in danger.

His gut had been tied in knots since he'd first tried to contact her at Tasnim's house, phoning when he'd been on his way from the hospital to Nimr's dinner, phoning again every ten minutes, feeling more and more desperate until someone finally admitted that neither woman had returned to the house.

If she'd left voluntarily it was because of him, and if something had happened to her, well, that was probably to do with him as well.

Somehow they got through their first full day of captivity, although Tasnim's mood swings took more out of Marni than the desert heat when she ventured outside during the day. Tasnim's first idea had been to write the word 'help' in big letters in the sand so the searching helicopter Ghazi was sure to send would see the message.

Although not believing for a minute Ghazi would send any form of rescue, Marni did write the word in large letters in the sand a few metres behind their shelter. But the wind that came up in the afternoon obliterated the word in seconds—*and* gave Tasnim a new idea.

'We'll put up a flag—use one of the wuzars in the pile of clothing.'

She dug around and produced a snowy-white length of material and Marni felt blood flowing into her cheeks as she realised it was the kind of undergarment Ghazi had shed on that memorable night.

Did Tasnim see that blush that she laughed and said, 'It's only a strip of cloth!'

As they'd agreed Tasnim should stay inside out of the sun, so as not to overheat, once again it was Marni who searched the dunes around their shelter for a stick long enough to hoist a flag.

But a flag with no message? Would it mean anything on the slim chance someone *did* come looking?

She found a stick behind the shelter where some small branches and bunches of dried grass had been stacked, presumably to provide fuel for a fire on a cold night. Digging around, wary of the scorpions Tasnim kept telling her to watch out for, she discovered another, smaller, though thicker stick. Taking it inside, she put the little gas lighter under one end of it, charring it all around so she could use it as a writing implement.

Tasnim objected to the word 'help' this time. It had been chosen when Marni had written in the sand because it was shorter than the local word, but now they settled on the universal 'SOS'.

It took over an hour, charring the stick, writing, charring again, until it was done. But where to put it? Their shelter was nestled between dunes, and even on the stick and somehow attached to the roof, it would barely be seen above the sand.

'You'll just have to climb to the highest dune,' Tasnim told Marni, 'and if Fawzi and Hari really are watching us then you'll get caught but I don't think they'd shoot you.'

'Well, that's comforting,' Marni grumbled, although she was becoming used to Tasnim's cheerful fatalism.

Ghazi stared at Mazur in disbelief.

'You're telling me those two idiots are holding Tasnim and Marni because they want me to stand down and declare Nimr the ruler?'

Mazur shook the six-page letter he was holding.

'There's a lot more than that—all kinds of rot about you having stolen Nimr's birthright and brought shame to the family's name, and not having any honour or integrity or cultural importance.'

'What the hell is cultural importance?' Ghazi demanded, then shook his head at his stupidity. As if it mattered what the pair had said about him—the important thing was rescuing Tasnim and Marni, although Tasnim would probably be happier to see him than Marni would.

'Phone Nimr, get him here immediately. If anyone

knows where those two reprobates might be holding the women, he should.'

Ghazi hoped he sounded more in control than he felt. His mind had been in chaos since Marni's disappearance, and now this! His chest was tight with worry, his gut knotted, and his neck ached with tension. It was bad enough that he'd hurt Marni with his thoughtless words, but to have put her into danger purely because of her connection to him—a connection he'd shamelessly used for his own purposes...

He'd kill those two.

'There are two or three old hunting shelters they use as bases when they're hunting.'

Nimr was striding into the room, his mobile phone in his hand. He crossed to Ghazi and put an arm around his shoulder.

'I was in the palace when Mazur called. Man, I'm sorry about this. We'll get them back. The one thing we can he sure of, they won't hurt the women. They might be stupid and infantile in their pranks but they would never hurt a woman.'

Ghazi acknowledged his cousin's words with an abrupt nod, but Nimr's arrival had brought more than hope.

'Did you want the job?' Ghazi had to ask, although he'd been sure they'd discussed this many times and Nimr's answer had always been the same.

'No way,' Nimr assured him now. 'And those two lamebrains know that! I've told them times without number that I've other things I want to do with my life and, besides, I've always known, just as my father did, that you're the best man to rule our country at this time.'

He gave Ghazi another hug, then bent over the map he'd asked Mazur to find.

'A helicopter, flying low,' he suggested. 'I'll pilot it and you be the lookout. We'll take the little four-seater Bell. It can fly lower without disturbing the sand too much so we'll still be able to see.'

He nodded to Mazur, who left to arrange the helicopter while Nimr pored over the map then glanced up at Ghazi.

'What about Tasnim? How do you think she'll be holding up?' He grinned then added, 'Are your obstetric skills up to date?'

'Don't even think about it,' Ghazi said, watching as Nimr traced a line across the map with a red pen.

Obstetric skills? The words echoed in Ghazi's head.

Tasnim was eight months pregnant and had been through a major upset. He phoned the hospital and asked if they could have a midwife with her obstetrics bag standing by on the heliport in twenty minutes.

The little aircraft lifted lightly into the air, Nimr confident at the controls, Ghazi already working out logistics. He would send Marni, Tasnim and the nurse out on the first flight and Nimr could return for him.

Once they found the women...

If they found the women...

Marni had expected Tasnim to be asleep again when she returned from planting her flag on the dune. Tasnim dozed on and off all day because her sleep at night was restless.

But Tasnim was awake—not only awake but naked.

'There must be something in the clothes, either some kind of bug or they've been washed in something that disagrees with my skin. Look!'

She pointed to where little red weals were showing on her belly.

'They're itchy and they're driving me mad.'

Marni examined them, wishing she knew more about general medicine than she did.

'They look more like an allergy than a bug of some kind,' she said. 'And I've not been bitten by anything. Lie down on the bed with just the sheet on you and I'll see what there is in the supplies that might help soothe the itches.'

Cold mint tea? she wondered.

But Tasmin refused to lie down, believing now that whatever had bitten her could be in the mattress. She went outside and sat on the sand in the small amount of shade offered by their shelter, scratching at the weals and crying softly to herself.

Aware just how brave and held-together Tasnim had been so far, Marni knew she had to do something to help her friend before she fell apart.

She poured cold tea into a cup and tore a clean strip of cloth off a wuzar, then went outside.

'Let's try this to see if it helps, otherwise there's salt—we can try salt and water—or oil perhaps. She kept thinking of bicarbonate of soda, which had been Nelson's panacea for all ills. Bathing in it when she'd had chickenpox had definitely eased the itchiness. But their little hut didn't provide bicarbonate of soda…

And Nelson wasn't here…

Ignoring her own momentary weakness, Marni concentrated on Tasnim.

The rash was spreading, and Tasnim was getting more and more upset, undoubtedly because she was becoming more and more uncomfortable.

Ignoring the dune where she'd raised her flag, Marni climbed another dune, back in the direction they'd come in from. Once at the top she shouted for the boys, alternating their names, yelling that Tasnim needed help, they had to come.

Her voice seemed a pitifully weak instrument out there in the vastness of the desert and she was certain they wouldn't hear her. She slid and slithered back down the dune, persuaded Tasnim to come inside and put on her own abaya, which she'd been wearing over her clothes when they'd been kidnapped.

Too tired and upset to argue, Tasnim dressed, then lay down to sleep—on the floor, not on a mattress.

She was still asleep when Manir heard the engine of a vehicle break the endless silence in which they'd lived since they'd reached the shelter.

'Come on, we're moving you,' Fawzi announced, when Marni met him outside the hut.

'Did you hear me calling? Tasnim's ill. She has a rash across her stomach and it could be affecting the baby. She needs to get back to town and see her doctor.'

'No can do,' Fawzi said, although Hari looked only too happy at the idea of getting rid of their captives. 'But it won't be much longer,' Fawzi continued. 'The imposter has our letter of demand and he'll be giving in any minute now.'

'The imposter? You mean Ghazi? Why is he an imposter?'

'Because he took the throne from our brother,' Hari said, apparently repeating a lesson Fawzi had drummed into him.

'But I heard Nimr didn't want the job,' Marni argued.

'He should still have taken it,' Fawzi said. 'It was his birthright.'

'Well, I don't understand the politics of your country and even if I did I'd have no right to comment, but it's silly to be standing out here in the heat. Tasnim's asleep so we can't leave yet, but if you move around the side into the shade I'll bring you some mint tea and biscuits.'

Hari, appearing only too happy to indulge in tea and biscuits, led the way, and Fawzi followed, though, Marni felt, more reluctantly.

She set everything out on a makeshift tray and joined them in the shade, knowing it would be to their advantage if she could make friends with the young men, rather than hitting them on their heads with rocks.

And as they talked, relaxing quickly as young people did, she realised just how much they loved their country, especially the desert.

'I'll get some of Fawzi's photographs to show you,' Hari offered, when he'd finished his tea.

He raced over to the car, returning with a computer tablet, opening it up at a picture of an Arabian gazelle, a beautiful picture, taken so close up you could see the reflection of the camera in the animal's eyes.

'How on earth did you do that?' she asked, and Fawzi explained that they had many hides in the desert, like this place, only built for photography rather than for shelter.

'So you're still hunters, the two of you, but your gun is now a camera?' she said, and Fawzi looked pleased that she understood.

She slid her fingers across the screen, looking at one photograph after another, amazed at how good they were.

'You should put these into a book. I had no idea there was so much wildlife in the desert. It would be wonderful publicity for Ablezia.'

'This is what people are forgetting,' Hari said. 'That's what Fawzi and I don't like about the way our country is going. People move into the city and lose their interest in the desert, forgetting that the desert is part of their hearts and souls.'

'I can understand what you mean,' Marni said, but her visitors' attention had shifted from her, and as she watched the tension build in their bodies and their heads turn skywards, she heard the distant thud, thud, thud of a helicopter.

'It's Nimr, he's found us,' Hari said, looking as if he'd like to burrow deep into the sand and disappear.

'Quick, we have to leave!' Fawzi stood up and looked ready to flee but couldn't quite bring himself to haul Marni to her feet.

'Sit down again,' she said. 'You can't go rushing all over the desert with a helicopter chasing you. That's only for the movies and even in the movies the vehicle usually crashes. And there's no way on earth I'd let Tasnim get into the vehicle with you. She's too far gone in her pregnancy. Stay here, I'll talk to Nimr. I'll show him we're both quite all right and you've been very kind to us and that it's all just been a joke.'

'Except Fawzi wrote the letter to Ghazi, telling him we had you,' Hari reminded her.

'Well, we can get around that too,' Marni said above the now loud clatter of the helicopter rotors. 'Ghazi isn't going to throw you into a dungeon. In fact, I doubt he'll even throw you into jail. We'll work something out.'

She didn't add that he might well have given them a medal for getting rid of her, if his sister hadn't been involved as well.

Perhaps realising the futility of escape, the young men stayed put, all three of them bending their heads low over their knees as the sand from the rotors kicked up all around them.

The little aircraft touched down as lightly as a butterfly and when the engine was turned off and the rotors started spinning more slowly a door opened and not Nimr but

Ghazi dropped onto the sand, followed by a woman with a large black bag and, finally, from the other side, Nimr.

'I'll kill you two,' Nimr roared, then proceeded to yell at them in their own language.

'Where's Tasnim?' Ghazi growled, anger in every line in his body, rage radiating from his pores.

Marni pointed towards the hut where a still sleepy Tasnim had appeared in the doorway.

Ghazi—although clad in jeans and a polo shirt there was no doubt from the way he held himself that he was Ghazi—led the nurse in that direction,

So that's what he thinks of me, Marni decided sadly.

Ghazi thought he'd held himself together quite well through the ordeal of not knowing where Marni was, or even if she was alive. But when he jumped out of the helicopter and saw her sitting on the sand, chatting happily to her kidnappers the tension that he'd held in check erupted into searing, white-hot anger.

Not wanting to let fly at her in front of so many people, he held it in check and sought out his sister instead, taking her in his arms and holding her close while she sobbed onto his shoulder. Her cries of relief were rising towards hysteria, her babbled words barely understandable. He soothed and comforted her, taking his time to calm her down before peeling her off his body so the nurse could check her.

By that time Nimr had joined the little group sitting on the sand, and they had obviously calmed him down because both his brothers were not only still alive but didn't seem to have been harmed in any way.

Ghazi walked towards the group and now, finally, the woman whose disappearance had nearly ripped his heart out looked up and nodded acknowledgement of his presence. She was pale, her hair coming loose from a plait and sticking out in all directions, but her face betrayed no hint of relief that they'd been rescued, or delight at seeing him.

'Nimr tells me the helicopter only carries four, Ghazi, so I think you should go with Tasnim back to the hospital,' Marni said, so calmly he wanted to throttle her. 'I know you brought a nurse, but Tasnim's been really strong up until this morning when she came out in a rash across her belly. I vaguely remember something called PEP, poly-something eruption of pregnancy that can happen in the later months. I think that's all it is but she's getting very anxious and upset about it and is desperately worried that it could affect the baby. If you're with her, you'll be able to keep her calm until she gets back home and her own obstetrician sees her.'

Ghazi stared at the woman he'd come to rescue.

Was that all she had to say?

Apparently not, because she was speaking again.

'That way, I can get a ride back to town with Hari and Fawzi, or Nimr's said he'd be happy to fly back out to pick me up once he's dropped Tasnim off.'

She had it all organised, this pale, dishevelled devil he'd fallen in love with.

And not a *hello Ghazi, nice to see you, sorry if you've been worried* to be heard!

She was unbelievable and, heaven forbid, unbeliev-ably beautiful to his eyes—even in an old kandora she must have found in the hut and smudges of exhaustion under her eyes.

Had he hurt her so much that she was treating him this way?

Like a passing stranger?

Or a *pretend* fiancé?

The pain in his gut suggested this might be so, but how could he say anything in front of Nimr and his brothers?

'Are you in agreement with this plan?' he asked Nimr. His cousin nodded.

'I think Tasnim will need you as well as the nurse,' he said.

Knowing Nimr was probably right, Ghazi turned to the young men.

'As for you two,' Ghazi he said, 'can you be trusted to stay here with Marni until we return or will you get some other wild idea and take off again?'

'We'll be here,' Hari said, so promptly Ghazi had to wonder what threats Nimr had already made to his brothers.

'I think we should go right now,' the nurse called from the doorway of the hut, and Ghazi, after one last, despairing look at the woman he loved, turned back to help his near-hysterical sister into the helicopter.

'Well, that went well,' Nimr said to him when they were airborne once again. 'Some little glitch along the road to matrimony?'

'Just keep flying,' Ghazi growled. 'And don't think for a minute you'll be flying back there, unless you want to ride home with your brothers—which might not be a bad idea. With you there, I'll be less likely to murder them.'

Nimr flew.

CHAPTER ELEVEN

NOT A PRIVATE word, not a touch—he hates me!

With Hari and Fawzi chattering on in their own language, Marni was left with her own gloomy thoughts.

You didn't exactly rush into his arms yourself, she reminded herself, which only made her feel even worse.

The problem was that, being the honourable man he was, Ghazi would undoubtedly feel he was bound to her in some way—apart from the pretend betrothal.

Enough to make the betrothal not pretend?

Probably, Marni decided gloomily, then became aware the other conversation had turned to English.

'Do you think Ghazi will banish us?' Fawzi was asking.

Marni studied the young men and saw fear and despair in their faces.

'I doubt that very much,' she said gently. 'You did a very silly thing but no harm has come of it. And you did it for reasons you believed in your hearts were right. I'm sure Ghazi will understand that.'

'You will speak to him on our behalf?' Hari begged, and although Marni knew her words would achieve little, given Ghazi's current opinion of her, she agreed that she would.

'But you'd do better speaking to him yourselves—

apologising for causing alarm. And I think he'd be more willing to forgive you if you can come up with more than just an apology. What do the pair of you do, apart from kidnapping women?'

'We hunt,' came the chorused reply.

'Hunt animals for food?'

The young men laughed.

'No, for the camera,' Fawzi said. 'You saw the pictures, and that gun I had, well, it was an antique—no way would it harm anyone or anything. We love the old ways but some of our desert animals are almost extinct. Some we trap and keep to breed from—out at the old palace—then we set the young ones free when they are able to live on their own.'

'Your photographs are brilliant,' Marni told him, 'but would it not be better for people to see these animals and birds in the wild? Could you take tourists on trips to the desert—not just to eat dinner and watch the sunset, the way tourism operators do now, but run specialist tours for photographers and wildlife lovers. You could mix the old ways with the new, as tourists want comfort—set up luxury tents and provide good food. I am sure that kind of thing would really take off.'

She saw the growing excitement in their eyes so wasn't surprised when the talk again excluded her—not that she cared. If this pair could find something useful to do with their passion, they'd have no time to be thinking up wild schemes, like kidnapping pretend fiancées.

Which brought her thoughts back to Ghazi, but what he must be thinking she had absolutely no idea.

Flying the little aircraft was second nature to him. He and his boyhood friends and relations had been flipping around in them since they had been teenagers, so he had time to plan.

No matter that Marni might hate him, he had to do the right thing by her, his honour demanded that much. He'd sort out the rest later.

He phoned Mazur and gave him orders to have every-thing in readiness at the old palace, for that was where he'd take her—where he felt most at home, and where he knew she would be safe.

'I'll need someone qualified to marry us. With the photograph as proof of her grandfather's agreement to the betrothal, we won't need anyone to stand in place of her father, and I'll use Nimr's otherwise useless broth-ers as witnesses, then send them packing back to the city and deal with them later. I want my quarters prepared, clothing and toiletries for Marni, and food laid on, but no hovering servants. She'll need privacy and quiet, Mazur, to get over the ordeal she's suffered.'

He tried not to think about what would happen beyond the ceremony he was planning—what might happen in his quarters. He knew what he hoped would happen but feared he'd damaged the tender shoots of their relation-ship beyond repair, not with his lovemaking but with the rash words he'd uttered afterwards.

Nearly there, and now he saw the brave little flag fly-ing from a dune beyond the shelter and knew she'd put it there. Kidnapped and left in the middle of the desert, she'd not only handled the situation but had done her best to get herself and Tasnim safely out of it.

He set the aircraft down, waited while the rotors slowed then dropped down to the ground.

Marni watched him walk towards them. Behind her, the two men stood, but she couldn't get her legs to move because this time Ghazi wasn't radiating anger. In fact, he appeared to be smiling and she was reasonably sure he wouldn't be smiling at Fawzi and Hari.

'You two get into your vehicle and get over to the old palace,' he said. 'I want you there as soon as possible. I've got a job for you to do.'

The pair looked shocked, but moved rapidly enough as Ghazi drew closer, his hand waving them away dismissively.

'But they wanted to talk to you about an idea they've had,' Marni objected, with only the slightest quiver in her voice betraying just how trembly she was feeling inside now she knew she'd have to face Ghazi on his own—be with him on *her* own!

'They can put it in writing—Fawzi's good at that!' Ghazi growled, coming closer and closer to where she sat.

She feared if she stood up her legs would give way on her, because just seeing him was causing palpitations, and quivering nerves, and goose-bumps on her skin, and too may other physical sensations to name.

'You,' he said, putting out his hand and hauling her unceremoniously to her feet and marching with her towards the helicopter, 'are coming with me.'

'Do you think this is the modern equivalent of one of our ancestors throwing his woman over a camel and riding off into the desert?' Hari whispered to Fawzi, loudly enough to bring another growl from Ghazi.

'Is Fawzi right?' Marni asked, because she had to say *something*. 'Are you throwing me over your camel and riding off with me?'

He had helped her into the helicopter and now stood outside, looking in at her.

'Would you like that?' he asked, his voice deep, his eyes, his face unreadable.

'I don't know,' she answered honestly.

Or was it honestly? she wondered as he marched around the chopper to get in behind the controls. She suspected that, somehow or other, she'd fallen in love with this man, without really knowing him at all.

Was that possible?

Or was it nothing more than the manifestation of the attraction that had flared between them from the beginning?

But would lust make her heart ache when she saw the tenderness with which he treated Safi?

Would it make her heart skitter when he smiled?

Not that there was any evidence of a smile at the moment. In fact, sneaking a sideways glance at him, she had to wonder if she'd ever see him smile again. Not any time soon, that was for sure.

'Are you all right?'

The demand came when they'd lifted into the air and banked as if to go even deeper into the desert.

She wanted to cry. Wanted to ask why he hadn't asked her that before. But he was all business, and she could do business.

'Desperately in need of a bath but apart from that, yes, I'm fine,' she said, and saw a slight frown mar the inscrutability of his expression, but it was quickly gone.

'You'll have time for a bath,' was all he said, or maybe he kept talking, but if he did, Marni missed it, too filled with astonishment at what lay ahead of them.

Rising out of the desert sands, barely perceptible at first, was what seemed like an immense building. High walls, sand coloured and seemingly endless, round turrets set at intervals, and where the walls changed direction, and within the walls, more walls, and domes, and spires.

'It looks as if it just grew up out of the desert sands like some fantastic plant.'

She breathed the words, lost in wonder as they flew closer and the immensity of the old palace—for that was all it could be—was revealed.

Now she could see colour—rugs hanging over balcony parapets to air, market stalls set up inside the walls, the sun glinting off brass and silver pots and pipes and urns.

Ghazi circled the building, allowing Marni a glimpse of an inner courtyard, green with trees and plants, then landed on a concrete pad at the back of the building but within the outer walls.

Speechless with astonishment and wonder, Marni followed Ghazi as he led her past a long row of stalls, with horses' heads poking out of some—horses here, not cars—and further on past different stalls—camels?—all the time heading towards the main building.

'You're late!' he said, as Mazur pulled up in a little electric cart so they could ride the rest of the way.

'You flew too fast,' Mazur countered, but when Ghazi slid in beside him in the front, Mazur clapped him on the shoulder.

'It's done?' Ghazi asked.

'All done, although Fawzi and Hari aren't here yet. Not that it matters. All you need are two adult males.'

Ghazi nodded but gave no explanation of this weird conversation. Not that Marni minded. Now she was finally somewhere civilised, all she could think about was a bath. She just hoped this place was stocked up with clothes and underwear, because second in importance to the bath would be clean underwear!

They drove through an arch into the courtyard, a wonder of green in the barren land. All around the courtyard Marni could see arched openings that led into the shade of the wide loggia, the covered outside sitting area.

Mazur stopped the cart at the bottom of shallow steps,

and Ghazi hopped out, turning to offer his hand to Marni. To her horror, she found that she was shaking—that the simple of touch of this man's hand had thrown her into a quivering mess.

She tried a smile and said weakly, 'I was doing fine up till now.'

He squeezed her fingers and she saw the familiar kindness in his eyes—kindness and something else she didn't recognise.

'You have been marvellous. Tasnim told me how you helped her remain calm.'

Marni shook her head, and tried a better smile.

'No, Tasnim did her bit. She told me it was the generations of desert women standing behind her that kept her going.'

Ghazi saw the bravery in her feeble smile and felt the tremors of post-traumatic shock shake her body. He wanted nothing more than to gather her into his arms and hold her close, tell her everything would be all right now—tell her things he barely understood himself.

But Mazur was there, servants appearing from inside the house, and a young woman, obviously chosen by his major domo here to look after Marni, was waiting in the doorway.

'This is Lila,' Mazur said, beckoning the woman forward. 'Lila, will you take Ms Graham to her suite and do whatever she needs you to do.'

So Ghazi had to hand Marni over to a stranger and hope she had the strength to keep going for just a little longer.

'Does the girl know what is planned?' he asked Mazur.

'Only that you wish to see Marni in the majlis in an hour.'

Ghazi heard the doubt in Mazur's voice—doubt and no little condemnation.

'I know she's exhausted but that's why I must do it now,' Ghazi told his friend. 'Once we're married she can rest.'

'Did you tell her?' Mazur demanded, and Ghazi shook his head, unable to explain that he hadn't been able to bring himself to mention marriage to Marni on the flight.

Because he was afraid she'd object? Refuse to go along with it?

'Then you should,' Mazur said firmly. 'I know you think you're doing the right thing, but you can't just drag the woman down the aisle with two witnesses—and why couldn't I be a witness might I ask?—and expect her to go along with marrying you.'

'It's for her safety and as for witnesses, she knows you and I need you to be there as her friend, not mine,' Ghazi snapped, then he strode away from his friend and mentor, angry, confused and heartsore.

'We must hurry,' Lila said as she led Marni along marble corridors and through jewelled archways, finally entering a room with a high domed ceiling, painted a deep, rich purple that matched the curtains around the huge four-poster bed.

'Why?' Marni managed to ask, as she took in the magnificence of this room, with its grilled windows looking out to the courtyard.

'Because we only have an hour. I have drawn a bath, it is all ready for you. I will wash your hair while you are in it, then perfume you and do just a little henna design on your hand because although no one is supposed to know, you will be marrying our prince today.'

'I will be *what*?' Marni demanded, the words muffled

as she'd been pulling the long tunic off over her head as she spoke.

'Getting married,' Lila said, obviously very excited about the upcoming event.

'No, and, no, and, no!' Marni stormed, although she did step into the bath. She could hardly argue with Ghazi stark naked—*dirty* and stark naked. 'I'll have the bath but I'll wash my hair myself and while I'm doing it you find whoever you have to talk to and get a message to your prince that I'll see him in my room in twenty minutes.'

'Oh, but you can't do that—not in your bedroom,' Lila protested.

'No?' Marni muttered. 'We'll see about that! You just get the message to him. And leave some underwear and something I can wear on the bed before you go.'

Sinking into the water, delicately scented and bubbling around her, was pure bliss, but having set her own deadline she couldn't lie back and enjoy it. She wet her hair and lathered it with shampoo that was handily placed on a shelf alongside the bath, rinsed it off and rubbed conditioner in, then let her hair absorb the treatment while she scrubbed her body clean of sand and dust and dirt.

Emptying the bath water, she stood up beneath the overhead shower and showered off the conditioner, then stepped out of the bath, wrapping herself in a super-soft towel and growing angrier by the minute that she hadn't been able to revel in the luxury of her first bath in three days.

The memory of when she'd last showered brought a rush of embarrassment, and she wondered if summoning Ghazi to her room might have been a mistake.

No! She had to talk to him. A pretend betrothal was one thing, but being rushed into marriage was just not on.

Wrapped in the towel, she went back into the bedroom, to gasp in wonder at the clothing Lila had apparently deemed suitable for her wedding.

Various packets of lacy underwear offered her a choice of colour and size, but it was the garment that would cover it that gave Marni pause. It was a simple enough gown, long and straight like the tunic she'd been wearing in the desert, but there any similarity ended, for this garment was apparently made with spun silver—fine and delicate silver—elaborately embroidered around the sleeves, neckline and hem.

It was something that should be in a museum, not about to be worn by any ordinary mortal.

She searched the walls of the bedroom, knowing there'd be concealed wardrobe and dressing room doors somewhere, and within those rooms there'd be other clothing—something else she could put on.

The doors eluded her, so she found underwear her size among the packets then returned to the bathroom, sure there'd be a robe there she could wear.

No such luck, but the towels were huge, and choosing a dry one she wrapped it around herself, then went across to a small sitting area by one of the windows to await her confrontation with her betrothed. Talking to him in the sitting area was slightly better than anywhere near the bed, but the bed still seemed to dominate the room.

And her thoughts!

Seeing her clad only in a towel was very nearly Ghazi's undoing. To hold her, smell her skin, feel her still damp hair against his face, peel off the towel—

'So, what's this all about?' the woman in the towel demanded, and he jerked his mind back to reality.

'No, don't bother answering that,' she added, before he could reply. 'It's your sense of chivalry, of honour that you're insisting on this marriage business. And sit down, I can't keep arguing with you when you're towering over me up there.'

For some reason he wanted to smile—perhaps because she should be at such a disadvantage in the towel, yet here she was issuing orders to him.

He didn't smile, knowing that would only make her angrier, but he did sit, and, sitting, could take in the clear pale skin of her shoulders—was that a bruise or the remnant of a love bite from the other night?—and the shadows of tiredness beneath her eyes.

His arms ached to hold her, to kiss away those shadows, to feel her body tight against his—where he was sure it belonged.

But was she sure it was where *she* belonged?

He had no idea, which was why he had to tread carefully.

'It's a matter of keeping you safe,' he said, forcing his mind to take control of his wayward thoughts. 'I need to have the right to protect you for as long as you remain in this country. As my wife, you would have a status that makes you, by tradition, untouchable. We don't have to stay married for ever or have a marriage in anything but name, but what has happened once could happen again, and next time your kidnappers could be more dangerous than a couple of stupid young men.'

She frowned at him and he wanted to wipe away that frown, to smooth the skin above her neat little nose, maybe kiss the frown away.

'They're not stupid, they just don't have enough to occupy them and that always leads to trouble with young people,' she said, and Ghazi was so lost in thoughts of kisses it took him a moment to catch up.

'You mean Hari and Fawzi? I've been telling Nimr that for ages, but we're not here to talk about them, surely?'

'Not exactly, but it's the same thing in another way. Those two, well, we've worked out what they can do— run wildlife safaris for photographers and animal lovers. But they did what they did because they could—because no one's ever said no to them or their wild schemes and I suspect it's just the same with you, no one's ever said no to you so you dream up this stupid idea of us getting married for whatever reason and don't stop to think what I might have to say to it.'

Now he did smile, and if the delicate flush of colour on her chest above the towel was any indication, he didn't think he'd made her angrier.

Marni had thought she was doing quite well with the conversation, considering she was sitting practically naked in front of the sexiest man in the world, and her thoughts were rampaging on about giving in to her body and letting the towel slip, and then he smiled and her mind went blank.

'What *do* you have to say to it?' he asked, the smile still lurking because she could see it shining in his eyes.

To what?

She'd totally lost the thread of the conversation, if it had ever had a thread.

And *she'd* summoned *him*, so presumably she was the one who was supposed to be in control.

'To us getting married,' he said in such a kindly man- ner she wanted to slap him—or perhaps kiss away the little quirk of a smile on the corners of his lips. 'After all, we are betrothed, and as I said earlier it needn't mean anything, but it would give me the right to protect you, Marni, and I think I owe that to your grandfather.'

'Pop! Oh, heavens, I'd forgotten all about Pop. I need to phone Nelson, I need to find out—'

Ghazi touched her gently on her knee.

'Your grandfather is doing well—far better than his surgeon expected. I have spoken to both the surgeon and to Nelson every day. It will be a long convalescence, as you already knew, but he's progressing extremely well.'

Marni wasn't sure if it was the assurance or the hand on her knee that brought a rush of relief to her body, and with the relief came a release of the tension she'd been feeling for days.

And a burst of gratitude to this man who thought of everything.

Except she didn't want to be feeling grateful to him— she didn't want to be feeling anything!

Not that she'd have a hope of stopping the physical stuff!

But right now she had to get past that and get her brain working again, so she could explain why she wasn't going to marry him.

Wouldn't it be easier to just give in and marry the man? Then she could sleep.

Except…

'You say we're getting married so you can protect me but if I go back to being plain Marni Graham, a theatre sister, and live in a flat at the hospital, go to and from work there, then there'd be no need for protection. Now I know you better I know you can handle your sisters, so we can dispense with the betrothal business and everything can go back to normal.'

Her heart grew heavier and heavier as she spoke, yet she knew it was the right thing to do.

'Can it?' he asked, while the strength of the attraction between them was such that she could feel his body against hers, his mouth capturing her lips, although a full metre of palace air separated them.

'Of course it can,' Marni said, but the words didn't come out as strongly as she'd hoped they would. In fact, they sounded feeble in the extreme.

She took a deep breath and tried again.

'It's not only the protection thing that's pushing you,' she told him. 'I know you well enough to understand you feel you have to marry me because it's the honourable thing to do, and that's just nonsense. What happened happened, and I wanted it as much as you did.'

'What *happened* was that I hurt you,' Ghazi said, his voice full of regret. 'Hurt you with my foolish words, but it wasn't that you'd disappointed me in any way, but that, had I known—'

'You'd have pulled back,' Marni said. 'Don't bother denying it, it's happened to me before.'

The pain in her voice was too much! He stood up, lifted her out of the chair and sat down again with her on his knee. He brushed the hair back from her face and kissed her gently on the lips.

'Maybe,' he said, running his hand over her hair, enjoying just holding her, 'but only until I could make it special for you, make it easier and more enjoyable—slower and more careful, so it was more pleasure than pain for you. But how was I to know?'

He looked into her eyes, filmed with tears, although a brave smile was hovering around her lips.

'That I might still be a virgin at my age?' she asked. 'Not many people would think it. It wasn't that I was keeping myself for someone special, or that I thought my virginity precious, or anything that definite at all—it just happened.'

She was studying his face as she spoke, as if hoping to read understanding there.

'You see,' she continued, 'I was brought up by two elderly men, who loved me as dearly as I loved them, so early on, at school and university when all my friends were experimenting with sex, I couldn't quite get into it, afraid Pop and Nelson would be disappointed in me, that they'd think less of me. I knew if someone did come along that they'd like and approve of, then probably it would happen, but no one did, and then I was older and suddenly it was embarrassing to be a virgin and that made it harder and harder and—'

He cupped his hands around her face and kissed her gently on her lips.

'And when you did tell someone you thought might be the right man, he mocked you, hurt you with cruel words and snide remarks?'

She nodded and rested her forehead on his chest while he wound his fingers through her hair and held her close.

'So, now that's sorted,' he said, 'how about we go and get married so I can show you just how wonderful it can be?

Marni eased her head off his chest and looked at him.

'You could show me anyway,' she teased. 'The bed's right there, and no matter what you say, you're marrying me because you feel it's the honourable thing to do, aren't you?

He was and he wasn't but how to handle it?

Could he, who'd never opened up his heart to anyone, not even his closest friends, open himself up to this woman?

Couldn't that lead to loss of power?

To vulnerability?

To pain?

Yet, holding her, knowing her as he now did, he knew nothing less would do.

He stood up and put her back in her chair then knelt before her, taking both her hands in his.

'You're right about the honour,' he said, trying hard to get the words he needed—to get them right. 'Yes, I believe marrying you is the right thing to do, and even if you feel you don't need it, I want to be able to protect you—to protect you, provide for you and care for you.'

Deep breath because this was it—this was where he laid bare his soul.

So she could trample on it?

He had no idea.

'But most of all I want to marry you because I love you more than I have ever believed I could love anyone. These last few days have been the vilest kind of torture, because not only did I not know where you were, or even if you were still alive, but because I'd hurt you before we'd parted, and not knowing if I'd ever be able to explain—to make things right between us—well, that was the worst agony of all.'

Marni stared at him in utter astonishment.

'But you never said—'

'Did you?' he countered, smiling up at her in such a way she felt her entire body melting.

'How could I? I was worried it might just be lust, although as I got to know you, saw your kindness, your love for your country and your people, the way you were with Safi, it felt like love, but what did I know about that? It was as foreign to me as Ablezia, so how could I tell? I just wasn't sure.'

'Not I until I lost you,' he admitted, then he lifted her hands and kissed the backs of them, before turning them and pressing a kiss into each palm.

'So we're good to go?' he asked, his voice shaking just slightly with what could only be nerves.

'I guess so,' Marni told him, although she was sad that Pop wouldn't be there on her wedding day. But then she leaned towards him, ready for the kiss that *had* to be coming.

Needing the kiss as confirmation of their love.

'If that towel falls off, we'll never make the wedding,' Ghazi told her, not kissing her at all but standing up and stepping back, needing space between them so the fires didn't start up again. 'Get yourself dressed. I'll send Lila back to help you.'

He headed out the door

EPILOGUE

MARNI WALKED THROUGH the suite of rooms she'd chosen for Pop and Nelson, checking everything was in readiness. This suite had a small kitchenette and she'd stocked it with their favourite snacks, brands of tea and coffee, and a refrigerator full of cold drinks.

It would make Nelson feel more at home if he could prepare small meals for himself and Pop and, as Pop was still convalescent, they'd both appreciate not having to join the family for every meal.

'Stop fussing, it's perfect, and it's time to leave for the airport.'

Ghazi had obviously known where to find her and he stood behind her, slipping his arms around her, one hand resting protectively on her belly where the surprise she had for Pop was just beginning to show.

She leant back against her husband, aware of him in every fibre of her being, aware of the love that flooded through her whenever he was near.

In six short months her life had changed so tremendously it still had a dreamlike quality. She'd soon learned the wife of the ruler had a multitude of duties to perform, but his family had been wonderful, even Tasnim, with her new baby—Marni—was constantly on the phone.

Like him, she was still learning 'the job' but it was

becoming easier every day—her reward for her diligence, the nights she spent in the arms of her lover—night after night of excitement, tenderness, raging lust and pure bliss.

Ablezia had certainly provided the answer to her 'virginity thing'!

'I can feel you thinking about sex,' Ghazi whispered in her ear.

'Not here, and there's no time anyway,' she told him, but she pressed her body against his and enjoyed the ripples of excitement even such a casual embrace could cause.

'We have to leave—the plane's due in within half an hour.'

She spun around and kissed him, her excitement over the arrival of Pop and Nelson now quelling other kinds of excitement.

Like most of the guest suites, this one opened onto the inner courtyard and Ghazi led her out that way and through the gardens to the garages at the back. This told her he'd be driving them to the airport—no driver for this private family meeting.

The courtyard seemed darker than usual, and only a few lights shone from the rooms around it, although usually the place was flooded with light.

'Austerity measures?' she teased, waving her hand towards the dark building.

'Probably a problem with a fitting somewhere,' Ghazi replied, 'and the electrician's closed off a whole section of the power.'

She forgot about it as they drove to the airport, although as they skirted the city, it, too, seemed to be less lit up. But Ghazi was talking about Safi, staying at the palace, in the harem, with his mother and younger brothers, awaiting his next operation.

One of Marni's projects was setting up a fund to raise money for the families of children who came to Ablezia for medical treatment—money that would allow family members to accompany the children and cover any loss of income they might suffer because of their absence from work back in their homeland.

They talked of it until they pulled up at the airport, driving to a private area where Ghazi's own plane would touch down.

Had touched down!

And there was Pop, using a walking stick but as upright as ever, Nelson right beside him, while a steward came behind them with their luggage.

Marni raced across the tarmac and threw her arms around her grandfather, tears coursing down her cheeks. She could feel his fragility as she held him, and that made her tears flow faster.

Eventually he eased away.

'See,' he said, 'that's why I sent you away. Couldn't have stood to have you weeping over me for six months. No more tears now. Say hello to Nelson then you'd better introduce this husband you seem to have picked up.'

Marni smiled through her tears and hugged Nelson, thanking him again and again for all he'd done, seeing Pop through his operation and recuperation.

'I know how difficult he can be,' she said, and Nelson smiled.

'And you also know I can handle him,' Nelson told her. He studied her for a moment then added, 'Ghazi being good to you, darling girl?'

Marni could only nod, the lump in her throat too big for speech. Then Ghazi was there, introducing himself, telling Nelson he remembered him, thanking them both for the gift they'd sent—the gift of Marni.

The steward had loaded the luggage into the car, and Ghazi seated Nelson beside him in the front, Marni and Pop in the back.

He drove slowly back towards the main road into the city, although maybe they were on another road for now all Marni could see that beyond the headlights was complete darkness.

'Is that desert out there?' Pop asked.

'Mostly, although this is a big highway and usually well lit.'

She'd barely spoken when the lights came on—and what lights! Strung between the tall lampposts were garlands of red and green, Christmas bells hanging from the centre of each one. The posts themselves were decorated with streamers, and along the road reindeer were picked out in fairy-lights.

'But you don't celebrate Christmas in Ablezia,' Marni protested, as more and more Christmas decorations came into view—huge banners hanging from high-rise buildings, streamers of coloured lights around the souk, Christmas trees in parks and gardens, and huge blow-up Santas atop any available chimney.

Ghazi slowed the car and turned back to look at her.

'I couldn't let you miss out on *your* celebration,' he said. 'Nimr took the idea to parliament, reminding everyone we have a lot of Western expats in our land. How better to welcome them and make them feel at home? he suggested. Then although Fawzi and Hari are busy with their safari plans, he got them busy organising it, seeing all the big corporations and explaining what we wanted.'

Marni shook her head, unable to speak for the wonder of what her husband and his people had done for her.

But the palace itself was even more breathtaking, for here everything was done in fairy-lights so the court-yard looked like a fairy wonderland, the tree in the majlis a miracle of silver decorations and tiny shining lights.

Still bemused by the whole thing, she showed Pop and Nelson to their suite, introducing them to the servant who would be on call for them at any time.

In Pop's bedroom they finally had time to pause, to hug each other again, and for them to study each other.

'How are you, really?' she asked, and he smiled his old, cheeky smile.

'Nearly there, my girl, nearly there. You know you can't keep an old dog down.'

Then the smile faded as he touched her cheek.

'And you? Are you happy? It's obvious he loves you, I can see it in his eyes. Do you love him?'

Marni smiled and hugged her grandfather again.

'With every breath I take, with every cell in my body,' she whispered, and Pop patted her on the back.

'That's good,' he said, then he held her at arm's length and she saw the twinkle in his eyes. 'So maybe two old men knew what they were doing, eh?'

'Happy?' Ghazi asked much later when she slid into bed beside him.

She shook her head and saw his frown. Kissed it away, and whispered, 'There has to be a better word than that for what I feel. Overwhelmed with love, that's what I feel, overwhelmed that you would do what you did for me tonight. You've given me so much with your love, and your trust, and bringing Pop and Nelson over for this visit, but to give me Christmas—that goes beyond everything I've ever known or expected or imagined.'

'So you *are* happy?' Ghazi pressed, as he gathered her into his arms.

'So far beyond it I can't explain, but maybe I can show you.'

And she did!

* * * * *

Merry Christmas
& A Happy New Year!

Thank you for a wonderful
2013...

A sneaky peek at next month...

CAPTIVATING MEDICAL DRAMA—WITH HEART

My wish list for next month's titles...

In stores from 3rd January 2014:

☐ Her Hard to Resist Husband — Tina Beckett

& The Rebel Doc Who Stole Her Heart — Susan Carlisle

☐ From Duty to Daddy — Sue MacKay

& Changed by His Son's Smile — Robin Gianna

☐ Mr Right All Along — Jennifer Taylor

& Her Miracle Twins — Margaret Barker

Available at WHSmith, Tesco, Asda, Eason, Amazon and Apple

Just can't wait?

Come in from the cold this Christmas with two of our favourite authors. Whether you're jetting off to Vermont with Sarah Morgan or settling down for Christmas dinner with Fiona Harper, the smiles won't stop this festive season.

Visit:
www.millsandboon.co.uk

Work hard, play harder...

Welcome to the Gold Coast, where hearts are broken as quickly as they are healed. Featuring some of the rising stars of the medical world, this new four-book series dives headfirst into Surfer's Paradise.

Available as a bundle at
www.millsandboon.co.uk/medical

MILLS & BOON®
Book Club

Join the Mills & Boon Book Club

Want to read more **Medical** books?
We're offering you **2 more** absolutely **FREE!**

We'll also treat you to these fabulous extras:

- **Exclusive offers and much more!**
- **FREE home delivery**
- **FREE books and gifts with our special rewards scheme**

Get your free books now!

**visit www.millsandboon.co.uk/bookclub
or call Customer Relations on 020 8288 2888**

SUBS/ONLINE/M1

In Real Life

Love, Lies & Identity
in the Digital Age

Nev Schulman

HODDER &
STOUGHTON

First published in Great Britain in 2014
by Hodder & Stoughton
An Hachette UK company

3

Illustrations on pp. 91, 105, 123, 124, 130, 158, and 188 by
Sean Donnelly (illus. on p. 188 based on original by Dallas Clayton).
Photo on p. 100 by Max Joseph; photo on p. 115 by Michael Hart;
photos on pp. 147 and 245 from the author's personal collection.

Catfish: The TV Show logo © 2014 Viacom International Inc.

A CIP catalogue record for this title is available from the British Library

Trade Paperback ISBN 978 1 473 60805 4
eBook ISBN 978 1 473 60804 7

Printed and bound by Clays Ltd, St Ives plc

Hodder & Stoughton policy is to use papers that are natural, renewable
and recyclable products and made from wood grown in sustainable
forests. The logging and manufacturing processes are expected to
conform to the environmental regulations of the country of origin.

Hodder & Stoughton Ltd
338 Euston Road
London NW1 3BH

www.hodder.co.uk

#IRLbook

About the Author

Nev Schulman is the host and executive producer of
MTV's No.1 series, *Catfish*, which 2.6 million people
watch in the U.S., plus millions more worldwide in
25 other countries.

@nevschulman / yanivschulman.com

Praise for *In Real Life*

'Nev is a great philosopher of the Internet and thereby a
critical voice for our generation. Whether or not you're
a *Catfish* fan, IN REAL LIFE is a must-read and shows us the
opportunities and pitfalls that are part of the digital era.'
Matthew Segal, founder of OurTime.org

'What I find most exciting about IN REAL LIFE is how it
explores the Internet's impact on our perception of gender
and sexuality, and how we portray our digital selves
to the world to that end.'
Kim Stolz, author of *Unfriending My Ex*

'IN REAL LIFE is so much more than a book about online
dating. It's about self-acceptance and being true to
yourself in a world where you're influenced by so
many people over the Internet.'
Jonathan Bennett, *Mean Girls* actor and host of MTV's *Copycat*

'Finally someone has written a smart and funny guide
that helps young people navigate social media without
letting it take over their lives.'
Maude Apatow, actress

To my grandparents,
Marvin, Phyllis, Lowell, Dianne, Toni, Marlene, and Hal,
for teaching me the importance of generosity, the value of humor,
and the meaning of family.

Contents

PART THREE
HOW TO LIVE AND LOVE OFFLINE, TOO

In Real Life

Introduction

It was 2:30 a.m. on an August night in 2008, and I was sitting in a rental car on a rural country road in Gladstone, Michigan. It was pitch black outside, with only one dim light illuminating a patch of yard, an empty horse trailer, and a barn. The girl I was falling in love with—a pretty young musician named Megan—was supposedly in that barn, helping a horse give birth to her foal.

At least, I *thought* she was someone I was falling in love with. The truth was, I'd never actually met her.

For eight months—ever since I'd encountered Megan online—she and I had been texting daily, spending hours on the phone every week, exchanging a huge volume of email and Facebook messages. We'd made attempts to get together—for me to visit her home in Michigan or her to come to me in New York City—but they'd all fallen apart for one reason or another. Still, we'd continued to grow closer, virtually befriending each other's friends and families. Even my mom loved Megan. I was in deep.

So why was I sitting in the car, silently freaking out? Why had I just engaged in a long debate with my brother, Rel, and my friend Henry, who had accompanied me there, about whether it made more sense to back into the farm's driveway (for a quick getaway) or drive in forward (so the headlights would illuminate the yard more)? Why was I not jumping out and running into that barn to finally see Megan, in the flesh, for the first time?

The answer to that question was way more complicated than I'd ever expected.

A few days before, I had discovered that Megan was lying about something—a seemingly small thing, but enough to raise a red flag. What else was she lying about? We'd had our first real fight. Rel, Henry, and I were in Vail, Colorado (where we were shooting a video) at the time, and decided to jump on a plane for a surprise visit to Michigan. I wanted to meet Megan once and for all so she could answer the questions that were starting to pop up in my mind.

What had started out earlier that day as an exhilarating, spontaneous trip grew more and more confusing the closer we got to Megan's farm. As we drove straight from the Chicago airport through Wisconsin, past Green Bay and along Lake Michigan, I had started to wonder: Was I headed for a thrilling encounter with real love, or a potential confrontation with a crazy person? The hours passed, and paranoia began to set in. Around midnight, we had stopped at Walmart to stock up on survival gear—bear spray and a case of bottled water, as if we were anticipating some sort of siege. Instead, our more optimistic and gentlemanly instincts took over, and we ended up buying presents for Megan and her family: CDs, a s'more-making kit, a ballet poster, and some dog toys for the family pet.

And now, finally, here we were. I was exhausted, yet high on adrenaline. I recognized the horse farm from the pictures Megan had sent me, so that was reassuring. When we opened the mailbox, just to confirm that someone named Megan actually lived there, we did find mail addressed to her. But it was mail *I* had addressed to her—some of it almost two months earlier. The postcards were stamped *Return to sender.*

Huh.

As Henry pulled the car into the driveway and then turned it around, I thought to myself, *This is the moment. This is the millisecond in the story of your life where you either go for it or don't. Either you walk up to that barn and your life potentially changes, or you flee.* And then, a more panicky internal voice: *If it's a horror movie, this is also the moment when you die.* But it wasn't a horror movie. It was real life. *My* life. And I knew that if I chickened out, I'd never get any answers at all.

Just do it.

I jumped out of the car, walked right up to the glass window of the barn door, and looked in.

———

If you are thinking right now that Megan probably didn't exist—you're right. I was about to be profoundly disappointed. It turns out I'd been "catfished"—a term that emerged out of the documentary that Rel, Henry, and I would make about my experience, and one that would quickly become a widespread meme encapsulating the growing phenomenon of online relationships based on fake identities. So, no—there was no Megan, at least not as I had known her. When I finally looked in that barn window, it was empty.

My experience trying to discern what had happened to me would end up becoming a documentary—*Catfish*—that would premiere at the Sundance Film Festival and turn out to be an international hit. It would spawn a TV show for MTV, in which I investigate online relationships to determine whether they are based on truth or fiction. (Spoiler: It's almost always fiction.)

Through all of this, I'd discover how universal my experience really was.

As we now know, "catfish" are everywhere. Every day stories turn up in the media—on *The View*, *Glee*, ESPN, *Vanity Fair*, and the *New York Times Magazine*, and those are just the ones that make it to the news. Thousands, maybe even tens of thousands of people are catfished every day. In the process of making *Catfish: The TV Show*, I've investigated dozens of these cases myself—and they don't even begin to scratch the surface. I receive hundreds of emails *every week* from people who believe they've been duped or are currently involved in a suspicious relationship.

Clearly, catfishing is an epidemic. But this book isn't just about being catfished.

The rise of catfishing has opened up the far bigger question of how we are living and loving in the era of social media. The vast majority of young people are now conducting their friendships and love affairs via social media, often (like me) with people they've never met in the flesh. Are you online? Then odds are you already know what I'm talking about: You've made friends, you've fallen in love, you've had *entire relationships* that never went past pixels on a screen.

There's always going to be a shortage of happiness. Thanks to Facebook and Twitter and Instagram and so on, we have a new way to search for the affection we crave. But far too frequently, we are engaging in Internet relationships—relationships that are founded on various forms of misrepresentation—*instead* of real-life relationships.

What I've learned in the course of making my documentary and TV show is that even though we have so many new ways of reaching out to one another, we don't know how to truly communicate anymore. We've distilled our interactions so that we don't have to deal with the sticky, complicated, uncomfortable reality that comes with expressing ourselves.

Instead of working our issues out, we fall back on white lies, half-truths, and downright dishonesty.

If you watch *Catfish: The TV Show*, you may sometimes feel frustrated by our brief explanations for some very complicated behavior. Well, where the TV show ends, this book really starts. Here I will dig into the deeper issues that motivate not just catfish, but everyone who spends significant time and energy on social media and their online relationships.

This book is for you if you find yourself looking at your smartphone fifty times a day instead of looking other people in the eye. Or if you find yourself worrying about your popularity online, obsessing over your profile photos, and counting your "likes." Or if you spend hours every day poring over Instagram posts and tweets, interacting with people you do not know, and disengaging from real life in order to stay connected to the online world.

This book isn't just for people who have been catfished—it's for *anyone* who lives online today.

Consider this an honest look at falling in love, loving yourself, and being loved in the social media age. It's a guide that addresses how to improve your actual life instead of living through your digital self.

We may all speak the same language, use the same emojis and acronyms, go to the same websites, but we've lost something important in the way we interact with one another.

We've replaced the spice of personal relationships—the benefits and burdens of being real—for the anonymity of social media; anonymity that allows us to create a persona free of the constraints of truth.

It's time to stop living *IRL*, and start living in real life.

PART ONE

Catfishing: A Primer

When I announced this book on my Facebook fan page, I asked my followers what they were most interested in reading about. I got hundreds of responses, ranging from "Tell us about your 'relationship' with your cameraman, Max" to "recovering from rejection" to "being so sexy it hurts 😊."

But by far the most common request was for more information about what you see on the show: You want a better understanding of who catfish are, why they do what they do, and what motivates them. What's the psychology behind catfishing? Why do catfish's victims believe every word they say? And how did *I* end up being hooked by a catfish?

This first section attempts to answer some of those questions. It reveals the complex reasoning behind some of the most bizarre stories we've uncovered. What does catfishing tell us about modern communication—and what does it say about us as individuals?

CHAPTER 1

My Catfish Story, Part One

The message that started it all arrived on a chilly December morning in 2007. I was at my new office on Broadway in Tribeca, a second-floor loft that I was sharing with Rel and Henry. The place was a disaster zone—boxes and papers and photographs and computer equipment everywhere. This small, chaotic space was home base for my videography and photography business and was where I worked as the media director for Morphoses / The Wheeldon Company, a new contemporary ballet troupe.

I probably should have been unpacking, or editing one of my many video projects, or—at the very least—cleaning up, but instead I was procrastinating. I'd already checked my Facebook profile a half dozen times when I decided to click over to Myspace, which I hadn't visited in months. There, I kept a fairly out-of-date profile under the title "Professional New Yorker."

In my Myspace inbox, I discovered a message, dated months earlier, from someone named "Abby Loves Ballet." It read, roughly:

Hi Mr. Schulman! My name is Abby. I'm 8 years old and live in Ishpeming, Michigan. I was in New York a few months ago on a trip with my mom. She took me to a performance of Morphoses. I saw your name on their web site and saw that you're a photographer. I really love your pictures. Anyway, since

I know you're a "professional New Yorker," I'd love to get your opinion on these paintings I just did of Central Park. I'm sure you're super busy. No worries if you don't have time to respond.

Peace and Love ~Abby

Later, I'd wonder whether the profile name Abby Loves Ballet had been created specifically to appeal to me and my love for dance, but at the time, I was charmed. Abby's profile picture was of a young girl with a big smile and long blond hair. *How funny and cute*, I thought. I clicked over to look at some of her paintings: They were pastel watercolor landscapes, mostly of trees and bridges in Central Park. I wasn't exactly a professional art critic, but I was sufficiently impressed. The paintings seemed pretty advanced for a kid her age.

It all seemed so genuine, which—after I'd lived my whole life in a city where cynicism is too often the default mode—came as a breath of fresh air. And I was flattered: It was the first time someone had reached out to tell me they were inspired by my photography.

I don't have the message that I sent back to her—my Myspace page is long gone—but as far as I can recall, my response went something like this:

Hey, thanks for your email. I checked out your paintings and they're really great. I particularly like the way you captured the light on the tree branches. Keep up the good work. Cheers.

And that was that. Or so I thought. Little did I know that she now had me on the hook. That one response would open a floodgate of more than 1,500 messages over the next nine months, and would ultimately change the direction of my entire life.

———

As an eight-year-old girl living in a rural town in the Midwest, Abby was pretty much my polar opposite. I was a twenty-three-year-old native New Yorker, born, raised, and educated within twenty miles of Manhattan.

Let me give you some background.

My family's roots in the city run deep. My name, Nev, is short for Yaniv, the result of the time my parents spent in Israel before I was born. My dad's family, the Schulmans, are a Jewish family that emigrated from Eastern Europe in the late 1800s. My mother's family, the Baraschs, are also Eastern European immigrants. Both sides were dirt poor but hard workers, and they ultimately found success in New York: The Baraschs owned a deli in uptown Manhattan and the Schulmans were dressmakers in Scarsdale. My mom's father, Marvin, started an insurance company with his brother that he grew into one of the largest in the country. My dad's father became a wealthy real estate developer, a golf course designer, and one of the most respected figureheads in the Northeast golf community. My dad followed right in his footsteps.

My parents married young, after a very brief courtship, and soon after that my mom was pregnant with my brother, Rel. My parents' relationship was already strained when I was born three years later, and not long afterward they decided to part ways. I spent my childhood bouncing between my mom's apartment on the Upper West Side of Manhattan and my dad's house in Westchester (and then, after he moved, his apartment eight blocks south of my mom's).

My mom is a wildflower tomboy. I inherited my love of motorcycles from her. She's an original, passionate and impulsive. Her taste is eclectic, and her home is always beautiful. She loves to try new things: She worked as a florist, and then at the auction house Sotheby's, and finally as an event planner before going back to school to get her masters in social work. I love how creative and artistic she is, and she truly taught me the meaning of unconditional love. (I'll tell you more about that later.)

My dad is a passionate guy, always excited about something. He's also a total creature of habit. Every day, he wakes up at 4:45 a.m. He drinks two coffees, then attends two back-to-back Bikram yoga classes. He is compulsive, a real "all or nothing" kind of guy. I remember that for months at a time while I was growing up, he'd eat only peanut butter out of the jar with a spoon, and then one day he'd decide to never eat it again. He'd find a pair of pants he liked and buy ten pairs of them. He cleans constantly and is hypercritical— of me, of the women he dates, of himself. That's probably why he was a perpetual bachelor when I was growing up, and although he did fine for himself, he never seemed to be where he wanted to be.

I grew up worried that I'd struggle with the same issue: having a productive life and yet feeling that I'd settled for a lesser version of myself. (It remains a battle to this day. Every morning when I wake up, my head races with all the little things I have to do. It's a constant fight not to sweat the small stuff—the easy tasks within reach—and instead to focus on the bigger picture, to slowly work toward something even if it doesn't immediately produce results.)

Maybe it was because of my parents' early divorce (I'll save that question for the therapist), but at a breathtakingly young age, I was already a professional troublemaker. By the time I was six years old I'd been kicked out of kindergarten for intentionally clogging all the toilets and urinals with toilet paper. It was just the beginning of my long and illustrious career as a juvenile delinquent.

I lasted at my next school—a snooty uptown private school called Ethical Culture—for three years before I got in a tiff with a teacher about the length of my hair (too long) and then cursed out the principal. I wasn't invited back for fourth grade.

By the time I arrived at what is now called the Trevor Day School my parents had realized that my hyperactivity was diagnosable. ADHD was the buzzword of the moment. Ritalin became my new best friend, and for a while, things seemed to improve. I had a therapist, and my new school had smaller classrooms and a more visual curriculum that appealed to me. The National Dance Institute visited the school once a week to teach the students dance, and I discovered an aptitude for it. It was the first time I'd ever been good at something. It was NDI that introduced me to dance and gave me an outlet for much of the energy and creativity I was looking to express.

Still, I was wound up. I was constantly getting in fights with my brother: It would drive me crazy when he came home and threw his dirty socks on the floor. Plus, I had a lack of inhibition that was unusual for my age, and couldn't stop myself from trying to be the class clown. I never kept my mouth shut. In my freshman year of high school, I was suspended for procuring a condom from the bathroom's new condom dispenser and waving the unraveled prophylactic around in class. (My female classmates didn't think it was as funny as I did.)

But my real problem was stealing. I stole DVDs from Tower

Records, clothing from Ralph Lauren, and a host of other miscellaneous items. My attitude was, *If they're not doing a better job keeping an eye on it, it's their fault.* I hadn't yet learned accountability; I didn't understand that even if I wasn't personally dealing with the consequences of my actions, someone else was. And I got away with it until my senior year, when I stole a Wi-Fi card out of my computer teacher's desk. I was a rotten criminal: I didn't yet understand how IP addresses worked, and the offending card was quickly traced back to me. That was the end of my career at Day School. They gave me my diploma, but I wasn't allowed to attend the graduation ceremony with my class.

I managed to talk my way into Sarah Lawrence for college—or, to be more honest about it, my mother did the talking for me. As an active alumna, she used her clout to get me in. (Let's be blunt, she begged.) Once I landed at Sarah Lawrence, I promptly began getting myself into even more trouble. I broke into my dorm's basement and set it up as a subterranean party pad, throwing massive bashes. I snuck into a defunct restaurant in Yonkers and stole all their booze, kitting out my lofted dorm room with an epic bar. I sold weed and mushrooms.

Then there were the car crashes. Between 2002, when I was seventeen, and 2005, I wrecked a 1980 Porsche (fell asleep at the wheel), a Harley-Davidson (going too fast on vacation), and a 1992 Acura Legend (old lady stopped too suddenly in front of me), not to mention countless small skirmishes with my motorcycle on the rainy and snowy streets of Manhattan. It's probably a miracle I'm still alive.

I never thought of myself as lucky, though. Instead, I was cocky and arrogant and thoughtless. I remember breaking into the Sarah Lawrence cafeteria kitchen with friends one night: We put condoms between the sliced meats and I took a dump in the cereal dispenser—a stunt that shut down the kitchen for two days. (I can't believe I just admitted that.) Another time, I got revenge on an enemy who I'm pretty sure slashed the tires of my motorcycle by emptying a fire extinguisher in his closet and taking a number of his things. Even though I later felt guilty and returned his belongings in garbage bags, it took some serious convincing to get him to drop the damage charges against me. I can't say I blame him.

He wasn't the only one who hated me. I was on the outs with everyone. I disappointed my family; I infuriated authorities; I pissed off half the kids at school. I spent the better part of my life being told that I'd messed up and apologizing. I'd tell people that I understood what I'd done wrong, that I'd fix what I'd broken, that I'd do better next time—but I wouldn't. I didn't have any real friends because I couldn't be trusted. It's not that I was a bad person, but I didn't have any perspective. My actions were aggressive. My mantra was, "I do what I want." I took every risk that came my way. I rarely considered the consequences, and if I did, I either didn't understand the seriousness of the situation or thought I could handle it.

But despite my talent for spreading chaos, my appetite for risk allowed me to become a budding entrepreneur. My sophomore year, my brother, who was in film school, was offered a job filming a bar mitzvah. Not having time, he offered me the job. It was a two-thousand-dollar opportunity that I happily accepted, immediately employing my suitemate and filmmaker friend Thomas to coproduce with me. The video was a success and I was quickly referred to many other NYC clients. One of them asked if I knew a good event photographer, and without hesitation I suggested myself. Of course, I didn't have the proper experience or equipment, so when asked about my fee I simply researched what I'd need to buy and made that cost my quote. It worked: I had successfully bullshitted my way into being a professional photographer.

As the jobs kept coming in, I decided to take a year off from school to build a photography and videography business. I started a nightlife photography website called TheContactSheet .com, which quickly became a hit. I loved working and making money, and by the time I returned to Sarah Lawrence my junior year, my heart wasn't in school anymore (not that it ever really was to begin with). Not long after my return, I decided to photograph the school's annual Sleaze Ball, a night of debauchery, drugs, and girls dressed primarily in lingerie. While I was photographing, an individual who didn't like that I was taking pictures attempted to tackle me and smash my camera on the ground. Since the camera was attached to a strap around my neck, I found myself in a very unpleasant situation, much like a dog with a choke collar. In an effort to free myself, I punched the person and ran off; when I returned minutes later, I discovered that the short, stocky, crew-cut-styled individual that I'd fought with was a woman—a fact that I hadn't been aware of in the heat of the moment. The next thing I knew, I'd been arrested.

The case was dismissed almost immediately, but Sarah Lawrence took the opportunity to toss me out once and for all. I never even finished my junior year. My attitude was, "Never mind. No big deal. I had it coming." It didn't matter much to me. But my mom was crushed. She'd already put her neck out for me more times than I could count, and now I was hurting her legacy at the school she loved so much. I'd finally screwed up so badly that it ended her relationship with Sarah Lawrence for good.

The upside of leaving Sarah Lawrence was that I was able to get more involved in the ballet scene. Even though I wasn't planning to pursue a career on the stage itself, I loved being in that world, taking photos and going to events. My videography company was growing, too. I made event documentaries, wedding videos, dance films, and corporate promos. My photos appeared in major newspapers. A still from a ballet documentary that I was shooting—a male ballet dancer holding a female dancer aloft in the late afternoon sun—was printed on a half-page in the *New York Sun*.

By the time the winter of 2007 rolled around, I'd managed to move on from my troublemaker days (at least to the extent that I hadn't been arrested, gotten in a fight, stolen anything, or gotten thrown out of a school in three years—in my love life, I was still proving adept at making messes). I had carved out a seemingly good niche for myself in New York City. I was making enough money to live in my own apartment and pay the rent on that Tribeca office. I traveled when I felt like it, bought and sold old cars and motorcycles, and had an on-again off-again relationship with a dancer named Katie. I worked as little as I could in order to have as much fun as possible. I spent hours every day fiddling around with social media.

Honestly, though? I wasn't happy. My girlfriend was great, but she didn't trust me, and I wasn't ready for commitment. I had a business, but I wasn't particularly driven or passionate about it. I was frequently bored. I was underperforming, and I knew it. I sometimes thought of my dad and his chronic dissatisfaction, his palpable sense of disappointment with his life. Was I falling into the same patterns? I was capable of so much more. What was holding me back?

Instead of facing this head-on, I found myself constantly seeking out distraction. I took my mind off my issues by filling my life with small tasks and fun adventures. My goal on any given day was simply to convince myself I was enjoying life as best I could.

All this was festering on the December day that I received that first message from Abby. And although I wouldn't know it for many months to come, my vulnerable mental state was the reason I would end up getting pulled in so deep.

_____

As far as distractions go, Abby turned out to be an A+. Almost immediately after I responded to her Myspace message, I received another Myspace message from someone named Angela Wesselman-Pierce:

Hi there, I'm Abby's mom, Angela. I hope Abby's not bothering you. My son was babysitting her and he wasn't paying attention when she emailed you. My apologies.

I responded to let her know that I thought her daughter was charming, and that I was happy to engage with her. By the end of the day, I'd received a new message from Abby.

One of my favorite photos of yours is the picture of the two dancers, the one that was in the New York Sun. Can I paint it and send it to you?

Of course, I replied. You can use any of my photos that you want.

And then:

Hi Yaniv!

Here's the deal, my Dad said he's ok with me painting from your photos as long as I send the original to you or destroy the original. I can't keep them or sell them because of my artistic integrity and whatever so if that's ok with you it's ok with me.

I looked at some of your Photos and you have like a bazillion photos that I would love to draw out! I also noticed that you dance too...sweet. I think that officially makes you THE Coolest person I've never met! And you have a Triumph?! too sweet!

I'm sooo grateful to have heard from you today! I was afraid my Mom was going to have me start drawing more old/dead people today. It sooo much sucks being 8!!!

Peace and Love ~ Abby

A week later, a box arrived in the mail. When I opened it, I found a meticulously rendered painting of my ballet photograph done in watercolor. It was surprisingly good. I figured that Abby must be some kind of prodigy, and I felt flattered that she was spending so much of her time and energy on me. I framed the painting and put it on my desk. I enjoyed having it in my office as a reminder of this interesting new twist in my life.

Hey Abby, I like the drawing.

I would also love to have any of the drawings that you make of my work.

More importantly, I would love to see you focus on some of my movement photos.

I think it would be a good exercise for you to try and capture the energy of dance since you love it so much.

Please feel free to use any of my photos and to post the paintings/videos on your myspace or youtube or whatever.

- Cheers, Yaniv

By the end of January, I'd received a second box, full of paintings that Abby had modeled on my photographs as well as a few other odds and ends she wanted me to have: two really old dollar bills, a T-shirt from her brother's band, an old edition of *Macbeth*, some photographs she'd taken. I didn't even have enough wall space to hang all the paintings, so I kept them in a manila folder until I could frame them.

Rel and Henry were amused by the whole thing. The first paintings and the emails seemed as legit to them as they did to me, and they were intrigued enough to pull out their digital video cameras and film me opening the boxes. But they grew more skeptical as my inbox began to fill with long, chatty emails from Abby. And my girlfriend, Katie, was starting to express her distaste for my "eight-year-old girlfriend."

Initially, my correspondence was primarily with Abby—she would write me with cute rambling stories about her family, her art, her school, her pet rat. But soon I was spending as much time, or more, emailing with her mom, Angela. Our Myspace messages quickly moved into email exchanges, and within a month of Abby's first contact, Angela and I were emailing several times a week.

Angela struck me as being a pretty cool mom, direct and pleasant and funny. She was almost forty with two grown kids—Megan and James—as well as Abby, plus two teenage stepsons—the twins Alex and Anthony. She lived with her husband, Vince, in an old Victorian house in Ishpeming, a tiny town (population 6,470) in Michigan's rural Upper Peninsula. Everyone in her family seemed to have an artistic bent: The boys had a band, Megan was also a musician, and Abby was a painter. Angela herself was a psychologist and social worker, but she dabbled in art and music on the side. She'd once owned a small cafe and gallery called the House of Muses, but it had burned down in a fire. For a mom of five, she was remarkably put together: The photograph on her online profile depicted an attractive older woman with a long dark braid and dreamy eyes heavy with green eye shadow.

In her emails, Angela would ask me about my photography and tell me about her life in Ishpeming, about having kids younger than she'd expected, and about trying to encourage her kids' artistic interests. "We recognize that Abby has a lot of potential to do great things but we don't want to force those things on her," she'd write me. "I'm not a pushy Mommy that's trying to carve out some career for a child, those people scare me more than a little."

Soon, Angela and I were Facebook friends. In fact, she became Facebook friends with my mom, too! Entering Angela's Facebook world was like joining her family: Almost immediately, I was introduced to and "friended" by everyone linked to her profile. Unlike my four hundred–plus Facebook friends, Angela's Facebook circle was limited to less than two dozen friends and family members. There were the older kids, Alex, Anthony, and James; her husband, Vince; assorted cousins; a few of the kids' friends. There was Abby's babysitter, Noelle; the local art dealer, Tim Hobbins, who I was told was starting to sell Abby's work; and Ryan, Megan's best friend. I was fascinated by the dramatic and chaotic life of this family of hillbilly hippies. I loved feeling like I'd been included in this whole alternate community. It was such a curiosity, such a departure from my day-to-day existence.

The only person who *wasn't* on Facebook was Megan, Angela's nineteen-year-old daughter from a previous marriage. I'd been hearing about Megan since the very beginning of my correspondence with Angela and Abby. Megan was a musician and a dancer; she loved to ride horses; she had graduated from high school the previous year. She lived and worked in Lansing but came home on the weekends to be with her family. Abby adored her half sister.

Megan first appeared in my inbox a few weeks into my correspondence with Angela and Abby.

Hello Yaniv,

Our parents went away for a couple days and left my brothers and I to take care of Abby.

The last thing my Step dad said before he left was "What ever you do don't let Abby e-mail Yaniv Schulman anymore, she's bugging the crap out [of] him!" Welcome to my world bawahahahaha! (that's my evil laugh) A word of advice, don't give Abby [your] cell number or she'll text you to death. She's the reason everyone in the family gets unlimited texting and our parents still pay our cell phone bills. She can be quite chatty, I'm sure you've noticed.

The reason I'm e-mailing you now is I need to know what Abby's painting next. Abby's about finished with the 18x24 painting of the woman in the field of flowers and she's getting ready to pick her next project. You mentioned "movement photos", what photos specifically are you referring to? If the paintings [were] going to end up in the fireplace I suppose it wouldn't matter but since she's sending them to you it makes

sense to me if you're going to end up with the paintings you
should be the one to pick the subject.

Thank you for being so kind to my sister, you're a Sweetheart!

Enjoy your New Years Eve!

-Megan

Megan's emails were sporadic in the beginning, but by
mid-February we were emailing at least once a week, chatting mostly about Abby's artwork, but also increasingly about
Megan's life with her extended family—about dogsledding
and ballet classes and horseback lessons and trips to Washington. She told me a tragic story about the sudden death of
Abby's best friend, Danny, the previous summer—a congeni-
tal heart defect had triggered a heart attack, and he died in
Abby's arms. I was touched. Megan seemed like a really sweet
girl; her life in the country seemed enchanted.

Intrigued, I asked Megan why she wasn't on Facebook.
"I've had my fair share of weirdness come from posting my
pictures on Myspace and Facebook," she responded (a comment that I would later find very ironic).

Finally, in early March, more than three months after my
initial email from Abby, I received a Facebook friend request
from someone named Megan Faccio. The profile picture was
of a stunningly pretty girl with big blue eyes, long blond-
streaked hair, and a coy smile.

I friended her back instantly. And that's when things
started to get serious.

CHAPTER 2

What Is a Catfish?

If you're reading this book, you probably already know what a catfish is. But for those of you who are new to the whole concept (in which case—Hi! Nice to meet you!), here's the UrbanDictionary.com definition:

> A catfish is someone who pretends to be someone they're not, using Facebook or other social media to create false identities, particularly to pursue deceptive online romances.

Maybe it's easiest to define *catfish* with a good story.

Let's start with Manti Te'o, a promising linebacker at the University of Notre Dame. For nearly a year, starting in 2011, he was in an online relationship with a pretty Stanford student named Lennay Kekua, who had befriended him through Facebook and Twitter. They had never met in person—after all, they lived halfway across the country from each other—but they spoke on the phone several times a day, so often that Te'o considered Lennay his girlfriend.

In the summer of 2012, Lennay called to tell Te'o that she'd been in a car accident, and as a result of her hospitalization, the doctors had discovered that she had undiagnosed leukemia. Despite bone marrow transplants, by mid-September Lennay was dead. A few days after getting this news, Te'o went out and scored a triumphant victory against Notre Dame rival Michigan State. Afterward, he told the sports media that Lennay's tragically premature death had inspired him to win. It made a great story—until the media did some digging and discovered that Lennay didn't exist, except as a Twitter and Facebook profile. There was no Stanford student, no car accident, no tragic battle with cancer. Instead, "Lennay" was a twenty-two-year-old boy named Ronaiah Tuiasosopo who'd been deceiving Manti all along.

It was a textbook catfishing case, and the mainstream media went nuts for it, with coverage everywhere from ESPN to *Vanity Fair*. You would have thought Te'o was the first person who had ever been duped in that way. But the truth is that since some caveman told the very first lie thousands of years ago, people have been pretending to be someone they're not, frequently in the name of romance. (Look at the themes of many Shakespeare plays and you'll see that identity deception has been a part of our culture for a while.) The difference today is that the Internet has made this much, much, *much* easier. Now, if you want to be a blond fashion model or a race-car driver or a Stanford student with a winning smile, you can be: All you need to do is find a photo, put up a Facebook page, and voila.

And in fact, that's exactly what's happening, over and over, in America and around the world. Catfish stories like Te'o's (and my own) are popping up with increasing frequency, and not just on my TV show. Consider this: Facebook admits that a mind-boggling 83 million Facebook profiles—8.7 percent of all profiles—are fakes or dupes. That's a lot of people who don't actually exist, conducting online relationships as if they are real people. This culture of deceptive online identity has grown so much that even social media profiles that *are* legitimate are increasingly riddled with lies.

In other words, catfishing has become so ingrained in modern life that many people do it unconsciously, in small but significant ways.

Even among those who set out to intentionally create a fake new identity, not all catfish are the same. Catfish tend to fall into a number of different categories, from fairly benign to incredibly malevolent.

Let's break them down, shall we?

CYRANO CATFISH

If you didn't learn the story of Cyrano de Bergerac in English lit—or see the movie *Roxanne*—here's a quick recap: Seventeenth-century poet with alarmingly large nose who believes he is unworthy of love agrees to help his handsome friend woo the beautiful Roxanne, whom Cyrano is also in love with, by writing her beautiful love letters for him. The Cyrano catfish takes that classic story and gives it a digital twist: Instead of love letters, it's Facebook messages, and instead of a handsome friend as a stand-in, it's a fake profile.

Of all the catfish I've encountered, these are by far the most common: people who seek, or unintentionally find, love under false pretenses. Cyrano catfish are generally insecure about themselves—their looks, their lives, their families, their jobs—and so they create fake profiles for the people they *wish* they were. And as those fake people, they have online romances.

Some of these catfish set out—as Cyrano did, and as Ronaiah Tuiasosopo also did—intending to fool someone specific. But they do so because they want to connect with another person. Others stumble into relationships accidentally. They don't set out to deceive someone in the pursuit of romance. Instead, they create their fake social media profiles as a coping mechanism for their feelings of isolation and loneliness, their insecurity and fear. In other words, they're trying to escape their problems via an idealized version of themselves. They think that under this new, more attractive guise, they will be appreciated for who they "really are" rather than being judged for how they look, or where they live, or the size of their bank account. They just want to be liked. Unfortunately, those fake profiles engage with real people. And the next thing you know, they are involved in a deceptive online relationship.

Take, for example, the case of James (episode 110), a guy who decided to reinvent himself in order to escape a less-than-exciting life and a criminal charge that had been dropped but was still associated with his name online. His Internet alter ego was Ja'Mari, a model and inspirational speaker with five thousand followers. Ja'Mari was who James felt he *could* be, if only he didn't have all his baggage. As Ja'Mari, James connected with Rico, a gay National Guard member, and what started as a friendship snowballed into a serious online relationship. Although James hadn't created Ja'Mari in order to ensnare Rico, when Rico found out about the deception, he was still hurt.

Cyrano catfish like James often know that what they are doing isn't exactly kosher. But that doesn't stop them from doing it. They need it. It gives them happiness, some sort of positive reinforcement, and the distraction from their lives that they crave.

REVENGE CATFISH

The revenge catfish is a different kind of beast. This is someone who sets up a fake profile not because they are looking to
genuinely connect with a new person, but because they want
to get back at someone they already know. The intention from
the get-go is to deceive and hurt somebody.

A good (if complicated) example is the story of Mhissy
(episode 104). Mhissy had a brief relationship with a girl
named Jasmine. After Jasmine ended the relationship, Mhissy
went on to date an ex-boyfriend of Jasmine's. When Jasmine,
who was now pregnant, contacted her ex-boyfriend to request
a paternity test, Mhissy, who was still pissed at Jasmine, got
mad. (Like I said: complicated.) Instead of talking to Jasmine
about it, Mhissy set up a fake profile of a handsome man and
started flirting with Jasmine with the intention of distracting her from her ex-boyfriend and messing with her mind. It
worked, for a crazy long time.

BENEVOLENT CATFISH

In rare cases, a catfish can set up a profile with the specific
purpose of trying to help someone. I've only come across a
few, but here's a good example:

Gladys (episode 201) had been best friends with Cassie
since grade school. When Cassie's father was murdered, her
life began a downward spiral—she began drinking heavily, doing drugs, and sleeping around. Gladys, desperate to

stop Cassie's self-destructive behavior, created a fake profile of a handsome guy and friended Cassie. Over the course
of two years, Cassie's new online boyfriend—and eventual
fiancé—"Steve," helped build up her self-esteem and pull her
out of the darkness. Gladys even enlisted her male cousin
to be the voice of the fake boyfriend (going so far as to have
phone sex with Cassie).

Of course, Cassie wasn't exactly thrilled to learn that she'd
been lied to—the phone sex in particular was pretty horrifying
to her—but she at least understood that Gladys had undertaken
this whole deception with the best intentions.

Another fascinating benevolent catfish story that I investigated (but that never aired) started with a girl who couldn't get
her deadbeat ex to pay his child support. Instead, she reached
out to his even more recent ex-girlfriend for help, and the two
of them collaborated to form a third, fake girl with the intention of using her to convince him to pay child support. (Yes,
I know that some of these stories are convoluted. That's what
real life is like.) Together, they made the girl that they knew
he'd think was perfect—and it worked! She flirted with him,
got him to talk about his daughter, told him she hoped he was
"really supportive" of her, and otherwise massaged him into
believing that the right thing to do was become a more financially responsible guy.

It all worked beautifully until he figured out that the girl in
the pictures was actually another girl—at which point the two
girls who started it all had to reach out to *that* girl, and got her
to participate in the ruse! Next thing you know, girl number
three was video-chatting with the deadbeat dad as the fake
girlfriend, too.

SWINDLING CATFISH

Swindling catfish are the ones that I personally have the hardest time relating to. For these catfish the exchange that takes place with their victim isn't for affection or attention, but for their livelihood. The swindling catfish's goal is to scam people for cash, or more.

This kind of stuff happens every day online (in fact, these types of swindles pre-date the Internet), and stories about it are becoming increasingly common. The most frequent story you'll hear is about men who get involved online with "women" from foreign countries and send cash to them for plane tickets or moving expenses, only to get stood up. Perhaps the most widely known case—featured on the cover of the *New York Times Magazine* last year—involved a world-renowned particle physicist who got involved with a Czech "bikini model" on an online dating site and flew to Bolivia to meet her. She had allegedly just left for a modeling job in Argentina, but asked him to bring her the suitcase she'd left behind. The suitcase was full of drugs, and the physicist was subsequently arrested. He has spent the past few years rotting in jail in Argentina.

Most of the catfish I encountered on the first two seasons of the show were people who believed that a false online personality was the best way to sort through some emotional confusion or an identity crisis they were having, rather than just trying to steal from others. But in season three, I encountered more of these Swindling catfish, people who created false identities with the intention of deception for their own material or financial gain. If you're going to get hooked, this is the worst kind of person to have on the other end.

CELEBRITY IMPERSONATORS

Then there are the all-too-common impersonating catfish, who pretend to be celebrities online. Even I've been a victim of this scam: Do a search for my name on Facebook and you'll come across more than thirty profiles claiming to be Nev Schulman, including a profile just for my chest hair. (Yes, it's exceptionally lush, but come *on*.) One of these profiles had 4,500 followers before it was shut down; the catfish who ran it was chatting with his "friends" every day as me.

Sometimes these impersonators are a type of Cyrano catfish (think Keyonnah and Bow Wow in episode 214), but usually they are caught up in the currency of having "fans," and they derive a strange emotional satisfaction from driving up their numbers, despite the fact that the whole thing has nothing to do with them.

The truth is, it's not just celebrities who are impersonated. Think about all those Facebook friends you have that you've never met. They have access to all of your information. They could be on your profile right now, downloading your photos and creating another *you* somewhere else in order to catfish someone. It's scary how easy it is to impersonate someone and how casually a catfish can damage the reputation of the person they're pretending to be.

Which brings me to...

EVERYONE ELSE

The fact is, there are catfish everywhere you go on the Internet. Anyone who has dated online has surely encountered profiles that use photoshopped or altogether false pictures and contain fudged information. That cute doctor you chatted with for weeks but never actually met? The hot exotic dancer who bailed on you three times because she had to work? There's a fair chance they were catfish.

Looking out at the Internet landscape, it's clear that false identities, from the mild prevarication to the jaw-dropping lie, have come to pervade every part of online life. A lot of people think that the catfish phenomenon is just a popular scam, just a digital deception. But in my experience, the issue of catfishing is so much deeper and more complex than that. It's the most extreme symptom of a trend in society away from the honesty and confidence that a face-to-face relationship demands and toward the isolation and cowardice of online connections. It's about the insecurity at the center of online life. About the fear of a real life lived in public that drives people to decide that it's better to pretend to be someone else entirely. About the way we *all*—catfish or not—curate ourselves online to be "better" or more "interesting" than we really are, presenting images and ideas that don't align with our real selves.

The rise of false online identities has opened up the bigger question of how social media is shaping both our romantic relationships and the way we function in our day-to-day lives. What is it about social media that compels us to lie? What happens when online relationships are based on small fictions or big deceptions; when *everyone*, intentionally or not, is participating in a culture of false identity? In a world where human interaction takes place through a screen, how do we learn to be honest and to trust that others are, as well?

CHAPTER 3

Fishing for Compliments: What Motivates Catfish?

W hat's *wrong* with those people?"

I hear this a lot about catfish. It's usually said in a dismissive tone: *those* people.

Since I've already touched briefly on the motivations of each type of catfish by defining the categories, I'm going to use this chapter to dig into what drives the most common type of catfish: the Cyrano.

You may wonder: What on earth would possess someone to pretend to be someone else and then get involved in a long-term online relationship, knowing full well that they can never meet the person they are "with" without blowing their cover? Anyone who does that must just be a crazy freak. Or so a lot of people think.

In my experience, it's not that simple. In fact, the motivations of your average catfish are both incredibly complicated and also far more relatable than you might expect. Often, there's nothing unusual or crazy about them at all—it's just that they use the Internet as an outlet for their issues in a way that other people don't (that is, in place of a therapist).

Let's start with a story.

A teenage girl named Kristen (episode 207) is in a terrible car accident. She loses one of her eyes and is bedridden for months. Her boyfriend dumps her. Her friends stop visiting. She gains weight. And then there's the matter of her glass eye, about which she's very insecure. She looks nothing like the person she used to be. She's miserable and lonely.

So what does she do? She creates a fake online persona, a version of the girl she wishes she still was. She keeps the details of this alternate "Kristen's" life similar to her own—the accident, her current enrollment in beauty school—but she changes her last name to disguise herself and swaps out her photos for those of a pretty acquaintance she feels she used to look like. It feels good to have people treat her normally again; cathartic; a relief. And using this new profile, she meets a boy on Facebook named Mike. They become friends, first talking on Facebook and then on the phone, ultimately speaking almost every day. He talks her off a ledge when she feels like ending it all. Soon, she feels like she's in love; she's totally emotionally dependent on Mike. By this point, Kristen is too afraid to reveal herself, knowing full well that if she does, Mike may reject her.

So she keeps up the charade. Until the day we show up at her door with Mike in tow and the whole thing falls apart.

So—what motivates these catfish? Typically, it's the same thing that motivates just about everyone: the desire to be liked and accepted. Usually, it's coupled with a sense of isolation. Insecurity. Depression. A negative self-image. So while your average catfish may not be a "crazy freak," they almost always have serious issues they need to work out. Most could probably use some therapy. (I speak from experience here: I've dealt with many of these issues myself, and since a very young age I've been lucky enough to see therapists regularly. Despite the cultural stigma against therapy, I honestly don't think I'd be where I am today if it hadn't been for my shrinks and their objective advice.)

Cyrano catfish create the version of themselves that they would like to be in order to see what kind of attention they would get if they were that person. It's easier than losing the weight (too daunting and sometimes not possible because of health issues), or going to college (not affordable or practical), or getting that great job (easier said than done). These catfish want to know what it would feel like to transcend their own issues. Often, their victims are collateral damage along the way.

I've encountered countless catfishing cases during the past few years, and every single one is unique (some are so complicated and convoluted that they're hard to even synopsize coherently), but I've come to recognize that there are a couple recurring themes. Personal issues that come up again and again. Every catfish may be distinct, but the root of their behavior often stems from the same place.

APPEARANCE

Yeah, it's a cliché, but it's true. The person behind that picture of an implausibly beautiful, skinny girl? In all likelihood, she's unhappy about her weight. Or maybe she just doesn't meet the impossible standards of beauty that society projects in ads, magazines, and movies, and is insecure about it. And that guy who claims to be a "male model" whose photos show six-pack abs? Yeah, right. Trust me: He's not so built in real life. A good third of the catfish who appear on the show have body-size issues or some deep-rooted concern about how they look that makes them miserable. (I can relate to that misery, since I myself suffer from the same affliction. Most notably about my build and body hair. Though I've come to love the way I look, it's nothing like the hairless pumped-up dudes I see in underwear ads and in movies.)

This is a symptom of our culture's obsession with appearance; our confusion about what beauty is and how we should feel about our bodies; and our compulsion to compare ourselves to the people we see on TV and on social media. Beauty is internal—related to energy and confidence—but we rarely remember this. Instead, most people, no matter their size or appearance, seem to feel like they've come up short. For catfish, that's often a trigger that sets off the lies.

Take, for example, Melissa, a girl I met in the first season of *Catfish* (episode 105). She had an unhappy life: At home she had a troubled relationship with her stepfather, and at school she was bullied for being overweight. Her self-esteem had bottomed out. But she discovered that on the Internet she could be thin and pretty! And when she was thin, people were nice to her! So she created a fake profile for a skinny blonde named Abby, met a guy named Jarrod, and the rest is *Catfish* history.

The ugly truth is that the world is often downright cruel to both women and men who are heavier. This nastiness can do a number on someone who is already suffering from a lousy self-image. When somebody absorbs that much negativity, it's no wonder they feel unlovable the way they are. Pretending to be a more conventionally attractive person on the Internet helps that person get the validation and attention they crave. It's easy to believe that once all our physical issues are hidden away, we'll be liked for being "ourselves." A new persona also makes it a lot easier to avoid having to face up to internal unhappiness.

Of course, all this serves as a distraction from resolving the real issues at play. Rather than getting up from their computer, taking a walk, and trying to improve their health or change their appearance, a person who is unhappy about their weight often uses the validation of their fake profile to avoid the issue altogether. This only drives the self-dissatisfaction further.

SEXUALITY

If appearance is the number one issue that leads to catfishing, sexuality is a close second. Another third of the catfish stories that I investigate involve men and women who are gay, bisexual, or transgendered. In many parts of the United States—not to mention vast swaths of the rest of the world—people are still closed-minded, and it's just not considered acceptable to come out as gay. Even in more liberal communities, a lot of gay kids have families that won't accept them.

Kids who grow up being taught that their homosexuality is wrong often turn to the Internet. There, they can flirt or even have "sex" with the same sex, using false identities, and no one will know. It's a stealthy and supposedly risk-free way to experiment with something that they are afraid to reveal to their (often religious) families and communities; to "sin" without really sinning, and to do it anonymously.

On the Internet, a confused gay kid can also find an outlet for feelings that he or she may not yet understand or know how to act upon. Kids who are bullied or are outcasts because of their sexuality can try on different identities in order to be accepted; maybe they even think that they can only be "loved" if they step into the persona of the opposite gender.

Take, for example, Aaron, whom I met in our first season (episode 108). As a gay high school sophomore living in small town Michigan, he set up a profile of a pretty blond girl named Amanda and spent the next five years deceiving straight guys online. "It feels better than being myself," he told us. "I realized other people had problems with me being gay, but when I went to Amanda I could convince a straight guy to like my personality. I don't want to be gay, but that's something I can't change." What he *could* change, thanks to social media? He could "be" a straight girl, rather than a gay guy, and play out his sexual interests in a more socially acceptable way. As Amanda, he could meet the guys he was too embarrassed to try to date in person.

Unfortunately, none of these relationships could ever materialize in real life, so they were doomed from the start.

CONTROL

It should come as no shock that a lot of catfish are people who feel like they have no control in their lives. Take Alicia, a twenty-three-year-old we met in the second season (episode 211). She was unemployed, physically unfit, and had been taken advantage of by a previous boyfriend. Her life was rudderless. So she began starting fake relationships online—in our case, with a girl named Aaliyah. Alicia pretended to be a lesbian in order to get Aaliyah "to fall in love with [her] and buy [her] things." Although at first this seemed like a swindling catfish case, there was more to it. Alicia had been hurt by life. At the heart of the matter was that instead of feeling out of control, she could be *in* control.

When they become catfish, previously helpless people suddenly feel like they are masterminds. From behind their alternate personae, they can manipulate the people around them; they can provide their characters with all the successes that they themselves lack. It gives them a sense of accomplishment and power that they can't seem to locate in their real lives.

Until, that is, they are exposed and the whole facade crumbles.

FEAR

No duh, right? Hiding behind a fake profile is a pretty good sign that someone is terrified of being themselves. But let's break it down further.

People who catfish are, for the most part, very fearful people. They are afraid of rejection. Something about who they are—their looks, their background, their home—strikes them as being unlovable. And so rather than risk their hearts in real life, they hide behind online profiles and digital barriers.

Take Derek, a guy we met in the second season (episode 204). For eight years he'd been chatting with a girl named Lauren, but he refused to video-chat or meet up with her in person. He wasn't pretending to be someone he wasn't or hiding some kind of physical issue, but he understood that in the real world, relationships often don't work out. And what he had online with his dream girl seemed so good that he didn't want to risk it falling apart. Simply put, he was scared.

And in a way, he was right. If you do make an emotional connection with someone online, what are the chances that you'll also have physical chemistry in person? If you aren't physically attracted, after all, it doesn't matter how much you like someone: It's just not going to work romantically. That was Derek's fear; it's the fear of almost all catfish. They're afraid that the magic they've found online will suddenly come to an end once they expose their true selves.

Even though there's a logic to this fear, the outcome is that some people never make that leap or take that chance; instead they end up living half a life. (The good news for Derek? We finally brought him face-to-face with Lauren, and they ended up falling in love for real and getting engaged. And subsequently breaking up. But hey, at least they gave it a chance. As Alfred Lord Tennyson wrote, it's "better to have loved and lost than never to have loved at all.")

Fear helps no one—not the catfish, and not the person whose feelings they are toying with.

ADDICTION

Imagine this: A catfish creates a whole new persona and unleashes it on the world. They have essentially given birth to a digital human being, an alternate version of themselves who is out there, engaging with other human beings. The catfish is responsible for the life of their creation, much like they would be for a pet or a child.

A lot of people find that very fulfilling. They think, "I've created this mini-me that people *like*. I can take care of him, send him on exotic trips, make him a model. My creative, artistic spawn can make other people happy!"

For a while, it does. But meanwhile, this digital creation's relationships are starting to get *demanding*. The fake person is connected with real people who expect responses to their messages. His profile needs constant maintenance and nurturing. It starts to snowball. The people he's talking to have real emotions, and things get complicated. The responsibility to the profile gets out of control. How does the catfish prevent someone who is passionately involved with this mini-me from coming to visit? They have to invent increasingly elaborate lies.

Catfish become hostages to their own creations, like Dr. Frankenstein. They may have breathed life into these digital personas, but now their monsters control them. It becomes a self-inflicted addiction. They don't feel they have a choice: Either they keep going, or they have to kill off the profile. And since they feel like their profile is a version of themselves, they are hesitant to murder their digital babies. They are hooked, and it escalates until it's completely out of control.

FANTASY

There's one common denominator that I've noticed in almost every catfish I've encountered over the past few years: an active fantasy life. Catfish use the Internet to fantasize the life they *want* into existence, in order to avoid dealing with the life they actually have.

Take Felicia, a season 1 catfish (episode 111). In her online relationship with Mike, she used real pictures of herself, but she changed many of the major details of her life. Instead of admitting that she lived in Orlando, where she was attending school, she told Mike that she lived in Jersey City and ran a salon that was in Orlando—which was her actual life goal.

Her online persona was simply a kind of projection, spinning out the life she hoped to live someday.

Many catfish we meet are doing some version of the same thing: imagining their desired lives into existence. "I'm a model!" "I travel a lot!" "I have a great big house and a nice car!" (You'd be amazed how critical a nice car seems to be.) They trump up their life accomplishments; they say they are attending college when they're not—but they *want* to be. Some are acting out extremely unrealistic versions of their lives, while others—like Felicia—are drawing a new life for themselves that's almost within reach.

You could argue that manifestation is a powerful tool, that envisioning your goals is the first step toward making them real. Unfortunately, the fantasy aspect of social media often gets in the way of real progress. Social media has come along and said, "You don't have to take real steps to actualize your dreams at all! You can 'have' the fantasy right now!"

Pretending online that you're living your dream life is free, it's immediate, and you're the only one who knows the truth. And yet, pretending to be successful is *not* the same as being successful.

So what motivates catfish, ultimately, is being unmotivated. The things they want—to feel good about their appearance, to be successful, to be lucky in love, to live the life they long for—are only achievable if they go out and make them a reality. But they don't. Instead, they hide behind fake profiles, "live" out their fantasies online, and let their day-to-day existence remain unsatisfying. The Internet is just an escape; the personal issues that have triggered their behavior will not go away until they step away from the computer and start dealing with real life.

CHAPTER 4

Hook, Line, and Sinker: Why People Fall for Catfish

All right. By this point, you probably get the modus operandi of your typical catfish. You know what makes them tick. But what about their victims? The people who buy into their hoaxes? What kind of person would fall for a deception that often looks mind-bogglingly obvious from the outside? Or are these "victims" even really victims? It takes two to catfish, after all.

I am probably one of the best-equipped people to answer that question. After all, I *am* that person. I was, as we put it, "on the hook" for nine months.

So why was I such a sucker? And how can people still be falling for this even after my show has been on the air for the past three years?

First of all, there are catfish, and then there are *catfish*. What I mean is that some catfish make eye-rollingly transparent claims (see: anyone who says they're an underwear model), but others can be extremely sophisticated liars. I managed to get involved with the latter. My catfish was creative, even sending me genuine newspaper stories that referenced (or seemed to reference) stories she'd told me. She set up Facebook profiles for at least fourteen people, ultimately building an incredibly complicated network of fake people that seemed, from where I sat in New York, to be totally real. She even had my mom convinced on a very personal motherly level. And if some of the stories that Megan, Angela, and Abby told me seemed amazing, who was I to know what life in rural Ishpeming, Michigan, was like? It was so radically distant from my urban New York life.

The nail in the coffin of my gullibility? The five hundred dollars I received in the mail, money that the family had promised me as a result of my influence on Abby's work. They wanted to pay me a cut of her painting sales, since those paintings were mostly based on my photos. Why on earth would these people have sent me that check if there wasn't a legitimate sale of a painting? And if that was the case, the whole story—about a child art prodigy; her goofy, fascinating family; and her alluring, flirtatious older sister—had to be true.

But even *that* doesn't really answer the hard question of why I became a victim. Looking back, there were plenty of red flags that I didn't pay attention to. Honestly, the main reason I chose to believe in my catfish's lies? It wasn't how convincing my catfish was. It was all about what was going on inside *me*. I chose to believe. I *wanted* to believe.

It's time for some more backstory.

At the time that Megan and I began to correspond, I was searching for something. I didn't know what it was, but I'd been searching for it for years. Sure, I'd started my production company with my brother at age nineteen and had built it into a reasonably profitable business, but did I want to be making bar mitzvah videos for the rest of my life? Hardly.

I also had a very light work schedule, to say the least—some weeks working twenty hours or less—so I had a lot of free time that I didn't know what to do with. I spent some of that time working on a photography event website—mostly shooting ballet parties and performances—as an attempt to reach out and be part of that community. But overall, I wasn't spending my time very productively.

My identity at that point in my life was heavily tied to my sexuality. That's where I drew my confidence; that's how I identified myself. I was a flirt. I was charming. And since I wasn't particularly fulfilled in my work life, I overcompensated by spending my time pursuing women. I got my sense of accomplishment from dating girls I wanted to date and sleeping with girls I wanted to sleep with. I was using my sexuality as a crutch. As a result, I had no shortage of relationships with women, but I couldn't ever seem to make them work. Big shock, right?

I wanted attention. A sense of value. I wanted to be needed. I'd go to parties, take pictures, get laid. But it wasn't fulfilling. It was surface. It was "lite."

And making matters worse, I'd recently made a lot of really lousy decisions. I'd been kicked out of college; ruined my relationship with my best friend, Mark, by hurting him badly in a fistfight (more on that later); and had a falling-out with my brother. I didn't like myself. I was disappointed, frustrated, lazy, and underaccomplished. I knew I could be doing so much more, but I felt stuck. And I knew that people didn't like me much, either. I had developed a reputation for being a rule breaker, a flirt, a loose cannon, and kind of a dick. I was not a particularly reliable guy.

Into this gaping chasm stepped—or, I should say, *typed*—Abby, Angela, Megan, and the rest of the Ishpeming crew. Here was a creative and passionate family who said that their

budding young artist admired me and drew her inspiration
from me. For the first time in my life, I genuinely felt a sense
of value: Something pure and meaningful and lovely was
happening as a result of my existence! I was thrilled to be part
of this exciting exchange. I was thrilled that they appreciated
my photos.

Better yet, it was an opportunity to start totally fresh, with a
clean slate. They knew nothing of my life in New York City, my
past fuckups. All they did was admire me. I could build a version of myself the way I'd *like* to be (sound familiar?), with new
people who had no connection to my family or friends or where
I lived. It was the ultimate reinvention—and, though I didn't
know it at the time, a close cousin to what my catfish was doing.

As a bonus, Megan was a great new distraction, an outlet
through which I could channel all my frustration and excess
energy. It was fun! Instead of pursuing girls in New York, or
working on my relationships, or building my company, I had
a new hobby—a potential virtual romance with this beautiful
Renaissance woman who admired me.

The people I've met who have been catfished (on the
show, we call them *hopefuls*) have similar stories to mine.
They have an almost universal desire to improve themselves. To be "seen" in a new and more flattering light, to be
respected and admired based on their personalities and not
their past actions. It's why so many people get easily lured
into these online relationships. They don't see a lot of value
in themselves. They are struggling to identify what makes
them happy. And then along comes this person online who
shows them that they *are* valuable. (And that's usually how it
works. You are approached: The catfish *chooses* you. A random
stranger contacts you and says, "I like the way you look and

the photos you post, and I want to tell you that I appreciate you." And you're hooked.) The catfish seems to get something meaningful out of communicating with the hopeful, and it gives the hopeful a sense of importance. At the beginning, at least, it's a symbiotic relationship.

It also feels like a very safe environment. Not only is the hopeful physically removed from the person they're communicating with, but they have the ability to perfectly curate how they are perceived. The words they type, the photos they post, how quickly they respond—all of it feels very controllable. The hopeful can show this new "friend" all of the good stuff and none of the bad.

That was certainly the case for me with Megan, Abby, and Angela. I thought I could put all the negative stuff away in a box—the hypersexuality, the lack of focus, the general dickishness—and work on trying to be the good person I *hoped* to be. I was attempting, through this relationship with them, to begin to identify how I could be a better version of myself. I was carefully controlling everything I told them. I was so in love with this idea of the new, improved me that I was totally blind to what was really going on.

Thinking about it now, I realize how similar my motives for *being* catfished were to the motives of a catfish. Hopefuls and catfish are, more often than not, simply two sides of the same coin.

————

So that's why *I* was emotionally vulnerable to a catfish. Most other catfish victims tell a variation of the same story: the insecurity, the lack of focus in their lives, the desire to be appreciated and to improve themselves. After all, no one gets hooked because they are stable, are in great relationships, and have their lives together. Instead, they tend to need some-thing emotionally that the catfish provides.

Consider the unforgettable story of Ramon, a nineteen-year-old guy living an unfulfilling life in Bullhead City, Arizona (episode 203). His parents were divorced, he felt unwanted and out of place everywhere he went, and he worked the graveyard shift at a casino, washing dishes. He had no love life and no prospects.

And then he met a cute girl named Paola on the Internet. She lived in Florida, but whatever, she was hot! Now he had a girlfriend he could brag about to his friends. After a while, she finally confessed that she wasn't "Paola" at all. She even revealed herself on a video chat, and she bore no resemblance to the girl in the pictures. But Ramon chose not to believe it! Instead, he demanded that she stop playing games with him—he insisted that *of course* she wasn't this new girl—and she went along with it, suddenly pretending that the girl in the video chat was her cousin and that it was just a test to see if Ramon really liked her.

So it went on. He bought her expensive gifts. He sent her money. He turned his head from the obvious truth. Why? Because his relationship with a "hot girl" gave him a sense of status for the first time in his life. The reality of what would happen should his relationship with Paola be revealed as a hoax seemed so much worse than just keeping up the cha-rade. So he willingly participated in this cycle of dishonesty.

Even if they aren't as willfully blind as Ramon, most hopefuls turn their heads away from the truth at some point. I certainly did. But the question remains—how can catfish victims remain ignorant of the truth for so long? In some cases, these online relationships with fake people go on for years and years, with no video-chatting or real-life visits. I was on the hook for nine months. Looking back through my archive of emails, I can see how ridiculous some of my correspondence with Megan really was. But at the time, I was totally convinced. Why?

First of all, it *felt so good*. I *loved* talking to Megan. A lot of the other victims I've talked to say the same thing: that talking to their catfish was the best part of their day. They looked forward to getting home and chatting or emailing with them. Why would they question a good thing?

And then there is the issue of the emotional and time commitments. By the time I started to notice things that should have raised red flags, I was in too deep to really ask the hard questions. I'd spent too many hours on these relationships; I'd revealed too many of my feelings to Megan. I'd told her my secrets: about the tramp stamp tattoo I'd gotten at age seventeen (yep) and deeply regretted; about the insecurity that lay underneath my bravado. I'd even sent her some artful nudes my friend Michael Hart had taken of me. I felt like I'd been vulnerable with her, intimate in a way that I'd never been before.

This is quite common among the victims I've talked to. They say things along the lines of "I've been talking to this person for months/years. We've taken it slow. I opened up and revealed my emotions and deepest secrets. I'm so invested in this that I need to see it through." In other words, to walk away now would make all of that a waste.

Finally, it's time to throw out the word *addiction* again. People on *both* sides of these relationships get addicted to the correspondence. Because, like a drug, it makes them feel something. Because, like gambling, it's a risk, an unknown. There's a mysterious jackpot element: "Could this be my dream girl/guy?"

Addicted, emotionally dependent, and in too deep, the catfished hopefuls end up turning a blind eye. Part of the brain decides, "I don't want to know this is a lie, because then I'll not only have been betrayed but also have wasted all this time," and as a result, the hopeful *just doesn't see.*

———

Almost everybody feels undervalued in some way. As I've seen during my travels and correspondence with both catfish and hopefuls, lots of people feel unhappy with their lives—just as I did. But all it takes to lift your spirits is the affection and attention of one person.

Often, when I ask catfish victims to explain the connection that's kept them going for so long—what it is they *talk* about with the person on the other end of the line—they can't really point to anything specific. "She's just always there for me," they'll say. This amazes me. *What do you mean, "She's always there"?* I'll ask. *She's not there. She's online!* "Well, no, but she would always text me. You know, 'Good morning, How you doing?'" In other words, the most basic kind of communication.

It's a matter of just getting a text message from someone in the morning. An email that says "I'm thinking of you." A chat about what you ate for dinner. People go through their lives feeling so disappointed, unfulfilled, bored, and lonely that even the most rudimentary relationship—a positive and supportive regular correspondence—helps lift them. If you can show someone that you are thinking about them, if you go out of your way—even with just a text message—to say "Hey, I hope you are having a great day," the power of that is apparently overwhelming. So overwhelming that it blinds people to the fact that they are being hoaxed.

This is key; it reveals how little it takes for people to feel valued these days. We are so desperate for external validation that we'll even accept it from someone who may be lying to us. We want people to tell us that we are worthy, and our connections online are about confirming what we already want to believe about ourselves.

One catfish victim I'll always remember was a kid named Dorion (episode 205). He'd had a rough life—he was raised by a single mother, his house burned down, his mom had gotten sick, and he'd spent time being homeless. As he was going through all this, he met an (implausibly gorgeous) girl online. Despite the many red flags in her profile, he was so smitten with her that after two years of online correspondence, he was even considering dumping his terrific real-life girlfriend for this unconsummated virtual relationship. "She has been by my side through everything," he told me about his catfish. When he showed me their texts and emails and IMs, I was expecting there to be tearjerking moments of intimacy and vulnerability. Instead, it was mostly your everyday correspondence, nothing that struck me as earth-shaking. But she had been a consistent presence during his darkest hours, and that was what he remembered. That consistency was so vital that it seemed to trump the girlfriend who'd known him only once his life was on the upswing.

This kid was smart enough to know that the photos his catfish sent him weren't really of her, but he didn't care, because she gave him affection and cared about him when he needed it the most.

And that, in a nutshell, is why people fall for catfish: They don't feel as if anyone else really cares about them. The catfish makes them feel special. They make them feel *loved*.

And isn't that the most compelling hook of all?

CHAPTER 5

How to Identify a Catfish

Never talk to strangers.

If you're anything like me, you probably heard this line from your mother about a million times while you were growing up. Well, sorry, Mom. Times have changed. We *all* talk to strangers now—all day, every day, everywhere we go online. It's just the nature of the world we live in.

So let's assume that—despite your mom—you are going to go out there and meet all kinds of strangers on the Internet. And, considering the number of fake social media profiles out there—like I said earlier, 83 million on Facebook alone—the odds are pretty good you'll run into a catfish at some point. How do you figure out if that fascinating stranger you're chatting with is actually who they say they are?

Believe it or not, I am not a clairvoyant catfish finder. I don't have access to supersecret government databases or mastermind software programs. And despite the fact that we've exposed several dozen catfish on my TV show, I'm not naturally adept at investigation. I had to learn my lessons the hard way.

In other words—everything that I do, you can do, too.

The good news is that most catfish can be identified with a skeptical eye, a little bit of common sense, and some basic Internet know-how. If you pay attention, you'll start to notice the little red flags that can prevent you from being hooked.

And so it's with a bit of hesitation that I now offer my advice on how to avoid being catfished. But I want to help, even if it means putting myself out of a job.

————

Here's a good rule of thumb to start with: If that person you've met online seems too good to be true—they probably are. I'm sorry to break it to you, but gorgeous, rich, successful, and busy world travelers typically don't have endless amounts of time to chat with strangers on the Internet.

If they have Abercrombie & Fitch abs? Red flag.

If they say they are a model? Big red flag.

Even someone who simply seems to like everything that you like should be taken with a grain of salt. Real people are more complex than that. Someone who seems to be your exact match in all things is probably tailoring the way they present themselves in order to appeal to you.

Through my years of observing catfish, I've learned that there are certain behavioral patterns that repeat themselves time and time again. For example: Catfish frequently disappear for days at a time, sometimes even weeks or months. They'll stop in the middle of an email conversation or Facebook chat and fail to reappear again for several days. They suddenly won't return phone calls or texts. What's probably happening is that they're having an internal struggle about what they're doing; they feel guilty about their lies, and they're worried about getting too close to you. Or they are cleverly manipulating you by being unavailable and mysterious in an effort to draw you in deeper.

If someone does this to you, and then returns with a vague or wild excuse for their absence, be very wary.

Similarly, catfish often seem to have terrible luck. Their lives are full of illness and catastrophe: car accidents, ER visits, family drama, even death. My Megan had a typical catfish profile, although I didn't recognize it at the time. In the eight months that I was in an online relationship with her, she was wrongfully arrested, got in several car accidents, had a brother get in trouble because of drugs, and nearly died while undergoing routine surgery. No one's life is that exciting all the time. No question, bad things do happen, but to that extent? Big warning sign. Especially if those dramatic events tend to coincide with plans to get together.

Catfish use this constant drama as a tool to both avoid conflict and draw on your sympathy: "Oh yeah, let's get together," they'll say. And then the day arrives and suddenly—"Oh no! My grandma is in the hospital! I'm so bummed out but I have to be with her." How can you be anything but sorry for them? Not only have they avoided getting together, but your empathy for their pain will draw you in even closer.

Catfish often pretend to be chronically ill, for the same reasons. (In fact, a widespread Internet scam consists of people pretending that they or their children have a terminal disease and then raising money from concerned online friends.) If someone you meet online tells you that they have cancer, ask them specific questions about their illness. If they're truly sick, they'll be able to tell you all about the doctors, medicine, and treatment. If they're not sick, they'll likely say something along the lines of "Oh, I don't want to talk about it." Of course, people who are terminally ill sometimes don't want to discuss their sickness, but if they have chosen to reach out to a stranger about their illness and then clam up when it comes to the details, it's suspicious. Use your logic and look for this kind of inconsistency.

Even if someone you've met online isn't exhibiting these behavior patterns, you still need to be careful. The first thing you should do when you meet *anyone* online, no matter how real they seem, is verify their existence. Are they really who they say they are? It may seem impossible to know, but honestly, the truth is not very hard to figure out. It's relatively painless, and it will save you a lot of agony in the long run.

When you meet someone online, Google them right off the bat. It may seem insane that I even have to tell people this, but I'm constantly shocked at just how many of our hopefuls on the show never bothered with this step. And don't just Google them and glance at the first few hits—go deep into the results. Make sure that what you dig up matches everything they've told you.

If you've watched the TV show *Catfish*, you already know that the next step is to hit up Google Images and search by image. Download any images your new friend has posted of himself and run them through this search engine. Check to see that the photos don't show up on someone else's Facebook page or website under a different name. Even if the person you're chatting with isn't lying about who they are, who knows what you might find: That photo might be posted on Sleazyguys.com by an ex-girlfriend who says that he's bailed out on child support. That's information you want to have.

Next, hit up Facebook.

Start by taking a good look at their Facebook friends. If they have an exceedingly high or exceedingly low number of friends, that's cause for concern. And are most of their friends either men or women, or is it appropriately mixed? Any girl that only has male friends on Facebook—or vice versa—should set off alarm bells.

Similarly, take measure of where most of their friends are from. Are these "friends" primarily people from around the world, or do they come from one area? Most *real* people are predominantly friends with people from their hometown, their college, and the places where they lived as adults. Of course, this isn't always the case, but if someone's friends hail from Africa and Australia and Japan, yet they have never left the United States, that's kind of weird. They probably don't know these people in real life. So what's the explanation?

Go through their photos on Facebook. If they only have photos of themselves, and no pictures with other people, that's definitely a red flag. (In fact, it's almost *worse* if they do end up being real, since it suggests that they are simply a self-obsessed egomaniac!)

Similarly, be skeptical if they have pictures of themselves with other people, but those other people aren't tagged. This applies to Facebook or Instagram. People tag their friends in photos. So if they're not tagging the people in their photos, it's probably because they don't actually know who those people are. Which means that *they* probably aren't who they say they are, either.

Look at what they've posted on their own Facebook page, and see what kinds of comments people are leaving on those posts. Are the people who are responding to them being specific? Do they sound like people who engage with this person face to face and attend real-world events with them? Or are their online correspondences just flattering banter from people who seem like strangers?

Martin $wagg

Amazing day. So excited for the beach this weekend.
Spent all day at the gym pumping up. Got my convertible ready!

Tiffani Gorge! Dying!

HOTTCHICA Crute

J'anell OMGILYSM 😊 🖤 🖤

BigBootyBabe Have my babies!

If everything checks out so far and you're still interested in getting to know this person, it's time to dig deeper.

Reach out to some of their Facebook friends. Message those friends directly instead of commenting on a public post, and ask them how they know each other. Yes, it's awkward, but if that person really knows them, they'll be able to tell you how.

Ask them specific questions about their lives. It's incredible how often I meet people who haven't asked the most basic questions of the people they are supposedly in online relationships with. What does he do? "He makes music." How? "I don't know. I haven't asked him." Well, why not? Ask them about their family. Ask them about their job. Ask them about their friends. Get names, dates, places. Not only is it a way to get to know a person you like, it's also a good way to find out if they're really doing the things they say they do. If they *are*, they should have an easy time boring you with details. If they're not, they'll be suspiciously vague.

Take note of their profile username. Often, people use the same username on multiple social media sites—not just Facebook, Twitter, and Instagram, but also on discussion boards and in online communities. Look up the username and see what you can find.

Look up their phone number, if you have it. What name is it registered to? If nothing else, just look up the area code and make sure it's from the place where they say they live. Sometimes this means paying a small fee or even registering with a site, but that $19.99 could save you years of heartache and wasted time.

Online yearbooks are still fairly rare, but they do exist. It can't hurt to check out their high school and college websites to see if there's an online yearbook you can use to verify their name and face.

If they've told you where they work, call that business and ask for them. If they say they work at Staples, call Staples and ask to talk to Jesse in Printers and Fax Machines. Maybe the person will say, "Sure, hold on." Maybe they'll say, "No one named Jesse works here." Even if you hang up before they get on the line, at least you'll have confirmed their story.

Get their home address. Tell them you want to send them a letter, a postcard, something you made them: Where should you send it? If they hem and haw or give you a hard time, ask yourself—why?

Ask them if they've seen *Catfish*. Gauge their reaction.

Get photo proof: Give them a series of specific objects to wear or hold in a photograph. A carton of milk, a roll of toilet paper, and a toothbrush. There's no way they'll randomly find a picture of whoever they're pretending to be holding those three things.

And last—but definitely not least—*always* video verify. Put a video chat session at the very top of your agenda from the start. If they say they don't have a webcam—which, these days, is increasingly rare—ask them to do it at a friend's house. And if that's not possible either, ask them to text you a short video of themselves talking to you directly. Everyone has access to cameras these days; there's just no excuse anymore. If they like you, and they're real, they should do it.

So much of this advice is common sense, yet many of the people I encounter don't do any of the above. They don't want to come off as stalkers. They especially don't want the other person to find out what they are doing and think they are weird or creepy.

I get that. I'm not saying you should take all these actions every time you encounter someone new online, but be smart about how you interact with people you don't actually know. If you're attracted to someone, you've been talking to them for some time, and they still haven't video-chatted with you or met up in person, it's time to take some steps to protect yourself. (See chapter 13 for safe ways to meet in person.)

Sure, it's awkward to sneak around someone's back asking questions. But how much more awkward will it be when you find out that your French supermodel girlfriend is actually a teenage boy from Kansas City?

CHAPTER 6

Catfish: The TV Show

Not long after the documentary *Catfish* was released, I began to get emails. Tons of emails. It was like the floodgates had opened, and everyone who had ever been involved in a fake online relationship was contacting me. They were relieved to finally have someone to share their experiences with. And it wasn't just people who had been catfished. I was suddenly the go-to guy for anyone who had gone through an experience online that left them feeling vulnerable, or unhappy, or concerned that they were being "had." Overnight I became an expert on all kinds of frustrating and enigmatic online relationships, a guru on digital love, as it were.

In a way, it was the perfect answer to all the frustrations that had led to me being a victim of catfishing in the first place. I'd gotten involved with my catfish as a result of my desire to be a better person, my longing to be useful and appreciated. Well, now I could really *be* that Nev.

Miraculously, I'd been the victim of a hoax and had handled it with sensitivity and compassion, had demonstrated an ability to listen to my catfish and to forgive her despite all the mistakes she'd made. I'd finally been the nonjudgmental, sensitive, caring, *nice* guy I'd always wanted to be, and it had—fortuitously—ended up on tape for the whole world to see. The whole world thought I *was* that guy. Which meant I had the rare opportunity to make Nice Nev the New Nev—permanently.

As these stories poured into my inbox—as strangers stopped me in the street to tell me about their experiences—I was both shocked and amazed. Clearly I'd tapped into a previously undiscussed issue that was plaguing our society. My experience was just the tip of the iceberg: There was a huge underground river of relationships taking place that were just like mine. And what surprised me the most was how many different types of people—of different ages, backgrounds, vocations—were experiencing the same thing. I was getting letters from teenagers and from senior citizens, from rich people and poor people, from all over the earth.

Finally, I turned to my brother, Rel, and said, "This is crazy. We should follow up on these stories and make a show about them." And so *Catfish: The TV Show* was born.

———

Catfish: The TV Show has been on the air for three seasons now. People come up to me all the time and want to know what goes on behind the scenes. For those of you who are curious, here's a (very) brief FAQ.

Question 1: "Hey, Nev, how exactly does the show get made? Who contacts who?"

First, people write in to our show, asking to be featured on an episode. It can be the hopeful or—more rarely—the catfish, who wants to confess. Whether they write in for help meeting the person they are falling in love with or are looking for the perfect opportunity to finally come clean, people come to the show with the same hope of finally having a physical interaction with the person they've been digitally pursuing.

We start by spending two full days with our hopeful—getting to know them, seeing where they live, often meeting friends or family, and also investigating this person they are in love with. It's interesting to note that when we come to help these people, they really have to put their lives on hold—take time off from their job, miss their classes. We arrive in their lives like a tornado and bring everything to a stop while we lift them up into the air and spin them around for a week. In a good way, of course. A gentle, loving tornado.

Then we travel with them to the hometown of their potential online love, and by our fourth day together, we are going to meet the catfish. Sometimes it goes well, sometimes it doesn't. On the fifth day we reconvene with the two of them and spend some private time with the catfish to help them open up and understand why they were doing what they were doing. And then, poof! We are gone.

The five or six days that we are there are arguably the most exciting, confusing, emotional, and difficult days of that person's life. During that time, a relationship in which they were incredibly invested either grows significantly or crashes and burns. We have to be *in it* with them. Max and I completely invest ourselves, engage with these people, and do everything we can to support, encourage, inform, and advise. We do our best to create a relaxed and comfortable environment so that people will open up to us.

To be completely honest, doing this show can be emotionally exhausting for us, as well. I often don't know how I feel about the lying catfish I just met, or even about the hopeful who has been engaged in this relationship for so long despite some incredibly obvious red flags. I often have no idea what to say to the people I am trying to help. I can't offer them an easy fix. And sometimes I feel like no matter what I say, I'm not going to get through to them. Anyway, who am I to help them, when I myself am often just as confused and uncertain about life?

At this point, I try to have a long conversation with Max or our awesome showrunner, Dave Metzler. They remind me that our purpose isn't to solve the problems of the people we meet. Instead, it's to listen and to give these people an opportunity to think about how they feel and what's driving their actions—sometimes for the first time in their lives.

Question 2: "Okay, Nev. But don't the people who contact you know that the show is usually about fake relationships? That it's almost always a hoax?"

Sure. But the truth is that I'm their last resort. They believe that the show is the best chance they have for finally meeting the person they are in love with and getting some answers. It's not news to them that they may be catfished. That's why they've reached out to me in the first place. Somewhere in the back of their mind, they know that this relationship they're having isn't quite right. And they are ready to learn the truth, for better or for worse.

But they also think they are going to be the exception to the rule—because exceptions do happen! They are holding out hope, clearly. What I love about our show is that we try to inform our hopefuls of what we've discovered prior to introducing them to their catfish face to face. It'd be so much more entertaining to not tell them anything we find, and watch the train wreck as they knock on the door—but we try to warn them, gently. We may be a reality show, but we try to be kinder and gentler than real life will ever be.

Sometimes, though, I still have to remind myself that this is someone's *reality*. I remember sitting in a car with Lauren (episode 204) on the way to meet her supposed catfish, Derek. Lauren was playing her cards close to the vest, so I kept pressuring her to think about the worst possible outcome in an effort to elicit some kind of emotional reaction. "What's wrong with this guy?" Max and I kept asking her. "Maybe he's hiding something? It's been eight years!" "Let's keep our guard up." We didn't want her to be blindsided.

Finally, to her credit, Lauren stopped us. "You're making me feel like shit before I meet him," she said. "You guys, it's not always bullshit. You do this all the time for people. But for me, it's new. I don't do this."

"This is not a show for you," I said, realizing. "This is your *life*."

"Yeah," she said, crying.

It was a really great wake-up call for both me and Max. We may always try to be nice and empathetic guys, but you can never really understand what someone else is feeling. Does the victim suspect their "love" is a hoax? Maybe, but emotions aren't that black-and-white. After Lauren called us out, we tried hard not to repeat the same mistake. We remind ourselves constantly that the feelings of a human being are far more important than our television show.

Question 3: "Don't you ever think, 'God, these people are stupid'? How do you maintain such a nonjudgmental attitude?"

Well, I'm heavily sedated through most of it. Just kidding.

The honest answer is that it *is* hard. Just like the people watching the TV show, I often want to roll my eyes when I hear outlandish stories of digital romance. But right before I succumb to the instinct to laugh or be dismissive, I remind myself that I had the exact same thing happen to me. Anybody who heard my story would have said the same thing: "How can you be so dumb? You don't actually believe that, do you? An eight-year-old selling her paintings for thousands of dollars?" But I believed all of it.

To the hopefuls having these relationships, it feels very real. There's a backlog of phone calls, text messages, and emails that we don't have time to show on air—if the hopeful even managed to save them all. We don't have the advantage of showing our viewers the slow, piece-by-piece trickle of how each relationship developed. When you talk to someone every day, you feel like they care about you, and they do! But when you fast-forward and sum up an entire digital relationship from the outside, it often looks totally implausible. Which is why I'm equipped for this job: I know how it feels to be in that kind of relationship on a daily basis.

So even if, in the back of my mind, I'm thinking, "This is so obvious; how can they not see this?" I remind myself that (1) *I* didn't see it; and (2) there's always a chance it's real. We've seen it on our show. The world is crazy; weird stuff happens every day. So I'm not going to make any assumptions.

Question 4: "Max! We want more Max! Tell us all about Max!"

I've known Max since high school. He and Rel met at a UCLA summer film workshop: Rel was walking down the hall, singing "The Confrontation" from *Les Misérables*—*"Valjean, at last, we see each other plain"*—when, directly behind him, he heard some guy singing the next line of the song—*"Monsieur, le Mayor, you wear a different chain."* It was Max. The rest was history. Max became my friend by default; I spent my high school years tagging along after him and my brother.

Max wasn't originally supposed to be on *Catfish* at all (I know; crazy, right?)—I had a different friend picked out to be my on-camera partner. Max stepped in to temporarily pinch-hit when my friend had a scheduling conflict, and after we saw Max on the screen, we all knew he was perfect. The yin to my yang. It's turned into an amazing three-year partnership. But he still holds that fact over my head: "I wasn't even your first choice!"

I've learned a lot from Max—especially how to be more self-aware and considerate to the people in my life. I marvel at his filmmaking abilities. He's taught me so much about storytelling. I feel lucky to call him one of my best friends.

We've had a few fights; for example, during season 2, we

were the only people sleeping at a bed-and-breakfast in Burlington, Iowa—even the owner wasn't staying there. I'd gone out for dinner with the crew, leaving Max at the hotel, and I decided to sneak back in and make haunted house sounds to mess with him. He got a little spooked—though he won't admit it—and then a lot annoyed, as I kept the sounds going far too long. When I finally revealed myself, he lunged at me, and we ended up wrestling in the living room. It ended when we realized that his nose was bleeding, and I ran to get tissues. We didn't want to hurt each other; it was just a best friends' tussle.

Question 5: "What's it like for you and Max, being on the road together so much?"

Max and I are total opposites in the way we travel.

Max can't wake up in the morning. He's a night owl—editing all night—and wants to sleep in. He sleeps with the shades totally closed: He's a cave dweller. You literally have to pull the sheets off him and jump on the bed to get his day started.

I couldn't be more different: I'm a bright, chipper morning person. I jump out of bed and am immediately energized. But once we are both up, Max puts on music—usually EDM (electronic dance music)—and we end up having a morning dance party.

Max gets to the hotel and it's as if his suitcase is spring-loaded. He opens the lid and everything erupts. His girlfriend, Priscilla, is a stylist and fashion blogger who takes him shopping and puts his outfits together. I give him a really hard time about that, probably because I secretly wish that I had my own personal stylist, too.

Meanwhile, I am always knolling. If you don't know what that word means, it's the process of keeping things neat, everything at right angles. (You can watch a hilarious Tom Sachs / Van Neistat film about knolling online.[1]) I'm constantly making sure that things are squared up and symmetrical. My hotel room always looks like the cleaning lady *just* left.

Max and I shared rooms in season 1 and—despite our differences—it was great. But these days, we get our own rooms. It's probably better for everyone.

Question 6: "Do you guys have a lot of material you don't use? What doesn't make it on the show?"

For every episode of *Catfish*, we have exactly forty-two minutes to tell the story of the online relationship we're investigating. In order to get those forty-two minutes, we spend five or six entire days with our subjects, eight to ten hours a day. Do the math: That's a whole lot of time we spend with these people that ends up on the editing room floor.

It's incredibly frustrating to me that so many of the storylines from these people's lives just won't make it into the final episode. Life is complicated. We work hard to draw all this information out of our subjects—their motives and all the nuanced details that explain why this person feels so strongly about that person even though they've never met. It often gets distilled into a three-second graphic of a text message that says "I love you so much, baby." That's not sufficient to illustrate a six-month—let alone a six-year—love affair.

Question 7: "Does being on the show ever change the lives of the people you've met?"

In most cases, the people we've met on the show have not spent a lot of time thinking about—much less talking about— how they really feel. No one has ever *asked* them, so they haven't pushed themselves to figure it out. Personally, I've been in therapy since I was a teenager (you've read enough of this book to understand why), and my expectations for personal insight are high. But that's not fair. Often, we think we know how the catfish and hopeful feel, and we're wrong. I have to remind myself, "I don't know how this person is feeling. I'm just here to encourage them to think about their feelings so they can make sense of their actions."

Sometimes the people on our show really do get insight into their behavior and motivations. So for those who are willing to do some soul-searching, I think the show does change their lives. But it always breaks my heart when I follow up with a catfish and ask them what they've learned and they say, "Don't get into Internet relationships." Because that's not the point of our show.

What *do* I want those people to have learned?

- Know what you want!
- Be comfortable with who you are!
- Demand respect!
- Treat others kindly!

The emotional issues that catfish face aren't so different from yours and mine. It's just that their behavior is more extreme. Through the people I've met while making the show, I've come to understand that catfishing reveals what's missing in *all* of our lives: true communication and self-awareness. The lessons that catfish and their hopefuls need to learn are the same ones that we all should learn.

Including myself. It's taken me thirty years—with a lot of help along the way—to understand how I should be living my life, why I should appreciate myself, and how to challenge myself. It may not be possible to transfer that hard-earned wisdom within the confines of a TV show, but my hope is that through the documentary, the TV show, and now through this book, I have at the very least begun a cultural conversation about how we are relating to one another and to ourselves.

PART TWO

How to Live and Love Online

Catfish are the symptom, not the cause, of one of the biggest challenges we face today: how to conduct ourselves in a world in which our friendships, love affairs, and day-to-day interactions frequently take place online.

More than ever, people are choosing to invest more in their digital lives than in their everyday experiences. An entire generation has shifted to feeling more satisfied by posting a photo on Instagram or receiving a hundred "likes" on a Facebook comment than by going to a party and interacting in person with their peers. It's become easier to maintain an online relationship than to make a real connection.

And yet social media encourages half-truths and downright lies, which undermine the bases of all those relationships. This is why it's important for everyone—not just catfish—to start living honest online lives. If we're going to live and love on social media, we need new guidelines to help us present our digital selves authentically, communicate wisely, and date effectively—not to mention how to protect ourselves against bullies, trolls, haters, and, yes, catfish.

Consider this section a prototype of the Golden Rules for Social Media, guidelines that I hope will help everyone lead a safer, more truthful, and more productive online existence.

CHAPTER 7

My Catfish Story, Part Two

Megan was gorgeous. No question about it. I spent hours combing through her Facebook photos, posting comments about how beautiful I thought she was. She told me how handsome I was, how much she wanted to meet me. Our emails to each other grew frank and flirty.

Hey Nev-

I have a confession to make. The only reason I went back on Facebook was to try to get to know you a little better.

———

Hey Megan-

...the feeling is mutual. No need for apologies at all.

We began to Facebook message each other almost daily. Soon, a pastel sketch arrived in the mail, stuck inside the latest package of Abby originals. It was a picture of me, a sketch that Megan had drawn based off my Facebook profile picture.

I think my favorite photo of you is the one that I drew you from. It's so quiet and peaceful. When I see it, it makes me think of falling asleep on your chest with your hands

laced through my hair. I think I should stop thinking now, I wish
I could.

Sweet dreams-
Megan

By mid-April, I'd sent her my phone number. The woman
who called me was breathy and soft-spoken. Her voice was
high and full of shy laughter, and although our conversation
was hesitant at first, we quickly grew comfortable with each
other.

Hey Nev-

It was so nice talking with you last night. You're so easy to talk
to and I love the sound of your voice. You're quite charming
with your wit and humor.

I hope to talk to you again soon. I was so nervous about talking
with you that I forgot most everything I wanted to ask you and
now I want to know so much more about you.

After we said our good byes I went and took my bath and fell
asleep in the tub. Abby woke me up at 3:45 and asked "Why
were you talking to Nev on the phone?"...I have to stay one
step ahead of that girl.

I have to get back to work.

I hope you're having a beautiful day!

Peace-
Megan

Within the week, we had each other on speed dial.

At first, I attempted to keep some kind of reality check on
the situation. After all, Megan lived in Michigan, she was

younger than me—and, oh yeah, I had a girlfriend in New York City. My emails to Megan often vacillated between brazen flirtation and cool standoffishness, sexy talk and hard truth.

Hey Nev-

I'm not trying to make you uncomfortable, I'm just being honest so please forgive me. Trust me, this is just as awkward for me as it is for you. I've been overwhelmingly attracted to you for sometime now. I'm not sure how or why that happened because honestly it just doesn't happen to me. So many things I see in you are qualities that I find attractive and I was hoping for something to happen between us. I think about you constantly. When I close my eyes I dream of being with you, going places, doing things together and so much more that I don't want to say for fear of really making you feel uncomfortable.

Peace - Meg

———

OK, Megan

I have to admit that through our getting to know each other over the past months, I have found myself thinking about you a lot also. There is a natural attraction between us that would be silly to ignore. The only reason I told you to cool down with the compliments was because it is just a little strange to have someone tell me that I have such a nice voice and how handsome I am. I would have told my mom to stop telling me that too, it wasn't my way of trying to give you a clue . . . it just feels funny to hear it.

That being said, I do think it's important for us to remember that our whole relationship is based on the mystery and improbability of it ever becoming something. At this point, it's clear that our lives will overlap in some way and I'm really happy about that. I just have no idea what our collective future will hold and don't want to go forward with any expectations.

Ok. I'm going to stop before I lose my focus.

Let me know what you think.

- Nev

Despite my attempts to keep Megan at arm's length, the truth was that we were talking every few days, and frequently discussing our attraction to each other. I was still officially with my girlfriend, Katie, but I wasn't exactly letting that get in the way of my flirtation with Megan. (Go ahead, call me a sleaze—you wouldn't be wrong.) I figured that I wasn't cheating on Katie just by emailing and talking to another girl. Megan lived halfway across the country! We weren't even having phone sex. (Well, not yet.)

But the truth was, a dangerously real-feeling relationship was developing. Even though I insisted to Megan—and everyone else—that we were "just friends," it was clearly a lot more complicated than that. So perhaps it was no surprise when, not long after the correspondence with Megan began to heat up, Katie and I broke up.

My and Megan's lives grew more and more entangled. Although my focus was increasingly on Megan, I was still heavily engaged with the entire family in Ishpeming. Abby's paintings based on my work were selling like hotcakes—well enough that the family could afford to buy an old run-down JCPenney in town and turn it into a gallery—and thanks to our business agreement I soon got my first check in the mail, for five hundred dollars.

Sometimes it felt like this fun, kooky Michigan family

was a sitcom, and I was the sole audience member. I had an exclusive front row seat to this exciting and weird show. Bored with my New York life, I latched on. Soon, I was emailing and instant-messaging not just with Megan, Angela, and Abby, but with Megan's extended family and friends. And they, in turn, were chatting online with *my* friends: my mom and Angela talked on the phone; my brother Facebooked with several of the Ishpeming crew; another friend of mine was constantly on IM and email with pretty much everyone up in Michigan.

Megan was my magical unicorn girl. She seemed to have it all: She was young, beautiful, active, flirtatious, and sexy. Her interests mirrored mine: She was a ballet dancer, an artist, a musician. She had focus: She was even a homeowner, buying a small horse farm before she'd hit twenty. She was a bad-ass who scuba dived and talked about going to work on a fishing boat in Alaska for the summer with her father. But she was also appealingly fragile and vulnerable—her family constantly told me to be sensitive about her low self-esteem. To top it all off (and perhaps this was where I should have gotten skeptical), she was a virgin.

I liked who *I* was with her, too. Usually I'd jump right into bed with the girls I met. This was the first time I'd been forced to take it slow. It felt like we were on a perpetual first date. And it's easy, on a first date, to curate how you present yourself, showing off only your most desirable qualities. I played up my kindness and generosity.

Another thing about first dates: They are full of potential. As Max says, mystery is the greatest aphrodisiac. Sure, I had plenty of girls I could pursue in New York, but this woman's lack of availability made her intriguing and exciting. *Imagining* sleeping with her was way more interesting than actually getting laid. The potential in this perfect virgin halfway across the country was way more alluring than the reality of being intimate with a complicated real human being in New York.

And wow, was there a lot of sexual titillation to keep me imagining it. At the end of May, Tim Hobbins—who, besides being Abby's art dealer, was a professional photographer— sent me a pile of photographs for which Megan had posed. They were highly sexy art photos: Megan naked, her back arched. Megan topless, with her hair coyly covering her breasts. Megan in sexy lingerie. Megan and Angela, naked, laughing. Megan in body paint. Megan in a fuzzy hat and jeans and nothing in between.

The pictures were stunning—and featured heavily in my nocturnal fantasy life (I'm sure you know what I mean). And in return, I sent her my own sexy art photographs—of myself naked, holding a stuffed deer head in strategic positions.

Hey Handsome-

I've been thinking about you all day. I kept wondering what it would be like to have you here with me. I would love to take the boat out just you and me. We could do some shallow dives where we wouldn't have to get all geared up, we could just free dive or snorkel. You'd be amazed at what you can see when you dive the shipwrecks here. They are hauntingly beautiful.

I'd love to set anchor far out from shore and lay on deck in the sun with you. Of course we'd have to put sunscreen on each other. I'd love to run my hands over your back and chest feeling your skin under my finger tips. I love your chest! I want to nuzzle into it while you lace your fingers through my hair. I also love when you have a little scruff of a beard. It makes me want to touch your face and kiss you. I would love to stay out on the water for hours just kissing you, touching you, exploring your body with my kisses. It makes my mouth water thinking of what could happen if you would let me have you.

I don't understand how I can feel so strongly for you when we are so different in so many ways. Your friendship means the world to me but I can't seem to keep myself from thinking that there might be something more between us. I keep trying to remind myself of the things you've already written to me about us not being able to be together because of the different stages we are at in our lives and how we can only be friends at this point but I can't seem to stop myself from wanting you in a more intimate way. I'm so anxious to come meet you!

Peace-
Megan

Not long after that, I Photoshopped myself into one of the half-naked pictures she'd sent me. We agreed that we looked great together.

Inevitably, it escalated into sexts:

Megan: I'm at home baking pies.

Me: Save a pie for me.

(Later)

Megan: I'm in the bathtub, thinking of you.

Me: Funny, I was thinking about you in the shower earlier.

Megan: Mmmm. I'd like to think about that. You know, I'll always have a pie for you, babe.

Me: Cherry?

Megan: Cherry. My body is craving your touch tonight.

Me: What exactly would you do if I had you there?

Megan: I'd have you in the tub between my legs…

I'll spare you the rest—and myself the embarrassment—but you get the idea. It was intimate. It was exciting. I'd never had an exchange like that.

As time passed, I began to think more and more seriously about going to stay with Megan, to see if she was everything I thought she was. Maybe I would even move up to Michigan. Try to be in a relationship with this girl. Life in New York wasn't *all that*, so why not uproot myself and start over in a whole new town with a whole new life? It felt like a really appealing option—and, although I didn't admit this to myself, an easy escape, a cheap solution to my chronic dissatisfaction.

In the meantime, Megan talked frequently about coming to visit me in New York. We made plans a half dozen times. But something always seemed to get in the way. (If I were investigating this relationship on *Catfish*, this is where I would raise a skeptical eyebrow.)

- In April, a family trip was planned to New York—Megan, Abby, and their stepbrother Alex planned to drive out—but it was aborted before it was even under way:

Hey Nev-

...I'm not going to be able to come to New York this coming weekend and unfortunately it doesn't look like Abby will be allowed to either.

My truck died last weekend and I missed an entire weekend of work. No work=no pay :(

To try to catch up financially I agreed to work Friday thru Monday this upcoming weekend.

- In May, Abby, Megan, and Megan's friend Josh tried a second time to organize a weekend visit to New York. My mother even corresponded with Angela about having Abby stay at her apartment. We bought ballet tickets in anticipation. They decided to drive out to save money. But not long after they got on the road to New York, I began to get texts from Megan. Abby was sick; they'd pulled over to let her throw up. Then the van had broken down. They were stranded in a small town two states away. Instead of forging on, they turned around and went back home. I was disappointed, but I wasn't upset—how could I be? They had it worse than I did.

- In June, a few days before she was supposed to come visit me, Megan went to the doctor to fix a deviated septum, a lingering problem from an old horse riding accident. When they sedated her, she had a reaction to the anesthesia, and she flatlined. The doctors revived her, but of course, the trip was canceled. And when I offered to visit her in the hospital instead, she refused—she didn't want me to meet her like that; besides, things with her family were too crazy.

- In July, Abby and Megan planned to come visit. But then Abby's father insisted that she fly out to San Jose to visit him instead. Megan decided to make the drive by herself, but fell asleep at the wheel in the middle of the night and crashed on a deserted road. She walked for two hours before she was picked up by the police, who arrested her on suspicion of a DUI. Instead of spending the weekend with me, she spent it in jail.

This girl seemed to have the worst luck *ever*. And yet I didn't question her stories.

Looking back, there are also countless emails and recalled phone conversations that, knowing what I know now, make it clear that I was talking to a catfish. There seemed to be no limit to her incredible stories—not just the near-constant drama and car mishaps, but also the father who was a commercial fisherman in Alaska, the former home that had burned down, the time that Alex and his friends were caught selling drugs (a story that Angela confirmed by sending me a news article about the drug arrest of some unnamed local teens). Or the fact that a nineteen-year-old student could buy a $225,000 horse farm on a part-time vet assistant's salary. Or that an eight-year-old girl could sell so many paintings that her family could open an art gallery.

But instead of setting off alarm bells, the stories just drew me in further and made me more sympathetic to the family's fascinating, problem-plagued life.

And no, we never video-chatted. Call me naive. But I didn't have a webcam, and neither did Megan. (This was 2008, before webcams were standard in phones and laptops.) Anyway, it never crossed my mind that I needed to video verify her. I'd seen a million pictures of her, and the photos had people in them who were active on their own Facebook profiles. People whom I was communicating with, too. How much more *real* did I need?

And yes, I had Googled Megan, and found nothing. But since she'd been telling me about her dislike and avoidance of the Internet since the first day I'd met her, that didn't surprise me.

Abby, on the other hand, occasionally nagged at me. Why weren't there any online articles about this young prodigy's artwork? I thought that was weird, but then again, it didn't prove or disprove anything. Besides, I was getting checks in the mail from her art sales. It was a dead end, so I didn't think much of it.

Some of my friends were skeptical—including Katie, my now-ex-girlfriend, and my brother, who by this point was filming my life incessantly, as he found the entire relationship to be incredibly entertaining and unusual. But for every question, I had a perfectly good explanation. And because I seemed so convinced, I was able to convince everyone around me. Which only convinced me even further: The more people believed my story, the more I believed it. I dug myself in deeper and deeper.

It turns out it's a lot easier to disprove the truth than it is to prove a lie.

———

Over the months of our friendship, Angela, Megan, and Alex had sent me music that their family had recorded together. Most of it was what you'd expect from a small garage band—as in, not gonna blow your socks off. But there were a few songs that stuck with me, including a pretty song called "Downhill," with Angela singing and Megan playing guitar. I was impressed and put it in heavy rotation on our office stereo.

The last week of July, Rel, Henry, and I headed to Vail, Colorado, for a two-week job making dance documentaries. I'd spoken to Megan about flying her out to visit during the trip, but we hadn't yet figured out the logistics. Not long after we arrived in Vail, during an evening messaging session, Megan mentioned that she and Alex were noodling around recording music. Was there any particular song that I wanted to hear?

Megan: I take requests
but piano you'll have to wait until tomorrow for
I don't have one at my house

Me: tennessee stud!!!
please please please do tennessee stud for me
real sexy

Megan: I think I can handle that

Me: ok, you have 15 minutes

Megan: lol

An hour later, an MP3 landed in my inbox. The recording was crappy, but the song was gorgeous: A throaty, husky woman's voice accompanied by an acoustic guitar. Rel, Henry, and I were all blown away. "I can't believe she just did that!" I bragged, and then, eager to show off the talents of the rest of Megan's family, I told Rel and Henry about Angela's rendition of "Downhill." One thing led to another—we wanted to find the lyrics to "Downhill," so we punched some of the words from the song into Google, looking for the original version... and moments later came across a YouTube video of a musician named Amy Kuney, singing a song called "All Downhill from Here."

It was the *exact* same song.

We listened to the recording again, stunned. It was unmistakably the same version of the song that Angela claimed to have sung herself. There was no question about it: Angela had lied. They had *all* lied, including Megan.

Curious, we next plugged "Tennessee Stud" into YouTube, and sure enough, there it was, on the fourth page of search results: an amateur recording of a girl singing "Tennessee Stud" at a bar in New York. By now, it was clear what was going on: Angela, Megan, and Alex were downloading live record-ings from YouTube and trying to pass them off as their own.

I didn't know what to think. Why would they lie to me about their music? They were so great; why did they feel the need to pretend to me that they were serious musicians if they weren't? I was angry enough to fire off messages to Angela, Megan, and Alex, telling them what I'd discovered and demanding an explanation. Instead of apologizing or admit-ting to their deception, they grew defensive. Alex claimed that they'd used the "Tennessee Stud" bar song as a model for their own recording, and that he'd simply accidentally sent me the wrong file; the original, rather than their cover.

As for "Downhill," they all claimed that it wasn't identical to the Amy Kuney song—it just *sounded* a lot like it because that was what they were trying to achieve.

Me: so?

do you have an explanation for why the songs sound so similar?

Megan: It's a cover song
they're suppose to sound similar

Me: maybe you should call me…cause im about to be very upset

Megan: I'm already very upset

Me: well me too
i can't believe you are lying to me
wow
im so shocked

Megan: WHAT!
Are you kidding me?

Me: right back at ya
we need to speak now please
im sure we can figure this out

Megan: It sounds like you have already made up your mind that
   I'm a liar

Me: no, but i would love to hear from you that its not true
   i want to believe you
   really

By now, I was pissed off and growing more suspicious by the minute. It was obvious they were lying; I thought it was ridiculous that they were spinning it to make me the aggressor. And I was also confused and hurt. I'd opened up to Megan, had become emotionally invested in our relationship. If the music was a lie, what else had she been lying about?

Rel and Henry were already on the case, proving their skills as amateur private investigators on Google. By the next day, we'd made a series of alarming discoveries. That horse farm Megan had told me she'd bought, the one where I'd sent her postcards? It was still listed as for sale. So was the JCPenney building in downtown Ishpeming that Abby had said she was renovating for a gallery. Maybe the listings just hadn't been updated, but in light of the lies about the music, that didn't seem so likely.

It was growing clear that Megan and her family had spun a web of lies for me. Why? The only explanation I could come up with was that maybe they were intimidated by my New York lifestyle and wanted to appear more cosmopolitan and accomplished than they really were. Maybe they were poor and wanted to appear rich (but in that case, why were they sending me money?). Maybe they just felt a need to impress.

The one thing that I never questioned was their existence. Not even when Rel, Henry, and I decided to spontaneously fly from Vail to Michigan and go confront them, face to face.

CHAPTER 8

A Brave New World Wide Web

Back when I was a teenager, in the late 1990s, there was no Facebook. (Yeah, I'm *that* old.) If I liked a girl, I didn't "poke" her. I didn't follow her on Twitter or post on her wall. I wrote a note—on *actual paper*—and passed it to her in class. Or I picked up a telephone and called her—on a landline, *at her house*, awkwardly having to ask her mom if she was home and available, since hardly anyone had cell phones. If I had something I wanted to say to her, I had to do it in person. If I wanted to learn more about her, I had to actually spend time with her.

Fortunately, I was born with the gift of confidence (or maybe I just didn't have the capacity to be embarrassed). I was fearless when it came to connecting with girls, whether it was writing notes as a kid or buying drinks as an adult.

It's a good thing that I *was* confident, because in those days, it was also a lot harder to meet new people. You didn't have access to a massive online network where you could contact hundreds of people who were loosely connected to you through some mysterious algorithm. Instead, your dating pool was limited to the people in your school or your after-school clubs and the kids you met on vacations. I remember going to "socials" at my summer camp, sharing one clammy-handed dance with a girl from our sister camp, and spending the rest of the summer sending letters across the lake to her. Not exactly modern romance.

By the time I arrived at Sarah Lawrence, in 2002, Myspace was big. I wasn't a fan; I had a page but I hardly ever checked it, and I didn't really get the hype. But by my junior year, Facebook had launched, and suddenly I was hooked. Being on Facebook felt like an obligation: It was the cool thing to do. In almost no time at all, if you weren't on Facebook, you didn't exist.

That marked the beginning of a seismic shift in the way people across the globe interact with one another. Thanks to the rise of social media and digital technology, everything about how we communicate has changed. The United States Postal Service is going bankrupt, while the average teenager sends 3,339 texts per month.[2] And if Facebook—nonexistent a decade ago—were a country, it would be the world's third-largest, containing one of every nine people on the planet.[3] We even date digitally now: A quarter of all "millennials" date online, often through increasingly enormous dating sites like Match.com but also just by meeting other people on the Internet.[4] As an alternative to dances, parties, or bars, social media sites are where we go to meet one another.

Everything now is about social media: There's Twitter (200 million users and counting); online gaming communities like Call of Duty and World of Warcraft; photo-sharing sites like Instagram and Pinterest; blogs and Tumblrs and Snapchat and Chatroulette and vlogs and Vines and whatever else will be out there by the time this book rolls off the press. Every day, it seems, there's a new social media platform, a new way for people to meet each other digitally. There are so many ways to be friends online that the idea of just going to grab a coffee with someone feels downright *archaic*.

Why do we like these social media platforms so much more

than the old system of telephones and paper and meeting in person?

People say that social media has opened up a world of information, and has helped us connect to share ideas. That's absolutely true. But books and stories have been doing that for centuries. And yes, the Internet made it easier to meet people! But why do we really love our social media? It's because online we don't have to deal with the awkwardness of real-time interactions and rejections; we feel safer behind the screen.

And yet this shift to a nonphysical way of interacting has created a whole new series of problems. Sure, the Internet has opened up an exciting spectrum of communication. It's changed the world in positive ways, allowed creativity to flourish, started revolutions, enabled new and profound connections. It can be an amazing tool when used correctly. But it's also taken us away from doing what, in my humble opinion, humans are meant to do: living our lives where we are, using our bodies and not just our minds.

————

There's a great short film from 2013 called *Noah* that captures the disconnectedness of a life lived completely online. It takes place entirely on the computer screen of a kid named Noah as he obsessively clicks from Facebook to porn to online games to Chatroulette and back to Facebook. His girlfriend, Amy, Skypes him, says something cryptic about the status of their relationship, and then hangs up. Rather than picking up the phone and talking to Amy about what's going on, Noah obsesses over her status updates, hacks into her private Facebook messages, becomes convinced that she's cheating on him, and ultimately gets dumped via online chat.

The movie ends with a lonely Noah desperately seeking some kind of interaction with a human, begging a total stranger on Chatroulette to talk to him.[5]

If you ask me, this film—much like *Her*, the terrific Spike Jonze film about a guy who falls in love with his computer's operating system—sums up what's going wrong in the Facebook era. We may think we are being more social thanks to the Internet—like Noah, we'll spend the entire day chatting simultaneously with friends, romantic partners, and total strangers—but in fact, we are being *less* social, since our communication doesn't involve any physical interaction at all. Sure, we're communicating more, but those interactions are not as meaningful or intimate.

> "Oh, great! I don't have to actually call my mom and talk to her on the phone anymore. I'll just email her!"

> "I have to break up with my girlfriend? Awkward! I'll just text her."

> "My friend's dad died and I don't know what to say, so I'll just post something on his wall. It's so much easier!"

And it is! It's *so much easier.* That's why the Internet is so successful: It took something difficult—human communication—and made it easy. It took away the vulnerability.

When we're far away from our friends and loved ones, these tools can be helpful and relationship-maintaining. But when we resort to them out of laziness or fear, we are eroding our relationships, not building them.

Don't get me wrong; I'm as guilty of this as anyone. I've gone weeks where I've talked with my dad only via text.

DON'T USE YOUR

TO COMMUNICATE.

USE YOUR

VOICE

Because talking to my dad—or mom, or grandmother, or friend—in person means *caring*. If I can hear his voice and he can hear mine, or if we are sitting face to face, emotions are involved. I have to show genuine interest, and if he says something that's difficult for me to hear, I'm confronted with a situation I can't avoid. And if I get up and walk away, it's rude or hurtful or embarrassing.

In person, it's hard to hide how we feel; we can't escape seeing the judgment in the expressions of the person sitting across from us, the way we can online. Then there are the heavy, awkward conversational silences, and the fact that we can't avoid responsibility for the impact our words have on the person sitting across from us.

In other words, when we are face to face, we can't ignore the emotions involved. It's riskier. But with social media and technology, there's a way to interact without any of that challenging emotional stuff. We have, over the past decade, turned to a form of communication that is devoid of all those things that make human interaction exciting. It's a safe way to communicate, but it's sterile and leaves no room for the thrill of a true connection. And instead of helping us, it's actually hurting us.

Because, like it or not, real emotions are a *good thing*.

———

The other thing that social media has given us, for better or worse, is a really exceptional outlet for pretending. Which is where catfishing comes into the picture.

Much in the way that it's less stressful to communicate with your mom via email, it's easier to present yourself online as someone more exciting or accomplished. It doesn't take as much effort to exaggerate or lie when you don't have to look someone in the face.

Online, we can pretend that our real lives are glossy and perfect, even—especially—if we are actually unhappy and unsatisfied. Social media is the perfect escape. We can go there every day to pretend for a few minutes—or for countless hours. For some people, the pretending consists simply of acting more popular or active than they really are; for others it's about trying on entire alter egos, and sometimes doing a lot of harm in the process.

I worked on a *Catfish* episode that didn't end up airing that focused on a girl who—for the sake of anonymity—we'll call Monica. In order to boost her self-esteem after a bad relationship ended, Monica began friending beautiful women online in order to steal their online identities—manipulating them into giving her video clips and photos. She'd create convincing new Facebook profiles with that information and use those new fake profiles to befriend yet more women, stealing their photos and identities, and so on.

For years, Monica lived vicariously through these alter egos, whose personae seemed so much more alluring than her own. But it didn't make her any happier. In fact, it made her even more miserable: Not only was she still depressed and lonely, but now she was also disgusted with her own dishonest behavior. She didn't think she was worthy of anyone's friendship.

What struck me when I met her was that her original unhappiness and loneliness could have been resolved long ago had she just put the same energy into improving her life that she had into faking those profiles. She'd wasted not just hours, but years.

When I meet with catfish like Monica on my show, I tell them what most people won't: *Clearly, you want a different version of your life, which is why you created it for yourself on the Internet. So why don't you do it for real?* It's a challenge that applies not only to catfish but also to all of us.

It's easy to say that one of the biggest issues with the Internet is that people can pretend to be someone else. That's a boogeyman everyone can get behind: *Catfish are bad.* But at the core of *that* problem is how we are relating to ourselves in the digital age. The truth is that when you're on social media, you are essentially having a conversation with yourself. We hide, and the result is that we prefer shallow relationships based on 140-character tweets rather than real conversations based on intimacy.

CHAPTER 9

The Myth of the Little White Lie

At this point, you're probably still thinking that the lies catfish tell don't have anything to do with *you*, right?

Wrong.

The truth that no one likes to admit is that we *all* lie online, to varying degrees. Dishonesty in social media is at epidemic levels. Surveys show that 25 percent of all Facebook users admit to lying on their profiles.[6] Teenage girls are even less honest: 70 percent say they lie on Facebook, according to a *Seventeen* magazine survey. And statistics show that up to 80 percent of people who date online are lying about *something* in their profiles—their height, their age, their weight, their favorite band.[7]

There are lots of ways we lie online. The vast majority of these are little white lies, of course—photos that don't quite tell the truth, status updates that pretend at better lives, profiles that exclude unflattering facts, even the perfectly lit high-angle selfie. Social networking almost *encourages* us to fudge things, from the filters we use to make our photos prettier to the way we upgrade our height/weight stats on Match.com or simply exclude certain unfavorable information about our job history on LinkedIn.

But so what? If it's just a little white lie, what's the harm? It's not like you're *catfishing*, right?

Let me stop you right there. Because, as I've learned from making *Catfish*, no one starts catfishing with a big lie. Usually, it's the little white lie that's the gateway drug to the big, bold lie. It's amazing how easily one or two small lies can snowball into something much, much bigger.

I'm not saying that everyone who alters their height and weight on Match.com is going to become a catfish. But it's all part of the online culture of dishonesty in which we're now living, a culture in which the lives that we present to our friends on the Internet are increasingly at odds with the lives that we really lead. And when this dishonesty is at the foundation of our relationships with our friends and our romantic partners, *everyone* suffers.

––––––

Who do you want to be? If you're anything like me, you are nowhere near your own ideal. Maybe you want to be more successful, or better traveled, or better educated, or plain old ridiculously wealthy. Me? I want to be a leader. I want to be someone people look up to and admire for my accomplishments. I want to feel like I've had a purpose and made a difference in people's lives.

Here's another question: Do you present yourself online as being far closer to those ideals than you are in real life?

We all have ambitions, goals, things about ourselves we want to change and improve. But getting motivated to actually *do* those things is far more difficult. What I see with young people—and I include myself in that group—is a lot of procrastination: a sense of endless time. *I'll get to that someday.* When it comes to things like going to school or really buckling down for some weight loss—the two subjects that the people I encounter on the show lie about the most—a lot of people fail to take that initial step. They may *say* what they want to do, over and over—"I'm going to get my GED and apply to community college. Maybe next year..." "I'm going to start that diet—next week..."—but then they don't do anything about it.

And that's fine. It happens. But what *isn't* fine is posting on your Facebook page that you're already going to school, or that you've already lost the weight. Don't fool yourself: Posting it doesn't make it a reality. Instead, you'll get recognition that you haven't truly earned from your online friends. This is the fantasy projection that I encounter so often with catfish, but it bears repeating for *everyone*. It's the issue at the core of this book. Thanks to social media and our culture of public consumption, the way you are perceived seems so much more important than what you actually are. The Internet lets you get that attention without having to do the hard work.

These kinds of little white lies actually get in the way of achieving what we want. They set up an emotional hurdle that we have to clear. Because due to our fudged digital profiles, we can now receive the same attention that we would get if we'd actually achieved those accomplishments. When we do this, we're getting real attention from real people, so it feels good... temporarily. But eventually that feeling fades and we have no real accomplishment to back it up, so we start to feel crappy again. It's easy to see how this cycle perpetuates itself.

———

Toward the end of season two of *Catfish*, I got to meet Brian, a former marine (episode 208). He'd been introduced to a girl named Jesse online, and they spent three years chatting before planning to meet in person. But on the actual day, he never showed up. It turned out that Brian had PTSD and didn't tell Jesse because he wanted her to believe that he was the happy guy he wanted to be. On the day of their meeting, he'd had a flashback, and had subsequently been arrested for being in possession of a shotgun. And—making matters worse—he was married (though he was separated), another fact that he hadn't wanted to tell Jesse for fear she'd reject him.

Brian wasn't a fake, and he wasn't pretending to be someone radically different from who he really was. His little white lies were lies of omission, wanting to hide the things he was insecure about. But the lies grew in scope the longer he failed to acknowledge them. The outcome of his dishonesty was that once she did get to know him—after they'd finally spent time together—he wasn't who she'd imagined he was. Even though they tried to work it out, their relationship was based on misperceptions, and everything fell apart.

So yes, the lies that we tell online can be obvious—about our appearance or our accomplishments—but often, they are far more subtle. Lies of omission; lies about our emotional state; lies about our vulnerabilities. Lies that are so subtle that we sometimes don't even admit to ourselves that we're lying.

Social media has put an incredible pressure on the Facebook generation. We've made our lives so public to one another, and as a result we feel pressure to live up to a certain ideal version of ourselves. On social media, everyone is happy, and popular, and successful—or, at least, we think we need to look like we are. No matter how well off we are, how thin or pretty, we have our issues and insecurities. But none of that shows up online. We don't like to reveal our weaknesses on social media. We don't want to appear unhappy, or be a drag.

Instead, we all post rose-colored versions of ourselves. We pretend we have more money than we do. We pretend we are popular. We pretend our lives are great. Your status update says *I went to a totally awesome party last night!* It won't mention that you drank too much and puked and humiliated yourself in front of a girl you like. It says *My sorority sisters are the best!* It doesn't say *I feel lonely and don't think they accept me.*

I'm not saying everyone should post about having a bad time. But pretending everything is perfect when it's not doesn't help anyone.

The danger of these kinds of little white lies is that, in projecting the happiness and accomplishments we long for, we're setting impossible standards for ourselves and others to live up to.

––––––––

As I've said, almost none of the catfish that we meet on the show start off by telling big lies. Instead, they start with little lies and escalate from there.

Once you start, it's hard to go back. With every little lie you tell, you dig yourself deeper into the hole.

We can't lie like this without being aware that it's wrong. It breeds self-hatred, since, after all, we *aren't* that ideal self we are presenting online. It's a vicious cycle: The more we go online in order to present ourselves in a certain way, the farther from that reality we'll become. The happier we appear online, the less happy we will be in real life. The more active we are online, the less active we'll be in real life.

CHAPTER 10

Avat-Are You Kidding Me?

How do you set up your online profiles? Maybe you pick a flattering picture of yourself...or a photo of someone else entirely. Maybe you describe yourself...or the person you wish you were. Maybe you tweak your profile with someone specific in mind in order to appeal to them.

Catfish are extreme examples of this—like my own catfish, Angela, who created online personalities that were designed to appeal to my love for bands, ballet, and photography—but we are all guilty of it, to some degree.

Including me. I've done it myself, more times than I can count: picked a photo that hides all my shortcomings or included only part (the most flattering part) of the story of my life. On Facebook, I've been known to look up the profile of someone I've just met to see what they are interested in—books, bands, movies, TV shows—and then, whether I like those things or not, add them to my Facebook page so that when I friend-request that person, they'll see that we have common interests: "Hey, we *both* like *Family Guy*!"

One thing I know for sure: Manipulating your photos and your online profile to "hook" people who wouldn't otherwise be interested in you is not going to improve your life. Sure, you may get a momentary thrill when someone shows an interest in those altered photos. But the truth is, you're setting yourself up for failure.

———

Ashley was an insecure twelve-year-old girl when she met a guy named Mike in a chat room (episode 210). She was really struggling with her weight. As a result, she'd become a kind of recluse, so insecure about her appearance that she wouldn't even allow herself to be photographed at family events. But she did have a Facebook page. And there, she posted photos that she'd run through Photoshop in order to trim herself a little. Nothing dramatic—she didn't pretend that she was radically thinner—but she'd lift her cheekbones, remove her double chin, and post only photos taken at one specific, flattering angle.

But in the meantime, Mike was also overweight, and he was also lying about his appearance. When Ashley asked to see Mike's photos, he sent bogus pictures of some handsome

Abercrombie & Fitch–like model with ridiculous abs. Ashley wasn't stupid. She didn't buy it. But she didn't say anything because she knew her own photos were dishonest, too.

This went on for six years, until we finally met them both. Each of them was terrified to reveal themselves. They never made plans to meet, because they were too embarrassed about their appearances. Instead, they hit a kind of glass ceiling on how close they could get. Luckily Ashley recognized that it was time for some honesty, and she reached out to us. Only when we showed up on their doorsteps did they feel ready to take ownership of their lies.

It didn't go well. They both realized that they'd been dishonest with themselves and each other. And that ended up getting in the way of more than six years of friendship—a beautiful, magical relationship that had been a consistent presence for both of them through some really awful ordeals.

When we left town, it looked like that was going to be the end. Fortunately, though, Ashley and Mike stayed in touch, and their feelings quickly regenerated. Soon, they admitted that they were in love and started moving toward being in a relationship. It was a rare happy ending, but it was also incredibly frustrating: All that time had been wasted. So much *could have been* if those doctored pictures hadn't gotten in the way. (Most devastating of all, Mike ended up dying a few months later, making that wasted time even more tragic.)

Technically, theirs was a catfish story—but it's also not terribly far from what countless other people do every day.

Take a look at the photos on your profile. If you're like me, you often take a picture a half dozen times to make sure you look *exactly* the way you want to before you post it. You add a filter and only post the most flattering photos. It's what everyone does, barring the handful of people who honestly don't care about how they look (they are rare, but they exist, and they tend to be comedians). We believe—and rightfully so—that we'll be judged on how we look. So we do our best to appear put together.

That isn't necessarily a bad thing. But it's something to pay attention to because it's a stepping-stone, a gateway into the realm of Internet identity addiction. Once you start adjusting your photos, what's next? What else don't you like about yourself that you can fix with a few keystrokes?

I hear extreme catfish stories all the time, stories about men and women who told massive lies and duped people for years. But the stories I hear the *most* frequently? They're the everyday minor deceptions, the people who tinker with their pictures. Especially in the world of online dating. I hear these kinds of stories almost every day: "I didn't get catfished, but I'm on PlentyOfFish and every time I go to meet the guy he totally doesn't look like his pictures." Or "It wasn't even him in his photos."

People do this because they know that when you're trying to catch someone's interest online, the most important thing—like it or not—is a picture. After all, if you don't like someone's picture, you're probably not going to click on their profile. People who fudge their photos justify their decision by saying, "It was the only way to get to know the person I was interested in." Maybe they are right. But it doesn't help them in the long term.

As humans, we want to believe that love is blind. That if

someone really loves you, it shouldn't matter what you look like. Looks don't last, and accidents can happen, but love is forever, right? There is no doubt some truth to this, but equally important is the truth that we are beings for whom romantic relationships are based in no small part on physical attraction. It's mammal science. I can't speak for everybody, but in my experience, no matter how much I've wanted to like someone or longed for it to work out, when there's no spark there's just no spark. You can't convince yourself to be attracted to someone.

I've learned this, over and over, from doing *Catfish*: No matter how close two people get online, if one person has lied in their photos, the relationship almost always ends when they meet for the first time. When a catfish is revealed, the hopeful almost never says, "Our relationship isn't about the physical, so your looks don't matter to me." (They also almost never say, "I don't like the way you look"—they're not that cruel.) Instead, they say something about not trusting the other person anymore (which is also true) and then quietly end the relationship.

Ashley and Mike were able to move past their fudged photos, but they were the exception, not the rule, and even then it was a tough hurdle. The truth is that romantic relationships require some physical attraction. Pretending you look different than you really do may help you *meet* someone online, but it won't help you develop a true relationship with them. Because the minute you meet that person in real life (and if you want a real relationship, you *will* have to meet up eventually) they'll know that your photos didn't tell the truth. And that's exactly where things will end: with a lot of wasted time and the potential for a broken heart.

I'M NOT
PERFECT
-BUT-
CONFIDENCE
-IS A-
STATE OF
MIND

(HOLD NEXT TO YOUR FACE + SMILE)

If you tell the truth, you don't have to remember anything.

—Mark Twain

It should go without saying that we should strive to be honest and honorable in everything we do and say, online and off. And it's not like we don't all tell little white lies in real life. (Try this one on and see if it fits: "How do I look today?" "You look *great!*") But online we tend to give ourselves far greater leniency with the truth. We tell ourselves, "I know this isn't true, but what's the difference? It's just my Facebook profile." But Internet life is becoming inextricably linked to (or at the very least, misinterpreted as) real life.

You may think that you bear no resemblance to the catfish on our show, but even the littlest lies can turn around and bite you in the ass. Trust is at the core of everything, so be honest.

Next time you start to fudge your profile data or upload a misleading profile photo, ask yourself: Am I improving my life by doing this? Or am I setting myself up for failure? Instead of hiding who you really are, strive for total honesty, even when it hurts, and use *that* as the launching pad for helping you become the person you want to be.

Only by embracing who you really are can you get the things you really want.

CHAPTER 11

You Are What You Tweet

Rebecca Sedwick was a pretty, normal twelve-year-old girl living in Florida—who just happened to piss off the wrong person. When Rebecca's ex-boyfriend began to date another girl, that girl took offense to Rebecca and began an online smear campaign against her. Soon, up to fifteen kids at Rebecca's school were bullying her, sending her nasty texts and posting taunts on her Facebook page, like "Drink bleach" and "Die."

So she did: In September 2013, she climbed a tower at an abandoned concrete plant and jumped to her death.

A horrible story, and if you read the news with any regularity, you already know that Rebecca was not an anomaly. In the year before her death, at least nine teenagers committed suicide due to cyberbullying. And that's just the tip of the iceberg, the ones who took the fatal step of killing themselves. Untold thousands, maybe even hundreds of thousands, simply live with online cruelty every day.

Bullies are just the obvious and extreme end of a broad spectrum of online unpleasantness. The Internet is jammed with all kinds of haters who think they can do or say anything online without consequences. Consider the trolls, who riddle the landscape of the Internet. Like catfish, they use the anonymity of an online identity, in this case to be mean: They criticize and bully without any accountability, discharging their negativity out into the world. You'll find dozens of trolls in the comments section of every blog, there for no other reason than to piss people off.

Online, we've fostered a culture of negativity where it's considered acceptable (even cool) to say things that are nasty, critical, and downright mean. Almost everyone is guilty of participating in this mentality at some point—whether it's posting a nasty book review on Goodreads, saying something snarky on a friend's Facebook page, or making a catty remark about a stranger's Instagram photo.

It always blows my mind that people follow me on Facebook just to post mean things on my wall—but they do. And this behavior isn't limited to high-profile people like me. Thanks to the Internet, *everyone* encounters haters, no matter who we are or what we do.

Sure, most of the unpleasant things that people say online aren't going to cause someone to kill themselves, but all the negativity still has deep-rooted consequences. It's time to start holding people accountable for their online behavior—and that means starting with ourselves.

Before we go out and start critiquing other people's words and hard work, we need to ask ourselves if we've earned that right by doing anything risky ourselves. Putting yourself out there—being creative—deserves support. It takes a lot of courage. Let's reward *that*, instead of diminishing it.

———

When I was growing up, if you said something mean to someone, you'd either end up in the principal's office or facedown in the dirt, getting your ass kicked. But now kids can be as evil to one another as they want, and then simply turn off the computer and walk away.

> *I think [cell phones] are toxic, especially for kids....*
> *They don't look at people when they talk to them*
> *and they don't build empathy. You know, kids are*
> *mean, and it's 'cause they're trying it out. They*
> *look at a kid and they go, "You're fat," and then*
> *they see the kid's face scrunch up and they go,*
> *"Oh, that doesn't feel good to make a person do*
> *that." But they got to start with doing the mean*
> *thing. But when they write "You're fat," then they*
> *just go, "Mmm, that was fun, I like that."*
>
> —Louis C.K., comedian, on *Conan*

The Internet is an amazing tool with which we all enjoy the freedom to express ourselves, with almost no legal or social accountability. That's an incredible thing. Most people use this freedom wisely. I am always so excited to hear about people who create amazing online communities in which they connect with people around the world. Many build businesses, raise money for charities, share art and culture...the possibilities are endless. I am inspired daily by the photographs and films posted online by people around the world with messages of positivity and love.

But social media has also given an outlet to millions of kids and adults who were victims of unhappiness, abuse, and bullying themselves, and are now releasing that same aggression on other people.

I've met plenty of bullies over the past few years. And more than one has told me that they believe that they can transfer their negativity. They say things like, "I feel shitty, so someone else should feel shitty, too. That way, I'll have balanced the world and made sure that *everyone* feels shitty."

Awesome logic, right?

Take the case of Mhissy, the first-season catfish I mentioned before. She created a Facebook page for a fake guy in order to mess with the head of Jasmine, a girl she once had a relationship with and who she felt had betrayed her. Mhissy seemed like a pretty unpleasant person, but when we dug down, we discovered her logic. She was hurting, she felt like she had no control over her life and the way she'd been treated, and so she thought to herself, "Jasmine hurt me. I want to hurt her back. That way I can make sure that she feels the same way I feel."

Hers was a one-to-one direct relationship, but a lot of people who go online to vent their frustration spread their negativity anywhere they can. For example: "My dad fucked me up, so I want to fuck someone else up; it doesn't matter who it is." It's a kind of pass-the-buck mentality—the inverse of paying it forward.

In our worst moments, we're all capable of this kind of thinking. If we're not careful, we can seed nastiness and hate everywhere we go. When we go online, it's just so incredibly easy to use social media as an outlet for all of our frustrations, to give in to our most unpleasant impulses without any consequence. The challenge we all face is learning how to spin our negativity into something more worthwhile. (More—much more—on that in a few chapters.)

We have all been haters at one point or another. No matter how nice of a person you are, odds are you've given in to a bad mood at some point and impulsively posted something unkind, written something anonymously, or gotten involved in an online flame war.

Look, we all do it. But I think we should try to be more careful.

Everything you say online you are saying to *someone*. That post didn't write itself; a robot didn't take that photo. There's a person behind every single image and word on the Internet, a person who took the time to create and share their feelings and ideas. So even though, in an instant, with zero accountability, you can make a negative comment—don't. Even a remark that feels insignificant to you *is* significant to that real person. A person like you. Just because you don't have to look them in the eyes doesn't mean it doesn't hurt.

I've come up with a few simple, commonsense guidelines for online accountability. If everyone tried to live by the following rules, the Internet would be a much nicer—and more productive—place.

- Remember that you're talking to real people. Don't say it online if you wouldn't say it to someone's face.
- Find a constructive way to express yourself rather than defaulting to a snarky shorthand. Say what you really mean, but say it nicely. Craft a thoughtful opinion.
- Before you hit "post" on anything, read your post out loud. Think about how you'd feel if someone said the same thing to you.
- Don't post anonymously as a way to vent. It's cowardly.
- Don't pick a fight just for the sake of entertainment.

RESOURCES

Sometimes, no matter how positive you try to be, the hate that you encounter online is just too much to shoulder on your own. Bullied teens like Rebecca Sedwick need serious emotional support, and I'm aware that in these cases, telling someone to try to spin their experience into something positive isn't going to cut it.

Fortunately, there are support groups out there that exist specifically to help kids who are bullied. Sites like www.endcyberbullying.org offer online counseling, and the National Suicide Prevention Lifeline has a great website and a hotline that's available 24/7.

And for those on the other side of that equation—the bullies—there's a great organization called Leave Out Violence (LOVE) that is focusing on helping teens channel their anger into more productive outlets. So you're pissed off? Don't join a gang or bully someone online. LOVE teaches teens to express their emotions through photojournalism, poetry, creative writing, and more.

CHAPTER 12

Less Is More (Except When It Comes to Chest Hair)

So, you've got an online crush. She likes you. You like her. You've chatted. You've texted. You've tweeted. You've "liked" every photo she's ever posted on her Instagram. It's *tru luv 4evr*. Now what?

It's time to take a picture of your junk, right?

Wrong.

At some point in the past few years, courtship took a left turn. Everyone from politicians to athletes to tabloid celebrities—not to mention teenagers everywhere—decided that the best way to show someone that you like them is to take a naked selfie. A hand-bra shot, sent via text message or Snapchat, became the modern equivalent of going to first base. Dick shots? More popular than love letters.

There are a lot of good arguments against sexting and naked selfies—the demise of romance and intrigue is a good place to start—but the number one reason that you shouldn't send them? You never know where they'll end up.

Consider what happened to four teenage girls in Etiwanda, California. All four of them had sent naked photos to their boyfriends; those boyfriends then passed them on to their friends. One of those friends posted the pictures online and bragged about it on Twitter. Pretty soon the naked photos were a trending Twitter topic. Those "private" shots the girls had sent to the guys they'd liked? Not just their entire high school, but the *whole Internet* was looking at them.[8]

Every day, it seems like there's a story about someone whose revealing selfies and sexts went viral—whether it's the Miss Teen USA who was blackmailed by a guy who hacked her social media accounts and stole naked photos of her[9] or the fourteen-year-old who got charged with child pornography after sending a naked photo of his ex-girlfriend to everyone he knew.[10]

The lesson here: No matter how private you may believe that picture is, you never know where it will end up. You may *think* you're in a relationship with someone you love and trust, but things go wrong. People lose their minds. It happens all the time. Seriously, I've seen some people go cray cray for real. And then they have pictures of you. It's just a mouse click to revenge porn sites, where scorned lovers go to post the naked selfies that their exes gave them.

Think it'll never happen to you? Think again. Remember those naked photos that I sent of myself to my online "girlfriend" Megan? Well, I would soon learn that someone else entirely had them, someone whom I didn't exactly want to have them. I feel a twinge of mortification every time I think about that. To this day, I worry that somehow those photos will turn up somewhere embarrassing and very public.

According to a study by McAfee, 13 percent of all adults have had their personal content leaked on the Internet without their permission. The same study showed that 10 percent of all exes threaten to publish their former lovers'

(There was another photo without the deer head.)

naked photos online, and a majority of those go through with it.[11]

It can get even worse, believe it or not. A growing number of teenagers are ending up as victims of "sextortion." Here's how it works: A girl meets a "cute guy" online (actually, a child predator) who offers to send her a naked photo in exchange for one back. As soon as he gets her picture, he blackmails her. She needs to keep sending him sexy pictures—or even perform live sex acts over a webcam—or he'll send her pictures to everyone she knows. Her school, her parents, her boss. So she keeps doing it.

It's horrifying, and growing in scope every year.

If there's one rule of social media to always remember, it's this: Everything that you post, text, and tweet can be used against you in the future. On the Internet, there is no real privacy. Before you do *anything* online—sexting, compromising selfies, photos, and comments of all kinds—remember that it's going to live there forever, for potentially anyone to see. Your friends. Your teachers. Your boss. Your future friends, teachers, and bosses. Total strangers. *Your mom.*

————

Sexy pictures are the most obvious no-no, but those aren't the only kind of shortsighted photos posted on social media. It blows my mind how often I see Instagram photos of people getting drunk, doing drugs, and smoking weed, including high-profile celebrities like Rihanna and Justin Bieber. People think they're untouchable online, but they aren't—just ask the fraternity in Florida that got itself suspended for hawking drugs on its Facebook page,[12] or the Milwaukee teen who was arrested after police saw an online video of him getting high,[13] or the young mom who was charged with a misdemeanor after posting a "joke" photo of her baby holding a bong.[14]

Even things that seem innocuous can come back to haunt you. Consider the woman who got fired from her job after making some critical comments about her boss on her Facebook page;[15] or the high school teacher who was fired after the school board came across her Facebook vacation photos, featuring a trip to the Guinness Brewery.[16]

Instead of being your own personal, private playground, your social media pages are actually a vast, permanent resource for any authority figure that wants information about you. And these days, *everyone* does. If you are applying for a job, trust me: Those employers will Google the hell out of you before they hire you. Do you think they'll want to hire someone whose Facebook page is full of stories about their love of Adderall and Goldschläger, or their disgust for their current place of employment?

When you apply for college, the first thing admissions officers now do is plug your name into Facebook. What happens when they come across a gallery of red-cup party pics of you—even if it's on your friend's page? If they have to choose between you and thirty thousand other applicants, they'll choose the applicant who *wasn't* getting wasted in their photos. Every time.

And think about your health insurance. Sure, you may not be worrying about this yet, but at some point, you will. Those companies don't have to rely on your own self-reported health questionnaire anymore, not when your Instagram feed is a better measure of how you're really living your life. It's not out of the realm of plausibility that they would jack up the price of insurance for someone whose photographs show him smoking cigarettes, drinking heavily, and eating junk food.

"But Nev," you say, "I have great privacy settings! No one but my friends can see my photos on Facebook." Great—but friendships and relationships fall apart, and when people get angry or jealous, ugly things happen. Digital information is incredibly easy to copy and disseminate. Incriminating photos of all kinds are a very popular revenge currency.

Even if your friends *are* one hundred percent permanently

trustworthy, accounts still get hacked. Phones get lost and stolen every day. You don't want some fourteen-year-old computer nerd getting into a cab and finding your boyfriend's phone loaded with naked photos of your hoo-ha.

"Okay, fine, Nev," you say. "I'll just use Snapchat." But there is no guarantee that that picture really has been erased forever. The person who got your selfie or the snapshot of you doing drugs can always screen-grab your photo, for starters. Plus, you just sent an image millions of miles through space, bouncing across hard drives and servers. Trust me: It still exists. It's been saved *somewhere*.

Once you publish something on the Internet, you lose ownership. The information you share over your free phone apps isn't private. Those app companies *own* it. They have access to it. Your posts on social media websites? Some of these sites have privacy policies that allow them to use those posts however they want—including using your face or words to endorse something.

Heck, even the government can watch you, if it chooses to. The NSA tracks everyone's emails, texts, and social media. Get noticed for the wrong reasons, and they'll start digging up that digital file with your name on it and every beer bong photo you've ever taken. Think that sounds paranoid? Maybe. But the government has already admitted that they do it.[17]

Did you know that lawmakers can subpoena your social media account? One suspect in a murder case was found guilty in part because he'd described himself on his Myspace page as an "outlaw" and a "criminal."[18] And Facebook status updates and comments are increasingly being used as evidence of cheating in divorce proceedings.[19]

Sure, these are pretty extreme examples that probably

won't ever be relevant to you, my law-abiding friend. Still, no matter how strong you keep your privacy controls, if you ever wind up in the public eye—not just because you did something wrong, but because you become famous or even decide to run for public office (you never know!)—you can bet that someone's going to go digging. The last thing you want the whole world to see is the first thing that will be used against you.

———

Fame has really changed my approach to social media. It's why I practice consideration and awareness of everything I post before I post it. It's why I'm more respectful of other people's privacy. Because everything I say online now is potentially material that anybody could use. An offhand tweet might seem insignificant to a couple hundred friends, but in my case, it's hundreds of thousands. My tweets get picked and published in newspapers. The news media uses my tweets as a source. When I put something online, I'm essentially publishing it, signing my name to it, and making a statement.

As a result, I'm very sensitive about what I say online. I want everything that I say and post, every link that I share, to be something I can really stand behind. I never want to post anything that will be offensive, or hurtful, or shameful, or embarrassing.

In my case, because I'm a public figure, my posts can have a tremendous effect on my career and reputation. But even if you're not a public figure, you have to consider the moments when you *will* be worried about your career and reputation. Because those moments *will* happen, whether you anticipate them or not, even if it's just the manager of the local 7-Eleven Googling you before they hire you.

We live in a time when we feel compelled to document

everything we do—good and bad—without stopping to think about the ramifications. We mindlessly post photos and comments all day long, every day. We are so concerned about constantly updating our feeds—making sure we always look popular, busy, and fun—that we don't think about the consequences of the particular photograph we've just uploaded.

The outcome? Our lives, good and bad, are out there for everyone to examine, exploit, and criticize.

So what should *you* do about it?

First, realize that your online identity is very much part of your real-life identity. It's not *"just my Facebook page, where I get to be silly and funny and free with my friends."* Nope. Not anymore. That social media persona is the *first* thing that any stranger is going to encounter when they look you up online.

In other words, it's time to start being mindful of your image on the Internet. Before you post a photo, take thirty seconds to think about it. Ask yourself: What would my parents think if they saw this picture? What would my school think? My boss? Could this affect me in the future? How does this reflect on my personality? Could this hurt my reputation? Could it be considered offensive by someone?

If it could be construed as having a negative reflection on you—don't post it.

Look, I don't want you to entirely avoid expressing yourself; I'm not saying that you need to be squeaky clean and opinion free. I just want to make sure that you can justify everything you post and that you are willing to stand behind your words and images. That you consciously control your online image, rather than letting it control you.

The same goes for photos that your friends post. It's nearly impossible to prevent yourself from ending up in other people's photos these days; I'm not suggesting that you avoid all camera phones, because if you did, you'd never leave your house. But if a photo of you drinking, smoking, or partying— doing *anything* compromising—turns up on someone else's Facebook page, *untag yourself*. And, more important, pick up the phone and have a conversation with that friend and maybe ask them to take it down. It may not even be a picture; it might just be an inappropriate message. If someone makes an unflattering comment on your Facebook page, reach out to them and ask them not to do it anymore.

Yeah, I know. No fun. But they'll understand. We need to start a global conversation about the importance of privacy, and the best person to start it is you.

(Of course, it goes without saying—don't post compromising pictures of other people on your Facebook page without asking them, either. Yes, I know that you're going to tag your friends in your photos—without that habit, social media would come to a screeching halt—but be considerate and respectful.)

A second maxim to live by? The more you value your privacy, the more people will value you. Set your privacy controls on all your social media accounts at the maximum security levels. You should be sharing your photos *only* with people you really know. (And by that I mean people you have met in person and have a real-world relationship with.) Hold people to a high standard and make sure they have earned your trust and deserve to see inside your life. Remember that you don't have to whore yourself out to be popular on the Internet, especially not at the risk of humiliation.

As I've come to realize, privacy is more valuable than you think. Remember what Andy Warhol said? *Everyone wants their fifteen minutes of fame.* Well, that may have been true for the past few decades, but the world is changing fast. We are becoming such a public society that I think in the future, everyone will want their fifteen minutes of anonymity. The more wealthy and successful we are, the less accessible we'll be. That's how status will be determined.

Already, the people *I* pay most attention to online are the ones who are the most mysterious. We all know there is nothing more frustrating and exciting than seeing a cute guy or girl "like" one of your photos on Instagram, but when you go to check out their profile: Alas! It's private. It makes me want to know more. It means that woman values her privacy; she doesn't let just anybody into her life. Her exclusivity is a self-respect that makes me respect her more.

Everyone wants to be part of the club that's exclusive. So make your life exclusive. And invite only people who are worthy.

————

Okay, one final note. Ladies: Keep your tops on. That hand-bra shot is not gonna make him like you any more than he already does. Guys: No more dick pics. There's nothing romantic about a photo of your junk.

Seriously, you're not doing yourself any favors by sending pictures of yourself naked. Sure, it's easy to do. But in romance, less is more. Subtlety is *powerful*. When it comes to love, people are interested in what they can't see. When you reveal yourself in full in a photo, there's no more mystery. You've showed your cards. Shot your wad. (Figuratively *and* literally.)

A better way to be sexy and flirtatious is to be coy, to reveal only a little bit at a time. A sexy picture of your eyes is more

Dear _____ ,

You are one of the most _____ people

in my _____ .

Every time I see you, I think to myself

_____ , that _____ is
   WOW / OMG / DAMN / UGH [CHOOSE ONE]

_____ .
   OUT OF THIS WORLD / SO SEXY / INSPIRING / KINDA WEIRD [CHOOSE ONE]

You always make me _____ when
               LAUGH / SMILE / RELAX / FART [CHOOSE ONE]

I am _____ .
        UPSET / ANNOYED / HUNGRY / GASSY [CHOOSE ONE]

The best part of knowing you is that I always have a

_____to go on _____
              CRAZY / STUPID / SILLY / SPONTANEOUS [CHOOSE ONE]

adventures with.

Looking forward to the next time you _____ me.

Let's get together soon for a _____ .
                         COFFEE / DATE / SNUGGLE / RUN [CHOOSE ONE]

_____ ,
   BEST / ;) / XOXO / LOVE [CHOOSE ONE]

_____

intimate and exciting than a blurry photo of you standing naked in front of a bedroom mirror.

Guys, if you really want to impress a girl and tell her that you like her, here are a few things that are far superior to that junk shot you were considering:

- Give her an actual handwritten love note.
- Buy or hand-pick flowers and leave them on her doorstep.
- Buy her an iTunes movie rental and invite her to watch it with you.
- Make her a personalized Spotify radio station.
- Send a cool picture you took of something *besides* yourself.
- Show up outside her dorm with a boom box on your shoulders.

Better yet, rather than sending her a text message, call her on the phone. Listen to her voice. I know—crazy, right? But more can be accomplished in a ten-second phone conversation than in hours of texting.

And your best option of all? Go out. On a date. A *real* date. It seems insane that I should have to tell people to meet each other in person, but judging by what I've seen over the past few years, I do. Social media has become a fallback for all human interactions—including sexual ones—but face-to-face communication is always the superior choice. I'll never forget the feeling of sitting at a movie with a girl and building up the courage to reach over and hold her hand for the first time. The exhilaration of having her turn to me and smile might just be one of the best feelings in the world.

CHAPTER 13

Love at First Skype; Or, Nev's Rules for Online Dating

If you're alive, single, and under the age of, oh, say, seventy-five, odds are good that you've looked for love online. Forty percent of all single people are using online dating services these days.[20] A full *third* of all married couples now meet online.[21] According to one MTV study,[22] traffic to the top ten online dating sites has actually tripled in the past few years. And that's just dating sites; even people who aren't using those sites are meeting and dating online—often through Facebook or other online communities.

Online dating may take all kinds of forms now—from people who hunt for mates on JDate, to people who fall in love while blasting aliens together in *Halo*, to people who spend their days flirting with strangers on Facebook—but the one common factor is how much time and energy it can consume. Online flirtation can suck up huge swaths of the day. Relationships that would have ended quickly if the people involved actually *met* in person get drawn out for weeks or months or years instead.

Clearly, the game has changed. And we still don't know the rules.

If you'll indulge me, I'd like to propose some.

NEV'S RULES FOR ONLINE DATING

Putting Up a Dating Profile

Congratulations. You've decided to take control of your love life; you're going to set up a profile on Match / OkCupid / eHarmony / FarmersOnly / PlentyOfFish / whatever launched this month. Here are a few things to keep in mind.

1. Do not lie in your profile. Period. Don't lie about your height, your weight, your job, your car, your college, or the name of your pet iguana. You're just setting up yourself—and the person you meet—for disappointment.
2. Use pictures that look like what you *actually* look like. Provide a full body shot, not just the most flattering angle shot. Choose a few good snaps rather than uploading a whole photo album: It's about quality, not quantity.
3. Don't use your name—especially your full name—in your profile username. Don't provide an address or phone number, either. Duh.
4. If you like something obscure—a quirky band, an interesting book, a sport, or a hobby—list it in your profile. Don't be embarrassed. You never know who else might be totally into naked tennis, too. It might even be the thing that brings you together.
5. Conversely, don't pretend you like things that you don't actually like. It will make for an awkward conversation when your date brings it up. *So, you're into football too, huh? What did you think of the second-round NFL draft picks?* Uh...

6. When you read other people's profiles, be open-minded to their interests. Don't discount them because of something they enjoy. Sure, maybe you don't like dubstep music now, but you might someday.

7. Be honest, but don't give away too much. If you are overly revealing on your dating profile (or your Facebook page, for that matter), it's easy for someone to study you and prepare a perfectly crafted strategy to appeal to you. This might seem great at first, but if that's not really who they are—especially if they're just doing it to get you into bed—you're facing a lot of heartbreak down the road. You don't want a stranger to play on your weaknesses. (We've all seen *There's Something About Mary*, right?)

8. Expect the best but prepare for the worst. That's an old adage that holds particularly true in this situation. There are a lot of weird people out there. If you date online, you *will* meet some of them. But you might also meet the man or woman of your dreams...And who knows? Your soul mate may even end up *being* one of those weirdos.

When You Meet Someone Interesting

Okay, your profile is up on a dating website. You've been pinged by a cute guy or girl. They have sent you a few flirty messages; you've flirted back. Mutual interest is clear. Now what?

1. Do your research. Hit up Google, Facebook, Twitter. See what their public profile is. Make sure they aren't a

felon or married. But also don't take an offhand Reddit post from five years ago too seriously. In other words, get an overall vibe on that person, but don't sweat the tiny details.

2. Trust, but verify. Don't be afraid to do your background research on this person, and double-check what they've told you. (Refer to chapter 5, "How to Identify a Catfish.") Keep in mind, though, that there's a difference between a background check for safety and stalking someone: Get enough information to verify this person's identity, but don't try to learn *everything* about them before you meet them. Leave some room to get to know them organically.

3. Do not Facebook friend them. Instead, wait until *after* you've met them to make sure they are deserving of your "friend"-ship. You don't want a total stranger to have access to your photos and private profile.

4. Skype before meeting. Save everyone some time and make sure the person is who they say they are. This is a good chance too to make sure there's some physical attraction. There is more to attraction, after all, than looks—there's the sound of a person's voice, the way they carry themselves, body language, and so on. (On a related note: Make sure your Skype name isn't your full name.)

5. And last but definitely not least: Don't just online date, *offline* date. Meet the person as soon as possible. Remember, the Internet is the means of *finding* the person, not dating them. Give every relationship a deadline to actually meet in person. Don't be afraid to give the other person an ultimatum.

VIRTUAL CONTRACEPTION

→ YOU SHOULD DO A CERTAIN AMOUNT OF RESEARCH — AT LEAST 10 MINUTES OR SO IS ENOUGH | ON ANY PERSON YOU'RE GETTING INVOLVED WITH ONLINE, TO PROTECT YOURSELF.

The First Time You Meet

Congratulations! This guy seems to be who he says he is. He's asked you out. You've made a plan to meet. *Now* things get interesting.

1. Meet in a public place, tell people you are going to be there, and keep your phone on. Have a friend do a check-in halfway through the date.
2. Don't discount someone just because you don't feel an immediate connection when you meet them. It might be the beginning of a friendship. Or they might introduce you to someone else.
3. Remember to remain casual. Yes, you've Googled this person. You've seen their social media pages. You know a lot about them. But don't let that affect your first date. It doesn't mean you are already intimate or that you're signing up for a long-term commitment the first time you meet in person. Let a first date be a first date.
4. Give yourself an out. Tell your date that you're meeting a friend later or that you have an appointment; if you are enjoying yourself, you can always blow the "appointment" off.

5. Don't overdo it. Just like your online identity can some-times be hard to live up to, the way you present yourself on that first date can be tough to maintain if you go over-board. Look your best, of course, but look like *you*.

Forging Ahead

So, you actually like this guy. There's a physical attraction. He seems like he's into you, too. Your phone is on fire with text messages from him. Now what?

1. Take it slow. *Take it slow. Take it slow.* I can't repeat it enough. Go out again. And again. Get to know each other. Don't decide someone is your soul mate after one date. Don't change your relationship status. Don't send a naked selfie before you've gotten engaged. (Matter of fact, don't send one at all. Ever.)
2. You've gone on three dates and you're still feeling it? Great; now it's time to become Facebook friends, fol-low each other's Twitter feeds, and start "liking" each other's Instagram photos.
3. But don't let an online relationship turn into a full-time job. Flirting on Facebook with a guy you are dating—or even just like—should not take up more than ten minutes a day.
4. Don't obsess over the small things, like Instagram "likes" and Facebook comments. Yes, it's fun to exchange "likes," but they are not important in the long run. Texts, "likes," and comments are the easiest, lowest form of atten-tion; they're what people do while they're doing some-thing else (even sitting on the toilet). They don't really matter. So don't worry about how much attention you're getting from the tip of their finger (unless you're naked

together, but that's a different story). The *real* gestures are what show you they care: A phone call. Inviting you out on a date. Introducing you to their friends. Sending you a present. Leaving you a note. *This* is the stuff worth obsessing over, not messages on your Facebook wall.

I can't reiterate it enough: Online dating is just a conduit to offline dating. Even if you can't meet in person—say, you live in different cities—bring the relationship into the real world as soon as you can. Skype. Send each other letters. Talk to their friends on the phone. Send each other mixtapes.

Perhaps most importantly, don't assume that just because a new relationship isn't working out exactly as you'd hoped that you should give up. Don't assume that Mr. Perfect is out there online somewhere waiting for you. Real love is a product of trust. Trust takes work. Relationships require commitment, compromise, and consideration. Just because we now have access to millions of people around the world doesn't mean that when we find a special person it will immediately be "happily ever after."

Look, I'm not a love expert. I'm just trying to share what I've learned. And although I can make a list of rules for you, I know that there are no hard and fast rules for love. No two relationships are the same: Sometimes you have to go with your gut, feel things through, and take risks. But take the right risks.

PART THREE

How to Live and Love Offline, Too

You know me from my TV show. Maybe you've seen the documentary, too. But the version you know of me is, in many ways, the exact opposite of the person I used to be.

I don't have all the answers to life. I'm not a psychologist. Just like you, I constantly struggle with fear, insecurity, and questions about how to make my relationships work.

But one thing I do know is that I spent many years of my life heading in a direction that I didn't want, and I was finally able—with a tremendous amount of work and struggle—to take control of the big wheel of my ship, stop the negative momentum, and turn my life around. My world may not be perfect now—no one's is—but it's a vast improvement on what it was. What I did that's fairly unique was simply spend a lot of time thinking and talking about myself, both in therapy and with my friends and family.

So while I can't tell you exactly what to do with your life, I know what *I* did, and I can share what I learned along the way.

And, thanks to my work on *Catfish*, I've also listened to a lot of other young people talk about their feelings and thoughts and ideas. While other people go to med school or law school, I've been doing my fieldwork in friend school. I've spent years exploring how the Internet has become a crucial part of the fabric of friendships, relationships, and communication. I've witnessed firsthand how it can be both wonderful and terrible at once.

Yes, I know I've talked a lot about the negative aspects of social media so far in this book, but I do believe that it can be terrific. For creative people, it offers an unbelievable platform that otherwise doesn't exist, a place to share your talent and passion and to connect with people and potentially even be discovered. One of my favorite places online is Vine, a totally unbiased democratic platform where you can achieve status by earning it through your work. Some of my closest friends now are people I've met on Vine—filmmakers and musicians and comedians like Nicholas Megalis and Jerome Jarre (who now works on *The Ellen DeGeneres Show* because of Vine).

Social media is also an incredible resource for communities, as we saw during the Arab Spring in the Middle East. It gives a voice to people who are otherwise voiceless. It allows people to fight oppression and garner support for events that will alter the course of history. In the United States, it's a serious outlet for otherwise marginalized points of view, allowing people to easily share and shed light on issues of great importance without the construct and filter of mainstream media.

And while I still love the charm and satisfaction of a physical photograph, there's no question that social media has made sharing photos and experiences with your friends and family infinitely easier and more immediate.

That said, I'm trying to start an honest discussion about how social media is affecting our lives.

I don't want to scream at everyone to "get off the Internet." But that's what the TV show *Catfish* is ultimately about—encouraging people to stop looking for excitement and love on the Internet, and to instead turn off their computers and look around them. It doesn't matter whether you live on the East Coast or West Coast; a small town or a big city; in Paris, Texas, or Paris, France—everywhere that we have access to social media, people are just not spending enough time in real life anymore.

What I've learned over the past few years is that all people are looking for a deeper connection. We're looking for happiness, success, self-acceptance, and love, but despite all the time we're spending on social media, we're not finding those things there.

This section is about where you *will* find them.

CHAPTER 14

My Catfish Story, Part Three

By the time Rel, Henry, and I arrived in the Upper Peninsula of Michigan, just a short drive out from Ishpeming, we were exhausted. We'd already stopped by Megan's horse farm only to discover that it was vacant. We'd found my postcards in the mailbox, marked *Return to sender*.

In the middle of the night, we finally collapsed at a weird little motel near Gladstone, right on some lake. By this point, I knew that Megan was lying to me about more than just her music. I wasn't sure how to feel anymore. In the days since I'd accused her of sending me those fake songs, our relationship had been strained. And yet, I *still* wasn't anticipating anything really bad when I met her. I *still* thought my mutual attraction with Megan would provide for an interesting encounter. I thought the whole family would be surprised and excited to meet me. After all, they'd talked for eight months about how they thought I was the greatest, how much they wanted to meet me, how much they wanted me to meet Abby.

If this goes well, I thought, *I could end up spending time here. Or being in a relationship with her and bringing her home.* I was still optimistic, despite everything that had happened the previous week.

But a nagging voice in the back of my mind kept saying, *If she's lying about the music and the horse farm...who's to say she's not lying about being the girl in the pictures?* I did my best to push this thought out of my mind.

Rel, Henry, and I stayed up late that night, talking through the possibilities of what might happen the next day. I revealed my last and most embarrassing card—I read out loud my sext message history with Megan. I knew the texts were silly and cheesy. I even felt a little guilty about them, because she was nineteen and a virgin. It was the last thing I wanted to share with my brother. But there was no turning back; tomorrow was going to be a defining moment, no matter what happened. I figured I might as well put all my cards on the table. Within hours, this intimate correspondence would either be a mortifying moment in my past or a part of a burgeoning future.

The following morning, we got up early to make the final drive to Ishpeming. Before we showed up on Angela and Abby's doorstep, we made a few final—and illuminating— stops in town. We wanted to have as much information as possible before meeting the family so we could determine whether what they were saying to us was true.

First, we stopped at the UPS store from which Abby's paintings had been shipped, where the nice woman who worked there told us that sure, she knew Angela—*She's always shipping her paintings to New York City. I even bought a few from her myself.* Huh?

Then we hit up the town art gallery, the store where Abby's paintings were represented by the dealer and family friend Tim Hobbins. No one knew who he was; no one had ever heard of Abby.

We drove by the old JCPenney store that Abby and her family were supposedly renovating as her personal art gallery; it was empty, with a FOR SALE sign in the window.

More and more pieces of the story were starting to fall apart. It was beginning to seem like *Angela* was the family artist, not Abby. And yet, although it was crazy that Angela had been lying to me about this, that part of the story really wasn't so important to me anymore. I was there for Megan.

Still, by the time we arrived at Angela's house—a pretty two-story wood-sided Victorian with a garden full of flowers—I had suspended any expectations about my relationship with Megan. I felt like I'd pressed a mute button on my feelings. Instead, I'd taken off my lover hat and put on my detective hat. I was on alert: I was looking for the truth, hoping to be as objective and unbiased as I could be without upsetting or hurting anybody.

After we parked across the street from Angela's house, Rel and Henry put a mic on me and hid it underneath my shirt. As I walked up to Angela's front door, carrying a bouquet of wildflowers, followed by Rel with a camera, I felt a certain heart-pounding thrill that can only be achieved by going out on the edge and being a little daring.

The woman who opened the door was Angela, but not the Angela I knew. Instead of the angular, exotic-looking sylph I'd seen in the photos and paintings, the Angela I faced now was plain, a bit frumpy, and bespectacled, although friendly looking. Whereas "my" Angela looked way younger than forty, this Angela looked older. The only point of resemblance was the incredibly long hair dangling down her back.

"Megan's not here," this strange Angela blurted almost immediately. "Abby's not here." But she hugged us, introduced us to her husband, Vince—who also bore no resemblance to the youthful, hunky Vince we'd met online—and continued: "Nice to see you. But you guys shouldn't have come."

It was immediately clear that nothing was as we'd been led to believe. Abby, Alex, Ryan, and Megan weren't at the house, although two severely disabled twin boys were—Ronald and Anthony, the latter clearly not the Anthony I'd met on Face-book. Angela was obviously their caretaker, and she was gentle and kind with them, despite their need for constant attention. The house was full of paintings, although it wasn't clear who had painted them. Oh, and by the way—Angela had ovarian cancer. She was starting chemotherapy that week, she told us.

For the better part of that day, Angela did her best to con-vince us that the absent Megan was simply in Gladstone (at the house we already knew was for sale) along with her broth-ers. Both she and I called Megan's cell phone over and over, leaving urgent messages, but none were returned.

Abby was easier to locate. Angela drove us out to the lake, where Abby and a friend were staying at a beach house. Abby was the only person we'd met who actually matched the pho-tos we'd seen of her—but she seemed to have no clue what we were talking about when we asked her about her paint-ing. Instead, she seemed like a normal eight-year-old girl, gig-gly and awkward and primarily interested in goofing around with her friend.

Finally, I asked Abby how often she saw her older sister, Megan. "I never get to talk to her or anything and I don't know what she looks like anymore," she said.

At that moment, it finally dawned on me that Megan, as I knew her, didn't exist. That in fact, Angela *was* Megan. In fact, Angela was everyone. She was Abby; she was Alex; she was Ryan, Tim Hobbins, Noelle. She was every single one of the fourteen Ishpeming friends and family members I had communicated with over the past eight months. She'd written every single one of the 1,500 emails that I'd received. This entire world that I'd been so deeply embroiled in? My online love affair? It existed only in this lonely woman's head.

I didn't confront Angela with the truth. I needed to digest it first. Instead, we spent a bucolic afternoon on the beach with the kids, making small talk and avoiding the hard truth that all of us knew would eventually need to be acknowledged. We finished the day with a promise to come by again.

Back at the hotel, Rel, Henry, and I tried to parse the facts in order to nail down the truth. Meanwhile, my phone was finally lighting up with text messages from Megan: *Are you seriously at my mom's? Stay there. I'm coming home!*

The next morning, one last text message arrived, supposedly from an inpatient rehab facility called Dawn Farms:

> I can't come home, Nev. I came here with Alex to get help. I have a drinking problem and it's serious. By now you know my mom is very ill. I can't continue to do this and neither can Alex. I have my farm up for sale. Sorry I've disappointed you. Peace, Meg.

I wanted to believe it. But by this point, I couldn't.

Later that morning, we met Angela and Abby at a stable where Abby took horse riding lessons. As Abby rode in circles around the paddock, I confronted Angela. "I'd like to meet the real Angela," I said gently, as Angela began to cry. "There's nothing to be upset about. You have a great imagination. It's pretty remarkable."

She confessed to everything. Yes, there was a Megan, she told me: her nineteen-year-old daughter, who was in fact in rehab at Dawn Farms. "Megan's" life was based on her daughter's life, Angela told me, although the real Megan hadn't ever communicated with me and didn't know that I existed. The girl in the photographs was a family friend, she said. Later, I'd discover that the photos were actually of a Vancouver, Washington–based model and photographer named Aimee Gonzales, who had never met Angela; the rest of the people in the pictures whom I'd "met" on Facebook were actually Aimee's husband and friends. Angela had downloaded Aimee's entire photo gallery off Myspace and ModelMayhem.com, relabeled the photos, and repurposed them in order to fashion an alternate universe for herself.

The paintings? They were Angela's, not Abby's. My correspondences with Abby about art technique? That was Angela, too. I'd never actually emailed with Abby, although the one (very) brief phone conversation I'd had with her had been legitimate. Alex, Ryan, Tim, Noelle, and the rest simply didn't exist in any form. And Vince knew nothing about his wife's Facebook activities—he'd been told that I was just Angela's art patron, her best customer, which, being incredibly supportive of Angela's painting, Vince simply took at face value.

That night, after Angela's confession, Henry, Rel, and I sat in our hotel room and discussed what we wanted to ask Angela when we could have a quiet moment with her. We went over the previous eight months and put together a list of questions. For Rel and Henry, the question was, *How had she done it?* For me, it was, *Why had she done it?*

Why? Well, it wasn't so hard to figure out. In Angela's day-to-day life, she was a struggling homemaker dealing with the all-consuming challenges of disabled children and regretting the life decisions that had left her artistic ambitions behind—but on Facebook, she was able to live out those dreams and be the person she'd always wanted to be.

"I guess I knew in the back of my mind that this would happen," she told me on our last day there. "I thought, 'I don't want to lose this friendship, no matter what. But if I'm lying, is that really a friendship anyway?' So it got harder. And I really thought you'd just end up hating me."

But I didn't hate her. Instead, I ended up spending four days with Angela and her family, four surprisingly enjoyable days. Her family dynamic was amazing: Vince was passionate about Angela's artwork, Abby was adorable, and Angela's commitment to her kids was admirable. Angela pleasantly agreed to be in Rel and Henry's documentary. We left hopeful that we would stay in touch and be friendly.

During those four days, I was able to roll my shock and disappointment and disbelief about the loss of Megan under the table. There were moments when it would hit me that I'd actually been having an online romance with Angela, but I managed to disconnect myself emotionally. I was wearing a lot of hats simultaneously: I was an impassive documentarian working on getting this amazing material on film; a baffled lover who had just had the rug pulled out from under him; an empathetic friend trying to fully understand the woman whom I'd been so close to without knowing her at all.

It wasn't until I got back to New York City that the sadness hit me. Suddenly, I was terribly lonely. The steady stream of emails and text messages and funny posts and Gchats that had filled my days were gone. It was very quickly apparent just how much time and energy I'd been investing in Megan and her family. I had all this free time I didn't know what to do with. In the center of my life, there was a void.

I *missed* Megan.

Which maybe explains why I was so quick to pin my hopes on an alternate Megan, the "real" Megan at Dawn Farms whom Angela had told me about. When we left Michigan, Angela had promised to put us in touch with her real daughter; sure enough, within the week I'd received an email from a girl named Megan telling me how sorry she was that her mom had done what she had. She was available to give me any answers I might be looking for. Her pictures, though bearing no resemblance to the provocative Megan I'd fallen for, depicted an appealingly cute, tomboyish equestrienne.

I felt like I knew her—even though I didn't. Somewhere, in the back of my head, I began to conflate *this* Megan with the Megan I'd believed in, a faint hope that compelled me to start emailing with this new girl on a near-daily basis. She told me stories about her troubled mother, Angela, and gave me some insights into her family's tumultuous life. I wondered—if the whole character I'd fallen in love with was based on *this* Megan's reality, then maybe *she* was the dynamic, active, sexy girl I'd fallen for, and maybe now that I'd actually found her, my correspondence with her could turn into something more. As crazy as that sounds. I was reaching for something to hang on to. I was feeling lost and sad.

Unfortunately, despite the steady stream of chats and emails, it was proving hard to get Megan on the phone, thanks to Dawn Farms' restrictions on phone use. For two weeks we made aborted efforts to speak in person before it finally dawned on me that this relationship with New Megan was starting to feel suspiciously like my former relationship with Old Megan. At that point, I called Dawn Farms directly and discovered that, although they wouldn't confirm the names of their patients, one thing they *could* confirm was that their patients had no Internet access. None at all. In other words, there was no way I could have been communicating with a Megan at Dawn Farms.

Angela had lied again. And she'd also lied about the cancer, as I found out after I called to confront her. She was emotional and apologetic, explaining that there really *was* a Megan who was her daughter, but Angela hadn't spoken to her in years; that the real Megan was the result of a bad high school relationship; that Angela had been a stripper with a drug problem when she was young; and that Megan had been raised entirely by her father.

"My grasp on sanity is a thin thread these days," Angela wrote me.

At that point I started to really feel used. I could no longer justify why I was still talking to this person. I'd made every effort to be as accepting and generous as possible, and yet she chose dishonesty again and again. No one had ever lied to me like that before; I felt betrayed and disenfranchised. The low feeling turned into anger, fury that Angela had abused my trust and wasted my time. Perhaps this was a much-needed dose of my own medicine. To finally know the confusion and disappointment of being lied to and hurt; of trusting somebody only to have them deceive you again.

For too long, I'd been living my life with one foot out the door, too heavily involved in an alternate—and, as I now knew, totally imaginary—reality in Michigan. It was time to start focusing on my life in New York again.

So I reached out and got back together with Katie. I threw myself into helping Rel and Henry finish the documentary by providing every email I'd ever exchanged with Angela, recalling stories, and facilitating interviews with all the people in my life who had been affected by our relationship. I told the story of Angela over and over, at dinner parties and gatherings with friends. I relived the experience on a daily basis, hearing about it, thinking about it, and reflecting on it.

Every day I felt like I had more insight into what had happened to me. And yet I still felt lost and confused, unclear as to what I should be doing with my life. It wasn't until the documentary was complete that I began to see a bigger picture, and the positive outcome of my catfish experience grew clear.

––––––

It took over a year for Rel and Henry to get a finished version of the documentary *Catfish* together, but once they did, the feedback was immediate. They partnered with two amazing producers, Andrew Jarecki and Marc Smerling, and took it to Sundance, where it sold almost immediately. I was surprised to realize that with the success of the movie came a small amount of celebrity for me. Because I was the guy in the film, I was suddenly interesting and desirable. It felt like a lucky break.

And yet I was still at sea; especially because Katie and I had broken up after Sundance yet again, this time for good. (It was my call this time, and for a pretty shortsighted reason: I was excited by the prospect of being the star of a movie and wanted to be single so that I could fully absorb the attention I was getting.) But as feedback on the documentary started to come in, I was surprised by how people responded specifically to my behavior in the film. Viewers would tell me that I'd shown real compassion for Angela; they were impressed by my empathy. It was strange to have my choices

Left to right: Marc Smerling, me, Ariel (Rel) Schulman, Zac Stuart-Pontier, Henry Joost, Andrew Jarecki

and experiences analyzed and reviewed—and given *positive* reviews—especially at a time when I wasn't feeling particularly present in my own life.

The emails started to trickle in after Sundance, and then, after the film was released in movie theaters, the trickle turned into a flood. The sheer volume of stories similar to my own stunned me. People were looking to me for answers, hoping I could help them understand what had happened to them. They saw me as a beacon, shining through a murky fog of confusion and dishonesty.

Throughout my life I'd always felt that I would eventually find *something*—or perhaps that *something* would find me—and everything would suddenly *click*. I would know in that moment that *this* was what I'd been waiting for, working toward.

Well, I was finally at that moment.

It dawned on me that my calling—my niche, my purpose—was to serve as some sort of mediator. I could be a leader of the vital conversation about how life and relationships are changing now that we spend so much time online. My experience with Angela—and, more importantly, the process of incessantly discussing and dissecting that experience—had led me toward some deeper understanding of myself and my choices, but also of the choices we are all making in the social media age.

I found that what I could bring to this discussion—what I had brought to Angela—was empathy. *I'd been there.* I'd been on Facebook since it launched, yet even as I grew more and more "connected" with the world online, I'd still been searching for and struggling with purpose, identity, sexuality, self-esteem, and happiness. I may never have catfished anyone, but I also knew that I wasn't always honest online. I knew firsthand how hard it was to evolve as a human being—to be present, positive, accomplished, and engaged; to be kind and generous—while spending so much time on the Internet.

I still struggle with these things. I'm still figuring life out; still learning what it all means; and even now, sorting out my feelings about the whole Angela experience. Like everybody else, I'm hurting and confused. Even though I now have a life that a lot of people would dream of having, that doesn't change how I feel inside. I'm constantly trying to move toward being the person I really want to be.

But what I learned—through my own experiences and through the stories that I've heard during the past few years of *Catfish: The TV Show*—is that we all need to take a minute to really think about the choices we are making. And not just about the choices we make on the Internet. The specific challenges of living and loving in the age of social media aren't just about the things we're doing online—they are, even more critically, about the things we're doing *offline*.

Before we can live happier, healthier lives in the digital realm, we need to take a look at the bigger picture of our lives. Only once we step away from the Internet and start living in real life will we be able to find what we really want: love, connection, and self-fulfillment.

CHAPTER 15

Repeat After Me . . .

Repeat after me: *I am awesome*. And you are. You have the potential to do great things. No matter who you are, what you look like, your background or your sexual preference or the balance of your bank account: The only person holding you back is *you*. I want you to feel great. I know you can.

The first step toward that greatness is being happy with yourself, and to get there you must be honest with yourself and others about who you are.

Consider Heather, who we met on the last episode of our second season (episode 215). She was an insecure girl, struggling with her weight, who had gone on PlentyOfFish and—with a friend—created a fake profile of a beautiful woman named Claire in order to test her friend's husband's fidelity. As Claire, Heather was messaged by a guy named Mike. They chatted and seemed to have a real connection, and within a week Heather had confessed who she really was. But when Mike saw Heather's real photos, he blew her off. Not only was he upset about her lie, he simply wasn't attracted to her.

Wounded, Heather created a second fake profile—using pictures of another girl—and pursued Mike again. As Caroline, she had an online relationship with Mike for almost a year and a half. She pretended to have cancer in order to avoid meeting him, even though she lived just a few miles away. Her obsession with him was so complete that she would drive by his house and tell him about it later, even leave notes on his car.

Heather felt that she had been unfairly judged: Mike had liked her before he saw her picture. Why should it matter what she looked like? But the consequence was that she ended up wasting eighteen months of her life pursuing a guy who had already made it clear he wasn't interested in her. And in the meantime, she missed out on pursuing guys who *could* have been interested in her.

Heather's big issue with herself was the way she looked. She dealt with that by pretending to look like someone else. But if she'd used that time and energy trying to get in shape, she could have found happiness inside herself. She could have set a goal to achieve the fitness level she wanted, rather than hatching a plot to hook a guy who simply wasn't attracted to her.

(To Heather's credit, after she was exposed, she decided to change her eating habits, go to a therapist, and start a video blog as a form of self-expression. Those are exactly the right steps to take—it's just too bad that she had to mess with Mike's head for a year and a half before taking them.)

The most powerful thing you can do is learn to love yourself, to embrace and accept who you really are.

You don't have to be thin and rich and stunningly beautiful to be happy with yourself, either. We've all met those people who aren't conventionally attractive, or who carry an extra ten or fifty or even a hundred pounds on their frame, or who are dead broke and wearing shabby clothes—and yet who walk into a room and *own* it. It's because they are happy with themselves, and they exude confidence. They don't believe that their "shortcomings" are shortcomings at all; they know that they've got something special going on. People are drawn to that like moths to a flame.

We all have weaknesses—aspects of ourselves that we believe are hard to love. They can be physical or emotional. Some of these are even things that we will never be able to change—physical disabilities, family background, and so forth. Hating yourself because of these things is a waste of time. If, instead, you can accept and embrace those weaknesses, you might even be able to put them to work for you.

Take me, for example. I was diagnosed with ADHD when I was very young. It was a big problem for me in school—my hyperactivity got me in all kinds of trouble. I was terrible at doing homework. I was kicked out of three different schools. I was constantly seeking attention, trying to be the class clown. I wasn't particularly easygoing or pleasant to be around. It kept a lot of people away.

I'm also a tiny bit OCD (obsessive-compulsive), with very high attention to detail. I don't have compulsions or weird superstitions, but I am hyperaware and sensitive to my surroundings, and I want my things to be organized and clean at all times. (You could eat off the floor of my house. I'm not kidding.) I know how I want things to be and have a hard time trusting people to live up to my standards.

For a long time, I took Adderall to cope with these issues. I went to therapy (lots and lots and lots of therapy). But at a certain point, I decided to stop. I was finally functioning well in my day-to-day life. And rather than trying to change what was at the core of who I was, I decided to make those "flaws" work for me. I embraced that I was sort of OCD, kind of hyperactive, and had a problem with paying attention, and I created a lifestyle for myself that made use of those things.

Sure, I was constantly distracted. But I was also really good at multitasking and focusing on tiny details. When it came to choosing friends and work colleagues, I knew what I was good at—practical matters, day-to-day chores, tasks—so I put my personality to use and teamed up with people who were much more patient and big-picture than me. My chosen partners, like Rel and Henry, were creative and needed someone like me to help them manage the smaller stuff so they could focus on the overarching issues. The things I couldn't do, I delegated.

I'm not going to pretend that I'm thrilled about having ADHD and OCD, but I am very comfortable with them now. I know how to make them work for me instead of against me. I know how to see my flaws as advantages, to see how they set me apart from other people and appreciate that.

Of course you can be confident and happy with exactly who you are, flaws and all. You *should* be. But *finding* that confidence can take work, real work. Confidence comes from within. Some people have it naturally, but a lot of people don't.

Maybe you're reading this right now and thinking that I'm just spoon-feeding you that sound bite we've all heard a million times before: *"You're special just the way you are!"* I'm not. The self-loathing you live with every day isn't going to suddenly go away, no matter how many times someone tells you to love yourself the way you are. Nothing you hate about yourself is going to magically fix itself.

So what if you can't accept and embrace yourself the way you are? The answer is simple: Change yourself to be the person you want to be.

Almost everyone has something about themselves that they don't like, something they'd like to change. Want to hear another one of mine? I have hyperhidrosis, which is a fancy way of saying I get really sweaty. I'm terribly self-conscious about it. I worry about how I smell, and I hate ruining my shirts. Especially on TV, it looks awful. So guess what? I started getting Botox. In my armpits. It stops the sweating entirely. (Yeah, call me vain, but let me tell you, wet armpits are gross.)

So ask yourself: What's preventing you from being happy with yourself? What's that issue that's getting in the way of your life? Identify what your issue or vulnerability is. And then, if you can't embrace it, attack it! Challenge it! No matter what you do, face it head on. *Face your fears.*

It's going to take real action. If you don't have the confidence to love yourself exactly the way you are, flaws and all, you can't just *will* that confidence into existence. You can't *think* your way to being happy. You have to *pursue* that confidence, taking the steps to turn yourself into the person you most want to be. Whether it means going to therapy, or doing community service, or joining AA, or getting a makeover, or signing up for boot camp, or taking further education classes, confidence comes from knowing that you're constantly improving yourself.

It can take a lot of work. You have to invest energy every day toward your goal, whether it's maintaining a physical appearance, a lifestyle, or a psychological presence that you feel good about. That requires things like exercise, diet, cultural exposure and conversation, and informing yourself so that you can be actively involved with the world around you. It means working hard, having a good job, earning money, getting an education. Put in the effort, though, and you'll feel a hell of a lot better than you did when you were just sitting in your room, hating yourself and feeling terrible.

Self-acceptance is a challenge. But as my girlfriend, Shanee, wisely puts it, "*Life* is a challenge. We are born into this thing to be tested, and you can't avoid the obstacles that you'll come across. You need to overcome them. You need to put in the work every day. That's the way you grow as a human being."

The best way to find love is not to pretend that you look or live like someone else; it's to make yourself into the person you want to be. When you're comfortable with yourself, people *will* like you. What Heather learned, through the eighteen months of her relationship with Mike, is that you can't change other people. You can only change yourself.

————

Metaphor time, people.

For more than five years, I walked around in pain. I'm talking about physical pain—my back and neck were really stiff and uncomfortable, all the time. I went to physical therapy, but they couldn't fix it, so I figured it was muscle tension related to stress. Frankly, I was afraid the doctors were going to tell me something terrible—that I had a chronic ailment or something that required surgery—and I didn't want to hear it. So instead of dealing with it, I decided to ignore it. For years.

Then last year, I pulled a muscle in my back, and it hurt so badly that I ended up having to get an MRI. After the doctors examined the results, they informed me that I had arthritic discs in my back. It's a common problem, easy to fix with exercise and stretching.

So now I know what I need to do to fix it. That doesn't

mean I'm gonna do my stretches every day. (I often don't, to my own detriment.) But at least I know that there's a solution, and I can pursue it.

A lot of people walk around in a general malaise. We put off seeking the proper help or admitting the real problem because we don't want to deal with the potential diagnosis. We need to understand what is making us unhappy, but we are afraid of hearing the truth.

Instead, we ignore our unhappiness, distract ourselves, or manifest our issues in ways that aren't productive—whether by wasting time on social media, catfishing, binge eating, or drowning ourselves in drugs and alcohol. But, as they say in AA, the first step toward recovery is admitting that you have a problem. It's all about accepting your issues, embracing them, and facing the truth: *I am unhappy because of X.*

Unfortunately, there is no MRI for the heart. No X-ray for sadness. It's not always simple to locate the source of your dissatisfaction. But there are lots of other ways to diagnose your unhappiness, and it all starts with finding outside help.

I'm serious here—*get outside help.*

Maybe you've heard this before, but here's another metaphor: Think of yourself as a car. You need gas, fuel, and oil. When things are broken, you need to get them fixed, but you can't always fix those things yourself. You aren't a mechanic; nor should you be. Like a broken-down car, you can't simply *will* yourself to be repaired: You need proper professional attention, or you won't drive.

When you are unhappy with something about yourself, and you can't find the solution on your own, seek out the proper mechanic, whether it's in books, from professionals, or from friends. Prescription drugs. Exercise. A therapist. A life counselor. A wardrobe stylist. Whatever it is that's bothering you about yourself, there's someone who can help you resolve it. Find someone to talk to—express that sadness. Don't just internalize it. People around you might have dealt with similar problems in their own lives and might have insights or advice to offer.

And here's the best thing you can do: Use your feelings to create something. Take that energy and *do stuff* with it. Make art. Write. You need to engage with your sadness. Go ahead and express it, whether in a journal or on a blog or through photography or paintings. It will make you feel better. Instead of numbing your pain with drugs, alcohol, social media, and other distractions, convert it: Transform it into something of substance.

There's a John Lennon quote I love: "Life is what happens to you while you're busy making other plans." If you're constantly distracting yourself rather than putting in the real work needed to accomplish something, you're never going to be satisfied. Just ask any catfish who has ever been on my show. No number of "likes" or "friends" is ever going to fill you with the sense of self and confidence you're seeking.

Instead, look at yourself in the mirror and commit to bringing about the change you need.

THE TRUTH IS

I FEEL _____

(PLEASE FILL IN THE BLANK)

CHAPTER 16

Friends versus "Friends"

Here's a surprising fact: I am not on Facebook. Yeah, I know. Hard to believe.

I *do* still have a fan page there, but I turned my personal Facebook page off in 2012. After years of spending hours on Facebook every day—a lot of them digitally pursuing girls—I decided that I was done wasting so much time. Yeah, sure, I had thousands of "friends" on Facebook—but were they *really* friends? Were they worth all the hours I was spending keeping up with them?

Nope.

I'd been an average Facebook user for years—which means I'd been spending far too much time on the site. Still, until the movie *Catfish* came out, I'd mostly been using it to keep in touch with my real-life friends. But after the film was released, I started getting a ton of friend requests from strangers. At first, I loved it. *This is great!* I thought. *So many people like me!* And in fact, many of the messages I received did end up leading to the TV show, as people used Facebook to share their catfishing stories with me.

But as my Facebook friend list began to grow and fill with people I didn't know in real life, I realized I wasn't using Facebook to communicate with my true friends anymore. I was using it to chat with "friends" I'd never met and to pursue the cute girls who were friending and messaging me. Some days,

I spent hours on Facebook, chatting with girls, looking up strangers' pages, commenting on the photos of people who lived across the country. Ultimately I got to the point where I had *too* many friends—I'd hit Facebook's limit, and no one could friend me anymore.

By November of 2012, I was simply tired of the distraction of Facebook. I just didn't have the time anymore—I was too busy actually *doing* something for the first time in years. I was producing a TV show! I had a new career! And I realized I didn't want the temptation of being distracted by strangers anymore. I wanted to put all my attention into my actual real-world relationships. Instead of wasting hours every day messaging girls I'd never met (and probably never would), I wanted to spend time with the people who mattered in my day-to-day life. The people I really loved.

In the age of social media, we've come to believe that it's a good thing to have hundreds—even thousands—of online friends. We've redefined the term *friend* to mean anyone who has ever clicked a button to acknowledge our existence. But the truth is that friendship—real friendship—is hard work. And avoiding that hard work by nurturing online friendships instead isn't going to make us happy in the long run.

———

If you're young and involved in social media, you probably already know how much of a time-suck online "friend"-ship can be these days. But if you aren't, here's a quick primer on how online relationships work.

First, someone you don't know starts following you on Twitter, or Instagram, or Facebook. They respond to something that you've tweeted, or they tag you in a post. To let them know that you saw what they did and that you appreciate their attention, you go to *their* Instagram or Twitter or Facebook feed and "favorite" or "like" one of their photos or tweets or status updates. This lets them know that you've checked them out, too. The farther back you look in their feed, the more interest you express in them.

Now multiply that times dozens—even hundreds—of people.

If you're under the age of twenty-five, this is quite likely what you are doing *all day long.* (Yes, *you,* I'm looking at you. I'm looking at *you,* and *you,* and *me,* and *them,* and all of us— we're all complicit.) Every spare moment you aren't absolutely required to apply your full attention to something else, there you are on Instagram and Twitter and Facebook and a dozen other social media sites, posting and "liking" and retweeting. You do it in class. You do it driving. You do it on the toilet. It's an all-consuming, reciprocal game: If someone does it to you, you're expected to do it back, and then they are expected to do it back again. And so on. Until you're spending all day long "liking" and tagging and "poking" and commenting and retweeting, trying to keep up with the countless people who are "liking" and tagging and "poking" and commenting and retweeting *you.*

And you don't even know most of these people!

I'd love to blame social media tools for the shallow connections and massive waste of time plaguing modern life, but the truth is that we as a society are responsible for the mire we find ourselves in. We've taken the tools that companies like Facebook and Twitter gave us and completely lost self-control. As a result, social media is kind of like quicksand: The more we thrash around, the deeper we sink, until we get pulled all the way under and we drown. I know because I was starting to drown, too, until I made a conscious choice to change the way I was spending my time and energy.

These days we have a heightened sense of how connected we are. After all, we can measure exactly how popular we are from minute to minute, quantified by the number of "friends" we have. I see people judging their worth by the number of likes they get on photos, declaring it a good day if something they posted garnered more than fifty likes. Or if a tweet got twenty retweets. We are measuring our value entirely on the attention we get on social media. Instead of thinking about our real lives and what we may or may not be accomplishing there, we worry about whether we have more Facebook friends than everyone else in our class.

For centuries, popularity was a nebulous thing, hard to quantify, hard to achieve. It's actually quite difficult to be popular in real life. Just ask anyone who's survived high school. But online you can be wildly popular very easily. There's an exact metric with which to judge it. And if your real self isn't popular with a lot of people, well, you can pretend to be someone you're not—you can curate out the bad and highlight the good. It's easy to have a gazillion friends! So much easier than real life!

But what this does is isolate us and keep us from having real connections. We can see that every day when we look around us—people sitting at restaurants, looking down at their phones instead of the person across the table; friends who are together and yet not together because both of them are too busy tweeting to talk. We are spending more time milking our online popularity than interacting with the people who actually know us.

Take a wild guess which one matters more, in the long term.

———

I'd like to pause right here for a mild attack on Facebook Inc. for hijacking the word *friend*.

It used to mean something if someone was your friend. You didn't get friend requests. Someone didn't *ask* to be your friend. They just *became* your friend because you spent time with them and showed them that you cared. They were your friend because they were present in your life, active in your happiness, and supportive of your ambitions. They were accountable to you.

But then Facebook came along and decided that all that's required of someone to be your friend is a mere click of a mouse. Instead of having shared life experiences with you as part of a balanced exchange of give and take, now your "friends" simply consume your photos and status updates. They are witnesses to your life, not participants in it. Your life online is just another content stream that distracts and entertains the people you are "friends" with, and your identity is like another channel for people to flip through, admire, or judge.

How is that in any way a friendship?

Let's just admit it: Being a "friend" with someone on social media means nothing unless you actually know that person, and know them well. Maybe social media was initially conceived as a tremendous way to share photos and stay in touch with the people you know and love. Certainly some people still use it like that. And that's great! That's what it should be used for! But something vital shifted when sites like Facebook and Twitter crossed the line into *suggesting* friends for you, people you "may know" simply because you and they share a friend. Suddenly, these sites and apps were cross-pollinating groups of friends to get you even more invested in the tools they provide. (From their business perspective, when you have more content to consume and browse through, you spend more time on that app/website and they can sell more advertising.)

Don't get me wrong: It's not bad to be connected to other people. But the way we are communicating is unbelievably shallow—it's become quantity over quality. You can be "liked" by thousands online and yet have very few friends in real life. I see it all the time. It's an escape from reality, a means by which people who are unhappy are able to justify the time they spend isolating themselves. They can claim that they are online "making friends"—but these people are not their friends. They don't know anything real about them.

Have you ever had that moment when you're
updating your status and you realize that every
status update is just a variation on a single request:
"Would someone please acknowledge me?"
—Marc Maron, comedian, in his book
Attempting Normal

So why are real-life friendships important, anyway? Why can't you replace a few real-life friends with a thousand online ones?

Let's try something right now. Go and post on your Facebook page that you're sick and could really use some soup.

Then see how many people call you on the way to your house with a hot bowl of chicken noodle soup.

I am willing to bet that you won't get many responses, and if you do, they will be people posting "Feel better" or a sad face. If someone does show up at your door with soup, it's probably someone who is already a close friend in the real world. Your mom, your best friend, your neighbor. Am I right?

That's real friendship. Isn't that one person who shows up with soup far more valuable than the hundreds of other people you spend your days dithering around with online? Stop wasting your time with those "friends"—and spend more time working on your relationship with the person who is going to show up at your door.

Here's how friendship works: There's a finite amount of connection that any one person can have with the world around them. You get to choose how to distribute that time and energy. It's like your bank account of friendship. If you have a girlfriend or boyfriend, you'll give a certain value of time and energy there. And then you have your family and your best friends, who take up more value. At that point, your account is pretty depleted. So if you want to make more friends, you'll have to take value away somewhere else. You can't spread the same amount of time and energy across an infinite number of friendships.

But the Internet tells us that we *can* be friends with *lots* of people, because each friendship requires an incredibly low level of investment. If you spend six hours a day online, you can say you are "friends" with thousands of people. That's a sexy, alluring concept for many of us—who doesn't want to be able to say that they have lots of friends? But in real life that's impossible. There's just not enough in your friendship bank account.

In other words, maintaining a friendship with someone on Facebook requires almost zero effort. In real life, the moment you stop actively working on someone's friendship, that connection begins to weaken. No wonder so many people are trying to take the easy way out.

A *real* friend is someone you can count on day or night—to help carry a couch down five flights of stairs or pick you up on the road when your car breaks down. You only need two or three of them. (Unless none of them have a car, in which case you need a fourth.) I can count my true friends on one hand.

When I think about what real friendship is, I think about the time my brother, Rel, was driving up to Boston. Halfway up I-95, he pulled over at a Mobil/McDonald's rest stop and parked in a yellow no-parking zone, over a gutter, so he could dash in and pee. As he was getting out of the car, he accidentally dropped the car keys in the gutter. No key = stuck in the middle of nowhere.

Luckily, Rel had a spare key in his apartment. He called me and asked me to drive into New York City from Westchester County (where I lived) and retrieve it. So I did—I drove into the city, got the key, drove another hour and a half up I-95 in order to deliver it, and then turned around and drove right back home again. Did I mention that it was ten thirty at night when he called?

But of course I was going to do it. It was for *Rel*—my brother and best friend. There was only one person in the world who was going to help him like that: me. Anyone else would have said, "It's too late; can you wait until the morning?" or "Get a tow," or they would have looked at the clock and rolled their eyes and simply not answered the phone.

I know that Rel would have done the same thing for me, if

I were in his shoes. And I also know that there are only a few people in existence whom I could count on that way. I cherish every one of them. And trust me when I say that *none* of them are "friends" that I met on Facebook.

_____

YOU DON'T NEED A CERTAIN NUMBER OF FRIENDS, JUST A NUMBER OF FRIENDS YOU CAN BE CERTAIN OF

I've had a lot of low periods in my life (see: getting kicked out of pretty much every school I ever attended), but there's no question in my mind that the rock bottom—the absolute nadir—was the time I broke my best friend's face.

Mark had been my best friend since kindergarten. When I was kicked out of grammar school for clogging the toilets with toilet paper? He was kicked out with me. In junior high, we briefly lost touch when we went to different schools, but we reconnected in high school and grew even tighter.

When I was at Sarah Lawrence, he was a short drive away at a different university, studying film. Soon, we'd formed a little film collective together with our brothers and were making short experimental films. By the end of my sophomore year, in 2004, we had been invited to be the crew for a film that the Neistat brothers, documentary filmmakers we'd met through mutual friends, were filming in Connecticut—a documentary about their ninety-three-year-old tap-dancing grandmother.[23] We jumped at the opportunity.

After a week on location, with the four of us crashing in one tiny hotel room and working around the clock, we were all exhausted and testy. But that's still no excuse for what happened on the next day of the shoot. We were at a Radio Shack when Mark picked up a megaphone and accidentally blasted it right in my face. Annoyed, I smacked him upside the head with an open palm and stormed out of the store. In retaliation, he followed me and smacked *me* upside the head from behind.

I was caught off guard, my ears ringing. I turned and looked at him. I remember thinking, "Just walk away. Cool down." But I didn't. Instead, I slugged him with all my might, right in the face.

There was blood everywhere. I knew immediately that I'd fucked up terribly, and I tried to help him, but it was too late. The damage was done. I'd broken his nose and fractured his skull. He was rushed off to the hospital.

After we got back from Connecticut, Rel sat me down. "I'm always going to be your brother. I'll always be there for you, and I'll always love you," he said. "But I do not *like* you right now. I don't want to be friends with you in your current state." He went on to explain that I was a bully, always aggressive in my interactions with other people—not so much physically, as I was with Mark, but also with my humor and my sexuality. My jokes were usually put-downs. When I hit on women, I didn't know when to stop. And he didn't want to be around that anymore.

Ever since I was a kid, Rel had been the most important person in my life: not just my brother, but my most important friend. I'd always looked up to him and often felt inferior to him. Aside from Mark, Rel's friends had been my only real friends when I was a kid. So when he rejected me, I was shaken to my core. *Oh God, I've lost my brother,* I thought. *Even he can't pretend to like me anymore.*

It was the worst moment of my life. But when I look back at it now, I can see that it was also the most important. It shook me up. Thanks to this moment of truth from Rel, I began the long and difficult process of redefining who I was and what friendship really meant to me. I realized that because of my behavior, I'd lost the two friends who meant the most to me— Mark and Rel. It was my own fault. And if I wanted to earn their friendship again—if I wanted to learn how to be a *good* friend—I needed to do some serious rethinking.

In retrospect, I'm so happy that I had someone who was willing to be honest with me, even if it meant hurting me deeply. His lecture was the spark I needed to really start doing the hard work of becoming the better person that I am today.

It didn't happen overnight, not by any means. I may have recognized that I no longer wanted to be the jester character who makes jokes at everyone else's expense, but it took me years to make that epiphany a reality. For a long time, I just licked my wounds and sulked. But ultimately I began to formulate a plan. Thanks to Rel, I started to understand both how to be a friend and what I should be looking for in a friend. And I learned the hard way that the best way for me to grow was to surround myself with people who inspired and challenged me, and who taught me things I didn't already know.

So I decided that if I could earn the trust and affection of creative, talented, meaningful people again—people like Rel and Mark—then I would have become a decent and meaningful person myself. My goal was to be the person whom the people I admired most would *want* to be friends with.

———

My transformation started like this:

My dad was a ballet groupie. Not long after I went off to college, he got involved in a summer ballet workshop called the Morris Center Project, led by Benjamin Millepied (the talented dancer who choreographed *Black Swan*, now married to Natalie Portman), that brought dancers and choreographers together for three weeks of creative exploration on Long Island. My dad hosted three dancers at his house; he invited me to come and observe them as they rehearsed. It was fun and inspiring. It reminded me of my childhood love of dance, a passion that I'd forgotten about over the years.

Soon, I was a total ballet groupie as well. My dad and I would go to the ballet as often as we could, serving as a de facto cheering section for our favorite dancers. We'd deliver flowers to the girls' dressing rooms, make NY City Ballet T-shirts, and host annual open-invitation Christmas parties for the ballet companies. We were the Ballet Boys.

After I broke Mark's face and Rel subsequently broke up with me, my awesome dad had a moment of intuition that I needed a little focus. He got me a job working on that summer's choreography workshop as a documentary filmmaker. For three weeks, I was a part of something exciting, and I even had a film at the end to prove what I'd done. I worked hard to be a positive, useful guy, and as a result, I ended up earning my place in a very small and cool group of ballet friends. For the first time, I was included because I'd proven myself worthy.

It was a turning point: I had the epiphany that I wanted to be a part of something. I'd found an art and lifestyle that I was passionate about; a group of people that I really admired and that I wanted to admire me. They inspired me to better myself—and that's the most important quality in a friend. Even if I was still feeling insecure and confused after the fall-out of my friendships with Mark and Rel, I understood that by associating myself with people who were doing good things, I too could be involved with something great.

So I started showing up at ballet events, offering my services as a photographer and videographer. I crashed NY City Ballet galas, took pictures, and posted them on my nightlife website, TheContactSheet.com. I talked my way into any rehearsal space or ballet institution having a performance and offered my filmmaking services at no cost. I'd show up and say, "I don't see anyone making a film of your rehearsals; mind if I shoot a piece?"

I wanted to be *the* New York City dance photojournalist. And soon, I was. Not long after the fight with Mark, I got kicked out of Sarah Lawrence (like I said, my epiphany took time to set in and affect my actions), and within a few years, I was right at the heart of the ballet community, capturing it. I was the guy with the camera. Just being around these talented dancers whom I respected and admired—observing their hard work and commitment to their art—made me feel better about myself. I challenged myself to be more productive, committed, and creative. I believed that my pictures would someday be important because the artists I was photographing were going to be important.

When you find something you are passionate about, *commit to it*. Make it your whole life. Take risks. Put yourself in front of the people who are already successful at that thing. That's what I did, and it paid off. My friendship with the New York City Ballet dancers ultimately led to a creative collaboration called *Opus Jazz*, a film we shot with those dancers in the summer of 2007. That led to a job with the Morphoses dance company, which led to a project I did with Juilliard. In turn, that led to real, inspiring friendships. It led to romantic relationships with talented ballet dancers. And it led to one of my dance photographs being published in the *New York Sun*, a photo that ultimately resulted in my relationship with Angela.

I'd found a great new community of friends in the ballet world. And yet, the most important person to me—the person whose respect I valued above all others'—was still Rel.

By my early twenties, I had turned my life into a full-time quest to be the kind of person Rel would want to be friends with again. My first epiphany, courtesy of my new ballet community? I understood that choosing where I wanted to physically locate myself and trying to be in service to the people whom I admired could play a big part in achieving my goals. So I set a goal: to get Rel and his cool new business partner, Henry, to move into a shared office space with me. I figured that would be a first step toward being closer to them. And if they were spending time with me, I could better show them the positive parts of my personality, traits and qualities that I'd been working on. I wanted to be useful to them.

So I rented an office space I couldn't at all afford on a cool New York street that was crawling with interesting creative people (including the Neistat brothers, Lena Dunham, and Red Bucket Films, to name a few), and I asked them to move in. It was a huge risk—way beyond my budget, and if they'd said no, I would have been screwed. Fortunately, they agreed.

And then I went to work making myself indispensable to them. I bought ink for our printer, did tech support, cleaned up after parties—anything I could to give them more time and space for their creative filmmaking. I volunteered to assist on their projects. I humbled myself. I paid my dues, and it worked. Within a year or two, I'd earned my way into their inner circle. (It's a funny thing: When you start taking actions consistent with who you want to be, one day you realize you've become that person.) We began working on projects together, even hanging out after work. We were, once again, real *friends*.

A successful friend once gave me a piece of advice that really stuck with me. "Don't set a budget for yourself that reflects your means," he said. "Instead, set a budget for the means by which you'd like to live. And then find a way to make it happen." In other words, start to live the life that you *want* to live and *then* figure out a way to make it work. Push yourself. Rather than renting the apartment that sucks, rent the apartment that costs a little bit more and force yourself to hustle to pay for it. Maybe you'll look for a better-paying job or take a few extra risks that will help expand your life. His point was that you have to challenge yourself, otherwise you'll never grow.

I'm not saying that you should go rack up a whole bunch of credit card debt. Bad idea. You shouldn't take these words as carte blanche to go out and buy that Lamborghini you covet. But stretching, in the right context, is a good thing. Just make sure that you follow through, work hard, and are fully aware of the reality of what you're taking on.

This advice certainly worked for me. I rented that office that I couldn't afford, because I knew that I wanted Rel and Henry nearby. I created an opportunity by taking a reasonable risk, and as a result shared an office with people who would become my very good friends and—ultimately—end up making a documentary about my burgeoning online relationship with a family in Ishpeming, Michigan. If I had been sitting at any other desk, without Rel and Henry behind me, that strange experience may simply have gone undocumented and may have just been dinner conversation instead of the defining moment of my life and career.

But the most important lesson that I took away from my breakup and makeup with Rel was about humility. You need to acknowledge that there are people who are more talented than you, more sophisticated, more mature. You need to challenge yourself to meet them at their level. You don't have to like all the same things, share the same opinions, or be in the same sorority or fraternity—after all, the best friendships are a give-and-take. But sometimes the best way to make someone a friend is to recognize when they need something that you can provide. So there's a cool person you admire? Aspire to be their friend. Find a way to involve yourself in their life. Be at their service. Figure out what they need and how you can help them.

And often, simply by having access to them, you'll build a friendship that will force you to grow into a better person.

————

If I were to pick one quality that is absolutely the most important one to have in a friend, hands down I'd pick honesty. That's the final lesson I learned from Rel's tough love. We all need to surround ourselves with good people who not only inspire us, but also will tell us the truth, no matter what.

I was incredibly lucky to have family and friends who were willing to tell me the difficult things I needed to hear in order to grow into a better person. If they hadn't, I'd probably still be the dick that I was in my early twenties. Not only did Rel tell me, truthfully, that he didn't like the person I'd become, but my parents also sat me down and gave me a talking-to. Instead of helping me out in the situation with Mark, they made me pay for Mark's hospital bills and surgery—at a cost of thousands of dollars. And then they told me that it was time for me to stop fucking up, and that if I did screw up again, they weren't going to bail me out.

I am thrilled that they did that. For the first time, I began to think about the repercussions of my actions. Instead of thinking "I want it, so I'm going to do it" the way I always had, I began to consider the fact that everything I did reflected on my family and friends. My parents' brutal honesty opened my eyes to the way my behavior affected the people I loved and admired.

If you ever plan on evolving as a person, you need to surround yourself with people who will point out your flaws and aggressively challenge you to improve yourself. Sure, you can also challenge yourself, as I did, but I was always inspired first by the honesty of my friends. You can't expect to grow or change if you choose friends who aren't willing to criticize you.

Often, we try to become friends with people who are similar to us—too similar. They'll share the same interests, the same jokes, and the same habits. As a result, they won't inspire us to grow. Often I notice that lazy people hang out with other lazy people, playing videogames and smoking pot, instead of hanging out with that friend who is really hustling to get a business started. Jocks hang out with jocks, type A's with type A's, the paranoid with other paranoid types, all of us feeding one another's habits and dysfunctions. After all, for someone struggling with their weight, the less painful choice is to hang out with the friend who can commiserate over food and the number on the scale rather than the friend who eats her kale salads and works out. We don't want to hear the hard truth about the mistakes we are making, so instead, we surround ourselves with people who are making the same mistakes.

Everyone needs a friend who tells them the hard truth. And not just when they mess up, either. As you go through life you're constantly going to run into situations that are difficult and confusing and emotional. An honest opinion and some heartfelt advice from a close friend is the foundation of every good decision. (I bet that at least half of the catfish victims I've met shooting our TV show would have ended their online relationships sooner if a friend had just sat them down and given them some tough love.) When you're looking for friends, seek out people who will be honest with you and whom you can be honest with, too.

To this day, Rel and Henry remain my closest friends and collaborators, the people who tell me what I really need to hear. My parents have never had to bail me out again. And I've made new friends, too; people who inspire me and who aren't afraid of really giving it to me when I deserve it—like Max, who recently called me out when I was being unintentionally insensitive to the hardworking crew on my show. He was totally right, and thanks to him, I went to work on improving my behavior. (Even now, eight years after the incident with Mark, I'm still working on becoming a better person. It's a never-ending process.)

And I'm also happy to say that my friendship with Mark—though maybe not what it perhaps could have been—is really strong again. For my last birthday, he sent me a short text: "Happy Birthday Penis." Believe me when I say that, coming from Mark, this is a term of affection.

CHAPTER 17

How to Apologize

I come from a long line of practical jokers and goofballs. Just one example: My grandfather Marvin used to think it was funny when women put on lipstick at the table after the meal was over. So one night, after dinner at a restaurant, when the wives all pulled out their compacts to touch up their makeup, he whipped out his electric razor and started buzzing his beard right there at the table.

My uncle Michael is cut from the same cloth. Sit near him at a restaurant and at any moment you might expect a bread roll to come whizzing by your head. Once, at a fancy fundraiser, he thought it would be funny to slip the expensive silverware into the purse of the woman sitting next to him—who happened to be of some royal European descent—and pretend she'd stolen it. Unfortunately, the forks and knives had already been used, and they ruined her incredibly expensive silk purse. She was not amused.

When I was growing up, Michael's wife—my aunt Candy—was constantly scolding him about his antics. And yet she always seemed to forgive him. No matter how badly he screwed up, it didn't seem to negatively affect their marriage. I always wondered: How did he get away with it?

Finally, when I was twelve, I asked him. The secret to his ability to get away with murder? "Never forget these words: 'I'm sorry. I was wrong,'" he told me. "It's just five words, and they will end an argument every time. Especially an argument with a woman. It doesn't matter what you're fighting about, or even if you know you're right. If you want to release the tension and move forward, just say it. 'I'm sorry. I was wrong.' "

I took his advice to heart and began a long and illustrious career as a profligate apologizer.

I had a lot to apologize for. I got in a tremendous amount of trouble. I was constantly making mistakes. After my uncle clued me in to his secret, I began apologizing constantly. It was my automatic response to any mistake I made, my get-out-of-jail-free card. *I guess I did something wrong because you're unhappy and I'm in trouble, so "I'm sorry!" Now we're all square, right? I said what I'm supposed to say, and that's it!*

I soon mastered the art of the apology: how to articulately state what I'd done wrong, say that I was sorry, and convince whoever was mad at me that I'd learned my lesson and felt really terrible about it. I apologized to my friends, my teachers, my family—even the police, when I had to. I could convince almost anyone that I was sorry and that I wouldn't do it again...right up until the moment that I *would* do it again. I'd play the part of the repentant screwup until the curtain dropped, and then I'd be right back at it. It was as if I had my fingers perpetually crossed behind my back.

I was the most disingenuous person I knew: I wasn't really sorry, I didn't really regret it, and my remorse was totally false.

For a long time, my uncle's advice seemed to work. Until finally, during one of the most critical moments in my life—when I punched my best friend in the face—it didn't.

Mark was in the hospital with his skull cracked open. It was totally my fault. Everyone was upset with me. So I whipped out my usual apologies and dispensed one to everyone involved. *I'm sorry, I was wrong. I'm sorry, I was wrong. I'm sorry, I was wrong!*

For once I really was sorry, but this time, instead of forgiving me, Mark stopped speaking to me altogether. My parents didn't buy my apology. My brother didn't want to be my friend anymore. I was like the boy who cried wolf: I'd screwed up so much without changing my behavior that no one actually believed my contrition anymore. I couldn't apologize my way out of this situation, because everyone knew that my apologies were meaningless.

That's when it struck me that I'd been writing bad apology checks for years, and now they were bouncing. My apology credit with my family had run out. I was broke. My words had no value.

At that moment I realized that I couldn't just *say* I was sorry—I had to actually *be* sorry. I had to *demonstrate* how sorry I was and make sure that it would never happen again. A true apology in that situation could never be expressed in words, no matter how well-crafted. It had to be an emotional, sincere, and observable change in behavior.

There's an implied commitment when you apologize for something: a promise that you won't do it again. My uncle's advice was only half of the story. Saying "I'm sorry" *isn't* a get-out-of-jail-free card. It's just the first step toward making a change.

But a real, genuine apology *can* be incredibly effective. People are afraid to admit when they are wrong and take that hit, but the ability to confess your mistakes and take steps to address your behavior is at the foundation of all real relationships.

These days, I take my apologies really seriously. When someone (say, my girlfriend) is upset with me, I don't just immediately say "I'm sorry." (Except for farts. Apologies for farts should be instantaneous.) Instead, I take a minute—sometimes ten, a couple of hours at the most. I *think* about what the person is upset about and really consider my behavior. And only then do I go back and apologize. It takes longer, but it's done with real consideration, meaning, and self-reflection.

And then, most importantly, I try to figure out how I can change my behavior to ensure that I won't screw up in the same way again.

That's not to say that it's gotten easy for me—it's a constant process of evolution. For example, at the end of shooting season 2 of *Catfish*, I found myself in Pensacola, Florida, with the rest of the production team, shooting the Mike and Heather/Caroline episode (episode 215). It was day two of the episode—our "investigation day." On the show, this looks like a fun process, full of twists and turns. But that's because you're only seeing four minutes of what's usually an eight-hour process. The other seven hours and fifty-six minutes we're doing painstaking, frustrating, and often completely fruitless Internet research.

This is hands down my least favorite day of the episode. On that day in Pensacola, I was particularly irritable. It was the end of the summer. We'd been shooting for five months. And I was cranky. A few hours into the investigation, we finally made a discovery: One photo of our catfish, "Caroline," turned out to have been geotagged. A "pin" on the photo showed us an apartment complex in Pensacola, a big two-story building with dozens of units.

Max immediately got excited: "Oh my God, the pin falls right on unit two-twenty-three! Let's go investigate that apartment!" But I blew off his excitement, saying, "Max, the pin is just a triangulated position within a hundred yards of that spot. There are forty apartments within that pin drop. It's a dead end." It turned into a heated discussion, escalating to the point where I told Max that he was being dumb and wasting our time. In those exact words.

Max shrugged and walked out of the room. Meanwhile, in front of the entire crew, I threw my iPhone in a fit of rage, shattering it.

A few minutes later, Max came back into the room and said, "Nev, sometimes you can be a real dick. You need to be more careful about the way you talk to people. You need *all of us* to make this show. If you're speaking down to us, we aren't going to want to work with you. You gotta get this under control. You're hurting people's feelings."

At first I was furious that he'd said this in front of the whole crew. But then I realized that he was dead on. "You're right," I said. "I'm sorry. You guys are like my family on the road. I take our friendships for granted because we work together." And I vowed that from that point on, I'd make sure that no matter who I was talking to, I'd try to be as kind and respectful and humble and pleasant as I could be.

It's hard, and I'm still working on it. But Max's confrontation was a turning point for me, a moment of honesty and self-realization that changed me. This was only a year ago, but I've taken significant actions as a result. Now I try to look at every email I write before I send it. I think about what I'm going to say before I say it. I make sure I'm employing the most constructive words to get my message across.

That was a real apology—one that resulted in me working on myself and showing through my actions that I'm going to change.

––––––

If you watch *Catfish*, you know that we hear a lot of apologies on the show. Almost every episode ends with one person—sometimes both—apologizing for the lies they've told. My experience with what happens *next* is proof that saying "I'm sorry" is only the first step in repairing your relationship.

The ugly truth of our show is that our hopefuls rarely forgive and forget. And why should they? This catfish that they've been communicating with for months or years has lied to them! Just saying "I'm sorry" isn't going to cut it, no matter how much the catfish professes their remorse. After all, if the catfish truly understood that what they did was wrong, why didn't they apologize sooner? Instead, for their entire relationship, they chose to hurt, deceive, and betray the trust of the person they supposedly cared for. So even though they are admitting that what they did was wrong, that isn't going to absolve them of their sins.

Instead, an apology from the catfish is just the first step. What needs to happen next? A total restart. They need to build a whole new relationship that's filled *only* with actions that express how contrite they are. Only once the catfish has reintroduced honesty and trust into a relationship can it reboot and grow again. After that, anything can happen.

The majority of the relationships we investigate and expose on *Catfish* never get past that initial "I'm sorry." The catfish apologizes, but the apology is empty. Nothing changes. The relationship is over for good. The catfish goes back to their life as it was before; maybe they even go back to catfishing.

Every once in a while, though, we expose a catfish who uses their apology as the jumping-off point for a whole new way of existence. And these moments can be truly inspiring.

Chelsea was a teenage girl who, for years, had been pretending to be a man online (episode 101). Using the fake Facebook profile of a male model named Jamison, she cultivated an online romance with a girl named Sunny. When we exposed her on the first season of the show, Chelsea wasn't apologetic at first. Only after we broke down her protective wall did she apologize. Sunny even accepted her apology. There was talk about the two remaining friends, and at first they did, but it fizzled out quickly. The trust just wasn't there.

But Chelsea took her apology seriously, and she went on to turn her experience into a real, positive, life-changing moment. She decided that she was finished with pretending to be someone she wasn't on the Internet. Instead, she embraced who she really was, and came out to her community as a lesbian. And then she started an online support group, helping other people like her. She now runs a Twitter support page. She's constantly fielding emails and phone calls from other teenagers who are confused about their sexuality and playing with false identities; she's become a real source of strength.

In her case, an apology *was* the starting point, rather than an end goal.

———

A lot of people avoid apologies altogether. It's easier to pretend you didn't do anything wrong than it is to apologize and have to address your mistakes. But the truth is that an apology can be incredibly cathartic. It's a chance to start fresh, even to become a better person. It is, in other words, a really great opportunity—even if it doesn't feel that way.

We're all familiar with that awkward, uncomfortable moment when you're in the room with someone you've hurt and you *know* you need to break the ice and apologize. Whether your parents are upset because you broke something or your girlfriend found out that you cheated on her, broaching that conversation can be really tough. But when you do, it's a relief to finally have it out on the table, rather than eating you up on the inside. Once it's out, it can be addressed, and only then can it be *resolved*.

But some people just won't do it. They let it linger. Tension builds. And relationships get really toxic because there's something festering, invisibly, that everyone is trying to ignore. I constantly meet people who aren't talking to their siblings or their best friends because they got in a fight and neither was willing to apologize. A day or two becomes a week. A month. Years go by. And what could have been resolved easily with an apology from both sides instead leads to a lifetime of bitterness and regret.

It may seem counterintuitive, but the fastest way to feel better is to be accountable and take responsibility for your mistake. It's like washing dishes—the longer you put it off, the more it sucks. Those dishes are never going to go away. They just get grosser and grosser, piling up higher and higher until you deal with them. But if you address them right away? The work is fairly painless. Your kitchen is clean, and you feel great.

Here's an example: My freshman year of college, I discovered a four-room storage basement in my dorm that the maintenance men had forgotten to lock up. I quickly appropriated two of the rooms as a party pad. I cleaned them up and dragged in a sound system, a minifridge, furniture, and fans. I decked the space out. And then I threw parties for all my dormmates and friends.

I totally got away with it, too, until the maintenance men came back and discovered my lava lamps and sound system. They locked the basement and put up a sign that read THE PROPERTY IN THE BASEMENT HAS BEEN CONFISCATED. Everyone in my dorm began to freak out: *What should we do? What if we get in trouble?* My friends began to worry about getting thrown out of the dorm.

I decided to curb the rising drama by going to confess. I walked up to the administration building, knocked on the door of the student activities director, and, to his surprise, said, "Look, I'm sorry about what happened. I know I shouldn't have done it. But can I get my stuff back?"

It's true that at this point in my life, I was handing out apologies left and right without changing my actions. Still, I took responsibility for what I'd done instead of hiding, even if I was not yet mature enough to follow through with changing the behavior that led to the apology.

It wasn't as if I skated off without punishment: I got put on housing probation. Still, it could have been a lot worse. By taking responsibility and apologizing, I quashed the whole issue. The drama blew over within a day or two, rather than escalating into a finger-pointing session that might have ended my friendship with my dormmates. Who knows, people might even have been expelled. Instead, my dormmates were relieved that I'd taken the fall, and we all moved on. It was cathartic for everyone.

I even got my stuff back.

Human instinct is always to avoid drama. But raising your hand when you are responsible, and raising it right away, is *always* the best way to deal with an issue. Because the problem isn't going to go away on its own. Even if you are able to operate "as usual," an unresolved issue will continue to weigh on you and the person you've affected. Once you've stepped up, taken responsibility, and apologized, not only can you start figuring out how to fix your problem, but you've also taken away the reason for the other person to be upset with you. Which, in turn, allows for healing the relationship.

So in a way, my uncle Mike was right after all. When used appropriately and sincerely, an apology is the best move you can make. It puts you on higher ground. It's a surefire way to feel better. Even though it might lead to a difficult emotional conversation that you'd rather avoid, an apology is always the start of a better life.

The sooner you learn to do it, the sooner you get to the good stuff.

CHAPTER 18

On New Year's Day of 2012, I woke up with the blinding sunshine of a Florida morning streaming straight into my face. Where was I? Oh yeah: the guest bedroom of my father's condo in West Palm Beach. My temples throbbed; my tongue tasted of sour alcohol; my body odor was beastly. I could feel a wicked hangover coming on. And—oh crap—I wasn't alone.

Next to me was a girl. I knew her name (well, I knew her first name, at least) but barely anything else about her. She looked as rough as I felt—her mascara smeared, her face puffy with exhaustion and booze. There was some kind of crusty infection in one of her eyes. Pinkeye? As I looked at it, I could feel my own eye starting to itch. Served me right.

My memories of the previous evening were hazy. There had been a nightclub and too much alcohol. I remembered hopping in a taxi to my dad's place with this girl in tow, and I also remembered having drunken, passionless, downright awful sex. So bad that neither of us had even finished what we'd started: Thanks to the amount of alcohol in my system, I wasn't exactly fully operational.

Looking at the girl asleep next to me—someone I didn't care about and wasn't even particularly attracted to—I felt gross. *This isn't working*, I thought to myself. *I'm never going to find the love of my life by picking up girls and having meaningless sex with them. Something needs to change.*

It may sound extreme, but in a moment of clarity, I knew exactly what I needed to do: I had to write off sex. It would be my New Year's resolution! *A vow of celibacy.* I liked the way it sounded. I felt *relieved*. It was simple: I would avoid all sexual contact for a year. No sex. No kissing. No flirting. No nothing.

It's not like I'd been a total man-whore, but I wasn't exactly a saint, either. To put it delicately, I'd had enough sex to feel compelled to make a list with the names of all the girls I'd done it with, so that my sexual partners didn't just become an accruing number. It seemed like a good idea: I wanted to remember who those girls were and where I was at the time. Maybe that in itself was a sign that I'd had sex with a few women too many.

But that was only part of the problem.

I was a notorious flirt, and had been since I was eight or nine years old. I'd always had confidence beyond my years. I'd taken to heart my dad's advice about women: "Just tell them what you think of them. Women love being told that you think they're beautiful." I had no shame about approaching women. If a woman was even remotely attractive to me, I would flatter and flirt—to the point where women would often feel uncomfortable.

By the time I was in my twenties, my sexuality was out of control. I cheated on my girlfriends. I flirted with friends' girlfriends. I had one-night stands.

And then there were the women on Facebook.

I had categorized a special group called "Cute Girls" on Facebook—my digital "little black book"—and I would browse these profiles on a regular basis. When I met women, in real life or online, I'd file them away in that Facebook group and then I would chat with them, text with them, conduct distracting Twitter flirtations. I wasn't actually dating all of them at once (most of them I never even saw in real life), but I liked the idea of always having a number of girls on the hook. After all, my dad had always encouraged me to be assertive and outgoing, to approach ten girls in order to get two phone numbers. "Enough to keep you busy," he'd say.

I loved the high of pursuing someone. The challenge of figuring out what to say. The hunt. The conquest. I made the pursuit of women a part-time job in order to justify how much time I spent on it. (And to justify the amount of time I *didn't* spend doing other, more productive things. Like working.) I pretended I was looking for a girlfriend; and sure, maybe I was. But I was going about it all wrong. It was like pulling a slot machine trying to win the jackpot. It just doesn't work. You might get a couple coins back and feel like you're getting closer, but you're not.

My relationship with Megan epitomized all of this. It was

surface, fun, seemingly intimate but ultimately shallow. It felt exciting, and sure, I had told her some secrets, but the relationship wasn't based on anything real or honest.

You'd think that experience would have taught me an immediate lesson. It didn't. Instead, as the *Catfish* documentary came out and my new notoriety helped me meet more women, I became even more cavalier. I broke up with Katie, my long-term girlfriend, because I thought I should be single and free (a decision I ended up regretting). I'd make dates with women and then skip out on them the minute I found something or someone more interesting to do. I was *that guy*— the unpredictable, selfish bachelor dude. (Trust me: You're glad you weren't dating me.)

By the time New Year's 2012 rolled around, my behavior was at its worst. And when I woke up that morning, hungover, with an itchy eye and a deep sense of shame, I knew it was the moment to find a new way. I was about to start working on *Catfish: The TV Show*, and I needed to focus all my energy on that opportunity. I wanted to clean up my act, eliminate the distractions in my life.

A vow of celibacy just made sense. It would be the cleanse I needed.

My friends were in shock when I told them. A group of them even put together a betting pool: two thousand dollars said I wouldn't make it the full year. I laughed along with them, but I knew that it wasn't just about keeping it in my pants for 365 days. It was about changing my behavior so that I was no longer interacting with women on a sexual level only. Instead, I would talk to them, listen to them, have (gasp!) meaningful conversations. I didn't ever want to have empty sex again.

I deleted my "Cute Girl" group on Facebook, and then, not long afterward, deleted my Facebook account entirely.

At first it was hard, but a month into the experiment, I started feeling really good. And then I started feeling great. I actually felt more confident about myself now that I didn't need a woman's attention to boost my ego. I enjoyed surprising women by *not* flirting with them—and it turned out that being the guy who *didn't* hit on them just made me more interesting. (Bonus! More women interested in me! Too bad I couldn't take them up on it.) Being in control of my sexuality felt awesome, and people noticed it. They were surprised at and delighted by my new energy, and that made me feel even better about myself.

You could argue that I also got a kind of thrill out of trying not to be sexual with the women I met. Maybe that's true. But—if I were to make an analogy—it was the difference between the way a lion hunts to catch and devour its prey and the way a squirrel collects and stores nuts for winter. I understood that I was investing in a longer-term, more sustainable satisfaction rather than a quick rush.

I was finally learning how to be comfortable alone. Nights when I went home by myself—nights when I normally would have felt lonely and texted a Cute Girl—I was now happy just watching a movie and going to bed. Being by myself was more satisfying than the inevitably empty exchange of casual sex, I realized. For the first time, I started to really like myself.

And that's when I finally found love.

Shanee was a woman I'd been dating on and off since the summer of 2011; a cool indie musician with a face straight out of a Botticelli painting. At first, I'd treated her awfully. As she'd told me during a quarrel not long after we started dating, "You are a selfish and self-centered guy who doesn't know what you want and pretends to be happy but deep down is really just afraid and lonely." She had me pegged, but I wasn't ready to hear it yet, so our relationship stalled after just a few months. Still, her words stuck with me, and after I took my vow of celibacy, I decided to make an effort to really build a friendship with her. Best decision ever.

Our friendship began to grow. I respected how she challenged me about what I was doing, forced me to answer hard questions about myself, and helped me realize that my aggressive sexuality was just a way to distract myself from my loneliness and fear. During my conversations with Shanee, I started to see that I'd never felt the connection to my girlfriends that I was capable of. I'd been using my "joie de Nev-re" to keep things very surface-level. I'd filled my life with things that were fun and appealing to girls—I had a motorcycle, access to my dad's weekend home in the Hamptons, a big social circle—but I didn't actually open up to anyone, online or off. I was never honest with myself and as a result couldn't be honest with them.

But I was being honest and vulnerable with *her*, for the first time in my life. We had a few more false starts, but by the summer of 2012 I began to feel real love for Shanee. And that's when my vow of celibacy started to get hard. Really hard. We would snuggle and take naps together, but believe me: It's not the same thing. Although Shanee supported my celibacy, she thought it was crazy to deny myself. "Why are you really doing this?" she would ask me. "It's not to see if you can go a whole year. That's stupid. If the point is to feel love, then when you feel that, you're done."

She was right. And so after 265 days, we made love. It was long enough.

(For those of you who bet against me, feel free to send me a PayPal invoice.)

———

I learned a lot of things during those 265 days of celibacy—including how much money I could save when I wasn't trying to seduce girls with overpriced cocktails at pretentious mixology bars—but the most important lesson was this: Being ready to love is all about tapping into the power of vulnerability.

Loving somebody isn't just about saying the right things, or just "being there." In order to really show someone that you love them, and to let them love you, you need to be vulnerable and open. That's scary. Often it means admitting that you don't know something, that you're upset and confused and afraid. It means exposing your weaknesses. Admitting when you're wrong. Allowing yourself to trust someone else with your most sensitive, deepest, darkest feelings.

Social media can get in the way of all this. Facebook and Twitter present a very unrealistic playing field where people are meant to interact and share but are never expected to actually conduct a meaningful exchange. It's easy to go on Facebook and present ourselves in a way that we think people will like. To be the best version of ourselves. In my case it was, *"Hey, I'm Nev! I'm this confident guy with a fun life!"* I never thought it would be in my best interest to expose the fact that I was confused and felt lost a lot of the time and was unhappy with who I was. Who wanted to hear *that*?

Instead, I presented a facade and absorbed "affection" from all those Cute Girls—but it caused more harm than good. It distracted me from what's real.

Here's the thing: You can *control* your Internet profile. You turn it on and off, you choose what to say and delete, and when you are uncomfortable you can log out. Real relationships aren't like that. By being so invested in our "easy" online selves, we often avoid taking the time to understand our more challenging actual selves.

Remember your blankie from when you were a kid? Your mom probably still has it in a closet somewhere. It's gross, and it smells, and when you look at it now you realize how flimsy and insubstantial it is. But back then, it was everything: the friend that kept you safe from monsters in the dark, from scary situations, from feeling vulnerable. It was a crutch.

It's not so adorable when you're dragging around that bedraggled blanket as a twenty- or thirty-year-old, though. So instead, as adults, what do we use? We're still afraid of being vulnerable—especially in love—so we've found a new crutch in the Internet. Another world, full of "friends" that make us feel safe. But social media is kind of like that stinky blanket: an inanimate object that doesn't give us real emotion or affection. Maybe it makes us feel less vulnerable, but that's only because it's distracting us from the important stuff. It's the grown-up equivalent of pulling a blanket over our head in the dark.

Connections and friendships can take all forms, and social media can be an excellent way to meet someone, but the truth is you're never going to have a meaningful relationship if you aren't willing to take it beyond the digital realm and be vulnerable in front of a real, live person. Social media provides the illusion of intimacy, but it doesn't deliver the real thing. If your digital friendships are replacing your real-life friendships—and if your profile persona is replacing your real-life personality—it's time to have some real talk with yourself about whether or not you are doing the work that will bring you real satisfaction.

With "Megan," I was in love with a Facebook profile; an idea; a voice on the phone. I was never really open and vulnerable with her; and so I was never really in love with her, even though I believed I was. Phones and computers are a filter, and there's no filter in real life; I never had to expose myself to her in an honest, face-to-face environment with a real risk of judgment. In the end, neither "Megan" nor I had any clue who the other person was.

It took disconnecting from the Internet and going out into the real world—disengaging from the fun online persona and really working hard to be more vulnerable—for me to find real love.

> *The rise of online-only relationships [has created] a*
> *phenomenon I've begun to call Soul Mate in a Box.*
> *A Soul Mate in a Box (Smiab, for short) is a person*
> *we rarely if ever meet and in some cases never speak*
> *to, but to whom we feel closer than anyone else....*
> *We're always searching for new ways of finding*
> *love that don't involve having to feel insecure*
> *and vulnerable... and we're fooled into thinking*
> *this may be a better and truer way of having a*
> *relationship.*
> —Daniel Jones, editor of the *New York Times*
> Modern Love column, in the *New York Times*

This is a book about friending yourself. If you are still reading (as opposed to Instagramming photos of your cat), it's because you are curious about how to better understand and live a life that is real, honest, and fulfilling. And sure, we need to be real and honest in the ways that we interact online—but we also need to be real and honest with *ourselves*.

What does it mean to be realistic with yourself? Sometimes it means taking ownership of your problems and saying, "This sucks, I'm bad at that, I don't like who I'm being right now." Or "I'm unhappy, what am I doing wrong, how can I fix it?" We need to stop pretending to be happy online and figure out how to *really* be happy.

Casey Neistat made a great short film about being a frequent flier on American Airlines. He flies so often that he gets treated like a king, gets tons of perks, and almost never pays for a flight anymore. He says that airlines are like women: None of them are perfect, but when you commit to one of them, that's when you start to see the rewards.

I know that *I'm* not perfect. And that there's no perfect girl. No perfect guy. No perfect couple. There are just people who are willing to try—to accept and compromise and see through the superficial to what really counts. It's never going to be easy. Any real relationship has issues and speed bumps. But the only way you'll be able to achieve a meaningful connection is if you're willing to commit and put in the work—with your partner and with yourself.

My celibacy vow started with a commitment to not be sexual, and right away that felt good. And then it was a commitment to be more communicative, and that felt great. And then it was a commitment to try to understand what I was doing and what my actions actually meant. And that was tremendous. I learned that the unbelievable satisfaction and excitement that come from just choosing to commit—from giving everything I have—is one of the best feelings in the world.

Everything starts with a decision, a simple moment: Am I going to do this? Yes or no? The only way to change and learn, to discover who you really are and be happy, is to go for it.

So what did I learn from my nine months of celibacy? That being ready to love has nothing to do with anybody else and everything to do with yourself.

> *Your task is not to seek for love, but merely to seek*
> *and find all the barriers within yourself that you*
> *have built against it.*
>
> —widely attributed to Rumi, Sufi poet

CHAPTER 19

Relationships and Self-Esteem

Hi. My name's Nev. And I'm a jerk.

Actually, it's fairer to say that I *used* to be a jerk. Specifically, I was a jerk to women. Even more specifically, I was a jerk to my (now) girlfriend, Shanee. When I met Shanee, in the summer of 2011, I behaved like one of *those guys*—the kind of guy you tell your friend she should dump because he just isn't treating her the way she deserves to be treated.

Shanee deserved a lot more from me than I gave her, but I didn't realize that at first. Instead, I was totally inconsiderate. I dated other women. I'd talk about how cute other girls were right in front of her. I'd text her instead of calling her. I'd make plans and then cancel them. We lost touch for a long time, for good reason. And then, after I took my celibacy vow and reached out to Shanee again, I told her that I wanted to be "just friends"—and yet every time we were together, I would try to kiss her neck or hold her hand.

My reservations about being in a relationship with Shanee were petty, at best. I had decided right off the bat that she was not my dream girl. She wasn't my physical type, to start: Having been in a three-year relationship with a professional ballerina, I was used to women who were outrageously toned and lean. Shanee had a more feminine figure. And she was an indie musician whose music I wasn't particularly moved by at the time. (I've since come to love her music!)

Tactful me, I actually told her this. "What you do doesn't excite me. It doesn't turn me on," I said one day, not long after we reconnected post–chastity vow.

But her response to this surprised me. Instead of getting pissed off or hurt or equivocal, Shanee made her determination perfectly clear. "Well, listen, I don't care what you think," she said. "I chose to follow my heart's desire even though it's not practical or profitable. I believe I will succeed because I have something to say."

At that moment, I began to seriously respect her. She had held her own against my criticism without backing down. Not only that, but she soon began to draw the line when it came to my completely unacceptable behavior. "You can't tell me you're going to meet with me and cancel at the last minute," she informed me. "You can't talk about cute girls in front of me. And I want you to talk to me on the phone instead of just texting me all the time—that kind of communication isn't real."

Every time Shanee challenged or confronted me, it separated her from all the other women I had dated. She was elevated, in my eyes, because of her confidence and self-respect. The more she drew the line with me, the more my interest in her grew.

Finally, she gave me an ultimatum. "What are you *doing*?" she said one night when I was attempting to kiss her neck again (yeah, it was getting harder and harder for me to maintain my chastity vow). "Look—I'd love to be your *friend*, but that's not what's going on here. I have feelings for you. If you acknowledge that I'm your girlfriend, and that this is how we're behaving, we can hang out again. Until then, I'm not going to spend time with you, because you're not respecting my needs."

For a few months after she laid down the law, we didn't speak. And I missed her terribly. I began to realize how important she was in my life; how much I wanted her in it. I reached out to her again. "I don't have many friends," I told her. "Our relationship means so much to me; please stay in my life and forgive me for being an asshole."

Maybe I wouldn't have chosen Shanee out of a potential-girlfriend lineup before, but I was starting to realize that what was inside her mattered far more than any idealized fictional girl. She *was* beautiful, of course. But the sexiest thing in the world is confidence, and Shanee was fully aware of who she was and *happy* about it. Not only that, she had the self-esteem to not let me walk all over her.

"We love each other for who we are, and it doesn't matter what we really look like, because love is on the inside." I've heard this line so many times from catfish on the show, but it's not true—at least not in that *Beauty and the Beast* Disneyfied way. Looks *do* matter when it comes to physical attraction. *But—* and this is a big *but—*if you're really serious about being in a relationship, your preconceived notion about how your part-ner should look doesn't matter quite as much as you think it does. Remember earlier in the book when I said that physi-cal attraction is key to romantic relationships? This is the other side of that. A chemical reaction between two people is essential—but it can come in an unexpected form. Sometimes one person's attraction to another has more to do with what that person projects to the world than it does with any spe-cific physical attributes.

What matters most? Self-respect. Confidence. Strength.

Shanee's confidence was attractive to me: It was what I wanted in myself. And her self-respect was what ultimately caused me to fall in love with her.

———

When you take a look at my mom, it makes sense that I was drawn to Shanee's confidence. My mom is also an incredibly strong, self-assured woman, and her positive influence on me has resonated through every relationship I've ever had with a woman.

My mom's confidence and belief in herself is blatantly obvious in everything she does—from riding a motorcycle to getting tattoos (she has lots), from her lifelong love of art to the eclectic way she decorates her home. She's gone back to school twice as an adult: once for a continuing education course in film production at NYU, and again, at age fifty-five, for a masters in social work. She's gone through several careers, and now she runs a chapter of the terrific nonprofit Leave Out Violence, which is working to end the cycle of violence youth to youth.

I never knew my mom when she was a teenager (obviously) but from what she tells me, her sense of self was severely tested when she was in high school. She was diagnosed with scoliosis at age fifteen and had to have her spine fused, top to bottom. The doctors made her wear a full back brace—you know, the Elizabethan collar that you see in movies about nerd kids? Yeah, that. *Shudder.* Before the brace, she had been a ballerina; after the brace, she was an outcast. But she kept her head down, focused on getting out of there, and made it to a great liberal arts college—even with people sticking magnets on her brace in the high school hallways.

By her early twenties, she was married with two kids (yes, I'm referring to Rel and myself). She wasn't happy, though. So, at age twenty-six, she decided to leave my dad and raise her kids as a single mom. It was a courageous move to leave behind the security of marriage, going against both societal pressures and the urgings of her mother.

Her clarity about what she wanted worked in her favor. Within a few years, she'd met the man who would be my stepfather, Sheldon. Once again, she set a high bar for herself: He was still technically married at the time, and she told him that she wouldn't date him until he was officially divorced: "I don't want to be a part of your issues," she told him.

So he got divorced in order to date her. And then, when he wanted her to marry him, she made him ask her a half dozen times before she said yes.

My mom knew what she wanted from life and wasn't afraid to set boundaries for herself. She didn't worry too much about what the people around her would think. I'd be lying if I said that my mom didn't care *at all* about what people thought about her. But she didn't let that get in the way of pursuing the things she wanted. She wasn't afraid to try things. She had a very strong sense of who she was. Her self-respect was—and still is—apparent to everyone around her.

———

It's not a great time to be dating. We "hook up" instead of going out. We text and text without ever really speaking. We don't make plans until the very last minute, because it's so easy to avoid the commitment of setting a time and place.

Meanwhile, we bend over backward in order to be loved. Instead of saying, "This is who I am and if you don't like it, fine," we pretend to be things that we aren't. We lower our standards. Both men and women do this, but I've witnessed a lot of women in particular sell themselves short. They buy into the Hollywood stereotype of being passive and waiting for Mr. Wonderful to sweep them off their feet. They start changing their priorities in order to be with a guy they really like. They worry more about pleasing the person they're dating than about pleasing themselves.

I'm sure you have a friend who does this. A girl who puts up with a guy who texts her at 2 a.m. for booty calls but ignores her the rest of the week. A girl who pretends that she's fine spending her "one-on-one time" with her boyfriend, watching him and his friends play videogames—because she is afraid to insist on going out, just the two of them. A girl who acts as if it's totally fine that the guy she is dating is never nice to her in public, because she secretly believes this negative attention is better than no attention at all.

As a man, let me tell you: Men aren't attracted to this kind of self-effacing behavior. In fact, it's the opposite. When you hold your own and know yourself, when you recognize what's important to you and are faithful to that above all else, *that's* when real men take you seriously as a human being. When you respect yourself, the world will respect you back. *You* set the stage for how you want people to treat you.

For generations, women have been conditioned to be adaptable to the men that they are with. Men have been conditioned to be the opposite—to be the leaders. But times are changing; the world is waking up. Roles have shifted a little. Men are more like the stereotype of "women," and women are more like "men." This is a great time for women to hone their sense of self, and find a real partner who loves them for who they are.

Far too many people are looking for the right person,
instead of trying to be the right person.
—Gloria Steinem, feminist activist

Unfortunately, the age of social media is making that shift harder than it should be. Instead of being forthright with the people we are dating, we try to glean clues from their Twitter posts and relationship status updates. We communicate via texts instead of phone calls. We spend our time together on Gchat and Facebook instead of going out on actual dates. A relationship that's based primarily on digital communication is not one that's rooted in confidence and self-esteem. It's about hedging around commitment, keeping your options open, and avoiding the hard realities of dating.

The culture of commitment-free digital communication may make it more difficult than ever to assert yourself, but confidence and self-esteem will always break through the noise. After all, if a guy balks when you ask him to call instead of text, is that really a guy you want to be with in the long term? Only when you raise your standards, assert your needs, and get your relationship offline will you finally find real love.

———

You can't rely on someone else to feel good about yourself. If you judge your worth based on the person you are dating or the people you are friends with, you will never be happy.

Love isn't the answer, either. Growing up, we're led to believe that love is a fairy tale. Love solves everything: Find it, and you're set for life. We believe in love at first sight, and that once you meet that perfectly fitting "soul mate" the rest is easy. There's no need to work on yourself, because the person you've found will love you unconditionally.

That couldn't be farther from the truth. In reality, relationships require constant care and maintenance. And you as an individual have to challenge yourself to grow and improve so you can bring that self-knowledge to your relationship. The only way to keep things interesting is to keep challenging each other.

Love alone cannot sustain a meaningful relationship. Rather, the most important part of a relationship is communication. You need to be able to have a really good, open dialogue with the other person. (Same goes for your friends!) Be honest, and be willing to address issues as they come up. Because there are *always* issues.

My relationship with Shanee was the opposite of the fairy tale. It was not love at first sight; things grew slowly, and making our relationship work was hard. And still is! But I've learned that things don't need to be perfect. There just needs to be a connection. There needs to be a willingness to do the work a relationship takes. And there needs to be confidence that you can get it done without losing yourself in the bargain.

CHAPTER 20

You Only Regret the Things You Don't Do

M_y friend Casey Neistat was born in New London, Connecticut, to a lower-income family. Like me, he was a troublemaker when he was young. At age fifteen, he got his girlfriend pregnant. By the time he was sixteen, he was already a dad. He dropped out of high school in order to work, and got a dead-end job washing dishes at a local diner. He lived in a trailer park with his son and his son's mother. He was on welfare to make ends meet.

That could easily have been the end of his story right there—going nowhere fast.

But that's not what Casey wanted from life. He had drive. His older brother Van had graduated from college, moved to New York City, and found a job as a studio assistant for an artist named Tom Sachs. When Casey heard about what Van was doing, he thought, "I can do that." So he drove to New York City, lied to Tom Sachs about his experience, and got a job as an office assistant—cleaning, organizing, and making more than he'd been making as a dishwasher. He was now surrounded by really interesting people who inspired him; meanwhile, he was also committed to helping raise his son, and went back to Connecticut every weekend to spend time with him. It was hard, but he found a way.

In not much time at all, Casey and Van had saved up enough money to buy an early iMac—the first computer you could edit video on. They maxed out their credit cards, bought a video camera, and started making short films. The first film they made was a rant about the iPod—one of their favorite toys—and how the battery was irreplaceable (when you called Apple to complain about the short battery life, they simply told you to buy a new one). Casey and Van put their film online, and it became (arguably) the first viral video ever, with millions of views.

Soon, Apple was changing its battery exchange policy. And the phenomenon of the Neistat brothers was born. As a team, they posted more short films online—sixty-seven at last count. HBO gave them a TV series. They produced two feature-length films.

Nothing Casey did with his life was conventional. He followed none of the predetermined paths toward success in commercial filmmaking. Instead, he blazed a new path with nothing more than willpower. He wasn't born with any advantages. He's not a typically good-looking guy (he'll be the first to tell you that), but he's very attractive to women because he's creative and confident. He believes in himself. He's committed to trying new things. And he is fucking fearless.

Casey's life is a perfect example of one of my favorite maxims: You don't regret the things you do—only the things you *don't* do.

Real life is scary. It's hard. Knowing what you want—and taking those first steps to get it—requires guts, perseverance, and patience. It takes *courage* to face real life, because with every triumph (like Casey's) there are also failures. Every high has a low. Every peak comes with a valley. You get the point.

We tend to want to avoid those disappointments. Understandably! Who wants to try and fail? So we don't bother taking those first steps at all. We distract ourselves. We follow the easier path, the path of least resistance—spending more and more time on the Internet. Online, we can do everything that *feels* like living life—make "friends," explore culture, join a community—without ever having to look anyone in the eye.

But when we do that, we end up missing out on the potential of our lives.

———

I'm not saying that the Internet won't help you succeed. After all, it enabled Casey's success; he used it as a platform for his creativity. It worked. But not because he was using it as a *consumer*. Instead, he was a *creator*.

A consumer is someone who merely "likes" and shares things that other people make and post on social media sites; a creator, on the other hand, is someone who is generating that original material, whether they are a comedian tweeting jokes or a blogger uploading their own videos. Creators have an original voice, and the Internet is merely the outlet for that voice.

Casey was a perfect example of the latter. He was doing things offline, and then sharing them online. He had something real to contribute and promote—and *that's* the perfect use of the Internet. It's one of the reasons social media is great: It allows people like Casey to be heard in a way that they otherwise wouldn't. In the days before the Internet, Casey might never have been discovered or found a like-minded community of fans. Social media worked for him. It gave him a voice.

But, if you've read this far in the book (and hey, high five!), you know what I'm going to say next: As great as social media can be, it can also be a big, fat waste of time. Sure, the stuff we find online can be fascinating and inspiring, but every second that we spend on social media actually reduces the likelihood that we're going to do something ourselves. Surfing the Web and consuming other people's content in order to feel more connected and involved actually lowers our chances of making any kind of significant achievement of our own.

The truth is that the majority of people online aren't creators—although often we think that we are, because we are "involved." We get a false sense of fulfillment when we go online because we are participating in a community, but it's a one-sided exchange. By "liking" and reposting and commenting, we're not contributing in a significant way. There's an imbalance between input and outtake that teeters dangerously close to passivity.

Using the Internet is the simplest thing you can possibly do. Going online requires almost no energy. You can do it from your bed. In your underwear. Unshowered. It requires no commitment—after all, you can log out at any moment. It has no expectations of you, comes with zero accountability, and (in many cases) carries no repercussions for your actions when you use it.

There's no "failure" online, in the real-world sense—but there's no achievement, either. The things that seem like "success" online—gaining more friends; having people "like" your pictures, repost your comments, read your Twitter feed—are, for the most part, ephemeral. These social media achievements are merely a kind of popularity contest. And being popular online doesn't get us any closer to the things we want to achieve in real life. (I know there are exceptions—but they are not the norm.)

Think about someone you admire, someone you follow online who you really like. Then ask the question—why? Why is it that you like that person? I think you'll quickly realize that it's because they are actively *creating* something in the real world.

Personally, the two people I admire most online are Matthew Segal and Jarrett Moreno, the founders of OurTime.org, a nonprofit that is trying to give young people a political voice. They created the organization while they were at Kenyon College, after they observed their friends feeling disenfranchised during the 2004 elections—thanks to voting lines that were too long and convoluted registration laws, so many couldn't even vote. Matthew and Jarrett started a petition, then founded an organization, and now use social media and online organizing to help empower young people to understand political issues and act on them. They want to advocate on behalf of young Americans and effect real changes to benefit our collective future.

Matthew and Jarrett are heavily involved in social media—they tweet, post on Facebook, run a blog—but none of it is empty noise. They share meaningful information and relevant, current content, trying to help other people improve themselves. Social media is just another outlet for the things they are doing out there in the physical world.

(Similarly, supporting the creative content of people you truly admire by "liking" and retweeting their posts makes sense. This is how ideas get shared, and it is a constructive use of social media. Unfortunately, because it's so easy to click the "like" button, we are often too undiscerning in the things we share, and end up doing it mindlessly.)

> *Twitter provides us with a wonderful platform to discuss/confront societal problems. We trend Justin Bieber instead.*
> —Lauren Leto, comedian

The most popular things that people share online are the true-life, incredible experiences that only happen in the real world. Wouldn't *you* like to be the person having those experiences and mindfully sharing them, rather than simply capturing the low-hanging fruit and meaningless barrage of content that constantly comes at you?

So if, like me, you want to be more like Matthew, Jarrett, or Casey, start by making a list of your goals in life. Write down the things you'd really like to do—the dreams. How many of them are things you can accomplish simply by being online?

Life is filled with amazing and inspiring encounters. Instead of passively documenting them for the people you (barely) know online, I want to challenge you to absorb these moments and *do something* with them—become a writer, an artist, a dancer, a thinker. Learn skills that you'll have for the rest of your life. Travel. Explore. Grow. Advocate a political issue. Write a book. Take up a new hobby. Pursue that relationship. Try to do something new, and hard, and interesting.

You may fail—and yes, that will suck—but at least you will have tried. And who knows—instead of being a failure, you may be one of the successes. The only thing I can guarantee is that you won't be either if you don't give it a shot.

CHAPTER 21

Digital Detox

Hey, you.

Yes you, the one reading this book. I'm talking to you, okay?

I know what you're doing. You're reading this book, but in between pages you're picking up your phone and sending a text. You're refreshing your Facebook news feed. You're "liking" your friend's recent Instagram post and composing a tweet and checking your email for the twentieth time this hour.

It's time to step away from your computer. To put your phone somewhere you can't find it. To unplug and focus on the real world.

We—and when I say "we," I mean pretty much anyone under the age of forty—suffer from a compulsive need to share everything we are doing and seeing. We sleep with our phones next to our beds and look at them immediately when we wake up. We can't look at a sunset without Instagramming it. We can't eat a meal without taking a picture. We can't go to a movie without tweeting about it before the credits have even rolled. We almost feel guilty if we don't stay up-to-date on the twenty-four-hour nonstop feed. God forbid we miss something that everyone else is seeing and laughing about.

Let's just say it, okay? We are all totally addicted.

I'm not saying you shouldn't engage in social media at all—it *can* be incredibly rewarding, helping you connect with people you admire, keep up with friends, and express your opinions. I know you want to communicate; you have things to say! But all too often, we're forgetting to be participants in our own lives. After all, if you are constantly looking down at your phone, you're not interacting with the real world. Instead, you are distancing yourself by not being present.

Consider my friend Frank. I love him to death, but he drives me nuts. I cannot get him to put his phone down. He probably spends 75 percent of his working hours looking at his phone—checking social media feeds, looking at sports scores, texting with friends, reading emails. I'm sure he spends three or four hours a day looking at his phone—which, sadly, is just about normal for someone in their twenties.[24]

Frank makes it his goal to be super connected, but as a result, he lives in a state of incredible distraction. Every time we're together, I feel like he's more involved with the three people he's texting, or with his hundreds of Facebook friends, or with his thousand Twitter followers, than he is with me, who is standing right in front of him. He's so busy Instagramming a photo of where he is that he can't even enjoy what he's seeing.

Like Frank, we are all growing more distant from the experiences right in front of us. And it's not making us happier—in fact, exactly the opposite.

A recent study at the University of Michigan tracked the moment-to-moment happiness levels of college students throughout their days. The result? The more the students were on Facebook, the less happy they were. The moments when they were using social media were the moments when they had the most dissatisfaction with their own lives.[25] Enough said.

I recently asked my Facebook followers, "Do you feel like you spend too much time on your phone instead of engaging with the world around you?" The answer was a resounding yes. These were some of my favorite responses.

Jessica: My boyfriend is constantly on his phone....When we're out to dinner it feels like I'm there alone.

Lauren: I literally just finished scrolling down Twitter and moved on to Facebook. There should be a social network rehab.

Korbin: I spend all day, whether working or enjoying leisure time, hovering over my fucking mobile. It's equal parts obsession and curse, but the way I look at it is that someday when I'm old and wrinkled I'm going to enjoy knowing that I have such a detailed account of my youth. It seems like a waste to some people but I almost find it liberating because it's a living archive of my time on this big rock. That being said sometimes even I annoy myself with how many times I log on to FB/Twitter/Insta. #dilemma

Nissa: I have a rule. When I am in the [presence] of company, phone is away. If my friends don't show the same respect for our time, I speak up and say something.

Katie: Honestly, I miss flip phones. I miss when you could go on dates and the only thing you could do was look at each other, and talk.

Lindsey: I constantly check my phone or my laptop...I feel like some of my friends & I have grown apart because we spend so much time talking on Facebook or texting... instead of making plans to hang out in person. Pretty sad... I'm ready to start connecting with people face to face again.

Since becoming kinda famous, I've experienced firsthand how people don't engage with the individuals and objects that interest them anymore: All they do is document things in order to share them online. For example, almost every day someone recognizes me and approaches me. But, without fail, I end up confused and disappointed by what happens next.

The person will say something like, "Oh my God! I'm such a big fan! Can I take a picture with you?" And without waiting for a response, they'll snap their picture and then flee, texting and uploading their photo immediately.

I'm left thinking, "That's it? You're a fan, you love my show, you have the opportunity to engage with me, and all you want is to take a picture to post to your Instagram? All you care about is showing people that you stood next to me for three seconds?"

I'm not a Madame Tussauds wax sculpture. Sure, if all you want is a picture, absolutely, take it. But don't be shy. Say something to me! Introduce yourself! Ask me a question! Let's have a conversation about the issues that we address on the show!

Surely that's more interesting and important than tweeting to your friends that I'm on your flight.

———

Let me lay out a familiar scenario for you. You're at a concert. The band has just started. What's the first thing you do? Take out your camera and take a picture, of course. Then you have to fiddle with that photo, worry about the exposure, and go in and out of applications, all before uploading it to Instagram. Maybe you even decide to record the performance, and end up watching the whole show through the two-inch screen on your smartphone. As a result, you're completely distracted during the entire concert.

These days, everyone is a photographer. We take photos and videos constantly, maxing out our hard drives, filling up our social feeds. It's so easy! After all, we all walk around with a camera in our pocket, thanks to the smartphone.

Photography, in its ideal use, is an art form, a way of capturing things that are important to you and saving them for the future. You shouldn't take pictures for other people; you should take them for yourself. But these days, we feel pressure to constantly take and upload photos for other people. Think about it. How many times have you thought: "I think this will get a lot of 'likes,'" or "That looks cool—I bet other people will think so, too," or "I want to film this concert so everyone knows I was here!"? It's not really about being inspired or memorializing a moment, is it? Instead, it ends up being something closer to bragging. Plus, on behalf of everyone behind you at the event, please know how distracting and irritating it is having your phone blocking my view the whole show.

Our default procedure, anytime we go to any event, is to take that camera out and start taking pictures. It's as if capturing the moment and sharing it later on is more valuable than actually *being there*. Without the proof that you were there, uploaded for other people's approval, your experience somehow doesn't count.

So before you whip out your phone, ask yourself this question: If what you are doing is so cool and so great that you want to take a picture, then why are you on your phone doing something else?

I'm not down on photography, of course. I'm a photographer by profession. For years, I lugged around my camera equipment everywhere I went. But it's all about intention. If you snap a single photo of a moment because you want to remember it, awesome. If you're taking pictures for a bigger purpose—an art project, your profession—and because you're inspired, then great. But if you're taking pictures just because you want to get recognition on social media? For the sole purpose of saying, "I was here"? Maybe it's time to rethink your intentions.

Photographers are, by definition, observers. Their job is to capture. And taking pictures is a second-degree activity. You are one layer removed from the action: You're literally looking through something. You're not seeing what you're looking at, because you're worried about framing and angles and process. If you're trying to enjoy yourself, taking pictures is a surefire way to ruin that. Trust me—I've taken a lot of photos. You can't have an immersive experience with a camera in front of your face.

In fact, you may not even clearly remember the experience at all. There was a fascinating recent study by a researcher at Fairfield University. He gave students digital cameras and then took them to an art museum, telling them to photograph some objects and simply observe others. The next day, the students were given a recall test. It turned out that they had far clearer memories of the things they *hadn't* photographed but had simply observed. As for the other objects? It seemed that subconsciously the students were counting on their photos to "remember" things for them, so they turned their brains off.[26]

If you go to a concert because you enjoy the music, then

you shouldn't be photographing or videorecording it. That's not your job. I can't say that there isn't something wonderful about the ability to capture and share culture on the Internet. It's an amazing thing. But your video of that song at that concert that you took with your phone from the nosebleed seats— the video where the stage is washed out and you can barely make out what the song is because the sound is so bad? Trust me, it isn't going to be as good as the music video the band has already made.

I'm guilty of doing this, too. It's hard to avoid in the culture that we live in. If I want to take really good pictures, I'll bring my real camera with me. I *like* to take photographs, especially at special events. But I struggle with this, because I know that I'm distracted when I photograph, and my enjoyment diminishes. So more and more I'm choosing to not take my camera.

I still bring my phone, though—it's unavoidable. And as long as it's in my pocket, I feel pressure to take pictures, because I have a following of people who want to see what I see. But every time I pull it out to take a picture, I know that it's not as good as the real thing. Not even close. It's a watered-down, miniature, low-res version of what's out there.

So lately, when I see something great and my first instinct is to take a picture with my phone, I take a minute to consider whether it's something I really need to photograph and whether my picture of what I'm seeing will even come close to capturing how great it is. Is my photograph going to be meaningful? Will it add value? Or will it be a sad reproduction of the moment? I find myself thinking, more and more, *I don't need to capture this—for me or for anyone else. It happened; I saw it. And that's good enough.*

So put that camera back in your pocket. Don't worry about sharing the moment with the people who aren't there. Just enjoy it.

————

But let's be honest, here—you're alive, and that means you probably have a smartphone, and you're probably pretty hooked on it. (Who isn't?) And I'm telling you to turn it off, to get off Instagram and Twitter and Facebook, to stop texting and tweeting and taking pictures. To step away from your computer and go out into the real world.

Easier said than done, right?

I don't have the easy, pain-free solution to unplugging. It would be amazing if I did. The truth is that we don't "go online" anymore, not the way we used to. The Internet is pervasive: We are constantly connected, through apps and social media and our phones. Technology is our life source, with no separation between online and offline. So sure, I can tell you to just turn off your phone, but we all know that isn't going to happen so easily.

So what's the answer? I have a fantasy about creating the perfect app, one that everyone would have preinstalled on their smartphone. The phone would lock you out until you engaged with one of thousands of different questions and suggestions—like "Do you really need to be sending a text right now?" or "Take a picture of something that inspires you, but don't share it with anyone else," or "Call your mom." The goal would be to make you think before you mindlessly tweeted/texted/commented/uploaded.

The app would also monitor how much time you spent online and what other apps you used—and it would cut you off when you were going overboard. You could set your own limits, and the phone would send you alerts: "You've spent 50 percent of your allotted time on Facebook." And if you felt like you were getting sucked into using certain apps too much, you could temporarily lock them out of your phone.

I haven't written that perfect app, but there are similar programs that already exist. The software programs Freedom and SelfControl both cut off all access to the Internet for a period of time that you set yourself; Anti-Social is a similar app, one that simply disables social media sites. RescueTime audits how much time you're spending on different apps and programs, giving you a graph of where you're wasting your time and how often you're switching between tasks. It's a kind of wake-up call.

But there are lots of ways you can work to reduce the impact of social media in your life without having to download an app to do it.

NEV'S RULES FOR SOCIAL MEDIA:

1. Start by turning your phone off. No, not forever—I know that's not going to happen. I'm talking about doing it for just twenty-four hours. Maybe you've already heard of the concept of a "Tech Sabbath"; if you haven't, the idea is to turn off your technology entirely for one day a week. Why not try it, at least once? Make it your challenge to yourself to leave your phone at home on Sundays. Make your plans the night before. Let your phone get some rest.

2. Set a new rule for yourself: If you are with someone, the phone stays in your pocket. Unless you are taking a photo or receiving an important cell phone call, *put away your phone*. No texts, no tweets, no email. Only use it when you are alone.

3. Set limits for yourself regarding social media. How many times a day do you currently post? Cut that number in half. No one needs to be posting ten or twenty times a day.

4. If you take photos at an event, don't post them to Instagram until you get home. Wait until the event is over, and *then* go through your photos to pick the one or two that you think are best. Be mindful in your choices.

5. Stop accepting friend requests from people you don't know! I'm not saying no new friends, but maybe you should consider more seriously whether you need to bring more strangers into your life.

6. Similarly, go through your friend list. If you don't know somebody personally, even if you have mutual friends, it's time to delete them. Fewer friends means less time spent catching up on news feeds.

7. When you feel compelled to text someone, stop and think. Why don't you call them instead? Have a real conversation—trust me, you'll get things accomplished a lot faster. While you're on the phone, ask them how they're doing. Make a plan to get together in person.

8. Every time you take out your phone to take a picture of a stranger, stop yourself. Go up to them instead and start a conversation. Ask a question. Find a way to engage with the people and things that catch your inter-

est beyond passively snapping a picture. Who knows what you might learn?

9. Similarly, instead of relying on your phone when you need directions or advice, go up to actual human beings and ask for help.

10. Start a No Phones at the Dinner Table rule. Some restaurants have already started to do this; why not apply it in your home, too?

11. Buy an alarm clock. The real kind. That way you won't feel so compelled to plug your phone in next to your bed at night. Leave it overnight in another room, instead.[27]

In his great book *Outliers*, Malcolm Gladwell lays out the "10,000-hour rule." Basically, in ten thousand hours you can become a master at almost any task: Become a chess champion, an NBA-worthy basketball player, a best-selling novelist. It seems like a Sisyphean task, right?

Well, with the average person spending three hours a day on social media—or far more, if you include all forms of Internet use—that's a *minimum* of one thousand hours a year. If you cut out social media entirely, with the time you saved you could be a Gladwell-style master at something in less than ten years.

Okay, yes, ten years is a long time. But what if you gained just a few months of time? What could you accomplish with that?

- Take up exercise and lose twenty pounds.
- Become a really good cook.
- Learn a new language.

- Master the guitar.
- Read ten great books.
- Train for and run a half marathon.
- Take classes in art, photography, writing—anything you can think of.
- Get to know someone new really well.

If it's making you truly happy, sure, go ahead and keep your phone in your hand and your eyes on it all the time. But if you're like me and want a life of experience and adventure and amazement (and I bet you do), put that thing away. There's no life in your phone. Life is what happens when you're *not* looking down at what you're holding in your hands. The smartphone is just a way to capture and share it.

Instead, invest in creating the content of your life. This will endure long after your last tweet has come and gone.

CHAPTER 22

Fame Fail

I grew up believing that movie stars had it easy. I'd look at someone like Leonardo DiCaprio and think that his life was a piece of cake. Someone had put him in a movie, and now he was set: He was rich, famous, and dating beautiful women. Wouldn't it be awesome if that happened to me? Maybe it could. It would probably solve all my problems. That was my impression of celebrity: It just *happens* to you. It's just the luck of the draw.

We live in a world where people are obsessed with celebrity. Like me, people think that fame is a matter of luck; that it can happen to anyone. Just take a look at the people on reality TV! We fixate on this. And as a result, it's getting in the way of our ability to live our lives.

In an increasingly overpopulated, underemployed society, we've shifted our focus away from traditional work ethic ideals and toward tabloid celebrity ideals. We used to believe that hard work paid off; now, we focus on easy fame. As a society, we center all our attention on a tiny segment of people who, frequently for no good reason, have been able to make truckloads of money doing nothing. Kids today dream of being a Bachelor/ette, a Real Housewife, a member of the Kardashian family, or an American Idol.

I get it. Real-world options are pretty bleak for a lot of people. Option A, the best-case scenario, for so many young people around the world? You get to take on a tremendous amount of work and debt in order to educate yourself, with the relatively low chance of getting a good job; and even if you do get that job, you'll have to work incredibly hard for decades in order to earn an at-best modest living, a lot of which will go to pay off your student loans and the rest of which will (hopefully) let you live in a semidecent house and support a family—eventually retiring in your seventies, if you're lucky.

Nope, it's not sexy. The middle-class norm has become a dream. That's why fame has become such an alluring idea, and why everyone fantasizes about option B: becoming a reality TV star. Young people look at the cast of *Duck Dynasty*—all *they* had to do was be extreme versions of themselves while the cameras rolled, and for that they made a couple hundred thousand dollars an episode. Just for hanging out. And being obnoxious.

We, as a culture, have elevated that. We've made it a worthy goal. Because it requires so little talent and effort, we believe it's an option within anyone's reach.

As difficult as it might seem to achieve option A, the odds of option B are worse than winning the lottery. As one of the few people who has (incredibly) won that lottery, I can give you the inside scoop: Most people on reality TV shows don't get paid a lot. In fact, most hardly get paid anything at all. Even if you do miraculously get cast in a reality TV show, there's a very small chance it will make it to a pilot, a smaller chance that the pilot will get picked up by a TV channel, and an even tinier chance that the show will make it past two episodes. And even if you are in that infinitesimal number that makes it all the way to season 2, you still won't make much money because of the standard contract you signed back in season 1.

Sure, should your show become one of the 2 percent of all TV shows that are smash hits, you'll make some money. Best-case scenario? The money will last for a couple years. I guarantee that you won't end up a millionaire and retire at age thirty unless you have an unbelievable business manager. Instead, you'll be a has-been reality star with an empty bank account and no skills worth mentioning.

You might be thinking, "But even if I don't make a ton of money, it's still a glamorous lifestyle!" Not exactly. Though I am not Brad Pitt, I can speak to the fact that hosting a reality TV show and being something of a celebrity does not make for a dazzling day-to-day experience. While I feel incredibly lucky to be doing what I do, I want to be honest with you. Being a public figure generally involves a lot of long airplane flights, early mornings, hard work, and very little time spent with friends and family.

Option A may be the less sexy option, but if you go to college you're improving yourself. You're growing. You're opening yourself up to the world, ideas, and people that will excite you.

As I travel for the show, I meet with a lot of young people who have a bleak outlook on life. "I come from a small town, a middle- or lower-class family," they'll say. "Maybe I can go to a community college or state school and not rack up too much debt. But *then* what do I do?" Or they'll tell me, "I don't plan to go to college, so I'll just get a job in my town, doing construction or working in fast food. That's life."

But people don't realize how many different kinds of careers are out there, how many truly amazing, interesting things you can do. Some may require college degrees, but a lot require only self-motivation and drive. We only focus on the top 1 percent of people who are crazy successful in their fields, the people whose names are recognizable to us. Pop culture doesn't really highlight all the other people whose behind-the-scenes jobs are critical in those same industries.

So you're into fashion? Don't aspire to be on *Project Runway* or *Fashion Star*. Instead, learn as much as you can about fashion and become a stylist or a personal shopper. Or you're into movies? Instead of focusing on being a movie star, think about all the other great jobs in the movie industry. Start as a production assistant, get an internship, or become a makeup artist or production designer or grip. There are so many possibilities!

Or you're really into social media? Make that addiction work for you. There are so many jobs in marketing these days. Companies are desperate for social media page managers. Mock up a Facebook page for a local business that's not online, then go in and show them. Offer to run it for them for free. See if you like it, and if you do, go to another business and say, "I've been doing this for another company and I'll do it for you for a hundred dollars a week." And then you've got a portfolio and you can go to another company, and then another. In a matter of months, you might find yourself with a full-time job running a company's social media campaign.

Make your own opportunities. Remember how I was really into dance when I was young? I recognized early on that I was never going to be a famous ballet dancer. As much as I loved dance, I just wasn't star material; I didn't have the abilities or talent required. So few people do. But I knew I wanted to be involved in that world somehow, so I found a place for myself taking photographs instead. I offered my services for free for a long time, just making myself indispensable. Eventually, I found myself making a living as a ballet videographer. I paved my own path, found a goal that was achievable, and went for it.

There's a big misconception that things just *happen* in life—that fame will find you if you're fabulous. But things only happen to you when you are out living life. Your prospects are only as good as you make them.

The reason most people (outside of reality TV stars) are famous is because they *do* things. That actor you love from that TV show worked really hard to learn how to act. He struggled through countless auditions and callbacks to get a shitty part that led to a less shitty part that led, eventually, to an okay part...you get the point. He *earned* every second of screen time he got. *That's* why people get famous. *That's* why people succeed. It wasn't just the luck of the draw, as I once believed.

The world needs more doers.

Good news! Most people are too busy worrying about the "likes" on their Instagram feed and followers on Twitter to actually be out there doing stuff. The fact that you are reading this book and not just looking at your phone means that you want to think, engage, and participate in life. You've got a head start.

So if you're reading this right now and, in the back of your mind, are thinking that there's something you wish you were doing, a job you'd like to have...*go do it*. You'll have a jump start.

As for the fame that so many people think will solve all their problems? Let me tell you, as someone who has experienced it—it's not all that. Don't get me wrong; I feel extremely grateful and humbled every day by my job. But it doesn't make me any happier. If anything, it adds pressure and anxiety—because now there are expectations. I have to be "always on."

Nothing gets fixed simply because you are on a TV show. No number in a bank account is going to help you with your girlfriend. You are not going to be magically happier if you have a million Twitter followers instead of ten. Your issues will always be your issues, until you address them.

CHAPTER 23

Put On a Smiley Face

Stay positive.

If you were to ask me to sum up everything I've learned since I was first contacted by Angela almost seven years ago, that's what I'd say. Embrace who you really are, both online and off; improve yourself if you don't like what you see. Try to remain optimistic. And learn how to create a good thing out of whatever life throws at you.

I know, I know, I'm not the first person to say any of this. But I think it bears repeating, ad nauseam, thanks to the state of the world we are currently living in.

We live in an online society of "likes." Social media culture is all about wanting to be loved. We want our Instagrams to be liked, our tweets to be retweeted, our comments to be reposted. Our public lives are our most intimate work of art, and we want only positive reviews of the curated self-portrait that we depict there, all day, every day.

It's an extremely unrealistic hope.

People have been weird and crazy and negative and afraid for a long time—think about the Salem Witch Trials or the Spanish Inquisition—but social media has really generated an epidemic of unhappiness. The outcome of living a life in public, on social media, is that we are not only battling our own loneliness and discontent but making ourselves susceptible to other lonely and discontent people who take their emotions out on us and try to bring us down for daring to reveal ourselves. Unhappy people who will look at that meticulously curated life and give it a bad review. Whether we like it or not, when we live our lives online we have to be prepared to cope with all this cynicism.

Try being informed instead of just opinionated.
　　　　　　　　　　　　　　　　　　—Anonymous

So what can you do about it?

We all have to be careful about allowing negativity to enter our minds, in any dosage. It affects us. Sure, it's good to be exposed to a diversity of opinions. But it's a waste of time to seriously consider the negative feelings of someone who means nothing to you—someone who is not important in your life and who in all likelihood you will never meet. You should never let that person dictate how you feel.

Because here's the thing about negativity: It in no way helps you. Every moment you spend being negative or angry has zero value. No product or achievement or success comes from negativity. It just wastes your time and gets in your way.

———

When the documentary *Catfish* came out, in 2010, most of the attention it received was incredibly supportive and wonderful. But not long after the movie's release, the negative fallout began. Certain online reviews called Rel, Henry, and me "rich, spoiled New York City kids" and accused us of exploiting my catfish, Angela, and her family. (That couldn't have been farther from the truth.) Posters on online bulletin boards called us liars and claimed that we'd faked the movie. Across the Internet, people were downright mean.

It tore me apart. These strangers were calling me exploitative and dishonest. But I'd never had a more real experience in my life. I lived it. I knew it was true. It was *crazy* to me that they didn't believe me. I let it get to me. Instead of feeling great about having helped make this fascinating and successful documentary, I began to feel depressed.

Finally, Andrew Jarecki—our producer, and a great documentary filmmaker himself (if you haven't seen *Capturing the Friedmans*, you should)—said something that really woke me up. As he read through the bad reviews, his response was, "This is great for us. Because if everyone liked something, it would be boring."

In other words, he spun the negativity into something positive: If Rel, Henry, and I were getting people enamored and excited—but also riled up and upset—it meant we'd done something right. When you succeed creatively, Jarecki continued, you will *always* run into people who will spin your success against you because they are dealing with their own issues.

Rel, Henry, and I had caught lightning in a bottle. We had busted our butts making a movie out of a true life experience that was incredibly unusual. But we ran into a lot of luck—luck not only that I had the experience but also that my brother was a filmmaker who happened to start filming what was going on. Luck that my catfish agreed to be in the movie. Luck that we hooked up with amazing producers who helped us get our film into Sundance. A million things had to happen to make the movie, all of which were hard to believe.

I realized that a lot of the film's critics, aspiring to artistic achievements of their own, saw our luck and success and were annoyed. They didn't want to believe our film, because by believing in what we'd done, they had to question their inability to achieve their own dreams. And that pissed them off, so they chose to tear us down instead.

Understanding this, I had a revelation: I *knew* what had happened to me. I was there. So as weird and frustrating and difficult as it was that these people online didn't believe me—who cared? These haters were making up their minds to feel a certain way because of who *they* were, not who I was. If they had the ambition to actually find out the truth, they could have—but they didn't want to. There was nothing I could do about that.

So I let it go. I decided that these strangers weren't worth worrying about. Instead, I accepted the simple truth that I couldn't control what other people thought. All I could do was try not to let it get to me, and channel that hate into something more productive.

After the *Catfish* backlash, I decided to use my experience as motivation to think about how I could use my platform to peacefully spread *positivity*. For the first time, I started really considering everything I posted on the Internet and how it could be perceived. I identified the morals and ideals that I wanted to be associated with and made sure that everything I said or posted was furthering those messages. I resisted the urge to post things that were snarky or even just mindlessly funny; I didn't want to be a curator of entertainment. I wanted to be someone who stood for real content and value.

The surprising thing that I discovered? People felt that positivity and returned it. By channeling my frustration into something more fruitful, I not only helped other people feel better, but also ultimately I felt better about myself.

————

When I was younger, I used to notice only the negative things around me. Stupid, silly things: people who walked too slowly, bad drivers, red lights. Anger became an outlet for my emotional energy—something I could identify and understand, as opposed to the murky feelings of negative self-doubt that I dealt with every day. And as a result, I ended up spending a lot of time and energy being angry, missing out on and ignoring things that were great and would have made me happy.

That's why, lately, I've been trying to change my perspective. It's the battle I'm actively fighting: Rather than noticing something I don't like or getting upset about a nasty comment I read, I now try to acknowledge the negativity and look elsewhere for something that *does* make me happy. I remind myself how much good there is in the world, how nice someone was to me today, how lucky I am. Even simple things, like great weather or the fact that I ate a meal and have a full belly, can help boost my mood.

I've noticed that doing this has an immediate effect on me. When you work hard at noticing positivity and good fortune, your brain and heart feel better. And when you start to feel better and think better, you perform better. Everything improves.

So I'll say it one last time: *Stay positive.*

You've heard that line a million times before, I know. It makes you want to roll your eyes. It's not that easy, you think. You have physical issues, pain and sickness; emotional stress; problems with friends and family. There are haters everywhere you turn, giving you negative feedback, saying nasty things. And in the middle of all that you need to make money, find love, build a life. It's hard enough just to survive, let alone be upbeat about it.

And yet, everything good in life ties back to the idea of positivity. If you're struggling with something—a relationship problem, a work crisis, friendship drama—take a moment to recognize how you feel, assess what you want, and then approach the problem using a positive thought process. If you do, you'll be far likelier to resolve the situation than if you march in pissed off and pessimistic.

It's easy to get discouraged or bogged down. But keep your focus on the positive and on what you truly stand for, and know that what you're doing is what you're *supposed* to be doing.

Conclusion

Even though Rel, Henry, and I coined the term *catfish* with our documentary, we never really intended the term to refer to someone who lies about their identity online.

During my stay in Michigan, Angela's husband, Vince, told me this amazing story. Fisheries used to ship these giant vats of live cod from Alaska to China, but they kept running into a problem. Upon arrival in China, the cod's flesh was mushy and tasteless from the fish being inactive on the journey. So some guy had the bright idea to put catfish in the vats with the cod to chase them around and keep them moving.

When Vince finished telling me this story, I knew that's what Angela had been to me—a catfish of sorts, who had kept me intrigued, eased my loneliness, made me feel like I had finally maintained a great relationship. She had gotten my blood moving and had been a catalyst of sorts.

It's time to redefine *catfish* in a more positive light: someone who breaks the rules and figures out new ways to do things. Someone who inspires, rather than deceives. Someone who keeps us intrigued—for the right reasons rather than the wrong ones. Let's *all* be catfish.

The world needs leaders that can guide us on matters both big—how to deal with the financial crisis around the world, how to fight hunger, or how to preserve our planet—and seemingly small—how to use Facebook in a more moral way, or how to implement a society based on positivity. There's no reason you—yes, *you*—can't be that leader.

You don't think you're ready to be a leader? Then be a follower. There's a great TED Talk by musician/entrepreneur Derek Sivers about how movements get started. He shows footage of a guy at an outdoor concert—the *only* guy who is dancing, and in a really goofy way. Everyone else stands and laughs at him. And then one person, maybe on a dare, goes over and starts mock goofy dancing with him. And then two other people go over, and then five, and suddenly the *entire lawn* is dancing. It's practically a mosh pit.[28]

That first dancer, the leader, was critical, but just as important? The first guy who joined him. Being a follower can be just as daring and courageous—because once a leader has a follower, that's when a movement can start to happen. And every member of a movement is critical.

Regardless of who you are, remember this: You are an important and a crucial part of the future. Your ideas and actions can change the world—you can inspire a thousand people to change the way they think. You could help start a revolution, like the first person in Egypt who was brave enough to speak up in protest and helped start the Arab Spring. Don't be afraid to be that person. As Bruce Springsteen once said, you can't start a fire without a spark.

The Internet can suck, but it can also be great if we use it right and harness its powers for meaningful change. You can be one of the creators, using social media to distribute groundbreaking new work and ideas that alter our social fabric. Find something you believe in, something meaningful, and let that consciously inform your life, both offline and on.

So my final challenge to you? Get out of your chair and

go out and change the world. We need people to set the tone and guide us, because now more than ever there's an opportunity for new and better direction. Don't make your goal to be liked on Facebook. Make it to stand for something. You may not feel as popular at first, but believing in something and sticking to it is what makes life meaningful. And personal meaning is at the foundation of self-respect, of confidence, and—ultimately—of love.

Acknowledgments

I would never have been able to write this book if it hadn't been for the unconditional love and support of my family. I can only imagine the heartaches and headaches I must have caused you over the years. You taught me how to be kind, humble, generous, and expressive. You encouraged my creativity and applauded my individuality. If every kid could experience the love and positivity that I received from my family, I know the world would be a better place.

I also want to thank Angela Wesselman-Pierce. Somehow our paths through this crazy universe ended up crossing and I am grateful every day that they did. I appreciate your courage. I admire your commitment and I recognize your creativity. Thank you for sharing your story with me.

I could not have written this book without the guidance and support of Janelle Brown. You are a wonderful writer, trusted confidant, and good friend.

I want to thank my brother, Rel, and my brother-from-another-mother Henry for being my role models, both personally and professionally. I couldn't ask for a better pair of gentlemen to call my best friends.

Of course it goes without saying that much of my success is a result of the talent and intelligence of Max Joseph. There isn't anybody I'd rather be out there with, and I can't express how much of a positive influence your advice and companionship has had on me.

To my representation, who has had to put up with me and my passionate frustrations and constant queries since the beginning: Thank you for believing in me and helping me navigate the murky waters of this business.

Thanks to the entire team at Hachette / Grand Central Publishing, starting with Pippa White for taking a chance on a first-time writer with nothing but a gut feeling that we were on to something. And for all the hard work of Sonya Cheuse, Jamie Snider, Brigid Pearson, Brian McLendon, Andrew Duncan, Jane Lee, Beth de Guzman, and Jamie Raab.

Shanee. No words can describe the intense feeling of satisfaction knowing that there is somebody on this planet who gets me. I feel loved. I feel needed. You give me purpose and I can't wait to share our lives together. I love you.

And finally, to all my friends throughout the years: Thank you for giving me a chance. Thank you for giving me a second chance and often many more chances after that. I know it took a while, but all of you played a part and made a huge difference in helping me become who I am today.

Notes

1. http://www.youtube.com/watch?v=s-CTkbHnpNQ
2. http://mashable.com/2010/10/14/nielsen-texting-stats/
3. http://www.economist.com/node/16660401; http://www
   .digitaltrends.com/social-media/facebook-could-be-larger
   -than-china-in-three-years-time/#!JOQrc
4. MTV "Millennials" survey.
5. *Noah*, Toronto Film Festival. Available online at http://www
   .fastcocreate.com/3017108/you-need-to-see-this-17-minute
   -film-set-entirely-on-a-teens-computer-screen
6. http://www.cnn.com/2012/05/04/tech/social-media/
   facebook-lies-privacy/
7. http://www.womansday.com/sex-relationships/dating-marriage/
   online-dating-profile-lies
8. http://www.dailybulletin.com/general-news/20130517/sexting
   -probe-leads-to-arrest-at-rancho-etiwanda-high-schools, http://
   losangeles.cbslocal.com/2013/05/09/students-face-possible
   -child-porn-charges-in-sexting-scandal/
9. http://www.cnn.com/2013/09/27/us/miss-teen-usa-sextortion/
10. http://www.seattleweekly.com/home/933841-129/
    crimepunishment
11. http://www.mcafee.com/us/about/news/2013/q1/20130204-01
    .aspx
12. http://www.cnn.com/2013/08/22/us/florida-fraternity-facebook/

13. http://www.jsonline.com/news/crime/greenfield-teens-facebook
-post-for-drugs-leads-to-arrest-131826718.html

14. http://www.cbsnews.com/news/baby-with-bong-facebook
-photo-arrest-fla-mom-rachel-stieringer-faces-drug-charges/

15. http://www.dailymail.co.uk/news/article-1206491/Woman
-sacked-Facebook-boss-insult-forgetting-added-friend.html

16. http://www.huffingtonpost.com/2010/07/26/fired-over-facebook
-posts_n_659170.html

17. http://www.nytimes.com/2013/08/08/us/broader-sifting-of-data
-abroad-is-seen-by-nsa.html?pagewanted=all&_r=3&

18. http://www.themevision.com/files/clark%20v%20indiana%20
admissibility%20MySpace%20page%20evidence.pdf

19. http://fort-greene.thelocal.nytimes.com/2009/11/11/
his-facebook-status-now-charges-dropped/?_r=0

20. http://www.match.com/magazine/article/4671/

21. http://www.nydailynews.com/life-style/one-third-u-s-marriages
-start-online-dating-study-article-1.1362743

22. MTV "Millennials" survey.

23. http://www.youtube.com/watch?v=WsYAXPqVnYM

24. http://www.marketingcharts.com/wp/interactive/social
-networking-eats-up-3-hours-per-day-for-the-average-american
-user-26049/

25. http://drdeepikachopra.com/the-well-list-1/social-media-dis
-connection

26. http://www.theatlanticcities.com/technology/2013/12/how
-camera-phones-modify-our-memories/7829/

27. Thank you to Deepika Chopra for the last three ideas in our list.
http://www.mindbodygreen.com/0-10977/10-tips-to-spend-less
-time-on-social-media-more-time-with-humans.html

28. http://www.ted.com/talks/derek_sivers_how_to_start_a
_movement.html

I finally met "Megan" from the photos.
(Me and Aimee Gonzales.)

An invitation from the publisher

Join us at www.hodder.co.uk, or follow us
on Twitter @hodderbooks to be a part of
our community of people who love the very
best in books and reading.

Whether you want to discover more about a book
or an author, watch trailers and interviews, have the
chance to win early limited editions, or simply browse
our expert readers' selection of the very best books,
we think you'll find what you're looking for.

And if you don't, that's the place to tell us what's missing.

We love what we do, and we'd love you to be a part of it.

www.hodder.co.uk

@hodderbooks

HodderBooks

HodderBooks